6/06

After the Rain

Also by Chuck Logan

Vapor Trail
Absolute Zero
The Big Law
The Price of Blood
Hunter's Moon

Chuck Logan

After the Rain

HEN

HarperCollins*Publishers*

HarperCollins books may be purchased for educational, business, or sales promotional use. For information, please write: Special Markets Department, HarperCollins Publishers Inc., 10 East 53rd Street, New York, NY 10022.

FIRST EDITION

Designed by Joe Rutt

Printed on acid-free paper

Library of Congress Cataloging-in-Publication Data
Logan, Chuck.
    After the rain / Chuck Logan.—1st ed.
      p. cm.
    ISBN 0-06-057018-0 (acid-free paper)
    1. Broker, Phil (Fictitious character)—Fiction. 2. Undercover operations—Fiction. 3. Ex–police officers—Fiction. 4. Explosives—Fiction. 5. Smuggling—Fiction. 6. Minnesota—Fiction. I. Title.
PS3562.04453A65 2004
813'.54—dc22

2003067618

04 05 06 07 08 ❖/RRD 10 9 8 7 6 5 4 3 2 1

FOR SLOAN HARRIS

Acknowledgments

Gary Siegrist, dealer in heavy construction equipment, Montrose, Michigan

George W. Crocker, North American Water Office, Lake Elmo, Minnesota

Sheriff David Zeiss, Cavalier County Sheriff's Department, Langdon, North Dakota

Chief Deputy Greg Fetsch, Cavalier County Sheriff's Department, Langdon, North Dakota

Dana R. King, North Dakota Highway Patrol

Cameron Sillers P.C., Attorney at Law, Langdon, North Dakota

Harold and Nancy Blanchard, Grafton, North Dakota

Sgt. Lawrence R. Rogers, City of St. Paul Police Department Bomb Squad, St. Paul, Minnesota

Sgt. David Prois, Fridley Police Department, Fridley, Minnesota

Dean Mattson, trainer, River Valley Athletic Club, Stillwater, Minnesota

After the Rain

Chapter One

The young brown guy, the slightly older black guy, and the old white guy had been in the room for thirty minutes and now the sweat was running down their arms. They didn't need to be reminded, but the black guy went and said it anyway.

"*Damn,* it's hot."

"It ain't so hot," the old white guy said. "Panama was hot. Somalia was hotter. Kuwait was really hot, but that was a dry heat. Now, you take your triple-canopy jungle in Laos . . ."

"Don't start," the black guy said.

The temperature in the windowless room had topped ninety degrees at ten A.M., and that was half an hour ago. The room was in a suite of unused offices in an almost vacant strip mall off Highway 12 on the western edge of the Detroit metro area. The building was deserted except for a one-room telemarketing sweatshop at the other end.

The white guy was closer to sixty than to fifty, and his shaggy white-blond hair was shot with gray, and he'd given up trying to hide the bald spot on top. Once he'd been cinched down tight all over. Now his skin and muscles were starting to look like they were a size too large. He shook his head, toed the dirty carpeting, and laughed.

"Figures. No A/C. No nothing. Lookit this place. Some op. Shows how much we rate. Where are we? Inkster? What kind of name is that?"

"Yeah, yeah," said the black guy, who was in his late twenties. Unlike his older partner, he enjoyed looking in the mirror every morning. His skin fit him nice and tight.

They wore Nikes and faded jeans and oversized polo shirts that did not entirely conceal the holstered Berettas, the pagers, the plastic hand ties and cell phones hanging from their belts. They were obviously exhausted. They had not shaved in the last twenty-four hours.

They were not cops.

Nobody would admit who or what they were now. Only what they'd been. The old one was former Delta, former SF. The young one had also been with Special Forces. They'd been through the looking glass and now they carried nothing in their wallets or on their gear that could be traced back to the military. They were simply known by their mission name: Northern Route.

They were volunteers, totally on their own.

An hour ago they snatched a Saudi Arabian businessman off a busy street, stuffed him in a Chevy van, and brought him to this crummy little room from which the air conditioning, the desks, and the chairs had been removed. There was a touch of method in the selection of this room: the sensation of slow suffocation as an interrogation tool. For now the prisoner remained blindfolded. A little later they would take the blindfold off.

So it was just the three of them, and a lot of sweat, and the worn gray carpet, the bare walls, and the gray ceiling tiles crowded overhead with their grids of monotonous dots. And now the walls, carpet, and ceiling started closing in to form a solid block of heat.

The old guy wiped sweat from his forehead and said, "The right way to do this is we should be sitting on a runway. Three hundred thousand Arab types down the road in Dearborn for these wrongos to hide out with. And there's not a single military base in this whole town. That's real smart."

"Hollywood, man—just cool it. It's only half an hour. They're on the way in from Willow Run to pick him up." On *him,* the black guy nodded at the third man in the room.

"What would be nice, Bugs, is for Omar here to tell us something."

Bugs shook his head. "Never happen. We can't make deals, that's for the suits. But my guess is this guy's hardcore Qaeda. No way he's gonna talk to anybody. Nah, I think he's gonna sit out the war on the beach in Cuba."

Hollywood nodded. "You hear that, Omar? Camp Delta. Nice eight-by-eight chain-link dog kennel. Got your little rug and your prayer arrow scribed on the concrete floor."

The third man in the room showed lots of brown skin, as he'd been stripped down to his jockey shorts. He sat stiffly on a metal folding chair, his hands bound tightly behind his back in plastic cuffs. In contrast to his scruffy captors he was clean-shaven, his thick dark hair was styled, his fingernails and toenails looked recently manicured. He smelled of cologne rather than sweat and fatigue. In further contrast, a comfortable two inches of belly flab drooped over his waistband. According to the word, he was the renegade nephew of a Saudi prince, one of the world's ultimate rich kids.

But right now he was seriously separated from his Rolex and his Mercedes, and he had a band of duct tape wrapped around his head, covering his eyes. The intell on him suggested he was a dilettante slumming in jihad, that he was soft, that he would crack. So far, the intell was wrong.

Hollywood scrubbed at the stubble on his chin with his knuckles, then he grimaced at the prisoner. He crossed the room in three swift strides, grabbed a handful of the prisoner's sleek black hair, yanked him to his feet, and shouted, "We know you're getting set to move something. So what is it, where is it, and who's doing it?"

The prisoner hunched his shoulders and drew his chin into his chest.

Hollywood's frustration blew on through to outright anger. He seized the prisoner with both hands and roughly spun him in a circle. "So which way's Mecca, Omar? Take a fuckin' guess!"

"Hey, hey, knock it off," Bugs said, moving in quick. Their good cop/bad cop choreography was getting out of hand. It was the heat.

"Yeah, right." Hollywood rammed the staggering prisoner's head against the wall.

"You goddamn redneck—you're way out of line. Back off!" Now Bugs was shouting as he stepped in between Hollywood and the prisoner, who had collapsed to his knees. They glared at each other, standing so close the sweat on their noses almost merged.

Hollywood squinted his pale blue eyes. "You young guys—you think this is some kind of extreme sporting event. Let me clue you. This is a war. This scumbag is the enemy. You better get some hate in your chest, son; 'cause if you don't, when the time comes, you're gonna hesitate . . ."

Bugs stood his ground and stared directly into Hollywood's eyes. "You got no cause to bad-mouth his religion."

"Wise up," Hollywood said evenly. "This raghead wants to kill your family *because* he's an intolerant Wahhabi creep, get it?"

"Fine, but I'm telling you, he ain't going to talk, not to us."

"Oh yeah? There's ways."

"Spare me."

"When I was in Nam . . ."

"It's too early in the day for the geezer hour," Bugs said. "And it's way too hot, besides." Rolling his eyes, he reached down, hoisted the prisoner by the arms, and guided him back to the chair.

Hollywood walked to the corner, stooped and plucked a half-liter plastic bottle of springwater from a twelve-pack. He got up, opened the bottle, and returned to the seated prisoner. Slowly he poured several ounces of the water on the prisoner's bare chest. The prisoner reacted to the touch of liquid, instinctively licked his lips. Thirsty.

"All you need is a gallon of water and a washcloth. Put the rag over his mouth and nose and just dribble the water. Slow suffocation. Works like a charm. Don't leave mark one," Hollywood said.

"They catch you doing that today you go to Leavenworth. Besides, evidence acquired through torture is not admissible in court."

"Court? *Court!*" Hollywood actually shuffled his feet in a brief dance of rage. "Oh great, why don't we read him his rights and have a séance and see if we can contact William Kunstler."

"Maybe you could pull that shit in Afghanistan, but not here," Bugs said.

Hollywood was quick to jab a finger at Bugs's face. "*You* weren't in Afghanistan, fresh meat." They were back to glaring at each other. Then Hollywood relented and took a step back. "I mean, you and me, we'd never do anything like she . . ." He paused, let his eyes drift toward the door.

Bugs followed Hollywood's gaze, narrowed his eyes. "You mean, give him to Pryce?"

Hollywood shrugged.

"I thought you didn't approve of Pryce," Bugs said.

"I don't. Pryce is a freak of nature. But it can't hurt to try."

"We got less than an hour till the suits get here from D.C. Can't be any rough stuff, not so it'd show."

"So we agree," Hollywood said, smiling. He now approached the prisoner with open hands to show Bugs his benign intent and removed the adhesive blindfold, pulling with steady pressure. The prisoner, still dazed from his trip into the wall, winced, losing a little hair to the tape. He blinked several times, adjusting his eyes to the light. Then he rallied, looked past the two Americans, and fixed his eyes with a disciplined stare on a bare patch of wall.

"Okay Omar, here's the deal," Hollywood said. "I know you got your engineering degree at the sore-fucking-bone in Paris. I know you speak French, German, and excellent English. So I know you hear what I'm saying. And I know you don't care to talk to us infidels and all. But I feel obligated to clue you to this one important fact." He yanked his thumb at Bugs. "Him and me, we got our differences but basically we're *guy* infidels, you sprecken the comprez vous?"

The prisoner, whose name was not Omar, continued to stare at the wall.

Hollywood leaned forward and spoke into the prisoner's ear. He dropped his voice to a low, amiable tone. "I'm just saying, *guy* infidels ain't all we got."

The prisoner shifted on the chair and then spoke in precise, unaccented English. "I would like to speak to my attorney and I would like to use the bathroom."

Hollywood was still close to the man's ear. He smiled a kindly smile. Conceivably he was someone's grandfather. "Number one or number two?" he asked.

The prisoner shook his head briefly, then refocused his fatalistic gaze straight ahead on the wall.

"Fair warning," Hollywood said as he and Bugs ambled across the room and opened the door. As they stepped into the hall, Bugs called out, "The A Team is off the court, you can bring in the bench. Oh, and he wants to go to the john."

"Rashid, my man! The Gucci Terrorist—actually you don't look so bad, considering how your day has gone completely to shit."

Hearing his name, Rashid looked up and for a fraction of a

second lost his concentration and fixed his gaze on Major Nina Pryce as she walked into the hotbox room. She came straight at him; no frills, no wasted motion, no bullshit. She was a rangy, athletic thirty-five years old and stood five feet nine inches tall and weighed one hundred and forty-three highly trained pounds. Dressed down for the heat, she wore cut-off Levis and a ribbed tank top.

Rashid was trying to force his stare back to its meditation on the bare patch of wall when their eyes met. Nina raised her arm and ran her fingers through her short flame-red hair. Rashid's eyes followed the movement and became tangled in the interesting play of flesh on her bare upper arm. He noticed that the lobe of her left ear was missing, just a shrivel of scar tissue. A skull-and-crossbones tattoo grinned on her left shoulder like a memento of a wild youth. He saw the old-fashioned 1911 model Colt .45 automatic jammed into her waistband.

Finally, he yanked his eyes away from her flaunted American body. The light in the depths of Nina's gray-green eyes adjusted as she noted the way he stared at her bare arms. Her tanned forehead, which was sprinkled with copper freckles, frowned slightly. *Uh-huh. So you're one of those guys.*

Then, as Rashid looked away, she studied the collision of revulsion and lust; the way it flashed in his eyes, then resolved into contempt. She'd pulled several tours of duty in the Middle East. She knew that look from certain Arab men. It was pre-Islamic, rooted in ancient taboos of the North African tribes: contempt for the strangeness they saw in the female sex. And nothing was more alien to them than a free woman packing a .45.

But quite possibly, in this case his cultural baggage could work to her advantage. So she smiled. And not a bad smile. Ten years earlier and a bit slimmer, she would have been considered downright pretty.

Today she'd still look pretty—but no longer Starbucks-early morning-coffee pretty; more like last-call pretty in a country-and-western bar. Which was fine, because there was a lot more country than Starbucks in her chosen line of work.

Her clear, strong voice had served her well singing alto in her high school choir; but that was several lives ago, before she cut a swath through the U.S. Army: first female to command infantry in action (Desert Storm); first female to be awarded the Combat Infantryman's Badge. Now she'd wrangled her way into Northern Route via Delta. No one called her major now. Rank didn't matter here, only the mission.

Her cut-off jeans, running shoes, and a close-fitting purple tank top were a practical choice for undercover work, given the heat this July morning. To Rashid, however, the attire was totally revealing of her upper body and lower legs. Breaking his concentration, he now stole glances at her. He averted his eyes from her bare arms and the tidy swell of breasts confined in a sports bra. Her shoulders and throat were trim, muscled, well shaped. The clean physicality of her American-woman sweat cut toward him through the stale air like a dangerously unsheathed blade.

She smiled knowingly when she saw him struggle to avert his eyes. She stepped directly in front of him so that she was in line with his point of concentration on the wall. She folded her arms.

"Let's understand each other from the start. We have a lot in common, because this outfit I'm in is sneaky and very results-oriented. Just like you guys. It's like . . ." She paused, cocked her head to the side, and gave him a thoughtful squint. "Do you have kids? Well, you know how when you talk to a little kid it's best to stoop down, get on the same level with them and make direct eye contact?" She leaned forward from the waist, planted her hands on her knees, and looked him straight in the eyes. "What's happened is, because of what you guys did, my government has quietly given a few of us permission to get down on your level, follow me?"

Very deliberately she extended her right hand and placed her open palm on his bare chest. The whites of Rashid's eyes enlarged as he shied away. She leaned forward and lowered her voice. "Is it true that Ali, the husband of Muhammad's daughter Fatima, said that 'God created sexual desire in ten parts; nine parts were given to women and only one to men'?" She removed her hand, straightened up, and said, "I just felt your heart speed up in your chest. I understand this is not the most comfortable setting. You almost naked, me . . . uncovered."

She placed her hands on her hips. "But the fact is, we don't have a lot of time, you and I. That's for other people; the suits who work in offices and flirt by the watercooler and generally fuck things up."

Rashid had turned his head away from her and now fixed his gaze on a different wall. So she reached over and gripped his thick hair in her left hand and drew his head back toward her. She gauged him carefully, the way he tensed and planted his bare feet on the carpet. An inch shorter than she, and soft in the middle, but he had powerful soccer legs.

With her right hand she shoved the heavy pistol to the side of her waistband and quickly undid the snap on her Levis. "Is it also true your imams believe the greatest insult the United States inflicted on the country of the Two Holy Places was sending female soldiers there?"

She flicked the zipper down and used the pistol to lever back a corner of denim and some panty, revealing a raised whorl and purple dent of scar tissue. The entry wound was located in the whiter skin and freckles west of her belly button.

"Kalashnikov round, from an Iraqi Republican Guard. He got me low and to the right. I got him higher, center mass. And so ended one of my several dramas in the sand dunes. Remember Desert Storm? Back when we were defending your backward medieval kingdom?" Elastic snapped, the zipper hissed back up; Nina deftly buttoned her jeans and jammed the Colt back in place. "Yeah, I been to Saudi. Back then, when we traveled off base, we had to wear the Halloween costume. You know, that black bedsheet you make your women wear?"

She released her hold on his hair. Rashid leaned back and unfocused his eyes, turning his vision inward. To Nina it looked like he was searching for his desert trance. But she noted that, while his eyes toiled to achieve calm, the BBs of sweat on his forehead were growing to the size of gumdrops.

"Rashid, let's be candid here. You're not the warrior type. You're a money guy. There's no percentage in you playing it tough. I'd check my jihad contract if I were you. Somewhere in the fine print I think it says guys like you don't get the paradise bonus if you, ah . . ."—she curled her fingers, pointed her index finger between his eyes, and let her thumb fall like a hammer—". . . get yourself killed by a chick in cut-offs."

She stepped back and gave him a moment to think. Then she said, "We know you raise money through a network of businesses in the upper Midwest. DEA has you as a major smuggler of meth precursor from Canada. You're also into identity theft and forged documents. We know you disburse funds to Al Qaeda cells. Is there anything you'd like to tell me about something coming south across the Canadian border?"

Rashid lost his composure for a few beats and bared his teeth at her in a silent snarl. Then he lapsed back into his trance.

Encouraged, Nina threw up her hands in genial exasperation. "Okay. I tried nice. But you don't want nice. So now I'm pissed."

With far more strength than Rashid was prepared to believe existed in her body, Nina jerked him up by hair and shoulder and thrust him toward the door. "Comin' through," she called out.

The door swung open. Expertly pulling Rashid off balance, she propelled him into the hall. Hollywood and Bugs stood at the ready, and several other men were positioned down the hall, screening them from the office in the front of the building.

"Now what?" Hollywood asked.

"Time to adapt and improvise," Nina said. "He wants to go to the john, right?"

"Say again?"

"Clear that room of any civilians." She nodded down the hall.

"Ah, that's the women's can," Hollywood said.

"If you please," Nina said, jockeying Rashid forward.

Hollywood went down the hall, rapped on the door, and sang out. "Man needs to come in—duck and cover." Then he entered the bathroom and emerged ten seconds later. "Empty, it's all yours."

Nina nodded and turned to Bugs. "Duct tape. In my go-bag."

Bugs knelt to an equipment bag, removed a roll of tape, got up, and tucked it under Nina's arm. Hollywood gallantly opened the bathroom door.

"Now Rashid and I would like some privacy," Nina said.

"No problem," Bugs said as he and Hollywood took up positions on either side of the door.

Nina and Rashid careened through the door, bounced off a wall and into the row of sinks. Rashid started to fight back. He swung his elbows and shoulders and lashed out with his feet. The roll of tape went flying into a sink. But there was more desperation than training in his attempt, and Nina easily spun him, dropped her shoulder, set her stance, and drove a short, vicious right fist into his soft middle. As he sagged, gasping for breath, she maneuvered him into an open toilet stall.

Before he got his breath back, she had seated him on the toilet, retrieved the tape, and spiderwebbed his cuffed hands to the plumbing fixture with the gummy tape. More tape looped his ankles.

"Great stuff, duct tape," she said, stepping back.

He glared at her; pure, hot desert hate. Hollywood would have admired the way she met his glare, hate for hate.

Nine spoke fast. "Listen, you. I won't give the lecture about all the creepy shit you keep under that rock you crawled out from: the stonings, the honor killings, the clitoridectomies . . . Let's just say what we got here, between you and me, goes way back. But at least you're up front about it." She narrowed her eyes. "Fact is, what bothers me is how many of our own guys have you inside them wanting to come out. First day I was in the Army, at the reception station they kept us girls separate. We woke up and there was this graffiti spray-painted on the barracks wall that said: 'Never trust an animal that bleeds five days a month and doesn't die.'"

She leaned forward and tapped a rectangular plastic dispenser bolted to the wall that featured a drawing of a smiling nurse and a blue cross.

"Doesn't it make you a little nervous, being in America with all the unclean women out and about, just walking around during a certain time of month? Touching money. Preparing food." Nina ran her finger across the raised type on the dispenser.

PERSONAL HYGIENE AND CLEANLINESS
SANIBAG
For Sanitary Napkin Disposal
PLEASE DISCARD IN WASHROOM CONTAINER

Nina carefully studied his reaction. She'd judged him correctly. The wobble of pathological aversion had bumped the fatalistic desert trance from his brown eyes. She reached into the dispenser and pulled out a slender white paper bag on which a line drawing of a red vanity mirror framed the red type: *For Disposal of Feminine Products.* There was also a decorative red butterfly and a little red basket of flowers.

"Definitely unclean stuff going on by Wahhabi standards, I'd say." Nina let the slim bag flutter from her fingers and fall into his lap. "This one's empty."

She spun, walked to the step can in the corner, by the sinks, removed the cover, and hurled the plastic container across the room so a scatter of the crumbled sanitary bags spilled into the stall at Rashid's feet.

He hissed something in Arabic and drew back as she knelt, rummaged in the trash, and found a red-and-white bag containing a cylindrical tampon. "Nah." She discarded it and plucked up another bag crammed with a thick overnight pad with wings.

"This is more like it," she said.

She held it up so he could get a good look. There was a loud rip as she tore a broad strip of tape from the roll. Deftly, she taped the bag that contained the discarded pad to Rashid's thrashing chest.

Then Nina turned and walked from the washroom, kept going past Hollywood and Bugs, proceeded down the hall and out the back door to the parking lot. Before the door closed behind her she could hear Rashid bellowing in English:

"I WANT TO SPEAK TO A MAN. I WANT TO SPEAK TO A MAN!"

Nina opened the door to the brown Chevy van, removed a pack of American Spirit filter cigarettes from the dashboard, picked up a BIC lighter off the seat, and lit the cigarette. She grimaced. This thing had put her back on the smokes.

She took a deep drag and let her eyes trail over the strip-mall clutter, west, toward Ann Arbor. She'd left her daughter, Kit, there with her aunt. Events happened so fast. Ten days ago Kit had been in second grade, in Lucca, Italy. Now they were a long way from Nina's last duty station on the Tuscan plain.

Then Northern Route got the green light. Since they were headed for the upper Midwest, Nina brought her daughter, thinking to drop her off . . .

Nina looked at the cigarette smoldering in her fingers. Seven-year-old Kit would give her hell if she smelled tobacco smoke on her. Nina paced and smoked and waited. She field-stripped the remains of her cigarette and lit another one. She felt a vibration in the heat and saw clouds coiling in the western sky. She'd rigorously disciplined her mind not to let her personal life intrude on her work. But they were flying by the seat of their pants on this one. She'd have to pack Kit off to her father in Minnesota. Fast. And that would be a can of worms . . .

Her thought was interrupted by Hollywood's triumphant howl as he jogged out the back door, stopped, grinned, and jerked his thumb back toward the doorway. "That lad has been seriously mind-fucked. Honor is due. You improvise well." Hollywood inclined his head and flourished his hand in an elegant old-fashioned bow.

"What can I say. Some Wahhabi extremists tend to be phobic about us girls and our plumbing. So I took a flyer," Nina said.

"Some flyer," Hollywood said. "He spilled his guts. Not bad, for under thirty minutes. I take back anything I ever said about split-tails not belonging in this outfit."

"Right. So?"

"It's a compartmentalized operation, so he doesn't know the target or the timing. But he bragged it's not just any bomb . . ."

"You mean?" Nina came up slightly on the balls of her feet.

"I mean we might have hit the big one," Hollywood said. He was not a man given to being sentimental. But his voice shook.

"Nuclear," Nina said, letting the suddenly frivolous cigarette drop from her fingers and grinding it under her heel. There are different levels of adrenaline boost: there's the surge of competition; there's getting shot at and shooting back. But now she felt a solid jolt of very major high-end juice. A whole different order of magnitude.

"They got one, *here*?" The idea dried up all her spit.

Hollywood paused, licked his sweaty lips. "When we took off the cuffs, he said, 'Hiroshima,' and did, like . . ." Hollywood made the sign of a mushroom cloud in the air with his hands. "And he said it's already in the mix. I get the impression he's giving it up because he thinks it's too late for us to stop it."

They locked eyes. Nina could feel her pulse throb in a vein in her throat. "Sporty," she said.

Not usually this dry, my voice . . .

"He gave us the name of a smuggler," Hollywood said, going past her, opening the side door to the van, coming out with an AAA road atlas of the United States.

"No fooling. We got a name," Nina said, leaning forward.

"Damn straight. And a location: Langdon, North Dakota."

"Jesus? That's . . ."

Hollywood thumbed through the atlas, held it up. "Canadian border. Wheatfields. Doesn't get more wide open. And, Nina, they're getting sneaky on us; it ain't an Arab. I mean . . . he's not a Middle Eastern type. Some of the new security must be working, because it sounds like they contracted the job out. It's one of us. An American."

Nina bit her lip, thinking. "Once Rashid talks to the suits . . ."

Hollywood nodded and held up his cell phone. "Yeah, we'll lose the jump. I had to phone it in. They're skeptical. Some desk-bound commando actually told me that interrogation was a bit over our pay grade. So fuck 'em. I say we just go with it."

Nina narrowed her eyes. "On our own?"

"Absolutely. We can't leave it to the headquarters pogues, not after what happened on 9/11 . . ."

Their eyes locked, more intimate than illicit lovers: *WE CAN DO THIS THING.*

Hollywood said, "They put us way out on our own. So why not run with it. What do you say?"

Nina clicked her teeth, grinned. "Just grab our go-bags and hit it. Get out ahead of this thing. What's the name?"

"Shuster."

"We dump Rashid with the advance party. Go in hot and hard," Nina said flatly.

"There it is. Just you, me, Bugs, and Jane. And the Hardy Boys for backup. Question is, how?"

"We'll think of something," Nina said.

Chapter Two

He sat in his car, *a silly smile on his face because he was staring at a wrecked phone booth. The door was off. The side panels splintered. Weeds grew in the cracked concrete floor. A phone booth in the middle of nowhere. But it still worked. And there he was, on the empty prairie waiting for an Arab terrorist to call.*

In just a few months his life had turned into a movie. It happened like this: these Arabs were sneaking some explosives across the border, and, by accident, he had stumbled onto their smuggling operation.

At first they were going to kill him. Just step on him, like a bug. On his knees—staring up into the barrel of a pistol—he talked fast to save his life. What had been a private fantasy became his salvation. His would-be killer had listened, then he'd lowered the pistol. He'd invited him to sit down, drink some coffee, talk some more.

He showed them how he could provide access for an attack that would be deadlier than 9/11. And how it couldn't be done without him. But he wanted something in return. To prove their sincerity, he demanded they help him settle one old score. It was the beginning of the plan.

It wasn't just the million dollars they were going to pay him. Now that his potential had been revealed, he wanted a new identity. A new life.

Soon, maybe tomorrow, he would leave this desolate flat land. He looked around. The rest of the country liked to laugh about how this was nowhere. Well, all the smug fuckers out there with their Fargo jokes better get ready for a big surprise. All his life he'd been taken for granted. No one had a clue that he was changing.

The idea jolted through him.

Sugar rush.

Charon drained the can of Coke and tossed it into the passenger-seat foot well, where it clattered on seven other empty cans.

Charon was his future name. Billy Charon. William Samuel Charon, exact future address as yet unknown. He'd had to come up with a name fast for the new identification they were providing him. He smiled broadly.

His new afterlife . . . as it were. There'd be a lot of talk about afterlife when the time came. His would be much more pleasant than a lot of other people's.

The Mole was not real happy with the name. It was unusual and would draw attention. But Charon insisted on it. People from North Dakota weren't dumb, after all. They had the highest high school graduation rate in the country. So he'd read a few books, even Greek mythology and some stuff about comparative religion. He'd picked Charon, not just because it was apt, but because he liked the antique implications. Specifically, as pertains to this project, he enjoyed the irony of how the name preceded, and so trumped, the current intermural fuss between the Christians and Islam.

But he believed in giving credit where it was due. He did take comfort from a line of the Koran. The one about he who kills one innocent person kills the whole world. Now that he had killed his first person, it helped him get over the problem of magnitude.

As he waited he turned the Pearl Jam CD up so loud the drums and guitars made the inside of the car jump. Too much, too loud. Back off. Remain calm. Like the Mole always said, don't draw attention to yourself. He tapped off the stereo.

In the sudden quiet he stared out the windshield at the panorama of sky. Far to the south two white pencil-thin contrails streaked across a solitary patch of blue: F-16s heading home to the Air Force base at Grand Forks. The rest of the sky was massive, stonelike. Endless piles of veined marble clouds. Far to the north, he could make out the dark ribbons of a rainstorm.

He was parked on the cracked concrete apron of an abandoned roadside attraction called Camp's Paradise Country Club: a miniature golf course, gas station, and general store some optimist had created back during the Missile Time. A few hundred yards away, next to an overgrown railroad siding, a collapsing grain elevator tilted against the sky like a North Dakota tombstone. All his life he'd been hemmed in by this horizon; blue and green bands of monotony in the summer, gray and white in the winter. Now he was going to be free.

And rich.

He'd go somewhere that wasn't flat, somewhere that wasn't so hot or so cold. Somewhere with an ocean.

Charon checked the digital clock on the dashboard, put the air conditioner fan down from four to one, and cracked the window so he could hear the pay phone ring in the booth several feet away. In fact, someone had used it already today because Charon saw their tire tracks in the orange mud and also saw that they'd dropped a jelly doughnut on the booth's damp concrete pad, in front of the broken door.

Dropped it and left it and now a mob of big sturdy black ants swarmed on it.

He wondered how long that doughnut had been out there. Probably only an hour or so, it didn't look that old. Self-consciously, he looked around. The urge started in his eyes and descended into his mouth, and he felt the saliva start at the back of his tongue.

He licked his lips and stared at the pastry.

The insect activity seemed to burst from a bulge of jelly on the side of the pastry. He squinted. The way the thin light hit the jelly made it look almost voluptuous, like a naughty fat lady's red titty nipple.

He pulled his eyes away. He had to control himself. Like the Mole said. Concentrate on the Big Picture. Charon grinned, remembering an old line from that TV show, where David Carradine played Kane, the kung fu pilgrim. *The greatest compliment a student can pay his teacher is to surpass him.* The man he called the Mole had admitted that Charon had surpassed all his expectations.

The phone rang, right on time. The Mole was punctual, as usual. Charon got out of the car, carefully stepped over the jelly doughnut, entered the booth, and picked up the receiver.

"This is Charon," he said.

"Listen, we have a problem," the Mole said.

"You mean the rain; I know. We got it to the site. But we'll have to wait for the rain to stop to get it in position."

"I mean in addition to the rain."

"Okay, what kind of problem?" Charon asked.

"Remember Rashid? You met him in Winnipeg for the demonstration."

"Sure. Rashid." The Saudi prick. "He didn't particularly like me, but he liked what I had to sell."

"Listen. He was taken in Detroit . . ."

"Taken?"

"Captured, arrested. He knows a lot."

"He doesn't know where. And he doesn't know when."

"But he knows about the weapon and the kind of target. He met us. He gave us an advance. He was trained in the camps, he should be tough. But it's been my experience they start to go soft once they get over here."

"Unlike you," Charon said.

"That's right. I'm a student of history, not the Koran. History tells me that one out of three talk during interrogation. And remember, we're not among the faithful, we're just the hired help. He may give them something; a place, a name, to protect his other operations."

"If he talks, how much time have we got?" Charon asked.

"No telling."

Charon's breath came more rapidly. The idea of the government sending agents after *him* increased his heartbeat. Looking down, he saw that the black ants had started climbing over his boots. Methodically, he stomped on them. Stomp. Stomp. Stomp. Then he said, "Are you getting scared?"

"This isn't funny. You should leave now, get in position near the target. Just meet me on the road," the Mole said.

"Okay, okay. But I get to do another one. That was the deal."

"That was the deal," the Mole said with an audible sigh.

"You don't sound real sincere. I can still pull the plug on all this. One phone call and it's all over," Charon said.

"A deal's a deal," the Mole said more firmly.

"Okay. So when we go do it, I want to take another one along." Charon's voice sped up. "To celebrate."

On the other end of the phone connection, the Mole marveled at the total imbalance, the complete lack of proportion. Giving credit to a Jew had never been his style, but Hannah Arendt certainly summed it up when she coined the phrase "the banality of evil." In his youth, he had killed out of political conviction. But now his former Marxism and Arab nationalism were seen as just another infidel pose. Jihad was the new battle cry back in the region of his birth. He had become a contract man. In the eyes of the jihadists he was a contemptible, but useful, smuggler of Western poisons: drugs, alcohol, and tobacco.

In turn, he held the jihadists in contempt: primitive fools, like the cleric in Egypt who urged his followers to go out and tear down the pyramids. But beneath the guise of his U.S. citizenship, he was still an Arab radical and was not opposed to killing Americans for money.

A lot of money.

But not for pleasure. He'd thought he'd seen it all. But he'd never believed in monsters, until now. And he had basically created this one.

"Well . . ." Charon demanded.

"Take your pick." He could not quite disguise the disgust in his voice.

"Good. Okay. So that's it," Charon said.

"Unless the FBI comes knocking on our doors, it all depends on the weather . . ."

"I'll keep an eye out, okay? And *some* of it depends on the weather. *Most* of it depends on me," Charon chided him.

"Yes," the Mole said carefully. Dealing with Charon was like walking on eggshells. Or live grenades. "Most of it depends on you. We need two days for the ground to firm up once the rain stops."

"That'd be my estimate. It's starting to clear to the west," Charon said.

"That's what I figure. But you should get moving. Your security's on the way."

"Oh, I see. You want to keep an eye on me? Whatsa matter, you don't trust me on my own?" Charon's voice cracked into a laugh. It was their personal joke. But the serious fact was, the operation was put together in such a way that only Charon could pull the trigger. The Mole wanted to make sure that nothing interfered with the rendezvous of Charon's finger and that trigger.

"Just as long as you keep your impulses under control," the Mole said, trying for humor.

"No problem there. See ya." Charon hung up the phone, exited the booth, and, without missing a step, leaned down and snatched up the debris of the jelly doughnut. He wiped the smear of mud away and most of the ants and took a bite. The jelly squirted out and he had to lick the sticky goo from his fingers.

Definitely a sugar rush!

On the Minnesota–North Dakota border, the man Charon referred to as the Mole walked away from his remote phone booth of choice. He got back in his vehicle and headed north along rainswept Interstate 29. He hoped Charon was right, that this was the last of the front moving through.

But every time he saw a shudder of lightning on the horizon he flinched.

Not good.

It was still raining back where the weapon had been delivered. He imagined the tendrils of lightning sending out impulses that tickled the circuits in the power source attached to the blasting caps they'd set so lovingly in all that Semtex.

A ton of it.

Semtex, the Cadillac of explosives. A push to get the ball rolling.

Far to the east the sky flickered, and he braced behind the steering wheel as he counted the seconds until he heard a low rumble. He didn't think that an electrical storm could prematurely power the detonators. But the technology was new to him; the combination of frequency and carrier-coded signal . . .

So he wasn't 100 percent sure.

Damn.

• • •

The weapon sat in the rain, mired in the mud.

Simplicity itself. It hid in plain sight. Poised. Washed clean. A gleaming tribute to Al Qaeda's brilliant high-concept, low-tech philosophy.

The things the Americans see every day will be the tools we use to kill them.

In very large numbers.

But the religious fanatics lacked the Mole's cold vision. They thought it was a great victory to knock down a few buildings, to wipe out a few thousand city dwellers.

He had enhanced Charon's original concept into something as grim as the plagues in the Bible. And, best of all, the whole world would get to watch it unfold live, in full color, on television. Unfold over days, weeks, and months.

There was only one complication.

The components for the weapon had traveled halfway around the world. They had been painstakingly configured, everything had been calculated for maximum impact.

The Mole hated leaving anything to chance. He had followed the weapon and had seen it delivered with his own eyes. Four hundred crucial yards now separated the weapon and its target.

After all the planning and work, there was one last ancient and durable obstacle to overcome. Like Napoleon at Waterloo, they had to delay their attack, confronted by a sea of mud.

They were waiting on the weather.

Chapter Three

Ace Shuster woke up feeling lucky.

And he'd be the first to tell you, it was a feeling that slanted uphill against the odds.

So he kept his eyes clamped shut and tried to hold on to the feeling, which was a challenge considering the ache that wrapped his body. But after a few moments he ascertained that the pain was all surface, the fatigue of a hangover, not a specific injury. And that was a good sign.

For five long minutes he explored the velvet throb on the back of his eyelids. He'd wait a while, get real prepared before he opened his eyes. This was a habit from the old days when guaranteed trouble would be perched on his bedpost, waiting to pounce.

First he moved his tongue around in his mouth and found all his teeth were still where they should be. Then he moved his fingers and toes; then his neck, his arms, and his legs. Nothing hurt, so he was pretty sure he had come through the previous night reasonably unscathed. Tentatively, he snaked out his hand and prodded around in the bed and determined he was the sole occupant. He thought on it and assumed he'd been mostly drinking beer last night. He allowed that he'd made a few passes at the hard stuff around midnight.

Yesterday, his younger brother, Dale, had given him this rock-bottom nugget of wisdom about drinking: *Don't put it in your mouth, dummy.*

Check it out. Reduced to sitting still for advice from his concerned but severely limited nerd kid brother.

It wasn't out of the question to wonder where he was, so he braced himself and finally opened his eyes. A curling baseball poster was Scotch-taped to the wall. Slowly Ace raised a slightly shaky hand and saluted Roger Maris. Same poster had hung over his bed back on the farm when he was in high school.

So far, so good. He recognized the room. He'd managed to make it home. Then, as his senses unclogged, he heard the familiar sounds that he'd heard all his life. The wind doing its low howl down from Manitoba. The steady backbeat chug of a tractor somewhere out in the green grain ocean. Another enslaved North Dakotan, addicted to adversity. Dumb shit. Probably trying to pull a swather through his flax in this weather. Ace shook his head. The goddamn wind and the goddamn wheat and the goddamn tractor going on forever.

He saw a corner of clotted gray sky in the window over the bed. He smelled a moody ferment of rain in the air. Barley, durum wheat, and the pungent perfume of canola. God, would it rain *again* today?

As if on cue, the tractor stuttered and then quit.

Had it rained last night? He couldn't remember. Which meant he drove home blacked out. From where? Okay. Work it back. He got a snapshot of a dark-haired woman with a pretty face, except when she opened her mouth her teeth were too big. There was an Old Milwaukee beer sign over her shoulder. He didn't remember the woman but he recognized the sign.

At the bar in Starkweather.

Where else.

Ace shook his head. Dumb to go back there. Like picking at a scab.

Then he got the flash again. Why not something fast and pretty just for him? Why not today?

Damn. Just something . . .

Ace rolled over and planted his bare feet on the floor. Originally this room over the bar had been his dad's office, then it was a storeroom. Next they'd converted it to a one bedroom apartment, then a hangout for Friday-night poker games. Then they'd rented it out again. When they ran out of renters it was converted back to a storeroom. Ace rubbed his eyes. Since he and Darlene split up he'd been storing himself here.

He stood up and tested his balance. He had talked Darlene into no lawyers—a friendly separation and division of resources, she getting the lion's share, of course, plus alimony and child support. Like in the old joke about fires, floods, and twisters. Hurricane Darlene got the house in the end. She promptly sold the house and moved back to Bismarck, where they had malls and designer coffee.

Downstairs, he heard Gordy working at the hyper rate of a meth-addicted beaver—stacking crates of booze for pickup on the loading dock in the back of the storeroom.

Gordy Riker was the dark side of the relentless prairie work ethic. He labored to consolidate a corner of the smuggling in the county. Ace's dad's network was his present coup. Ace didn't care to continue the family franchise, so Gordy worked hard, selling off the equipment, cleaning out the last of the inventory. Through hard work and attention to detail, he was inheriting the network of Canadian drivers who ran the booze and cigarettes north, and folding them into his plan to bring drugs south. Ace just signed off, took his cut, and sent the rest to Dad in Florida. The plan was to sell everything. After four generations, the Shusters were leaving North Dakota.

The feeling came back, a warm honey spiral in his chest, a sensation of sparkly gold dust—*snap*—just like that, in his fingertips.

Lucky.

But reluctantly now, reality came creeping in and he admitted to himself that he started every day like this, wanting to believe that something different would happen. Something just for him.

He got up and went into the shower and sloughed off the top layer of hangover in strong jets of hot water. Eyes shut, he shampooed and shaved by feel. Then he toweled off in front of the wash basin. The mirror was a murky cloud of steam, like his memory of last night. He rubbed a tiny circle in the fogged glass. Just enough to see one bloodshot blue eye staring back at him, like coming from way off there in some deep shit. Which pretty much summed it up.

But thirty minutes into the day, the good feeling accompanied him into the small living room. His space was sparse and tidy; short on furniture and long on books. As a young man he became a dedicated reader; during a twelve-month stay at the James River Correctional Center at Jamestown, the state farm east of Bismarck. Wrapped in a towel, he sat down at his desk, opened the middle drawer, and took out two items; just like he'd done every morning for the last month. It was his little comic ceremony, which, nevertheless, contained a dark grain of truth.

First: he placed the well-worn Vintage paperback on the desk. Albert Camus. *The Myth of Sisyphus.*

Second: next to the book he placed the old .38-caliber pistol Dad used to keep under the bar. The pistol was not real clean but it was real loaded.

He open the thumbed pages to the first chapter and read the first couple sentences: *"There is but one truly serious philosophical problem, and that is suicide. Judging whether life is or is not worth living amounts to answering the fundamental question of philosophy."*

The lucky feeling was still cooking in his chest as he closed the book, so he put it and the pistol back in the drawer and stood up.

• • •

Ace dressed in faded jeans, a faded red T-shirt with the neck and sleeves scissored out, and a pair of old running shoes. He came down the stairs into the main room of the bar, which was a dogleg that wrapped around the old kitchen, now an office space. The booths had been removed and sold to a new malt shop on Main Street. The place had been stripped bare, just an empty mirror and three bar stools. One table and some chairs remained in the main room where Ace usually had his coffee and read his morning paper. And there was the old pinball machine. Ace wasn't going to sell that. No way. That would go with him.

A dozen framed newspaper photos hung on the wall in the alcove off the bar. A small flag. Ace made a mental note to take the pictures and the flag off the wall and box them. He'd promised them to the North Dakota Room at the county library.

He nodded to Gordy, who was behind the bar drinking a can of Coke for breakfast. Sweating standing still, Gordy was strapped into a black Velcroed back brace. Square and muscular, always unshaven. Even as a little kid, Gordy had lots of hair; a cross between the Energizer Bunny and a werewolf.

"Late night, huh?" Gordy asked. Friendly enough except for his restless, calculating eyes. He was, still, for all his ambitious plans, the hired help. And you could never tell when this hung-over shadow of Ace Shuster would experience a lethal two-minute relapse back to when he was the baddest thing in three counties.

Ace nodded and climbed on a bar stool. Gordy put two Alka Seltzers in a glass, poured in some water, and pushed it across the bar. Ace drank his breakfast. Gordy poured a cup of black coffee, slid it over along with a copy of the *Grand Forks Herald*.

"So what's going on?" Ace asked.

"Nothing much. Just the last few pickups tonight, tomorrow."

Ace nodded. They were cleaning out the last of the booze. Pickups after ten. There were only three full-time deputies and one highway patrol in the county. They seldom staffed from ten at night to six A.M. There was more Border Patrol around since 9/11, but they seldom patrolled the prairie roads the Canucks used when they came down to shop for the whiskey.

"Don't suppose anybody called?" Ace said.

"Nah."

Figured. Liquidation. Ace thought it a fitting word to describe the demise of a drinking joint. Everything must go. The license, the building, the chairs, the cash register. Ace himself. Ace's function was to preside over the dismantling of the Missile Park Bar. Just like Dale was selling off the last of Dad's heavy equipment at the shed across the road. Dad moved to Florida, picked up a golf club, and never looked back. Ma, expert at denial and rationalization, went to church and played bridge.

Ace sipped his coffee, lit his first Camel of the day, and opened the paper.

"I already looked, nothing new on Ginny," Gordy said. Ginny Weller, a town girl who'd moved to Grand Forks, had gone missing last month.

Ace nodded, scanned the section anyway, and turned to the commodities markets in business. "Three-dollar spring wheat," he said and shook his head.

"Umm," Gordy mumbled. He was a town kid whose father ran a string of failing gas stations. He'd never sat on a tractor in his life.

Ace passed on sports, repelled when he saw a lot of Minnesota purple in the feature football art. He came to the daily crossword and settled in on 1 across. "Four-letter word for southern veggie," he said.

"Corn," Gordy said.

"C'mon numbnuts. It says *southern*."

"Ah, grits?"

"*Four* letters," Ace said. He checked 1 down. Dark yellow. After a moment he penciled in "ocher," which gave him an O for 1 across. Okay. He got it. He was starting to pencil in "okra," when he heard tires crunch to a stop on the weed-choked trap rock out front.

Ace and Gordy exchanged surprised looks when they heard something they hadn't heard at the Missile Park in a long, long time: female voices. And these female voices were on the shrill side, pitched high, banging back and forth at each other.

Ace winced and looked at Gordy, who shrugged, came around the bar, went to the front, and looked out the window.

"Two chicks and a little girl," Gordy said.

"What are they driving?"

"Looks like a red Volvo. Hard to tell the way it's all dusted up. With Minnesota plates. Got an old green Wellstone sticker on the bumper. And, ah, this rainbow-type decal."

Ace's expression jiggled between a wince and a grin, "A Volvo, huh? Boy. They're lost for sure."

"I hear you. Jeez, busy day—old Chevy truck just pulled in, too. Arizona plates."

"So what are they yelling about? The women."

"Ah." Gordy craned his neck closer to the window. "Sounds like one of them wants to use the john and the other one ain't buying it, says it's just an excuse to have a drink. Now the other one and the little girl are trying to talk her out of it."

"What's she look like?" Ace asked.

"Which one?"

"The one who wants a drink."

"Ah, she's a redhead, not bad; kinda tough-looking."

Ace came forward off his stool. "How do you mean, tough?"

Gordy grinned. "Tough like the grim-fucking-reaper. She's got this skull-and-crossbones tattooed on her shoulder."

Ace nodded. Gordy would like that. Like it better if she had a Harley logo tattooed on her ass.

Just then the door opened. And Ace expected to see a tough redhead walk through. Instead, it was a leather-tanned older guy wearing this flowery, flowing orange and red Hawaiian shirt, with a full head of hair going white. Ace sat up and took notice. You don't see that many older guys with forearms like that, who walked so light on their feet. Who came into a room checking everything with those pale quiet eyes. Ace had seen eyes like that on serious lifers during the month he spent on orientation in the Bismarck state pen before they sent him out to do the easy time on the farm.

"I'd get near a phone if I was you, call nine-one-one," the guy said, jabbing his thumb over his shoulder. "Got a cat fight goin' out there." He walked to the bar, sat down, and stared at the wall full of pictures.

Gordy came up. The guy said, "You serving any lunch?"

"Sorry, the kitchen's closed. We've sort of gone out of business," Gordy said.

Very clearly Ace heard one of the women yell, "Yeah, well, I didn't drive all the way out here to watch you crawl into a bottle in Nowhere, North Dakota, goddammit."

Gordy and the guy drifted to the window and stared into the parking lot.

"Which one's that?" Ace asked.

"The other one," Gordy said.

The guy nodded, "The dark-haired, dikey-looking one."

Ace and Gordy perked up and raised their eyebrows thoughtfully. *The dikey one. Uh-huh.*

The guy shrugged. "Minnesota plates. That's a dead giveaway. Twin Cities is a regular dike pit. I feel bad for the kid."

Ace and Gordy nodded again, thoughtfully.

"Aw, screw lunch, gimme a beer," the guy said.

"All we got left is Old Milwaukee," Gordy said.

"That'll do." When he had a beer he gestured at the walls of an alcove to the right of the bar. The framed pictures, newspaper articles. A military unit flag. "Yeah. This is the place."

"How's that?" Gordy said.

"I was here once, back in the seventies. Came to visit my brother when he was in the Air Force, in the 321st Missile Wing. Was stationed down in one of those control pods, tending to ten of those big mothers, the Minutemen. We sat in this bar and had a beer."

Ace smiled. And Gordy said, "Sure, during the Missile Time."

The guy nodded. "Usually I take Route 2 across, but, hell, thought I'd swing up through here, not in a big hurry. So when did they pull the missiles out?"

Ace stared at his coffee cup. In the shadow of those missiles he'd had something like a happy childhood. Whole damn town had . . .

"You fucking bitch! You are not going to pull this shit after all we been through . . ." The angry voice screeching through the front door. The floor snapped back on its hinges, rattled off the wall.

Then, *"Mommm . . ."*

That was the kid. A wail full of shattered innocence that got to Ace like a dentist's drill—kid suddenly figuring out, hey, my world is falling to shit here. That nothing's for sure anymore. Something kids shouldn't have to bend their minds around. Ace understood it perfectly from arguments in the house back in town. His eight-year-old son Tyler, and six-year-old Trevor . . .

Ace shook his head. He'd started losing to Darlene when he let her stick those foo-foo names on those boys and he never did catch up.

And then Ace got a look at the redhead.

Chapter Four

She came spinning through the door fast. Ace thought he caught a whiff of sulfur—but also roses—so he sat up and took a hard look as she wheeled around and confronted the dark-haired one, hands on hips.

"Back off, Janey . . ." Real strong no-nonsense voice.

The redhead was built, but not that built. And she was pretty—but not stun-gun pretty, to Ace. What struck him was her presence. Her stance, the tattoo on her shoulder, and the set of her eyes hinted at danger.

Not just trouble. Trouble in a woman was appealing to scavengers who like to nose around in weak, messy lives.

Uh-uh. Just lookit the way the energy pulses around her. Like a swarm of hornets.

He saw real danger in her too-intense green eyes—and Ace was thinking, *Damn if a redhead couldn't look like she invented anger.* Eve, the first woman, was probably a redhead. This one was mad and fed up as a woman could be; short red hair frizzed out like static. She wore flared jeans with cargo pockets, this iddy-biddy white top with spaghetti straps and short at the waist, so her flat

belly'd show. And sandals. Red lipstick; red polish on her fingernails and toenails starting to chip like she'd picked at it all the way
from Minnesota. All that red hit his eyes at once, like warning flags.
Clear across the room he could see the pale stripe of untanned skin
on the third finger of her left hand where she had recently removed
a wedding band. Her worn leather saddlebag purse caught his attention; gray quill leather he couldn't place. And the way it seemed to
overflow with too many things, Ace read the purse as a sign.

Like her life, maybe.

And then their eyes caught briefly in some fast barroom magic.
Ace had to work at getting his breath. He felt the smile roll into his
face, rubbing out the hangover. Figure the odds.

Damn.

You spend your life standing out under the biggest loneliest sky
in the world and you're just bound to get hit by lightning . . . eventually.

And, aw shit, her eyes were that kind of sticky hot that transfix a
guy if he ain't real careful. Damn if he didn't feel the tug clear across
the room. And he was sure he knew her just a little bit. *Not real
sure if you're a saint in the kitchen, but I'd bet my last dollar you're
a whore in the dark.*

Ace Shuster just had to go with it.

And it was like the feeling he woke up with this morning had
climbed in the catbird seat and was driving him the way he'd
pushed all that big iron for Irv Fuller's dad all those years. The tug
just kept getting stronger and more complicated with him ad-lib-
bing a few self-dramatic flashes of redemption and rescue and de-
liverance. So he just had to stand up and clear his throat, like he was
waiting on a formal introduction.

Goddamn, Red. I been waiting to meet you all my life.

The dark-haired one was inside now and read his face quick and
fired a hostile look right through him.

The dark-haired one . . .

And for a moment Ace almost took a sensible step back because these women had all the right curves but he didn't see an ounce of softness showing and that should be a caution—but his curiosity had the better of his common sense . . .

And then he thought, *Uh-huh, like the guy said, the dark-haired one could be a lesbian.* Maybe that's what he was picking up? She was younger. Cleaner of muscle—no, strike that—more like colder, with permanent moody shadows burned right into her like beautiful bruises. Witch-black hair, styled short on the side, longer on top. No makeup, no purse; green designer fatigue pants and heavy black boots. And carrying a lot of metal, gleams of it notched the outline of both ears and pierced her left nostril. *More at her throat, a coke spoon on a silver chain,* Ace thought. He squinted and saw it was a little double-bladed ax.

"Girls, girls." Gordy tried acting big and easy and gracious. Coming forward, the peacemaker.

"Girls!" hissed the redhead. "You see any fucking *girls* around here?"

"Mom!" The little girl made a face.

Gordy swallowed and said, mollifying: "Ladies."

"I'll settle for the *ladies room,*" said the redhead, raising her eyebrows.

"Ah, that door past the pinball machine."

Ace eyed Gordy, who raised a reassuring hand. "No problem, I cleaned it this morning."

Ace nodded and turned his attention to the kid, who was around six or seven, in beat-up tennies, shorts, a yellow T-shirt with *North Shore* printed across the chest. She was angular like her mom, with the same freckles and the same thick, burnt-crimson hair, but longer, pulled back in a ponytail. Dejected, she plopped down on a chair at the table and folded her arms across her chest.

The dark-haired one lit a cigarette. The kid waved her hand in disgust, got up, stalked across the empty bar, past where Ace stood and brooded at the pinball machine in the corner. She went up on tiptoes and studied the glassed-in bumpers and lights. Touched the flippers on the side.

Aware of Ace watching her, she asked, "What kind of video game is this?"

Ace was impressed. Cool kid. Staying focused through all this bullshit. He smiled. "Well, it ain't a video game. This is what you call a machine. Got no computer in it. There's springs and pulleys and stuff like that."

The girl made a face. "Springs?"

"Yeah, you put in a quarter, pull that knob, and these five ball bear—"

"*Kit!*"

The dark-haired one hurled it with a sharp huff to her voice, almost like a snort, like when a doe warns a fawn.

The girl smiled tightly and stepped away.

"Not supposed to talk to strangers, huh? That's good. Tell my own kids like that," Ace said with a nod, leaning back.

The mom came out of the john. Her hands busy around her waist in a reflex, tucking in an imaginary shirt. The dark-haired one got up and approached her. "Well," she said.

"There was a theater in town, maybe you two could take in a show." Eyes darting. Still some mad in her voice, dismissive.

"While we're taking in a show, where are you going to be?"

"Here maybe. I'll hang out for a while. I need some time to think about things."

"Things."

"Us. You and me. I need some time to think about us," said the redhead.

To Ace the words were barbed. Like big muskie lures swishing in the air. Whatever they had going had burst through normal restraints.

"You bitch," said the dark-haired one. "I took time off work. I walked out on Debbie to play nursemaid to you. Now you're slid-ing back into it." She shook her finger in the redhead's face. "Hang out here, huh? And drink, right?" She stuck a finger in the red-head's face. "You're the one who has to get drunk to tolerate sex with a man, remember."

The redhead slapped the hand away. A crisp focused slap that cracked like a whip and brought Ace forward on the balls of his feet.

"No, please," the kid cried.

The dark-haired one seized the redhead by the arm and yanked her toward the door. The redhead resisted, they began to shove each other. The kid screamed, got between them and both women tried to move her out of the way. Tug-of-war.

The kid came away wincing with red Indian burns on her arm.

The dark-haired one was coiled to hit back but Ace was up and moving, amazingly light on his feet for a man with a bellyful of hot hangover gravel. Going in, he noticed that the old guy at the bar had put down his beer bottle and stood, hands loose at his sides, watching in a certain way.

"Hey, take it outside," Gordy yelled.

"Mom. C'mon, let's go," yelled the kid, grabbing at her mother's arm.

"Not now, okay? Just, not now," the redhead said. Then, in an eruption of nerves, she shoved her daughter away. "Look. Mom needs a time-out. *Okay?*"

"That's it, hands off the kid," Ace said.

The guy at the bar was bouncing slowly from foot to foot, watching them carefully with those flat dead lifer's eyes. Ace sig-naled him, firm but not belligerent. *Back off. I got this.*

Gordy rolled his eyes. "Ace, you're making a big mistake here. Walk away, man."

Ace ignored Gordy, threw open his arms, swept the women for-ward, and marched them through the door. They banged down the porch steps and into the parking lot.

"What'd I tell ya," the guy said as he and Gordy hurried out the door. To watch. "A cat fight."

"I don't know. I'm sure not buying this. Uh-uh," Gordy said.

Cats?

Ace was thinking: *More like cougars, jock cougars, padded with muscle.* It took all his strength to move them and then a full minute to untangle them and get them separated. Enough time for several cars to pull onto the shoulder of Highway 5 to rubberneck the goings-on. Ace sensed more than saw the drivers hunching to their cell phones. As he held the women at arm's length he was panting and sweating with the exertion, and his hangover had started banging like a drum.

But he felt good, younger, in step with fortune.

"Okay," he said, "it's like this. Red, you sit on the porch. And you . . ."

"Jane," the dark-haired one snarled.

"Jane—you go stand by your car. We're going to calm down for a minute. Then we're going to talk, one at a time."

"Where do I go?" the little girl said, rubbing a fist over her tears.

"You stay right here with me," Ace said as he gently lowered a protective hand on her shoulder.

It took another muscular minute to manhandle them into their separate corners. Just about the time he got them quieted down, Ace saw the black-and-white Crown Vic with the Cavalier County five-pointed gold star come up fast and turn into his parking lot.

Chapter Five

County Deputy Lyle Vinson had graduated in the same class with Gordy and Ace's brother Dale. With *his* bulk augmented by a Kevlar vest, Lyle looked like the product of a union between a fireplug and a sumo wrestler as he eased from the car.

He hitched up his service belt and took a thoughtful sip from a twenty-ounce plastic bottle of Diet Coke, set the Coke on the roof of the car, and hitched his belt again. Studied moves. Letting some seriousness sink into this situation. Then he eyed the two angry women. Then the crying little girl. Finally he settled his gaze on Ace.

"Couple people called dispatch about a ruckus in your parking lot," Lyle said. "Little early in the day for a drunk bar fight, ain't it, Ace? Seeing's how they ain't been a fight at the Missile Park for going on ten years."

"Nobody's drinking—*yet*," Jane said.

"Nobody's drinking, period," Ace said. "The redhead came to use the bathroom and the other one and her got into an argument, so I helped them outside and separated them and . . ."

Lyle held up his hand, "Let's see some ID, folks. License and registration." The two women went to their purses, then the glove compartment of the car, and produced their driver's licenses and the title to the Volvo.

Lyle raised an eyebrow. "You just bought this car yesterday in St. Paul?"

"Yes, officer," the redhead said.

Lyle took the licenses back to his squad. While Lyle ran his checks, Ace played uneasy referee and cautious explorer. He discovered that when he looked at the redhead, the resolution on things sharpened up and the day acquired this pleasing velocity. He listened to the suddenly playful wind. Felt it ruffle through her hair.

He tried to read the driven energy centered in her hollow cheeks, those hungry eyes.

Definitely strung out.

He could understand strung out. And when he dared to listen with his heart he heard a rushing, as if they were both leaning into the same white-water rapid that was about to sweep them away.

Ace blinked and caught himself as Lyle returned, handed back the licenses. "No wants, no warrants," he said, then he knelt next to the little girl. "Hi there, what's your name?"

"My name is Karson Pryce Broker."

"That's a lot of name," Lyle said.

She nodded. "My dad calls me Kit."

"And where is your dad?"

"At home, in Devil's Rock, Minnesota." Her lower lip trembled. "They had a fight, so we went on a trip with Auntie Jane." Then she lost it and her whole face transformed into a red tear gusher.

"Oh boy," Lyle said. Then he patted the girl on the shoulder, stood up, and looked at the redhead. "How'd she get those marks on her arm?"

"I was trying to move her out of the way so she wouldn't get caught in between," the redhead said.

Lyle eyed Ace. Ace nodded and said, "Wasn't intentional."

"Maybe I grabbed her a little too hard."

"Just a little," Lyle said, judiciously, with a whiff of copper menace.

The redhead heaved her shoulders and said, "Look. I'm sorry this happened. My husband and I had this ugly fight back home. So my friend and I thought we'd take a road trip. We were on our way to see the Peace Gardens." She shot a cross look at Jane. "Looks like we didn't make it."

"We were doing fine until you got thirsty," Jane again.

"Oh, right, as long as you thought *you* were getting what you wanted . . ."

The two women surged at each other and the anger creased their faces like war paint. Lyle stepped between them.

"See what I mean?" Ace said.

"Okay, okay," Lyle said holding the women apart with his outspread arms. "This is how it is. I want you two in separate corners and then you got thirty seconds to convince me this kid isn't in jeopardy and I don't need to call Social Services and stick her in protective custody."

"Custody? Hey, wait a minute." The redhead grimaced.

"No, *you* wait a minute. I bring in Child Protection and they contact Minnesota where you live for a background check. You understand?"

The kid sobbed, "I want my daddy."

"I told you we shouldn't have brought her. We should have left her with her dad," the redhead said.

Jane toed the trap rock, said nothing, looked away.

Lyle laced his fingers together, placed them on his chest, and cocked his head. Reasonable. "Perhaps we could call her dad and arrange something. Maybe he could come and get her," he said. "Then you two could continue to work out your problems, hopefully down the road in the next county."

The tension eased a notch as the women looked at each other.

Clearly there was room here to negotiate. Then the redhead said to her daughter, "Kit, honey, why don't you go inside and play the pinball machine so Mom and Auntie Jane can talk alone with the policeman." Her charged eyes drifted up to Ace's.

Ace shifted from foot to foot, absorbing the redhead's creeping voltage. "Sure, uh, c'mon, honey, let's go inside. Let the grown-ups talk." He held out his hand.

Lyle squatted down on Kit's level and said, "That'd be a good idea, Kit."

Eyes still downcast, Kit said, "Am I going to get to go home?"

"We're working on it, honey," the redhead said.

"Okay." Kit turned and walked toward Ace.

"Thanks," the redhead said.

"No problem," Ace said.

Seeing the eye play between her companion and Ace, Jane said, "I know what you're up to. This really sucks."

Lyle held up a hand indicating silence while Ace walked Kit into the bar. Then he spun on the two women. "Thirty and counting. Talk to me."

"Okay, okay, we'll work it out. There's a motel in town, right?" the redhead said.

Lyle nodded. "The Motor Inn."

"I know what you're pulling here," Jane said. She shut up when Lyle held up a beefy palm.

Practical now, and more than a little demure and deferential to Lyle, the redhead ignored Jane. "You're right, officer. We need a time-out. A couple hours. Then we talk, call Minnesota, maybe arrange something."

"There you go. Clear the air," Lyle said.

"He's right, Jane. Couple hours, then tonight we have dinner. Figure out how to put Kit with her dad and you and me start fresh. What do you say?"

"Do I have a choice?" Jane said.

"Sure. Take the wheels. Leave," the redhead said, taking a small step forward, showing some edge.

They stared each other down. Jane dropped her eyes first. "Okay, a couple hours."

The redhead folded her arms across her chest. "You take Kit and get a room. Settle down."

"What about you?" Jane said.

"C'mon, Jane, it's what? A quarter-mile into town. I'll take a walk. Breathe some fresh air."

"Okay, good," Lyle said. He removed a card and a pen from his chest pocket, wrote on the back of the card, and then gave it to Jane. "My cell's on the back. Things don't work out, you call me and we go to plan B." He turned to the redhead. "You follow me?"

"I understand," she said.

"Okay, now go in and get the little girl," Lyle said.

Kit was up on a chair hunched over the pinball machine, letting her third ball bearing fly into the clattering bumpers and buzzers and flashers.

"So, what do you think?" Ace asked.

Kit wrinkled her nose. "It's okay but I like Age of Empires more."

"Age of Empires, huh?" Gordy said, moving up to the machine.

"It's a computer game, ancient civilizations at war," the redhead said, walking up to them.

Kit nodded her head. "Assyrians have the best ballistas."

"What happened to dolls and dress-up?" Gordy said.

"She was playing it on Jane's laptop in the car," the redhead said.

"Uh-huh, and while she's playing on Jane's laptop Jane's playing on your lap . . . ," Gordy said softly.

"Don't even try to get your mind around it, farm boy; we'll have to wrap you in duct tape to keep your head from exploding," the redhead said slowly.

Ace was impressed the way she thrust her hip and let her hands dangle loose in this great bring-it-on stance. And now that things had calmed down a little he noticed her left ear peeking from her askew layered hair. The lobe was missing, just a lump of scar tissue. Like it had been cut off.

Sonofabitch! I bet she's got some stories.

A lazy morning, lying in bed, smoking, looking at the water-marks on the ceiling . . .

"Watch it," he said. His words were quiet but aimed right at Gordy.

Gordy was undeterred. He leaned over closer to Kit. "So what's your daddy do?"

"He's got these cabins on the lake. We rent them to tourists."

"Uh-huh."

Kit straightened up, looked around, and thrust her hand toward the window. "He drives one of those sometimes."

Across the highway, a rusted white Bobcat was frozen in front of a large pole barn. Chest-high weeds fringed the building and poked up in the trap-rock parking lot. A rusted windmill revolved in the soft breeze.

"C'mon, honey," the redhead said, helping her daughter off the chair.

Gordy moved next to her. "So your husband drives a Bobcat. What is it you do?"

"Hey." It was the older guy, who was still hanging around, following the action. He'd come back inside to finish his beer. "Can I get some of that beef jerky?"

Ace nodded at the customer. He puffed up some. He ordered, "Go wait on the man like you're paid to do."

Wheels revolved in Gordy's eyes, like he was thinking of challenging Ace. But he decided to wait and returned to his post behind the bar. After squirting a little wolf pee in Gordy's direction, Ace put a hint of strut in his walk as he escorted the redhead and her daughter out onto the porch.

When they got outside, the redhead leaned down and kissed Kit on the forehead. "You go with Jane into town and get a motel room. I'll be along in a little while."

There was more cynicism than innocense in the kid's frown. "Promise?"

"Go on, scat," the redhead said. Obediently, the kid went down the steps. They stood on the porch and watched her and Jane get into the Volvo.

"Now what?" Ace said.

"According to Officer Friendly's intervention plan they go in town and get a room. I'll walk in, see the sights, hook up in an hour or so when everybody's cooled down."

"Well, good luck cooling down in July in North Dakota," Ace said.

"You got a point. A girl walking down a hot highway probably could use a lift," she said.

"That's true."

She rolled her eyes slowly over the bleached brick facade of the Missile Park Bar. "This is fine and all, but is there anyplace around here to get a drink?"

"Like, what did you have in mind?"

Bang. She hit him dead on with a full frontal look. "Surprise me."

They were standing absolutely still but Ace could feel them rolling side by side like dice.

The red Volvo had pulled on the shoulder, Jane leaning out the driver's side, looking back. She pounded the horn.

Lyle walked up to the porch and said, "You want to walk or I could drive you around a while and drop you off?"

"I'll walk, thank you," she said.

"Well, then," Lyle said.

"In a minute. Unless I'm breaking any laws standing here," the redhead asked politely.

"No, ma'am, but funny you should say that, considering where it is you're standing," Lyle said.

"What's that supposed to mean?" she said.

"Long story," Ace said.

"Right," Lyle said.

Across the highway a heavy-set guy in a long-sleeved black shirt came out of the equipment shed, walked to the road, and yelled.

"Hey, Ace! What's the problem?"

Lyle waved him off. "Nothing. Just talk."

"You all right?" the guy yelled.

"I'm fine," Ace yelled back

The guy nodded, peered at the redhead for several seconds, and then retreated back into the shed.

Ace held out his hand to the redhead. "Ace Shuster."

She raked his face with her conflicted eyes and almost smiled. Then she closed up her face, took his hand in hers, and said, "Nina Pryce. Pleased to meet you."

She turned and started walking toward the town.

Ace heard Gordy come up behind him.

"We gotta talk before you go do anything," Gordy said. Ace didn't respond at first, he was very involved in watching Nina stride away along the gravel shoulder. Gordy tapped him on the shoulder.

"What, her?" Ace shrugged. "She's just looking for a party."

Gordy shook his head. "C'mon, Ace, look at her. She's way too put together to be some lush."

Ace grinned. "You check out that ear? Like it got cut off or something. That's different. Little skull-and-crossbones action on her shoulder . . ."

"I ain't joking here. Take a look around. Where are we?"

Ace exhaled. "You're ruining my morning, Gordy."

"Nobody comes here except for weddings, funerals, or to deliver something . . ." Gordy paused and plucked at his sideburns.

"Deliver something," Ace repeated, mulling it. But still staring down the road.

"Yeah, like say a subpoena, or a warrant, or a wire."

"You think she's a cop," Ace said flatly. He turned and faced Gordy.

"Just saying keep an open mind, like she *could* be some kind of snitch thrown in the mix, kinda off the wall," Gordy said.

"How sure are you? Hundred percent?"

Gordy scrunched up his face, thinking. "Well, the kid . . ."

Ace nodded. "One hell of a novel approach for a cop outta Bismarck, I'd say. The kid was *good*. I'm keeping an open mind. But the kid was for real."

"They got satellite cameras that take pictures from space, man. They got infrared over the border now. They can come up with a kid."

Ace turned and squinted down the road. He could just make out one last flash off the sweat on her shoulder blades. "An undercover? Why now? I'm not breaking any laws, am I?"

"We been through this with the state cops. Now that the volume is scaled way down, you're not drawing any heat. Hell, man, you're up for sale. You're history."

A shadow passed behind Ace's eyes. "What about you? You and your biker friends up north? You guys and that meth shit are all over the front page."

"Very funny." It was a sore subject.

"Answer the question."

Gordy shrugged. "I ain't into nothing that would involve you," he said slowly. "Not specifically."

"Not specifically, huh? That sounds like splitting hairs, like lawyer shit." Ace measured out each word. "If she's a cop, she's *your* cop, not mine."

"I'm telling you, this little thing I got on the side is nothing that involves you."

"Right, half your drivers still think they're running Dad's cargo. And Dad just handled booze, not that bulk ephedrine you buy wholesale up in Winnipeg, that you can't get down here cross the counter . . ." Ace cut Gordy with his first real sharp look of the day.

Gordy folded his arms over his chest, took a step backwards.

Ace continued. "I ain't dumb. Same couriers. Same transport— different contraband."

Nina was about two hundred yards down the road now, going past the Alco Discount, coming up on the Dairy Queen. Distracted by Gordy, Ace had lost the fine detail. A pickup went by, slowed to take a look. It occurred to him that some other enterprising shit-kicker was going to give her a lift, buy her a drink . . .

"Hundred dollars says she ain't a cop. But she sure is something more than she's letting on, and I just gotta find out what that is. So I'm gonna go along with her," Ace said abruptly, making his decision as he reached in his jeans for his truck keys.

"You never bet," Gordy said.

"Hundred bucks."

"You'll lose."

"Maybe. Probably. So how about another hundred on the side?" Ace grinned slow, with just a drop of the old nasty in it. "Like, what intrigues me is—how far will an undercover go? She goes all the way, we're even."

"Ace, you ain't thinking very clearly."

Ace shrugged and headed for his Tahoe. "What the hell. Not like there's a whole lot else going on."

Chapter Six

Ace walked around the back and braced himself as he came up on his new Chevy Tahoe. A crease ran the length of the right fender and petered out halfway across the door. He had no idea where or when or on what he'd left the paint last night.

Four minutes later he eased up beside her, then stopped the Tahoe a few feet ahead on the shoulder and zipped down the window. When she came up even with him and stopped, he spoke up.

"So, you still want to get a drink?"

Nina pursed her lips and regarded him warily. "Let's you and me get something straight. I appreciate you helping out back there. But don't get your hopes up. After what I been through in the last twenty-four hours, the next guy I fuck is gonna be wearing so much latex he can be dive certified . . ."

"Whoa. Hey, I'm here to listen," Ace said, marveling. Must be some gearbox she had in there, the way she could speed shift between full-bore hot and cold.

Five minutes later they were settled in a booth in a dark freezing lounge back of the bowling alley, off Langdon's main drag. They studied each other over a pair of double gin and tonics. Her choice.

"Good summer drink," Ace said diplomatically.

"I kinda want to ease into it," she said.

They clinked glasses. As Nina took a sip, she noticed that the waitress who had brought their order was standing at the cash register, very involved in girl talk with two women in shorts and halters who were real suntanned and would never see thirty-nine again. All three craned their necks to get a look at Nina with a certain proprietary interest.

"Friends of yours?" Nina jerked her head at the trio.

Ace frowned. "I was hoping to hear the story of your life, not mine."

Nina shrugged. "I went to high school in Ann Arbor. Put off going to college to join the Army."

"That where you got the tattoo?" Ace pointed to her shoulder.

"No, I did that on a dare, in Minneapolis, after the Army, during my brief bartender career."

"Why brief?"

She took a long pull on her drink. "Because I met this guy and put off going to college a second time to marry him."

"And you been with him ever since," Ace said.

Nina finished her drink and emphatically thumped the empty glass on the table. "Not now I ain't."

"Look," Ace said. "The way I see it you can call your husband and have him come pick up your kid and continue on with the lovely Jane. Or you go back with him and give your marriage another try, which is better for the kid."

Nina's eyes flashed up. "Really?"

"Yeah. Kids from intact bad marriages do better than ones from broken homes."

She regarded him carefully. "You figure that out on your own?"

"Nope, this counselor told me and my wife that to keep us from splitting up. Didn't work. But my mom stayed with my dad, which probably kept me and my brother and sister from turning out even worse than we did. What about your folks?"

She shrugged. "They stayed married but he was never there when I was growing up. He was in the Army." She chewed a lip, shook her glass so the ice at the bottom made a chilly rattle. Then she looked away. "And then one day he was really gone.

"Missing, they called it. Twenty years later, the Vietnamese turned over his remains: 1995." She held up her empty glass until she had the bartender's attention, then she turned her smoky eyes back on Ace. "So those are my two choices?"

"Or you could try something different." Ace said, trying his best to look reasonable and helpful.

"I just tried something different." She looked him over like a piece of merchandise when she said that, and Ace couldn't tell if she was deciding to buy or walk away.

Then, after a few seconds, she said, "You're staring."

"Tell me what happened with your ear."

She shook her head. "Nah, not yet. Maybe when I know you better. Try again."

"Okay. Pryce, is that your husband's name?"

"Uh-uh. His name's Broker."

"So you didn't take his name."

"And he didn't take mine."

"*O-kay.* What about your pal Jane? That hatchet thing around her neck," he said, exploring.

Nina smiled. "You ever hear anybody call a woman a battle ax?"

Ace thought about it. "Sure, my Aunt Bea."

"Was Aunt Bea a sweet soft thing, dependent on a man?"

"More like leather braid soaked in vinegar. Outlived two husbands."

"Uh-huh. See, Jane says it's one of those clues buried in the language. That ax is called a *labrys.* In ancient Greek paintings, like on vases, there's pictures of the Amazons carrying them in battle. A lot of lesbians and feminists are into the symbolism."

"I can dig it," Ace said, warming to the gin and the conversation. "I'm sort of into Greek mythology myself. You ever read *The Myth of Sisyphus*?"

She squinted, thought; decided how to play it. "The guy chained to the rock. The birds come every day to tear out his guts."

Ace shook his head. "That's Prometheus."

"Okay, then Sisyphus is the other guy with the rock. He pushes it up a hill over and over as punishment."

"Bingo. The original uphill battle. I got this theory that Sisyphus is really a German-Norwegian farmer who's trying to make a go on eight hundred acres up on the border by Hannah," Ace said as his best grin spread over his face.

"You're turning out different than I first expected," she said frankly.

"Yep. I'm not like the others." He held her gaze for a moment. "So Jane's an Amazon, huh?"

Nina sniffed, retreated back into her foul mood, and sounded irritated. "Jane wants to be a lot of things. Since I've known her she's wanted to a poet and a caterer but what she really does is wait on tables in this restaurant in Minneapolis."

Ace squinted, thoughts revolving just behind his eyes. "So how'd you two . . ."

Nina jerked the corner of her lip up in a sort of smile. "That turns you on, huh? The two of us . . ."

Ace shrugged.

Nina laughed. "Men don't mind the idea of two women in bed together. You know why?"

Ace couldn't help smiling. The way she rolled over you like a wheel, mostly hard parts but now and then enough of the soft showing through to keep you interested. "I got a feeling you're going to tell me," he said.

"Damn straight. It's 'cause you can see yourself sandwiched in there with them, huh?"

Ace felt his face get hot. "I guess."

She leaned across the table, her face softening, lips going mobile, probably from the whiskey. "But if I told you it turned me on to think of you and a guy naked together . . ."

The way Ace sat up straight, narrowing his eyes, put Nina on guard. Hit a nerve. But she pushed on, wagged her finger and said, "Double standard, Ace." The joke withered in his cold stare and she was more careful now, signaling that she read the palpable heft of danger in his body language. She sat up primly. "Moving right along," she said.

He studied her for several beats. "So what you gonna do, Nina Pryce?"

She tipped her eyes toward the bar. "Maybe I'll go back to tending bar right here. I could talk about you with the sun-fried sisters."

"I don't think you're up to all the sky, wind, wheat, barley, canola, and flax," Ace said.

"You ever read that play *Streetcar Named Desire?* Tennessee Williams?"

Ace shook his head. "I read a lot of Louis L'Amour once."

"Well, in *Streetcar* there's this woman named Blanche who winds up alone, and she says how she's always relied on the kindness of strangers."

"So that's me, huh? The kind stranger?"

Nina raised her shoulders and let them drop. "Maybe *kind* isn't the right word. I just hope you're not mean . . . Your friend with all the hair . . ."

"Gordy."

"Yeah, Gordy, he strikes me as being on the mean side. I get the feeling he doesn't like women."

Ace watched her carefully; the way she cast it out there like a lure. Was this where she set the hook? Gordy probably had her pegged right. Some kind of cop. "Maybe he just don't like you," he said.

"But he doesn't even know me."

"You ready for another drink?" Ace said as he swirled the ice in the bottom of his glass.

"Yeah. Something stronger."

They drank together and began the slow dance, bold with their eyes, less and less cautious with their words as one drink followed another and the tabletop became a field of interlocking water rings. They were coming up on the moment of truth.

"So what are we doing here? You and me?" Ace said.

The smoky eyes came up. "You can buy me drinks all night, Ace Shuster; don't mean I'm going to give it up to you or anybody else for a long time."

"I ain't that ambitious. I mean, like where you planning to spend the night?"

"Motel, I guess."

"Only one good motel in town and Jane's in that. Course, so is your kid."

"Let me tell you something. My kid could use a break. And Jane's good with her." Real direct.

"Speaking of Jane. I remember what she said back at my place about you needing to get loaded to be with a guy. Did that bother your husband? You drinking?" Just as direct.

Nina couldn't stop the flush creeping up her neck. She lowered her eyes. "Not like I had to get falling down . . ."

Ace held up his glass of scotch and peered into it. "I don't need the details. And sure, I'd like to fool around but I'd kind of like you to be sober. How's that?"

Nina's grin was wary and amused. "If that's the wager then it looks like nobody's getting laid."

Ace shrugged, drained his glass, and signaled for another round. "You can stay at my place tonight. Got an apartment over the bar.

No games, no bullshit, no hidden agenda. I already made up my mind to sleep on the couch. But tomorrow," he winked, "we're going to sober up, you and me."

The drinks arrived and Nina raised her glass in a toast.

"To tomorrow."

Nina fished her cell phone from her purse. "I'm going to call Jane, tell her I won't be back tonight, and explain things to my daughter." She looked around. "And I gotta use the john."

Ace nodded, pointed toward the rear of the place. "Door in the hall on the right."

Nina got up, walked down the bar, and went into the women's john. She took a seat in the stall, latched the door and flipped open her cell phone, thumbed down through the phonebook, selected Jane's number, and pushed "send."

"This is Jane."

"Nina."

"How's it going, Mata Hari? You catch that four-pound walleye yet?"

"Very funny. So far so good. I'm invited to his pad for the night. He says he'll sleep on the couch. And I sort of believe him. He's this odd mix of Eagle Scout and the Sundance Kid. I can't tell if he's going for it or going along with it."

"We gotta try, right? Hollywood wants to know how you assess your security."

"My first impression, he's got some dangerous baggage but it takes a while to get down to it. The other guy in the bar was more edgy. But this Ace, he's . . ."

"He's a tricky guy, Nina; and he's got some social skills and maybe even some depth of character. But so did Darth Vader."

"I hear you. So far he hasn't discussed his business."

Hollywood came on the phone. "We can't cover you all the time, Nina. Not in a small town. We talked about this. If you go forward you're on your own."

"Understood."

"We need some idea of his pattern, his contacts, any sign he's anticipating something big."

"I got it, Holly."

"Okay. And we set the ball rolling. Jane has the local cop hunting down your husband."

Great, Nina thought, but said nothing.

"I said . . ."

"I heard you."

"Okay. Here's Kit."

Nina shut her eyes. The bathroom smelled of cheap disinfectant on monotonous yellow linoleum. The walls and floor closed in; claustrophobic. She was quick to fight it off. *It's not a question of one kid; thousands of kids out there could be potential victims . . .* Still, she had used her daughter, like a private soldier, to gain position.

"Hi, Mom."

"You did great, honey. Thanks."

"Are you done working yet?"

"No, I got to keep going a little while longer. But, hey, Dad's on his way to pick you up and take you home. What are you and Auntie Jane going to do tomorrow?"

"She said there's an outside pool, in a park."

"Remember, you need lots of lotion even if it's cloudy."

"I know." Then Kit's voice quavered. "Are you going to come home, too?"

"C'mon, honey, we talked about this." Nina tapped her teeth together.

"Fine," Kit said sharply. "I know—don't quit, don't cry unless you're bleeding." Kit had obviously mastered Jane's cell phone because suddenly the call was over. The connection went dead: she had hung up on her mother. Nina couldn't afford the luxury of remorse when she was working, but she couldn't stop a memory. Eight years old, about Kit's age. An elementary school in Ann

Arbor. *A one-page story assignment: What I did this weekend.* "*My mom and I went to the VA Medical Center to help the wounded soldiers . . .*" The teacher, in beads and a peasant skirt, had said, "That's okay, Nina, it doesn't mean you're for the war . . ."

Focused now, she finished up in the bathroom and washed her hands. She regarded herself in the mirror. The alcohol she'd consumed dragged on her, like the middle of a Ranger run wearing full equipment. Deliberately, to test her timing and reflexes she applied fresh lipstick, taking pains to perfectly match the line of her lips.

She blotted her lips on a paper towel and surveyed her makeup. *So far so good, you floozy.*

Well, this is what she wanted. To be a D-girl and hang it way out there, going after something big. On her own.

Which brought her to the subject of what was going to happen tonight. Nothing in her training had exactly prepared her for this assignment.

Would Ace change his story when they were alone and expect to sleep with her tonight? Would he get rough? She took a fast inventory of the men she'd gone to bed with in her life. More than half of them had been a waste of time.

This was the first time she'd had to evaluate a potential sexual encounter professionally. Like a hooker or a particularly calculating trophy wife.

She squared her shoulders, grabbed the doorknob, took a deep breath, and pushed it open. *Hu-ah.*

She walked back to the table, sat down, and said, totally spontaneously: "I'm a lousy mother."

"You'll live. C'mon," Ace said, standing up.

"Where to?" Nina said.

"Take a ride. Eat supper. Get you a toothbrush."

"Big of you."

"Got nothing else going," Ace said.

Chapter Seven

An hour later they were in another bar and Ace was still playing Dr. Phil. "I mean," he said, "we only got a few more years of this."

Nina screwed up her face. "What do you mean, *this?*"

"I mean, what are you—thirty-five, thirty-six? 'Bout the same as me. We ain't like wine, you know. We don't get better as we age. Like, right now—today—bang," he snapped his fingers, "you can walk into any bar, anywhere, and make something happen because you got some looks and a body. But in five years . . ."

Nina slouched in the booth and held up her glass in a grudging salute. "Forty," she said glumly. She didn't have to fake this conversation. Uh-uh. This was a subject she thought about all the time.

"And you know what the stats are on divorced women over forty getting remarried. Ain't pretty, sweetheart. Us boys definitely got more shelf life."

"You're depressing the shit out of me. No wonder the population of North Dakota is rock bottom, if this is the way you court your women."

Ace shrugged. "Just saying, you should probably give the marriage a little more work, that's all. Bird in the hand."

Nina leaned forward. "A bird in the hand bites. My husband is a total *asshole*."

They stared into their empty glasses. Nina had switched to vodka sevens. She'd had a lot of success drinking vodka with a crazy bunch of Russian paratroopers in Kosovo. A new round of drinks arrived. The way Ace spread his hands before he spoke, Nina could see him behind a pulpit.

"Okay. It's like this," he said. "You're strung out. Strung out means you talk a little too fast. And there's off-the-wall thoughts come out of nowhere and bash through the conversation at random times. Like just now."

"You know this for a fact?" Nina said.

"Sure. I'm strung out, too. But mine is more long haul, more like holding off deep space. Mine's sadder. Yours is madder."

"So what do we do?"

"Drink. Booze tames down the brightness and buffs the edges off so it don't make the air bleed."

"Jesus. You been thinking about this stuff way too long, Ace."

"I'll say."

And that's the way the afternoon went into sunset: the ironies of marriage counseling, Ace's slow-hand seduction and booze. One bar, two bar, red bar, blue bar. Not quite a blur. Maintaining. Hey. They were both obviously competent folks.

They drove east out of town and he got her talking. About growing up an Army brat, schools on bases all over the South. How she'd gone into the Army, served in the Gulf War in a signal company, and moved to Minnesota after discharge. How she was tending bar in this joint called the Caboose by the U of M when she met her husband.

They stopped, gassed the Tahoe at a Super Pumper. Ace made good on his promise and bought her a toothbrush. They went to dinner in Cavalier, the next town east, and she talked about having a kid, thinking it would improve the marriage.

They drove back to Langdon in the dark.

Then Ace suddenly switched off the headlights and the night outside Nina's open window jumped up so black and shot with stars it took her breath. "God-*damn*."

Stars like she'd seen on night patrols in remote stretches of Bosnia. But more of them here. More sky.

"Welcome to the prairie, gateway to the Great Plains," Ace said.

But then the grandeur plummeted as she looked north. Anything could come across the border and filter down through the empty grid of back roads, run this deserted highway. The interstate just an hour away. Then she looked at Ace Shuster, who was good with women, but who might do anything for money. Him and his pal Gordy.

He switched the lights back on and drove into town, slowed in front of the Motor Inn, and turned to her.

"You want to see your daughter? Say anything?"

Nina shook her head.

"You sure?"

"Look. I thought about this a lot. I need a clean break or it'll be a tar baby, I'll get stuck in it all over again. Jane. My old man probably coming to pick up Kit. I mean, I took her and didn't tell him face-to-face. Just left a note, for Christ's sake. I just need some . . . time."

"Okay, okay," Ace slowly accelerated past the motel and continued west on 5 toward the Missile Park.

They found Gordy rolling a dolly, wheeling four cases of booze at a time off the loading dock onto a truck bed. He scowled at Nina and went back to work, hairy and furious. Nina turned to Ace and said, "Maybe you're right. He doesn't like me."

They went inside and Nina pointed to the cases of booze stacked along the wall by the basement stairway.

"You got a lot of booze for a bar that's out of business," she said.

Ace scratched his head. "Long story. Tell you all about it in the morning."

Nina gathered herself and followed him up the stairs into the apartment. And—hello—it was much cleaner than she expected. Dishes washed and put away, the drainboard in the kitchen clean. And lots and lots of books. A beat-up, old-fashioned desk and a swivel chair. Another well-worn armchair with an ottoman and a lamp.

No televison.

One whole wall was a blowup photomural of grazing buffalo.

"Moved in here when I split with my wife," he said as he stripped the bed and put on fresh sheets. She watched him make the bed, smoothing out the wrinkles, folding and tucking in tight hospital corners.

"You sure you weren't in the Army, the way you make a bed?" she said.

"Prison," he said.

He took the old sheets out to the couch. Then he handed her a T-shirt and showed her the bathroom. She took the toothbrush from its cellophane wrapper, used his Sensodyne and brushed her teeth, undressed, and put on the shirt. The shirt was an extra-large maroon cotton number that came down to mid-thigh. The sleeves and neck had been cut out way down the side so the shadowed dents and curves along her ribs peeked out.

She folded her clothing and came back into the living room.

Ace smiled and looked her over. "Picked the shirt to go with your hair and eyes." They stood a foot apart, watching each other.

"Another one of your little touches, huh?" Nina said as she hugged herself. Her word *touches* turned slowly in the close space between them like a silky scarf, slowly descending. "Now what?" she said, too abruptly, awkward, clearly on edge.

"Good night," he said simply.

Nina, wary, went into the dark bedroom almost on tiptoe, walking a plumb line to the bed, not wanting to disturb or touch anything, fearing sexual trip wires strung in the dark.

Alert. She braced for him coming through the door.

Chapter Eight

The first moment of truth came in Detroit two days ago, just after they broke Rashid. They'd had a real quick sit-down with the Colonel, who'd provided the intell that located Rashid. One of the "Squirrels," a pure intelligence network so spooky nobody knew its origin, the Colonel was their unofficial link to the databases back at the Pentagon. He could not say yea or nay to their preemptive mission. He could only evaluate. He had a chalky air-conditioned pallor acquired in some unnamed Pentagon sub-basement. He'd told them, just the three of them who were the sharp end—Hollywood, Nina, and Jane:

"We believe the intelligence is too provocative to pass up. They may have something, possibly a suitcase; one of those KGB tactical nukes. They could be bringing it into the States through North Dakota. Virtually anybody can claim refugee status and enter Canada. We know there's Al Qaeda activity in Winnipeg, just to the north of Langdon. So it could already be here, and maybe there's a fresh trail."

He told them it was a real long shot. They'd be going into a very fragile intelligence matrix. He concurred with Nina's plan, given the target, to lead with D-girls. He advised them to plan their approach carefully. He bid farewell saying, "This meeting never happened." Then he packed his briefcase and departed.

Fragile intelligence matrix.

That meant a small town where everybody knows everybody and strangers stick way out.

The information on Ace Shuster was already spitting out of the fax machine.

Wonderful. He killed a guy in a bar fight. Although, even in the official record, the incident looked like self-defense. But Shuster was convicted and did a year on a manslaughter rap at the state farm.

Then—Jesus—the FBI had pictures of him in the spectators gallery at Waco. This raised the specter of anti-Semitic American militias finding common cause with Al Qaeda.

No subsequent arrests. No known militia affiliations.

Shuster's father had been investigated repeatedly as a major player in the liquor traffic along the border, but the charges never stuck. He wasn't breaking any North Dakota laws.

The Colonel had put together a fast synopsis after a consult with Shuster's former probation officer. Shuster had served his time, went back into the community, and caused no real trouble. He'd had his conviction reduced. Probation described him as an underemployed heavy-machinery operator, and real smart. But the brains went wasted, because he tended to brood and drink. The drinking was probably self-medication for moderate depression. He'd dabbled in sports, smuggling, and women. Possibly peripherally involved with the biker gangs who ran the smuggling on the Canadian side of the border. No solid evidence linked him to the looming meth traffic. Remember, he was smart. He could be mixed up in almost anything out in all that empty country. Potentially a very dangerous guy, but not so's you notice it right off.

A ladies' man.

Nina had looked out the window toward Ann Arbor, where Kit was staying with her mother's sister, and came up with the idea.

"It could work if it's bold enough," Holly said.

Bold enough . . . The gloves were off. They were in the serious black on this one.

"You still sure you want in?" Holly said.

The serious black. Lie, cheat, steal.

"We're not carrying copies of the Geneva Convention in our kit," Holly said.

Jane, the sharp tack, cracked wise. "There's killing in combat and then there's murder. You ain't talkin' about combat."

"Correct. I ain't necessarily talkin' about combat. And there's other things you might have to do."

"Things?" Jane had said.

"What, I gotta draw you a picture?" Holly said pointedly to the two women.

So Nina told Jane, "He means like whatever it takes. Like you might have to suck some smuggler's dick. Not your favorite thing, Jane."

Jane came back fast. "Just as long as it ain't Holly's."

D-girls. Nothing but hardcore. Behind the bravado they were all picturing Paula Zahn on CNN going zombie-cottonmouthed, trying to get her words out while in the background a nuclear plume mushroomed over downtown Chicago, or Kansas City, or . . .

Fuck it.

Nothing else mattered. Mission first.

But the way the plan worked, Jane drew a pass. Jane was in the motel in town probably reading *Harry Potter* and the *Sorcerer's Stone* to Kit. Nina got the duty and now here she was in a smuggler's bed, listening to him putter around in his living room just beyond the closed but unlocked door. Jesus, his place was clean. Did that mean he was clean? What if he was a bareback kind of cowboy who didn't want to use condoms?

What was the statistical probability of contracting AIDS from unsafe sex in remotest North Dakota, anyway? Better or worse odds than being the first dummy rolling out of a Black Hawk on a hot mountain LZ in Afghanistan?

Numbers. Odds. Probabilities . . .

Nina slid between the clean sheets.

Downstairs she heard the dolly scurry across the floor. A one-man ant colony, Gordy went back and forth, loading the crates of whiskey. The rhythm of the work, the rolling dolly wheels, the thud of the cases being hefted in place drummed like a harsh lullaby.

Exhausted from the alcohol, Nina's mind wandered.

The mission.

Her first job was to survive insertion. *Boy, there's an example of military lingo falling flat on its ass.*

Think about other things.

Like her ex-husband . . . no, that wasn't right, they were just separated. Her estranged husband. Better.

It occurred to Nina that her asshole *estranged* husband would be right at home in these shadows. He'd lived this life for years on end working the margins, hiding out. A lot of people thought he'd done it too long. Not much for small talk, Broker. Not real great social skills at a cocktail party. Good with Kit, though.

And no one was better in the fog.

It was Broker who had taught her about compartments. The necessity to keep various parts of your life scrupulously segregated. And right now she had her daughter in one box and her husband in another. So she just cracked the door on Broker's cubbyhole, because if she wasn't careful all this stuff would come rushing out.

Stuff she didn't need right now.

Emotional stuff.

She realized she was holding on to her discipline like a chin-up bar. Hanging by it. White-knuckling it. Below her the rest of the night waited.

In order to function she had to sleep.

But sleep would leave her vulnerable.

She had to let go and drop into the darkness.

She had duty-trained herself to do so many things—among them, to drop into a fundamental animal sleep almost at will. She had learned how to sleep standing up, to catnap, to meditate.

So she relaxed her grip on the strange day, finger by finger, and started to slide down into the blackness. Sinking, she caught a fleeting notion of Broker and how he'd handle the news that Kit was left hanging in some motel room in North Dakota.

So, Broker, how many women did you sleep with in the line of duty?

But then she had to smile. He wasn't gonna like it the way she reeled him into this one. Uh-uh. Boy, was he gonna be pissed.

And that's exactly how they needed him.

Chapter Nine

The rotary phone in the booth at Camp's Corner still worked long after the golf course failed and the gas station and store closed. People drove out of their way to show their kids this dinosaur from the days before wireless. The county had originally asked the phone company to keep the line open so farmers working during spring planting and the fall harvest could make calls in an emergency. Which was good, because the man pacing back and forth next to the booth was facing a crisis.

Close to midnight and the city lights of Langdon, miles to the north, pushed a dome faintly against the sky. Overhead, a sickle moon wedged between the clouds. Lots and lots of mosquitoes swarmed around.

He was torn over the decision he had to make as he swatted at the bugs. Across the road, a spooky thread of moonlight outlined the Aztec dimensions of the Nekoma radar pyramid. He hugged himself, shivered in the muggy seventy-nine degrees, and looked up. Jeez. It was creepy out here, suspended between the ruins of the Cold War and this slender Muslim moon.

As he paced, he put his right hand, palm open, over his heart, like when you sing the national anthem. Except he was searching for his sluggish heartbeat. He suspected that a catastrophic illness lurked inside him, coiled up, something part diabetes and part cancer, that lapped sugar from his blood the way a dog laps water.

Sometimes he saw things.

Shapes jerked at the corners of his vision. He caught fleeting glimpses of movement he thought were people darting away through doorways.

At first he thought he might have paranormal powers. Lately he had come to believe that it was a sign his death was near. If this were the case, he reasoned, the closer he came to it the better he could see into the world that existed just the other side of death. Since his body and its functions repelled him, the idea of leaving it was a kind of comfort.

He had entered "out of body experience" in his computer's search engine one day and found his way to research papers about NDEs—near death experiences. The more he read about it, the more he surmised that the shapes he detected were presences transiting a zone between the sputtering energy of life ending and the total void of nothingness.

Near Death Experience.

The subject intrigued him and he'd investigated the sensation of what it might feel like with the help of a drug called ketamine. Abusers of the compound called it "going in the K-hole"; the dreamy scary sensation of leaving the body.

He had always suspected, and now he knew it for sure.

He was different.

It was time. Charon picked up the phone, inserted coins, and dialed the number. The Mole picked up on the other end but didn't say hello. Charon pressed the receiver closer to his ear and could feel the building anxiety—the whole attack plan hung in the balance. Finally Charon broke the silence: "It's me."

"Where the hell are you?" the Mole asked.

"Still in town. You know, Rashid must have told them some-thing, 'cause I think they're here."

"Shit. How many?"

"Three. Two women and an older guy."

"I repeat. Why are *you* still there?"

Charon took a deep breath, steeled himself, and made his demand: "One of the women—I think she's my pick. I mean, she came all this way to meet me."

Only by a great act of will did the Mole resist shouting a string of obscenities. This was absurd—jeopardizing the operation because of a woman? So many things could still go wrong, and now this.

"But she could be an agent, for Christ's sake," he said incredu-lously.

"It's got to be her. And that's that."

The Mole heard the finality in Charon's voice and took a deep breath of his own to calm himself. After all, he had unleashed Charon. Why be surprised when he tried to flex his new muscles? So the Mole held his temper and savored the element of risk. Almost like a stab from his youth. He said, in a level, measured voice, "We'll get her for you, but we have to do it fast."

After the Mole hung up, he was back on the phone in an instant, making a call of his own: "First, you should both be at the target, I don't care about the rain business. Second, Rashid talked, and now we may have agents snooping around in Langdon. And our friend's next girl-toy selection could be one of them. He's going to blow the operation if we don't get him in line. You have to go back in and get him out. Now."

The Mole hung up the pay phone and then, finally, he swore—in English, and then in Arabic. How was he suppose to get the job done with these homicidal clowns for help? Shaking his head, he walked across the deserted parking lot. Security dictated that he use an unfrequented location where he could observe anyone who might be following him. So he chose this abandoned truck stop on the interstate. The gas and diesel pumps had been pulled out. They'd scrawled CLOSED in soapy letters on the empty diner windows. But the pay phones still worked.

He leaned against the hood of his car and studied the sky, wanting the clouds to clear. Wanting this thing to be over. His hand drifted to the open neck of his shirt. Before this all started, he used to wear gold chains around his neck. Kept the top two buttons open so the gold gleamed, nestled in his thick chest hair. Now, instead of the gold, he fingered a small silver religious medallion. His Christian mother had given it to him as a child.

Saint Charbel, in the lore of the Lebanese Maronite Church, had performed miracles after his death. The Mole himself had been practically dead for decades; exiled to this wilderness. Now, like Saint Charbel, years after his death he was about to perform a miracle.

The world of his birth was no more: Beirut when it was the Paris of the Middle East. His family had mirrored the city's pre–civil war cosmopolitanism; his father had been a Sunni Muslim who'd preferred Karl Marx to the Koran. His mother was a Maronite Christian. His father had also been a member of the Ba'ath Party, an agent for Syrian intelligence, and a businessman heavily invested in growing cannabis and poppies in the Bekáa Valley.

Smuggling ran in his blood.

In 1982, an Israeli air strike killed his young Palestinian wife and infant son. One month later, a sixteen-inch shell from the American battleship *New Jersey*, firing in support of the Lebanese Army, killed his parents, his brother, and his two sisters.

Seeking revenge, he volunteered for a suicide mission against the Americans. His superiors counseled patience. This was before the collapse of the Soviet Union, and his left-wing guerrilla group was advised by a KGB handler. The Russian interviewed him, and, seeing that he possessed intelligence and quality, suggested a long game: send him to America to live anonymously with his mother's Christian family. Let him sleep among the Americans, become one of them, go to their schools, serve in their army.

So they sent him to the United States to ply his father's trade. He would buy and sell and quietly learn the rhythms of smuggling across the Canadian border. Someday he would prove useful.

But that day never really came. The people who sent him had perished in the endless combat against the Israelis. The Soviet Union ceased to exist. The Mole was sentenced to prosper among the people he had sworn to kill. He remained faithful to his mission, going through the motions of his shadow life, running drugs, funneling money back to fund Hamas and Hezbollah. He got soft, he got married. He built a business. His two teenage sons were in high school. Christ—just yesterday he had taken them to soccer camp.

And then the knock at the door finally came. Not from his old group, the leftist Popular Front for the Liberation of Palestine; not even from Hamas or Hezbollah. There was a new ascendant movement, inspired by the flyers of airplanes into tall American buildings. They were consolidating their fund raising. And asking favors. The dapper Saudi businessman named Rashid had impeccable knowledge of the Mole's background. And he needed a ton of some unspecified material moved from Winnipeg across the border. No questions asked. And that's how it began.

Now they were within hours of making it all work.

He believed Charon about the agents showing up in Langdon. And Charon wouldn't leave until he got what he wanted. So an alternate plan was called for. Something . . .

The Mole squinted into the darkness. Made a decision. To keep the thing alive he'd have to take some risks. He'd have to divert them away from Charon.

He spun on his heel, walked back to the phone booth, and picked up the receiver.

Chapter Ten

Goddamn sonofabitch Nina!

The red label on the prescription bottle warned: "May cause DROWSINESS. ALCOHOL may INTENSIFY this effect. Use care when operating a car or other dangerous machinery."

Broker took two of the white Vicodin pills, washed them down with bad roadside coffee, and stepped on the gas. If there was any dangerous machinery in the immediate area, it was him.

He was driving Milt Dane's Ford Explorer pretty fast down a two-lane highway. A road sign flashed up, then disappeared: black rectangle framing a white silhouette of an Indian in profile with war bonnet; black number 5 centered in the white, the letter N in one corner and D in the other; WEST spelled out in the smaller panel over the sign.

He was headed west on North Dakota State Route 5, going mostly over 90 mph. Yet it seemed like he was standing still the last couple hours—ever since he pushed north of Fargo.

He'd forgotten that North Dakota was basically you and the sky.

After Fargo, the sky was no longer behind things, like the horizon. It became the main thing. It was too much. Along with too many clouds and too much flat for his north-woods instincts. The problem was—no cover. Broker was a man who understood the advantages of cover; he'd perfected an eye for the subtleties in human and geographic landscapes, for blind spots he could slip in and out of.

Looking around here, he saw no place to hide.

Talk about being too exposed. Christ. He caught himself hunching his shoulders, almost ducking behind the wheel. *C'mon, uncramp. Sit up straight, stretch.*

Broker had reluctantly entered his later forties. He was tending toward lean and hungry this season, from compulsive exercise and a mild interest in Dr. Atkins' diet. He'd cut his dark hair extra-short, almost military. He'd even trimmed some of the bushy ends off his eyebrows that grew in an almost solid monobrow. He had a fix to his gray eyes, a hollowness of cheek, and a flatness to his belly of a man who had taken vows, who was on a pilgrimage, who was in serious training.

There was some other stuff that affected his mood.

Like: a little over twenty-four hours ago he had been shot in the left hand. At the moment he was thinking, in a sweaty, feverish way, that taking a bullet was a mere nuisance, a distraction, compared to what was waiting for him down this highway. What was waiting for him was Nina Pryce. His wife.

He shook his head. People like him and Nina shouldn't get married.

They shouldn't be allowed to breed.

And now she'd ditched their daughter with strangers in a motel in North Dakota. *Goddamn sonofabitch Nina! What are you up to?*

He'd lost the sugar-beet fields when he climbed out of the Red River Valley. Now he passed through a haze of strong-smelling clover and was into serious wheat. The fields stretched out to the horizon like a deep green comforter quilted with chrome yellow patches of canola and spashes of iridescent blue flax.

There was so much sky, he thought he could see ten thousand miles, clear past summer into fall, all the way to the chill breath of the first frost. Gunmetal on oatmeal on concrete. And no blue. No sun. Far to the north he saw a curtain of rain, a shudder that could be lightning. But far away. Well into Manitoba.

No sun since Friday. Saturday it had started to rain in Minnesota. Saturday . . . He blinked sweat, refocused. Saturday, which was yesterday . . .

Not now. Think of something else. He'd had heavy rain as he drove across Minnesota. It tapered off just past Grand Forks. He'd switched off the metronome slap of the wipers and opened the windows. Now he was sweating from more than the muggy air.

Infection had set in in his left hand where the slug from the .38 had bit a chunk of meat from the heel of his palm. So Broker had been shot with an old-fashioned low-velocity full-metal-jacketed round. Through and through. Which was apt, because he tended to be an old-fashioned wood-and-steel kind of guy.

Another scar.

The bullet had missed the bones and ligaments and the big nerve. So the hand still worked. The wound had been treated at Lake View Emergency in Stillwater. Last night the bandage was crisp gauze and white adhesive. Now it was turning a wrinkled funky gray, coming loose, with a ragged cockade of stiff brown blood the size of a silver dollar in his palm. It throbbed like hell.

Broker had been doing a favor for a friend.

The friend was a sheriff. As it turned out, he knew too many sheriffs. And now he was on his way to meet another one.

Back in Minnesota, he'd agreed to a temporary stint as a special deputy to the Washington County Sheriff. The favor had resulted in a struggle for a gun and him getting shot. Yesterday, just before noon.

An hour before getting shot, at ten A.M. yesterday morning, Phil Broker had been sitting on the deck of Milt Dane's river place sipping coffee. He had been house-sitting for Milt. Getting away to think. Rain clouds were rolling in to break a record heat wave.

That's when another sheriff called. This one was his neighbor, Tom Jeffords, up in Cook County, where Broker owned a small resort on the North Shore of Lake Superior.

Jeff had been called by the Cavalier County Sheriff's office, in Langdon, North Dakota. It seems that Karson Pryce Broker, Broker's seven-year-old daughter, whom he hadn't seen in four months, had popped up in a motel room in Langdon.

Minus her mother.

A woman named Jane had complained to the cops that Nina Pryce had abandoned the child. Then, before he could contact this Jane person, some real life had intervened and Broker got shot. So he called Jane from an emergency room. Vague on details, Jane said she'd stay with Kit until Broker showed up to claim her.

Immediately, the red flags started popping up.

Jane's voice came across with a relentless high-voltage undercurrent, the kind of energy that thrived on fatigue and crisis. A voice with a trained meter and cadence that she couldn't quite disguise.

The last address Broker had for his estranged wife, Major Nina Pryce, U.S. Army—who had informal custody of their daughter— was in Lucca, Italy.

Goddamn sonofabitch Nina! What could be so damn important that she dangled Kit out there like a loose end? It was time to confront the thing straight on.

He hooked his injured hand in the wheel and used his good right hand to pry open his cell phone and thumb in the cell number for this Jane person.

"This is Jane," answered the efficient voice.

"This is Broker. I have a fire mission. Can you copy. Over."

Silence on the connection. Then she said, "Very funny."

"Tell me one thing. Are you guys wearing uniforms?"

Broker listened to Jane's second loud silence. Then he said, "My guess is you're not wearing uniforms. So who are you, Jane?"

"I'm a friend of Nina's."

"Uh-huh. So where's Nina?"

"Concerning that, ah, it's better if you should talk to me first."

"Not the cops who came looking for me?"

"I think it'd be best to talk to me first." She was letting him fill in the blanks.

"Where's Kit?" Broker could guess. The connection was good. He heard kids laughing and the sound of bodies splashing in water.

"She's in the community pool here in town. You want to talk to her?"

"Sure."

Broker counted to ten and then his daughter's strong direct voice came on the connection. "Hi, Dad."

"Hiya, hon, whatcha doing?"

"Auntie Jane is teaching me to dive."

"Great. How's your mom?"

"Ah . . ." There was a pause, in which Broker imagined Jane giving his daughter stage directions. "Ah, Mom's working."

"Great, hon, I'll be there in about an hour."

"Bye."

Jane came back on. "She's good. We just got here, so we'll hang for a while. She's looking forward to seeing you. The pool's in the park two blocks north of the highway. You can't miss it."

"So, Jane. What's up?"

"See you soon, Broker. And like I said, come here first."

Like he'd just received an order.

Right. Pissed, Broker immediately punched in the number for the Cavalier County Sheriff's office, got dispatch, and left a message that he'd be there within the hour. The dispatcher informed him that Sheriff Norman Wales would be in his office and was looking forward to meeting him.

Hmmmmmmm.

A lazy herd of buffalo grazed behind an insubstantial barbed-wire fence. An unmarked but heavily fenced and abandoned-looking concrete structure bristled with antennae. The vast green rug of wheat. The endless clouds. Broker slumped behind the wheel.

So this was what his rodeo marriage came down to.

In the past, he and Nina had tried to work things out in a friendly manner. No lawyers involved. Ever since Kit had been born her father lived in Minnesota and her mother deployed all over the world. For the first four and a half years of her life she had stayed mostly with her dad.

About the time Kit started kindergarten, the battle lines were drawn. Nina wanting Broker to migrate to Europe and play "officer's spouse" to her career. Broker wanting the family under one roof in the States, which would require Nina to give up the Army.

Standoff.

In the interim, Kit wound up traveling back and forth.

That arrangement was about to end.

Broker had been around. He was a trained, competent man who could be utterly unsentimental in action. But all his experience failed when he pictured his marriage reduced to pieces of human machinery that had stopped working.

They didn't pack instructions on how to take a marriage apart.

His saliva dried up, his tear ducts started, and the muscles curled inward in his belly. Painful work, breaking a marriage apart and packing it into two separate boxes. Tearing a seven-year-old in half . . .

He pretty much knew what ripping a marriage in half sounded like. It sounded like Kit crying.

But goddammit, it was lawyer time. His kid wasn't going to be raised by strangers in Army day care all over Europe anymore.

Or mysteriously pop up in North Dakota motel rooms.

It was time for Nina to choose. She could be a mother or she could persist in her Joan of Arc soldier fantasy.

She couldn't do both.

But . . .

All the little hairs on the back of his neck had stayed at full alert since Jeff called. Because Nina wasn't just your ordinary insanely driven, ambitious soldier gal clawing for recognition . . .

His cell phone rang. Thinking it was Jane again, he fumbled at it one-handed and barked, "Now what?"

"Phillip?"

He sagged and caught his breath. Only his mother called him that. "Hi, Mom."

"Do you know more yet? About Kit?"

"I just talked to her. She sounded fine. I'm almost there. I guess Nina got called away quick . . ."

"It's not her fault. She really can't help it." Irene Broker said. "Nina's a triple fire sign and—"

"Yeah, Mom. You already told me." Mom had a Merlinesque faith in astrology and believed that Nina was in thrall to her heroic stars.

"Her basic energy comes from Sun in Aries. Her inner feelings come from Moon in Sagittarius. And her behavior is anchored in Mars in Leo."

Aries, Mars. He didn't need a starbook to plot that trajectory. Plus she had the Scots bloodline. Well, *fuck* Nina and the meteor she rode in on. He pictured her going naked into battle, like her ancestors, with her pubes dipped in blue woad.

"C'mon, Mom, give me a break," he said. Sun in Aries. Right. He looked up to where the sun should be and saw only gray woolly clouds.

"Well, are you going to drive Kit back? Because if you're not for some reason," she said presciently, knowing her son and the kind of work he still sometimes performed, "your dad is talking to Doc Harris about flying in and picking her up."

"That'd be good to follow up, Mom."

"I thought so. Now, just don't get ahead of yourself. And give her a chance to explain. You know, practice your listening."

"I will."

"Good. Well, keep us posted."

"Right, Mom."

"And, Phillip, remember to listen." *Said it like she used to say* "*Make your bed. Wear a hat. Don't talk back to your father*"—the tone of her voice reducing him to about twelve years old.

"Goodbye, Mom."

Broker ended the call and stared at the moody cloud cover. Calm down. Think. Listen. Okay.

Nina was not dishonest. She just omitted virtually everything about her last assignment to a classified military unit popularly known as the Delta Force. But ever since 9/11, communication with Nina had been increasingly spotty.

Broker was not dishonest either. But he also left a lot of things out. When people met Broker casually, he'd angle around direct answers. A sketch emerged of him suggesting a background involving a successful landscaping business in the St. Croix Valley to the east of the Twin Cities. Then he'd drop a few hints how he'd got out of landscaping and put his money in a little resort up on Lake Superior before the real estate up there went through the roof. This was the truth, up to a point; but the landscaping gig was a cover. In fact, Broker had left the St. Paul cops and joined the Minnesota Bureau of Criminal Apprehension fifteen years ago. Then he proceeded to clock the longest run of deep undercover work in the history of Minnesota law enforcement.

Then, about eight years ago, Nina Pryce had launched a genteel bayonet charge into his life. She had an agenda. She had a skull and crossbones tattooed on her shoulder. She had a map to buried gold in her hip pocket.

Broker followed her to Vietnam, where they found several tons of Imperial gold ingots on a beach on the South China Sea.

They came home quietly rich, pregnant, and eventually married. More than two tons of the gold found its way into a bank account in Hong Kong. Broker lived on credit cards linked to that account.

Five years ago he'd helped the FBI penetrate the Russian Mafia. An informal arrangement evolved. The Feds let him keep his loot as a kind of open-ended retainer.

Broker and Nina's marriage, conceived in high adventure, could not survive ordinary life. After Kit was born, Nina nursed her for six months, woke up one morning, saw the dishes in the kitchen sink, experienced a panic attack, and hurried back into the Army.

Some cops in Minnesota, who were not exactly fans of Phil Broker, saw a measure of poetic justice in the complications of his marriage.

Karma coming back to him, stuff like that.

So.

For a number of reasons, all of them having to do with airport security, Broker had decided not to fly into Grand Forks. And though he still had a deputy badge and ID, a routine phone check with the Washington County Sheriff's office would elicit the friendly reminder that he should have turned the badge in yesterday. These minor details would complicate flying commercial with the .45-caliber automatic, the two magazines, and the box of ammunition he had tucked under the front seat.

The circumstances he was driving into struck him as very odd. Broker was familiar with Nina Pryce's flaws. But those flaws ran to vainglory, arrogance, and compulsive overachievement. Quitting on any task or abandoning her people were taboos in her strict warrior code. He could not imagine Nina abandoning her daughter as long as there was still breath in her body . . . Broker knit his bushy eyebrows and smiled an unhappy intuitive smile . . . But she was capable of using their daughter in some cockeyed special-ops ploy, if the stakes were high enough.

Goddamn sonofabitch!

But even angry, wounded, and full of painkillers, Broker remained focused. He took several deep breaths and let his eyes travel over the empty landscape.

He was driving through some of the least populated territory in the United States. So what was a Delta Force operator doing in Langdon, North Dakota? . . . His eyes drifted north, past the wheatfields to his right. For the second time he flashed his unhappy grin as a line from *The Magnificent Seven* time-traveled into his mind. He heard the sound track, saw Yul Brenner and Steve McQueen banter back and forth about something they had going . . .

"*. . . in this little town below . . .*

"*. . . the longest undefended international border in the world.*"

So. When it came down to it, he wasn't in a mood to rely on other people to protect his daughter.

Twenty minutes later, two blue water towers, some grain elevators and a micro dish antenna rose out of the fields and he drove into Langdon, North Dakota. It was one-thirty on a Sunday afternoon, no sun, gray clouds like an overcoat over ninety-seven humid degrees. The air was heavy and sweaty, hovering over a million acres of ripening wheat.

The first thing he saw was the four new white Tahoes with Border Patrol markings parked at the motel. Okay . . .

The county building was low red brick on his right. A leafy main street nestled in shadow on his left. Keep going? Find the pool? Or talk to the cops?

Kit was waiting in the park two blocks away. Broker doubted that Jane was alone. Assuming Jane and company were Nina's comrades, Broker figured his daughter was at this moment the most well-defended child in North Dakota. She could last another half-hour.

Broker reverted to one of his basic commonsense rules, which in this case was the Waco Rule of Thumb. The WRT posited that in 99.9 percent of all cases the locals knew the ground far better than the federal interlopers, were less arrogant, and would return straight talk in kind.

So he ignored mysterious Jane's admonition to check in with her first. He drove around the county offices until he spotted a small sign on a rear entrance by the parking lot: SHERIFF'S OFFICE. He parked, checked the note he'd scribbled to himself again. Sheriff Norman Wales. Then he went in through the door.

Something had to be up. Why else would the sheriff be in his office on a muggy Sunday afternoon?

Chapter Eleven

Broker gave his name and came under the intense scrutiny of a very curious dispatcher the moment he was buzzed in through the security door. She directed him through the radio room and pointed to two men, one in uniform, who appeared in a doorway. Then she immediately reached for a phone.

"We'll walk you down to Norm's office. Jim Yeager," said the husky one in jeans and a T-shirt, extending a hard farmer's mitt. "This is Barry Sauer, state highway patrol," he said.

Broker shook their hands in turn. Sauer was obviously working today. He wore a dark brown shirt and tan trousers and had a full service belt strapped around his waist. He had the creased and spit-shined military bearing that the people who bossed state cops liked to see in their troops. Yeager and Sauer kept glancing at Broker's bandaged left hand. But there was more to their curiosity.

They came in to look me over. Word's out.

They were old-fashioned cops, like Broker's dad had been. Two of the biggest, strongest guys in town. But they had quick eyes and were light on their feet and Broker decided that strong did not imply dumb with this bunch.

Stay alert.

Sheriff Norm Wales, like his deputy, Yeager, came in special today. He wore jeans and a golf shirt and stood waiting in his office doorway. He waved the two cops off and they retreated back down the hall. "That where you got shot?" he asked, pointing to Broker's hand. The remark got Broker's attention. Wales was letting him know he was up to speed. He had a soft, reserved voice, sad, blue basset-hound eyes, sandy brown hair, and thirteen-inch wrists.

"How'd you know?" Broker asked back as they shook hands.

"I had this little sheriff's convention to get the book on you. When I heard you were coming I talked to Jeffords in Cook County again. He handed me off to Eisenhower in Washington County, who says, by the way, you forgot to turn in one of his shields." Wales paused and cleared his throat. "In case you were thinking of flying any false flags. We seem to have a rash of that going on last couple days."

Broker shifted from foot to foot. This prairie cop had done his homework.

Wales indicated a chair in front of his desk. "Go on, sit." He closed his office door, went around behind his desk, sat down, and said, "Your daughter is just fine. She's up at the municipal pool, swimming laps. We've had people watching her ever since this started. But the fact is, looks like she's running in some pretty heavy company." Wales gave Broker a very direct look. "Wouldn't you say?"

"I just got here," Broker said, as he dropped into the chair.

"Your kid got very strangely abandoned in my town and suddenly I got sheriffs coming out of my ears. Gets a guy to thinking. So I took a flyer, had the county attorney call somebody he knows who works in the Minnesota AG's office," Wales said.

"Who?" *Uh-oh.*

"Tim Downs. My guy met him at a seminar at the University of Minnesota. I believe you're acquainted."

Shit. "Sure. Downs and I worked in St. Paul together some years back. We were never what you'd call close."

Wales tugged an earlobe. "Right. Downs had a knack for Internal Affairs and you had a knack for undercover. Not exactly compatible assignments. And, well, Downs did go to law school . . ."

They let it cook between them for a few seconds and then Wales resumed: "Downs says some people back in your state think you're one of the bad guys. Eight years back you dropped out of police work, showed up in Vietnam. The story goes you dug up a shitload of lost gold bullion. To hear Downs' version, you're a cross between a mercenary and a pirate." He paused. "You want some water or something? You don't look so hot."

Broker held up his hand. "Infection."

"Uh-huh. So—are you some kind of freelance pirate, or what?"

Broker defaulted to his basic operating persona. He maintained strict eye contact and kept his voice flat and steady. "Wales, I own this little resort up on Lake Superior. We got pretty good walleye and lake trout fishing if you're ever up that way."

"Yep. Downs told us. He also told us you're married to Nina Pryce, a gal in the Army who's stirred up enough controversy that Downs says she got her name in *Newsweek* a couple times. Saturday, I got Nina Pryce showing up in my county. Sunday, I got you."

Broker watched Wales furrow his forehead, the sheriff thinking he might try to stare Broker down. Wales decided not to and nodded. "Okay?" He opened his large hands in a reasonable gesture. Broker noticed he wore a copper bracelet around his right wrist. "I'll make this simple. The federal undercover population of my county has just shot up considerably in the last two days. All I want to know is—are you part of the problem or part of the solution?"

Broker was exhausted from the drive, his hand hurt, his head hurt. All the unflappable reflexes he'd cultivated over the years failed him utterly. He was an angry dad whose kid had been deserted. Fuck a bunch of feds. "Goddamn bitch," he muttered. "All I know is, I came to get my kid," Broker said hotly.

Wales sensed a chink in Broker's surface and his demeanor toughened perceptibly. "You and your wife are broke up, right?"

"What are you getting at?"

"Well, just what is it that your wife does in the Army?"

"Last I heard she was in Italy." Broker hoped that was general enough. *Goddamn you, Nina, I'm going to wring your neck.*

Wales squinted at Broker. "She's a long way from Italy now."

"Guess so. We've been out of touch."

Wales leaned back and steepled his fingers. He stared briefly at a county road map that hung on the wall. "How do I say this?"

"Try straight ahead."

"Straight ahead it is. Nina showed up with this Jane lady and they put considerable effort into looking, ah, like they were *involved* together."

"Say again?" Broker came forward slightly in his chair.

"Traveling as, ah, a quarreling couple," Wales said.

Broker stared at him.

"Actually, we don't have a whole lot of experience with this sort of thing out here . . ." Wales talking slower now, deadpan, drawing it out and studying Broker's feverish face for a reaction.

"C'mon, Wales. You don't strike me as a guy who talks sideways," Broker said.

"Alternative lifestyles. I believe that's what you call it in Minnesota, ain't it?"

"Wales?"

"Out here I guess we're less kindly disposed toward . . . alternative lifestyles, but naturally we're working on it," Wales said.

"What exactly is it you want to tell me?"

"This Jane lady Nina's traveling with works real hard at looking sexy in a strident way that excludes men. She comes across queer."

"Ah," Broker said as a jagged fever spike flared up through the roof of his mouth and jabbed into his brain.

Wales continued his careful scrutiny. "Gotta give them an A for effort. You worked UC, you know how hard it is to put an agent into a small community. I didn't buy it at first look, but there's some who did. Like maybe their intended target. Or maybe not. Maybe he's just bored and this gambit amuses him."

"You might as well tell me the whole story," Broker said in his best neutral voice.

"Sure, I can do that. Yesterday around noon this soap opera rolls into town. We get a call, two women having a domestic in the parking lot of a virtually closed local bar. They got a little kid with them. So our deputy goes and cools them out. Various accusations pass back and forth. My cop separates them. Gets them to agree on a plan to diffuse the conflict. The plan is to locate you to come get your kid. Jane gives my guy a contact person to find you. Jane takes your kid and checks into the motel. Then Nina . . ."

Wales paused, massaged his right wrist where he wore the copper band. "Arthritis. Copper's s'posed to help. Anyway, when Nina doesn't show up at the motel, Jane calls my deputy as per the arrangement. He calls the contact person who turns out to be the sheriff in Cook County, Minnesota. Now, we get to wondering—why is a county sheriff involved?

"Then Sheriff Jeffords calls me and asks me, as a favor, to make extra sure nothing happens to your kid on account of you and him are buddies. Meanwhile, your Nina runs off with the bar owner. Seems they saw they had something in common from the git. To wit: a drinking problem."

"Aw god." Broker sagged forward, elbow on knee, face in his hand. "Go on," he said. The fever had now divided into a lot of little spikes that started to seethe behind his eyes like flames, or maybe snakes. He struggled to keep a straight face.

Very casual, very sly, Wales hit Broker with his crack shot. "By the way. Nina and Jane rolled into town in this broken-down Volvo."

"*Volvo*," Broker said in a strangled voice.

Wales grinned. "That's how my guy read it. He said that underneath their bullshit, these two chicks had the look of folks who might arrive by Humvee, or in a Bradley Fighting Vehicle, or by fuckin' parachute . . ."

Broker held up his hands. "I give up. You're right. The people she hangs with would turn Volvos away from her funeral."

"And those people would be . . ."

"Nina never brought her work home." Broker clicked his teeth together. "The fact is, she ain't brought herself home, either, the last couple years."

"You ever heard of the Purple Platoon?" Wales asked.

Broker shook his head. "Where'd that come from?"

"Your friend Downs, he's got a photographic memory, I guess. From an article he read. What about the term *D-girls*?"

Broker stared at him. "Got me."

"C'mon, Broker," Wales said softly. "Try D for Delta."

Broker slumped his shoulders. "Wales, man, I don't know. I just come here to get my kid clear of whatever's going on."

Wales leaned across his desk and said, "Maybe."

They stared at each other.

Slowly, employing a reasonable tone of voice, Wales said, "Look. The guy she took off with is named Ace Shuster. He did a bit for manslaughter ten years ago. Everybody, including me, believes it was self-defense and the jury stuck it to him. A case of personal and local politics. He drinks too much and considers himself a ladies' man. And his dad had a moment of notoriety a couple years back as the biggest whiskey smuggler in North Dakota. But the way they do it, they haven't been breaking any state laws. The dad split for Florida and left Ace behind to sell the family bar. And probably, from time to time, Ace ships a little booze north, like a thousand other saloons between here and Washington State. But his heart ain't really in it, because the truth is, Ace ain't such a bad guy. We also believe, but cannot as yet prove, that the little asshole who runs Ace's bar, Gordy Riker, is moving methamphetamine precursor, and anything else that pays the freight, down from Canada . . ."

Wales' voice was picking up momentum. "I talked to people in Bismarck who never bullshit me. There is no state operation aimed at Ace Shuster currently in the works."

Broker stared at Wales' face. It was a rugged, compassionate face, like the perfect uncle or the perfect sergeant. Wales narrowed his eyes. "Let me tell you how it is. I got three full-time deputies for this whole county. There's one state highway patrol copper . . ."

Broker interrupted. "I saw a bunch of brand-new Border Patrol Tahoes parked at the motel on the way in."

"Right. After 9/11 they started sending guys from Texas through here on thirty-day rotations. We got three official border crossings in the county. They close between ten at night and six in the morning. The BP sits at the customs stations each night just in case Al Qaeda comes trotting down the road in platoon strength chanting the Koran."

"I wish I could help you, Wales," Broker said.

"Lemme put it to you this way, Broker. You remember Gordon Kahl?"

Broker nodded. "Tax resister, Posse Comitatus type. There was a shoot-out here in North Dakota, early eighties. They got him later someplace down south."

"Arkansas. But the scene here is what I'm getting at. Feds came strutting into Medina and brushed the local cops aside. Dumb shits. Set up an ambush on the road. Two federal marshals were killed and Kahl got away. Lot of people think that wouldn't have happened if they let the local sheriff handle it."

Wales smiled tightly and paused to let his words sink in before he resumed talking. "I got two hundred miles of wide-open border, and, like I said, three official crossings under the watchful eye of the

U.S. Border Patrol." He stood up, planted his wide knuckles on his desk, and enunciated very clearly: "And I got twenty-three prairie roads cutting through the fields that people been using for a hundred years. Some of them are graded and can handle a semitrailer."

He paused and took a breath. Then he said, "So I only got one question: *WHAT THE FUCK IS ARMY SPECIAL OPS DOING IN MY COUNTY!*"

Chapter Twelve

Broker left the sheriff's office pissed, but also experiencing fits of wonder and disbelief at what Nina and her crew were up to. He got back in the Explorer, continued down Highway 5, and found the city park sign and an arrow pointing north. Two blocks later he passed the elementary school.

Like Jane said, it was hard to miss.

Broker stared up at a perfectly restored Spartan missile at the edge of the park grounds. Looming fifty-five feet tall, the antiballistic missile was painted white with accurate black tail and fin markings and a vertical stack of uppercase letters spelling US ARMY.

He left the Explorer on the street and walked up to the missile and read the plaque at the granite base, which announced that the missile was given to the people of Langdon and Cavalier County during deployment of the Safeguard Anti-Ballistic Missile Facility.

Only then, looking at this memorial, did it finally dawn on Broker that he was in the heart of the old ICBM, ABM belt. He remembered back to the 1970s and '80s, all the talk about the good life in Minnesota until some party pooper pointed out that the state was right in the path of the prevailing winds from the missile fields in

North Dakota. In other words, if the worst happened, North Dakota would take the first hit, but Minnesota would catch all the fallout.

Nina had picked an interesting locale.

He crossed the park grounds and entered a low building that abutted the fenced-in swimming pool. He told the employee behind the counter he was here to get his kid and went out onto the pool area.

Summer squeals and splashes greeted him, kids in water wings throwing balls, riding on Styrofoam snakes. Parents sat along the poolside, a few dangling their legs, more of them at tables under umbrellas.

Broker spotted her in the pool putting serious moves on the water. Even in his wounded hand he felt the instant ache of absence, four months' separation. Kit Broker, seven years old, in an apricot Speedo swimsuit, goggles, hair pulled back tight in a ponytail, was busting her butt, doing a fairly decent crawl, cranking out laps all alone in the right-hand lane.

A watchful presence who had to be Jane paced her up and down the pool. Broker recognized her voice from the telephone as he walked up:

"Long and strong, Kit. Long and strong. Short and fast won't do it. Let's try for twenty strokes on this next lap."

She wore a plain black tank suit over a sleek coat of fast-twitch muscle. Dark short hair, the sides showing a flash of scalp, a touch of style to go with hoops of metal pierced into the edges of her ears. All together it added a glint of pagan wildness to her tired brown eyes. Not flashy and not subtle. And Broker disagreed with Wales. Jane didn't look especially sexy or dikey. She looked exhausted. And, sure, she was sharp—as in sharpened to too fine a point. And just plain dangerous, the way someone strung out on speed is unpredictable.

As Broker came up to the edge of the pool he scanned the crowd of parents and watchers and settled on the older guy with sandblasted ash hair. He had the deep face and arm tan of a man who works outside. His muscular legs were pale in comparison. The leisurely wide shorts and oversized orange and red Hawaiian shirt didn't go with the face, whose pale blue eyes, relentlessly tracking the scene, had forgotten how to relax over twenty years ago.

The moment Broker started toward Kit, Hawaiian Shirt uncoiled out of his chair with slow intensity. His large blunt hands, attached to thick-veined forearms, moved to a hover near his waist, eyes scanning.

Then the eye contact, the recognition, the easing back.

Okay. So Sheriff Wales did have excellent instincts.

Kit was swimming with the sharks.

"Dad-deee . . ."

Kit shot up, gleaming, out of the water, hoisted herself out of the pool, and ran to him, a blur of freckles and red hair. She jumped into his arms. Broker grimaced and grinned at the same time, hugging the happy squirm of his daughter as he got covered in wet kisses and chlorine. Taller by a good inch since he'd last seen her, Kit was starting to show some of the lean lioness density she inherited from her mother. Broker got thoroughly wet in the process and grimaced when her knee banged his injured hand.

"Kit, hey, look at you."

She had her mother's eyes and color. She'd acquired her mom's scary habit of totally focusing her attention. The habit of picking up small details she got from both of them. "What happened to your hand?" she asked.

"Oh, I hurt it working."

"Can I see it?"

"Okay. But later. So where's Mommy?" Broker asked, managing to keep his voice cordial.

Kit knit her brows—the brooding expression came from her dad. "Mom's at work," she said. Then she brightened. "I helped. We were in a play."

"You were, huh? So who's watching you?" He hefted her in his arms, settling her weight on his hip. She laid her cheek along his neck and nestled in, molding into his hollows. She raised her eyes and said:

"Auntie Jane and Uncle Hollywood."

"Uncle Hollywood?" Broker nodded, turned, and stared at the gaudy Hawaiian Shirt. "And this must be Auntie Jane." Broker turned to face the woman in the black swimsuit.

She extended her hand. "Jane Singer. How you doing?" Her grip was a little too firm. An edge of challenge in her eyes was ambiguous and sexually nonspecific. Like a dare to guess where she was really coming from. She's young, overtrained, and very very tired, Broker thought.

Kit interrupted their mutual inspection, squirming from his embrace.

"Daddy, can I show you something?" She scrambled from his arms, looked to Jane for a second, and then crouched in racing-dive position at the end of the pool.

"Swimmers, take your mark. Get set. Go!" Jane said.

Kit sprang forward into the air, swept up her arms for more loft, clasped them over her head, and cleanly cut the water with nary a splash.

"All *right*!" Broker said, impressed.

"She has talent," Jane said simply.

Broker briefly watched his daughter go down the pool. She *was* a strong swimmer. She was also the only kid in the pool not playing. And that was probably as much his fault as Nina's—poor kid, condemned to a life sentence with Broker's and Nina's genes. He turned and stared at Jane.

She met his eyes in a level gaze and said, "How's your hand doing? We heard you got dinged yesterday."

Broker decided not to ask her how she got her information.

"You gonna tell me what's happening here?" he asked.

"Sure. Let's put Little Bit in the shower back at the motel and talk."

Broker waved to Kit. When she scrambled out of the pool he bundled her in the towel that Jane held out. Four months ago when he'd done this he'd thought of her as a baby. Something different now. It had to do with the way she used her eyes, how she held herself. She'd changed into a miniature woman. When Broker started to lead his daughter to his truck, Jane gently intervened. "We have a system. Follow us to the motel."

Broker decided not to fight the system just this once. He followed Jane to the famous red Volvo, pointed to his Ford. She nodded, got in with Kit, and drove away. A dusty gray Chevy truck pulled in behind her. The Old Man And The Sea was at the wheel. Broker came last.

They parked at the motel, went up a flight of stairs to the room.

"Go take a shower and wash your hair. And use the conditioner—you gotta get the chlorine out or it'll turn your hair green," Jane told Kit.

"Okay." Kit gave Broker a hug and raced into the bathroom. A moment later the water started running.

"She seems to be holding up pretty well," Broker said.

"She's very on-task and mature for her age. Plus, she understands what her mom does for a living," Jane said.

"What's that supposed to mean?"

"At the very end in Vietnam, you were in MACV-SOG with Nina's dad. Everyone was leaving, but the two of you went back in to bring out your Vietnamese agents . . ."

"I knew Ray Pryce," Broker said simply.

Jane studied his face and said, "Only one of you came back out. For most of Nina's childhood, her dad was deployed in forward areas. Nina was raised by her mom back in the States."

"So?"

"So, the shoe's on the other foot and you don't like it. You should be big enough to handle Nina's success . . ."

Broker looked around. "*This . . .* is *success?*"

"Hey. Deal with it. You married a soldier, mister," Jane said. Touchy.

Broker looked away from Jane and scanned the room. A fancy laptop on the desk along with a cell phone's travel charger. His eyes stopped on a large equipment bag on the floor along the wall. He went over, grabbed the handles, and hefted the bag. He was lifting about thirty pounds of steel that shifted and slid like guns and ammo.

Jane watched him, then asked, "So? What are you thinking?"

"That I walked into a classified Army unit that's wandered off the reservation. And you got a kid along. My kid." Broker let the bag drop with a crash, then turned and studied her.

"You didn't *walk* into shit. You were *summoned,*" Jane said.

Broker did his best deadpan, working hard to master a powerful resentment at the way this was unfolding. He changed the subject. "You and my daughter have been spending a lot of time together, huh?"

"Yeah." Jane did a little provocative number with her eyes and eyebrows. "You got a problem with people like me?"

"You mean young, insecure, with a chip on their shoulder?" Broker said carefully. "One thing I do know, I don't want my kid to have a chip on *her* shoulder."

"Cut the shit, Broker. You been filling in the blanks. Tell me what you really think." Jane folded her arms.

"I think you guys are flying by the seat of your pants and you're out of your depth. I'm pissed that you put Kit in the middle of it."

Jane shrugged. "We told her it was like a play at school. She even had some important lines."

"I talked to the local sheriff."

"That was a mistake," Jane said in a flat voice.

"He said there was some kind of fight at a bar? A deputy took you and Kit off-site. Nina stayed with the bar owner."

"So far so good."

"Tell me, is Nina playing Little Drummer Girl a promotion or a step down?"

"Very funny. Look, Kit was onstage for less than five minutes. Nina wasn't packing, but we had five guns outside that bar when it went down."

"I only see two of you so far."

"We had three more in a surveillance van." Jane paused, then added in a dry voice, "They peeled off for now."

"Sounds serious. Too serious to put my daughter in the way."

"We disagree. But it's moot. She's out of it now."

The phone rang. Jane moved to it swiftly. "This is Jane." Pause. "Good, c'mon down. We'll make the call." She turned to Broker. "There's somebody you got to talk to." She smiled again. "What did you think? Kit just got lost between the cracks in some half-assed scramble and needed a ride home? There's a plan. Kit had a part. And so do you."

Goddamn you, Nina. "A part?"

"Yeah. There's something Nina needs you to do."

There was a knock on the door. Jane squinted through the security peep and opened the door. Hawaiian Shirt shuffled in.

"Broker, meet Holly," Jane said.

Broker shook hands cautiously, circling slightly, sniffing Holly out. Too much sun and too much accelerated living had leached away all his excess body weight and emotions. About 180 pounds of callus and scar tissue remained. His pale bemused eyes impressed Broker, the way the dead spots and the live spots comingled.

Jane watched them do their signifying, amused. "Back before Cro-Magnon walked the earth . . ."

Holly had a voice to match his eyes, soft over steel. "She means back in the Nam."

"They called him Hollywood because he was showy," Jane said. Holly smiled.

"Now we call him Turner Classic Movies," Jane said, returning the smile.

"Eat your heart out, slit. You're never gonna do twenty pull-ups, ever," Holly said.

"And you're never going to have a multiple orgasm," Jane said.

"That's 'You're never going to have a multiple orgasm, *Colonel*,'" Holly said with a hint of a growl.

Kit came out of the bathroom. She had one towel wrapped around her waist and another, turban fashion, around her head.

"Sorry, Little Bit, grown-ups gotta talk shop. Back in the tub," Jane ordered. She handed Kit a Rubik's Cube to play with.

Kit knit her brows at her dad. "Do I have to?"

"Just for a while," Broker said.

Kit put the cube under her arm and held out her hands. "I'm gonna be wrinkled like a prune." She returned to the bathroom.

There was a table and two chairs in the corner. Retro etiquette bred into Broker's bones prompted him to offer one of the chairs to Jane. She rolled her eyes. Broker and Holly sat.

"So what do you have in mind?" Broker asked.

Holly gave a perfect Gallic shrug and said, "Wait one."

Broker waited while Jane punched in numbers on her cell phone. Holly said, "It's easy. All you got to do is get mad at your wife for leaving home and deserting your kid in the middle of nowhere. Think you can handle that?"

"Oh yeah, but why should I?"

Jane held out the cell phone. Broker put it to his ear. A voice he hadn't heard in more than a year said, "Hey, Broker, how you doing?"

Broker took a moment to focus. Then he said, "Lorn Garrison?" Several years ago Broker had helped Garrison, then an FBI agent, penetrate the Russian Mafia. Garrison had left the bureau and was now a sheriff in Kentucky. If they could casually phone up Lorn and get him on board, then Broker was being seriously handled— which meant that Holly, Jane, and Nina were into something big-time real. He relaxed his voice but his mind raced. "Not bad. How's yourself?"

"Can't complain. Down here tight as a tick in all the good things Kentucky's famous for: whiskey, tobacco, racehorses, and hot browns."

"This ain't a social call, is it, Lorn?"

"Nope. All about street cred. Some real serious folks you're with. They're hanging way out there 'cause they might have caught a piece of The Big One."

"Are you mixed up in this scene in North Dakota?" Broker asked.

"Uh-uh, just some heavy people in D.C. wanted me to give you a heads-up."

"What heavy people?"

"You heard how CIA took off the gloves and is putting covert operations back together? Well, Pentagon doesn't trust CIA *or* FBI for squat, so they put together their own black bag of tricks out of Bragg with a domestic agenda. And let me clue you, to this aging G-man it all sounds illegal as shit."

"Yeah."

"Well, that's who you're running with. Some bunch from Delta. Put together real fast. The operation is called Northern Route."

"Do I get to know what they're after?"

"Sure. Your wife is trying to go undercover and get next to a guy they think is a contract courier for Al Qaeda. The intell says this guy's bringing something into the country. Hold on to your ass, Broker—they think it could be one of those fucking suitcases we were so worried about."

Broker paused to let the word cycle through his brain.

Nuclear.

"A tactical nuke. No bullshit?" he said. Maybe he didn't hear right.

"No bullshit. So they want you to perform one small service and then get out of Dodge. Naturally, the usual threats are implied—you don't help these guys, I suspect the feds will start messing with your bottom line. You know, all that bullion you and Nina pirated from Vietnam."

"You know me, nothing but public-spirited," Broker said, staring at Jane and Holly.

"You got it?" Lorn asked.

"I got it," Broker said. "Check you later." End of phone call.

Holly handed him a black-and-white photo that showed a man holding up an open briefcase. The inside of the briefcase was cleaned out to make room for a metal cylinder and a bunch of gadgetry, computer boards, wires. "Worst-case scenario," Holly said, "they really have got their hands on a Russian KGB suitcase. A one-kiloton, 105 tactical nuke round, configured in a suitcase. Put it in midtown Manhattan, it'll kill a hundred thousand people, easy."

Jane stepped forward. "Two days ago we acted on a tip from one of our squirrels in Lahore, Pakistan. We took down an Al Qaeda financial officer in Detroit. He talked. He gave us the name of a courier for something nuclear. And a location. Shuster in North Dakota. We ran 'Shuster slash North Dakota' in every computer we could think of."

Holly held up a mug shot of a young blond guy with chiseled features. His hair was on the long side. The date was 1992.

"This is the target. Ace Shuster is a second-generation smuggler—"

Broker held up his hand. "I talked to the sheriff. He's got you figured out, up to a point. He already told me about this guy."

Holly scowled. Broker ignored him, got up, went to the desk, opened a drawer, took out the local phone directory, thumbed to the S's and read: "Gene and Ellen Shuster; Asa Shuster, Dale Shuster. I come up with three, four counting Ellen."

"Okay, smart-ass," Holly said. "What about this?" He handed Broker another photograph that showed a muddy road, parked cars, and a crowd of two dozen peoples, mostly men, standing around, low rolling scrub in the background. Two faces in the gathering were circled. Jane tapped one of them. "Ring any bells?"

Broker exhaled. Everybody in America now recognized that lean shovel chin. "Tim McVeigh."

Holly's finger moved to the other circled face at the opposite end of the picture. To help Broker out, he held the mug shot from Shuster's dossier next to the photograph. It was him, a little older but the same guy.

"Ace Shuster and McVeigh standing on a road, with a bunch of people in between," Broker said. "So?"

"So, what they're looking at is the Branch Davidian Compound. They were in the gallery of Koresh supporters."

"Are you saying this Shuster knew McVeigh?" Broker asked.

"We know their paths crossed at least once." Jane shrugged. "It sure got our attention."

Broker squinted at Jane and Holly. "Al Qaeda in Detroit to militia nuts to petty crooks in North Dakota? I didn't think Islamic fundamentalists had truck with nonbelievers."

"Yeah, well, we ain't gonna sit around and find out on CNN again," Holly said with absolute conviction.

"Not after the way those desk pricks in CIA and FBI fumbled warning signs on 9/11," Jane said.

"You know what you guys look like? Like you haven't slept for days," Broker said. "The local cops are onto you. Probably this Shuster guy is onto you . . ."

Holly put his hands on his narrow hips. "Look, Broker; we don't have the luxury of playing cop. If a cop's bad guy slips by, that's cool, they'll catch him later on something else. Cops can afford to wait and let the system grind along. Protect and serve. Life, liberty, and so on and so forth. The guys who wrote the Constitution thought in terms of threats being a British fleet taking weeks to cross the pond. A nuclear event is an entirely different order of magnitude."

Broker studied him. How exhausted and wired he was. "What if the local sheriff hauls you in for questioning?"

"What's the charge?" Jane said. "We're just citizens. None of us are carrying any military ID or equipment."

Broker pointed at the bag next to the wall.

"Nope," Jane said. "Everything in there is available in the economy."

"And what are you taking to stay awake?" Broker said.

Jane and Holly exchanged fast looks. Holly shrugged. "A little speed now and then. We been on one hell of a road trip . . ."

"Flush it. These local cops *might* be Andy of Mayberry, but I get the feeling they are seriously underemployed, highly trained, and itching for something to happen. Plus, they are very wired into their history. The sheriff gave me a lecture on Gordon Kahl."

"Kahl was a wacko," Holly said.

"Yeah, and the feds botched the job, pissed all over the locals, and got two of their own killed," Broker said.

Holly glowered. "We ain't the goddamn federal marshals."

"Right," Broker said. "The marshals are trained to uphold the law. You guys are trained to blow people away. Get rid of the dope. The locals just might shake you down for the hell of it. If they find drugs, you're no good to Nina sitting in the county jail."

"Point taken," Holly said. "But if the sheriff makes a phone call, no one, nowhere, will admit to our existence."

"*No one*," Jane underscored.

Broker understood her emphasis. They were expendable. Nina was expendable. He wondered, too, if, push come to shove, Kit would have been expendable.

"Whose idea was this?" Broker asked.

"Nina. We just got in the van and drove and made it up on the way. We stopped in St. Paul to pick up the car," Holly said.

"The Volvo from central casting," Broker said.

"Nina again. We found the car and staked it out, then practically mugged this walking liberal cliché near Macalester College in St. Paul. A *serious* feminist type, you know—got a housekeeper, nanny, personal trainer . . . But she took a pile of money for the car." Jane dropped her eyes, looked up, almost catty. "Outfitting Nina at Victoria's Secret, however, was my idea."

"Oh Christ," Broker said.

Jane shrugged. "This great pair of cargo harem pants and this really foxy rib tank. She's way past being cute, but, hey, she can still look pretty damn raunchy if you put a few shots of booze into her."

"Thanks for sharing that," Broker said.

"You're welcome."

"So. That's what's happening," Holly said. "We didn't coordinate any of this with the FBI or Homeland Security. We don't have time for them to hold a committee meeting and put it tenth on the agenda behind their budget requests. As the old Rum Dum himself is fond of saying, 'We are leaning *way* forward.'" There was a definite edge of sarcasm in Holly's voice.

"Shit," Broker said.

Holly and Jane stared at him. Holly cocked his left wrist in a reflex gesture, checking his watch; but he wasn't wearing a watch, and to Broker the mannerism had a chilling operational feel that brought back a lot of bad memories. Basically, he felt like a prong they wanted to plug into their socket, use one time, and throw away.

"Shit," he repeated. Then, "Okay. What exactly do you want me to do?"

Chapter Thirteen

Nothing happened the way she expected. She woke after ten straight hours of unmolested sleep to the soft buss of sunlight on her cheek. A bare trace of buttery warmth managed to squeeze between the clouds, leaked through the window and teased across her face. She opened her eyes and saw the brief flicker on a faded poster curled on the wall. Roger Maris, the old Yankee hitter. Then it went back to shadow.

She smelled fresh coffee.

She'd got out of bed and tiptoed to the door, very carefully eased open the knob, and looked into the living room. He was sitting at his desk, his back to her. Already dressed. Then he turned slightly and she saw he was holding a pistol in his hand.

Oh boy.

But he quickly put the pistol in the drawer and shut it. He'd got up, went to the kitchenette, and returned holding two cups of coffee.

"I don't know how you take it, so I got one of each: black or with half-and-half. You need an Alka-Seltzer?"

"The black's mine, and I'll pass on the seltzer," Nina said.

"No hangover?"

"Just a little tired."

"You slept in. It's almost noon. Here, this'll help." He handed her the coffee and she took a sip. Her facial expression showed her approval.

"I order it special from a place in Bismarck. Use that plunger-dealie. Seems to work pretty good," he said.

Some of the strangeness had worn off. They knew each other a little now.

"I'm going to make some breakfast. Bacon and eggs all right or are you a granola person?"

"Over easy," Nina said.

She took her time in the bathroom. Enjoying the hot water, the shampoo and conditioner, using his razor to shave her legs. She inspected the contents of the cabinet over the sink: maybe a little more aspirin and Alka-Seltzer than usual, but nothing prescription or illegal.

She dried off, finger fluffed her hair, and decided to skip the makeup. She stared at yesterday's clothes as the smell of frying bacon drifted in the humid air. She decided to put the peekaboo T-shirt back on along with the change of underwear she carried in her purse. Then she inspected herself in the steamy mirror, twirled.

Five more good years, he'd said.

Get serious, you're working, she reminded herself and went out the door.

Breakfast was eggs, bacon, cottage fries, and toast. He apologized: he was out of orange juice.

They sat at the small table in the kitchen nook. Downstairs they heard the door open, the heavy scuff of shoes.

"Gordy," Ace said.

"You and him seem pretty different," Nina said. "You know what he reminds me of? That movie, *The Time Machine*—those guys who lived underground, the Morlocks."

Ace smiled at the reference and said, "You know, I seen that movie, they were cannibals." Then he shrugged. "Gordy's not exactly a walk in the park, but he ain't as bad as he'd like to be. He came with the territory. My dad hired him to run the bar. He went to school same class as my brother. Works like hell."

"So bar manager isn't your regular business?"

"Big iron."

"Come again?"

"I drove heavy machinery for Fuller Construction—crawlers, dozers mainly, belly loaders," he said. "You name it, I ran it. Now Fuller's gone, like my dad."

Nina looked around. "I just thought . . . all these books?"

Ace smiled dryly. "Nina, this might come as a shock, but all the smart people don't necessarily go to college."

She frowned and ducked her head in mock fright.

He laughed and cleared away the plates, topped off the coffee, then sat back down and lit a Camel. "So," he said, "what are we gonna do with you?"

She peered into her coffee cup. "By now Jane's probably called my old man. Or that cop has, so he'll be coming to pick up Kit." She set down the cup and raised her hand, fingers spread as if holding off an invisible oncoming weight. "Once he gets here, I'll have to talk to him."

"What's he like, your husband?"

Nina didn't have to fake a word. It came out straight and honest and she wasn't planning to hold Ace's eyes so directly when she said it but she did: "Hard to read. Sorta like you. Lives mostly below the surface."

"All things being equal, if he'd a met you like I did yesterday, coming off some bad rebound scene, and you half-tanked, would he have . . . ah?"

"Taken advantage of me?"

"Yeah."

"Probably not. He told me something once. About barroom at

tractions. Maybe I shouldn't say this, but, he said when something comes at you out of nowhere, it's probably not attraction. Probably it's more a question of propulsion."

Ace made a soft reeling motion with his finger, asking for more.

Nina shrugged. "He's a good dad."

Ace repeated the reeling motion. Wanting more.

Nina pursed her lips, then bit down hard on the words, not having to fake this one either. "Just that the fucker thinks he can tell me what to do!"

Ace leaned back respectfully. "I get the message. We'll take it one day at a time."

Nina stood up. "I'll do the dishes."

He cocked his head and studied her. "No you won't. I can tell. It just ain't your thing."

Perceptive, she thought. So she didn't argue and went for her purse to get her cigarettes. She paced back and forth, smoking while he did the breakfast chores.

This wasn't the way it was suppose to go, was it?

She was starting to like the guy.

Nina excused herself to use the bathroom, and when she shut the door she heard Ace go down the stairs. As she was finishing up, she became aware that she could overhear voices; Ace and Gordy talking in the office. Stooping and listening carefully, she soon figured out that the water pipes under the sink ran down through a hole in the tile and floor joists. The hole was masked off with a piece of plywood, split to fit around the pipes. She knelt down, removed the plywood, and put her ear to the pipe.

"So, did you get any?" Gordy said.

"Oh yeah, went all night. Whips, chains, she tied me up and slapped peanut butter in the crack of my ass. It was wonderful."

"Bullshit. You didn't get any. You'd be in a better mood and you'd've sent her on her way. Look, I gotta go gas up my truck, be right back," Gordy said. "Almost forgot, George called."

"George, great. Lemme guess," Ace said.

"Where is she?" Gordy lowered his voice.

"Aw c'mon. Cut the shit. Upstairs putting on her face."

"Man, you are one pussy brain."

"Yeah, yeah. So? George?"

"Sounds like one of his moonlight packing specials."

"I'll take care of it," Ace said.

Nina squirmed to get more comfortable and pressed her ear closer to the floor. She heard Gordy leave, heard the door slam, then a moment later heard a muted truck engine start up and drive away.

Then Ace was on the phone talking.

"Hey, George, you old bootlegger. What's up? . . . Aw, man, I don't know, at this late date. Why don't you get Gordy to pick it up? . . . Okay. You got a point. I don't trust him on something serious, either. Just let me know. Bye."

Nina waited another five minutes. She spent the time putting on eyeliner and lipstick. Then she took her cell phone from her purse and went downstairs.

Ace was standing in the empty alcove to the right of the bar. He'd brought a chair and set a cardboard box on it. He was taking a picture off the wall. It was the framed yellowed front page of a newspaper. The headline read: LANGDON—MISSILE CITY, USA.

"Hey. You could help me take these down and wrap them. I promised them to the county library."

"Can I see?" she asked as she left her phone on the bar and came forward. He handed over the frame. Nina scanned the page. A picture of the town's main street. A map showing Sprint, Spartan, and Safeguard sites.

"See?" said Ace. "They put in the Minutemen in the late sixties, so then they started building the ABMs to protect the Minuteman silos. That's how the bar came about. They built this big trailer park for the construction crews right across the road. This place used to really jump back in '71, '72."

Nina noticed that he was unguarded, remembering—there was a softness to the depths of his eyes that was at odds with his physical persona.

"Yeah," he went on, "the population of the town doubled. The work crews brought their kids, and we had students in our schools from every state in the union." He took the framed page back and wrapped it in newsprint and put it on the box. "Mom used to joke how we had a rush hour when the crews changed shifts. Just like in a big city."

It started as a tightness in her chest and traveled up into her throat, her chin, and tugged on the corner of her lips. A feeling of . . . what? Was it sadness? No, more like trespass.

I wouldn't feel like this, goddammit, if he was more . . . bad.
But he wasn't.
Or was he? Who was George?

She remembered seeing him earlier with the pistol. Casual, charming, putting it away, never mentioning it.

"Dad brought in the equipment dealership, thought he was going to really cash in on all the construction contracts. But then, like a lot of things around here, it all sorta dried up and blew away."

He pointed to another picture, a massive snarl of interlaced steel reinforcing rods. "Nixon's pyramid. Government put out close to two hundred million bucks for that pile of concrete. Just south of town at Nekoma. I'll show it to you if you're still around. Was supposed to house the radar for the ABM system. Never used it. Jimmy Carter. SALT II."

Nina looked away, saw another newspaper page under glass. A quote in the center of the page: "If North Dakota seceded from the Union it would be the world's third-largest nuclear power." She turned and studied him, wrapping faded mementos in newsprint.

What was he doing? Dallying with her? Pretending to accept her and her sad little personal story?

If he was who they thought he was, he had to be suspicious.

"Is there any coffee left?" she asked.

"Sure," he said, not even looking up from his wrapping. "Gordy keeps a Mr. Coffee in the office."

She walked directly to the office, went in; there was a desk, computer, fax machines, printer . . . and wouldn't you know it?—next to the phone: a caller-ID unit.

A second later she pushed the review button. The data materialized on the tiny gray screen, a time, today's date, the number, and a name: Khari George. She grabbed a pen off the desk, removed a Post-it note from the pad beside the phone, scribbled the number, then slipped it under her shirt and into the waistband of her panties. The coffeepot sat on the edge of the desk, half-full of black tarry liquid. She selected the cleanest-looking one from a lineup of several mismatched mugs, filled it, and went back into the bar.

As she came out, Ace was reaching up with both hands, his back to her. He was taking down a faded military pennant that showed a wedge of stars and the wreathed heading: 321ST MISSILE WING.

Seeing him like that, back turned, vulnerable, she had the impression that he was dismantling and packing away pieces of his own life, not just picture frames. She remembered his blithe bar chatter about depression. And how Gordy sounded suspicious of her. Yet Ace was casual to the point of folly. She remembered a suggestion from his dossier; that his charming drinker's act was likely an attempt at self-medication.

What if she were stalking a cripple?

And if so, was it an advantage or a disadvantage? What would Broker say?

Ace turned, saw her watching him, and asked, "Are you all right?" Just then she heard Gordy's truck pull up in front. A second after that, her cell phone rang.

Chapter Fourteen

Broker did not enjoy the smile on Jane's face, or the way she relished each word she spoke: "You know all about domestics, right? What we have in mind is the domestic from hell. You're pissed, hurt, and dead tired. You're the perfect estranged husband."

"The bar is called the Missile Park," Holly said. "Shuster's got a pad on the second floor. It's just west of town on the highway, on the left. Go in there and read her the riot act."

"Yeah, make it real, take it to the edge." Jane chanted her encouragement like a cheerleader as she punched numbers into her cell.

"I get the impression you and Nina can come across as pretty authentic. Like, real pissed at each other," Holly said.

"We're counting on it," Jane said, cell to her ear, and as her call went through she sneered into the phone, "Hey, bitch, where *are* you?" Pause. "Why am I not surprised. Yeah, well, your old man is here to take Kit back. He's coming down to drop off your things." She turned to Broker, winked. "She says go fuck yourself."

Jane ended the call, then released Kit from captivity in the bathroom. Holding up pruned hands like fulfilled prophecy, Kit hopped on the bed, captured the TV remote, worked into the cable menu, and found the cartoons. Almost immediately the Road Runner honked his signature *beep-beep* on the TV.

Broker went over and kissed his daughter. She half-responded; brows knit, wrapped up in her cartoon, she said, "This is where the boulder falls on Wile E. Coyote."

"Great," Broker said without enthusiasm.

Holly clapped him on the shoulder and handed him a worn leather travel bag. "Some of her stuff. Go."

Swearing under his breath, Broker plodded out into the strange town, the immense hovering sky, the almost liquid humidity.

He was a realist, he told himself. He was attuned to ruthless practicalities. He didn't court notions like karma. Or destiny. He certainly didn't believe in poetic justice.

But this sure as hell felt like payback.

And he could imagine Nina smiling as she pictured him acknowledging the uneasy sensation of being swept up in someone else's undercover cliff-hanger. He shifted from foot to foot and stared north, toward Canada; imagined Wahhabi soldiers tiptoeing through the endless wheat with suitcases strapped to their chests.

It was not out of the question. So . . .

Onward.

Dutifully, he drove down Highway 5, spotted the bar, which was a wreck, and parked the Explorer next to a tan Tahoe that had a dented left-front fender. He got out and hefted Nina's bag. The Missile Park had seen better times: the porch sagged, bricks were falling out of its facade. Unlike the monument in the park, the badly proportioned missile painted over the door had faded almost to invisible. It was partially obscured by a FOR SALE sign.

Broker walked up the steps, opened the door, and commanded his heart to start manufacturing ice cubes. He took a deep breath, exhaled, and stepped inside.

The direct approach. An exercise any kung fu master worth his

chi would know as Fool Walks Into Lion's Den With Pocket Full
Of Lamb Chops.

Musty, dark, layers of slowly rising cigarette smoke. Lots of
mirror showing behind the bar. No bottles.

To announce his entrance he raised the bag to above his waist,
opened his hand in a stylized gesture, and let it drop.

Ka-thunk!

Three sets of eyes jerked up. Broker ignored a flash of thigh and
calf and bare shoulder, the red hair. The flimsy cotton dress. No,
goddammit, it wasn't even a dress. It was a T-shirt with the arms cut
out down to her hips almost. He scowled.

His T-shirt. Then—

Nina.

She sat at a table in the back of the room. And he paid no attention to the languid blond guy kinda poured into a chair next to her.
That would be Ace. He did take a half-second to register the second
guy in the room. He stood behind the bar. Shorter, wide in the
shoulders, wearing suspenders—no, not suspenders, a wraparound
Velcro back brace. Obviously the guy who did the heavy lifting.
Lots of bushy hair. Kept his shirt open three buttons down his
chest so the mat of chest hair climbed up like a ratty vine, connecting up with his mustache and his unshaven chin and his sideburns.

Like a freakin' badger. He'd probably be the other one the sheriff mentioned. Forgot his name.

Okay. Broker scanned the room. The bar was in the shape of an
L. To Broker's right, the short leg of the L formed an alcove off the
main room. A solitary chair sat in the space with a cardboard box on
it. Crumbled newsprint was creeping out of the top of the box.

Aware that the three of them were fixed on his every move,
Broker casually started down the bar, his own attention focused on
Nina, who was working through a Method acting exercise about
smoking a cigarette. Ace Shuster sat across from her. A newspaper
section lay on the table under his elbows. The crossword puzzle.

Great. The thinking man's smuggler. Their heads were bent forward, like comparing notes. Shuster's hand gestures and body language suggested someone wrestling with the dimensions of an obvious question. *Is this gonna be trouble? And if so, how much?*

Broker's eyes clicked back on Nina. He hadn't seen her in six months.

A complex scurry of emotions formed a knot in his stomach. Concern edged out anger; but not by much.

Nina looked right at him and rose to a half-crouch when their eyes met. Ka-pow.

Make it real. No problem.

It had always been there.

Not a planned marriage.

A pregnancy, a marriage to sanctify it. A daughter.

Other people found an equilibrium, hand and glove, yin and yang—complementary energy. Even darker partnerships found a balance—the enabler, the drunk.

They had never agreed.

They had always fought.

They never gave in. Rather than compromise, they had separated.

All his friends agreed. A match more suited to the boxing ring than the marriage bed.

And not real good for the kid.

Auntie Jane and that Hollywood character wanted a domestic? No problemo.

Broker wasn't used to seeing her show so much skin. Wasn't used to seeing her wear makeup. Wasn't used to seeing her with a glass of whiskey in front of her in the early afternoon.

She'd relaxed her martial precision into honky-tonk ripeness. No, more than that—a rawness. Palpably, from the set of her hips and her jaw and her eyes, she hungered after something, and this dumb shit Shuster probably thought it was some combination of booze and himself.

How'd she do that? Was it the funky shirt, the way she held herself? She'd never gone to any trouble to make herself attractive for him. But she was sure laying it on for this pretty-boy asshole.

Nina lowered her eyes and her fingers touched Ace's forearm; like just a little scared. So she had added vulnerability to her repertoire. Some mix of *catch me, fuck me, I can't help myself.*

He looked at Shuster's chiseled jaw and cheekbones, his touseled blond hair, his thick forearms. At exactly the wrong moment an old line he must have used a dozen times when he was younger jumped into his brain. *You ever notice how you have the best sex with the worst people?*

As if on cue, Shuster stood up. "My place, my rules," he said. "Talking is fine. So's yelling. But no hitting."

Broker tried, but failed, to ignore Shuster—because all of a sudden there was real anger, jealousy, and possessiveness churning in his chest. The kind of kid's stuff that could get a forty-eight-year-old man killed in a North Dakota bar.

Gordy did a fast eye exchange with Shuster. Shuster cooly warned him off as Broker took a few more steps. Now Broker had Gordy at his back. He stopped three feet from the table and aimed a casual snarl at Nina. "Brought your stuff, hon. Sorry, but Jane wouldn't part with the motorized dildos, or the whips and chains."

Nina just said, "Aw shit. You."

He stared at her. "So you dumped Jane already." Then he shifted his attention pointedly to Shuster. "At least *she* didn't have cowshit between her toes."

Shuster stood up a little straighter, loosened his shoulders, and shook out his hands. Not much, just enough. Broker heard Gordy's boots scrap the floor, coming around the bar.

Nina shrugged, definitely raw. "So much for trusting a fuckin' dike."

"Whatever. Look, I came to take Kit home before she's totally damaged by all this. Just what the fuck do you think you're doing?"

Nina's voice clotted, she showed her teeth and her knuckles.

"I'm not doing anything you haven't done, you asshole." The challenge in her voice conveyed a pretty convincing picture of a woman who might like to see two men fight on a hot humid afternoon.

"I want to talk to you—outside," Broker said.

Shuster nodded. "Like I said, talk is fine."

Broker shot him a look. "Is there a fucking echo in here?"

Shuster cooly stepped back. "So talk," he said.

Broker took a second look at Shuster, sensed Gordy at his back. He had been sizing up men for thirty years, and Ace Shuster looked like amiable trouble. Not dumb, or mean, just low-key dangerous. And Broker's quick study detected none of the overpressurized compulsion he associated with the true out-of-control asshole or psycho. This Shuster was trickier than that. He had some irony. Some of Holly's steel behind silk. He'd be full of surprises.

While Broker was pumping out the ice, Nina was going equal and opposite; fighting off a major meltdown behind her sternum, in the neighborhood of her heart.

Look at you, you sassy son of a bitch. Been a drag all year and now you're gonna make your one redeeming move. Like some major-league egomaniac pitcher who thinks he can go the distance, high on bottom-of-the-ninth, bases-loaded, full-count cool—twenty-four hours and here you are, standing in the same room with me.

"So talk," Ace said, stepping back to give them room. He made the briefest of eye contact with Broker, saw the bandaged hand, then looked back to Nina. A fast once-over that gave nothing.

"I suppose I got to talk about taking Kit back home," Nina said. Resigned. She stood up.

"Damn fool thing bringing her here in the first place." Broker clipped off the words, spun on his heel, walked the length of the bar.

Nina erupted in a wildcat snit, fast-stepping to catch up.

"Don't you turn your back on me," she yelled.

Broker spun just before they got to the door. The words tumbled out fast: "I don't know why in the hell we ever had a kid, anyway . . ."

She did this horrible puff-adder pursing with her teeth, lips, and cheeks. Her freckles glowed like grapeshot. She hissed: "I've thought about this a lot, you asshole. It was completely out of our hands . . ." Broker caught a spray of spittle from the force of her words. He smelled last night's whiskey on her breath, and tobacco. But her voice dropped low, just for him. "It was pure biological imperative. We saw each other and the drum didn't stop beating till the sperm penetrated the egg."

"Cunt."

"Prick."

As they pushed through the doorway Shuster and Gordy exchanged impressed glances. Gordy raised his hand and blew on his fingers, shook them, like, *Wow.*

They just had to follow them outside to the porch. An uneasy curiosity devoured their faces as they watched Broker and Nina jockey for good footing on the trap rock.

Shit, man, this could be a fistfight.

Half circling but moving away from the porch, Broker and Nina opened the distance until they were out of easy earshot.

Broker looked at Shuster, then at Nina, and then looked around at the bleak sky. "I been briefed. You guys are grabbing at straws. This is too small a town to pull this off."

"Agreed. So I could use some help. They explained, right?" Nina spoke flatly.

"Uh-huh. Move onstage and off like a piece of scenery."

"This is dead serious."

"I'd say putting Kit out on a limb is pretty serious."

They had started circling each other as they talked. Setting up a hostile rhythm with their bodies. Broker wanted to grab her and shake her. She sensed this and egged him on with a smirk. He was touched, never having seen this game, feline side of her before.

"You got shot in the hand," Nina said and jabbed a finger at him accusingly.

"How'd you know?" He glowered and hunched his shoulders.

"Garrison, the ex-FBI guy, told us. He tried tracking you yesterday. Talked to somebody in Washington County." She paused. "Look, you gotta get Kit out of here."

"For sure."

Nina grimaced at him. She was having trouble starting her words.

"Well?" he asked.

She clicked her teeth together. "Something about this scene doesn't feel right."

"You *bitch*!" Broker's voice rose to a shout, loud enough for Shuster to hear on the porch.

"What can I say? We're new at this sort of thing. I knew if Kit was here you'd come for her . . ."

"Nina." Broker's voice ended in a sputter.

"Can you get Kit back to stay with your folks? Charter a flight? There's a landing strip."

That was almost an echo of his mom's suggestion about Doc Harris flying in. "You been talking to my mom?" he said hotly.

In a fast change-up, she dramatically placed her fingers on her chest, raised her eyebrows. "Me?" Then she went back to her angry Mars in the House of Estrogen, or whatever the fuck Mom said her problem was, and gritted her teeth. "And maybe you could stick around?" Clearly it pained her to ask. "I gotta pass you something. It's in my left hand. A name and number off his caller ID. I can't chance using a phone. Have Holly check it out. Heard him on the phone. Sounds like a pickup."

"Christ, first I'm used. Now I'm working?" Broker's right hand shot out and seized her bare arm above the elbow. Hard.

"Ow."

It felt good to touch her, to feel her move. "Pass it to me when I grab your hand."

"Hey!" Shuster lurched up alert on the porch and called out. "Talk is okay. Grabbing is not okay."

". . . Turned into a regular little whore. Don't care who you give it to . . ." Broker's voice rose as he pulled her in close and they tussled, twisting her wrist with his good hand, feeling her insert the folded paper into his injured palm. Turning, he winced with pain as he slipped it in his pocket. He released her wrist and raised his hand, palm open, as if to slap her.

Nina's expression was suitably indignant and furious from a distance but, close in, there was a smirk, possibly even erotic, in her eyes. "God, I love it when you talk dirty," she said under her breath.

"You're enjoying this, whoring for George W.," he said between clenched teeth.

She whispered right back. "Oh really? What about that sleazy little cunt Jolene Sommer you fucked last year?"

"We were separated," he yelled, suddenly on the defensive, feeling the force drain from his raised hand. Should have never never told her about Jolene.

"Asshole!" she shouted back.

On the porch, Ace turned to Gordy. "I think I just won a hundred bucks, 'cause you can't fake that. Uh-uh. Those people are definitely *married*."

Nina stepped inside the arc of Broker's swing and slapped his face. Stung, Broker recoiled, recovered, and grabbed a fistful of her short hair and wrenched her head to the side. Then he held her at arm's length as she swung at him, a haymaker windmilling in midair . . .

Shuster came off the porch fast, athletic; he stepped between them and announced, "You're outta line, fella."

Broker reached around him to get at Nina. Shuster shouldered him, holding his hands up, all defense, not aggressive, trying to be reasonable. "I said, you're outta line."

Broker turned his attention to Shuster. He blinked, his face worked. His breath came in a rush. All his anger flashed like chain lightning, and he had to ground it somewhere or he'd just burn up right there. Before he realized it, he had squared off. Shuster's hands came up. But they were still open and signifying calm.

"Man . . ."

Broker changed up the speed, his hands a blur. He feinted right with his shoulder and fired a left jab, very crisp and fast, that piled into Shuster's right cheek—

BIGMISTAKE!!!!!!!

The force went out of the punch and his whole nervous system cringed and scream-balled up like a spider in a flame. His knees buckled, his good hand shot to protect his fiery left hand. Shuster blinked, surprised, raised his hand to his face.

Now Gordy trotted forward and muttered to Shuster. "Step back, Ace. You can't be mixin' in this. You got that DUI, remember? They'll throw you back in jail."

Gordy came straight ahead and Broker resigned himself to taking a punch for Delta Force, Donald Rumsfeld, and Homeland Security. *Goddamn shit!*

Gordy let fly, a powerful but sloppy overhand right. Like he was driving an engineer stake into hardpan. Jarred, seeing a starburst, Broker took it high on the left cheek and temple.

Broker staggered back, shook his head. Gingerly he tested his cheekbone. Unbroken. He'd have a black eye. A sore neck. Shuster restrained Gordy's cocked right fist. "That's enough, Gordy. Let him go," he said.

Gordy Riker bounced, doing a huff-and-puff number with his shoulders. Broker did a modified Charlie Chaplin pratfall, tripping as he stepped back. He fell on his butt on the damp trap rock.

Gordy hovered—porcupiney, short-fused, mean. Then, when Broker didn't attempt to get up, Gordy swaggered back to the bar.

Shuster walked Nina protectively back toward the porch, then stopped and came back to where Broker sat unceremoniously on his rear end.

"You don't gotta listen to me but I'm going to give you a little advice. I just been through a divorce myself, and one thing I learned is people need a little space."

Broker glared at him, all the while muttering deep inside how, granted, his left hand was under the weather and how maybe he should get up and introduce this hayseed to his right hand. Instead, he reflected that the ability to defer satisfaction was a sign of maturity; so he played his assigned role and remained on his butt.

Shuster joined Nina and Gordy and they went back up the steps into the saloon. Broker dropped his eyes and stared at a tiny procession of black ants picking their way through the pebbles.

Maybe you could stick around.

Yes, dear.

Broker grimaced and felt a puffy bruise swelling up below his left eye. He looked up and down the deserted highway. Just the green fields, the low gray clouds. Across the road he saw a rusting Bobcat sitting in weeds in what had once been a parking lot. A fading John Deere logo painted up on the front of a large washed-out yellow pole barn. Weather-beaten letters spelled SHUSTER AND SONS EQUIPMENT. Thought he saw the shadow of someone standing in the doorway, watching. When he looked again, the guy was gone.

"You're asking a lot," he said under his breath as he slowly got to his feet.

Chapter Fifteen

Dale Shuster stood in the doorway of Shuster and Sons Equipment and watched the commotion across the road in front of the Missile Park, thinking it had been a long time since anybody'd got in a fight in that parking lot. And it didn't turn out to be much of a fight, anyway, so eventually he turned away. The woman had showed up on Saturday. By the next afternoon, she had guys fighting over her. He shook his head. With his brother Ace it was always women. And not just the kind of women who went with booze. Women liked him.

'Cause he's good-looking, lean, and has that smile.

The opposite of me.

Dale got a pretty good look at her, and she seemed to be a short-haired redhead, kind of trashy and skinny.

Whatever.

He paced the interior of the pole barn and heard his boot soles echo faintly on the crumbling concrete slab. Empty like a cavern in here. Dale had this habit that, if he didn't concentrate, he saw things the way they looked when he was a child. Like this place. He remembered it full of big iron—bright-yellow backhoes, crawler dozers, loaders, and graders. Back in the missile time, when Dad was in the money; always chewing a cigar, talking on the phone in the front office, his brother Ace jockeying the big machines around the lot.

Before they got the house in town.

When they still had the farm.

Dale blinked. He was staring up at a dull speckle of light. Holes sprayed in the corrugated sheet metal where Ace, age sixteen, had become exasperated with the pigeons and grabbed the shotgun and pumped off a few shells of birdshot. That was Ace, impulsive. Dale would have been six . . .

Unlike his brother, Dale was methodical. That's why their dad left him in charge of shutting down the equipment accounts and selling off the last of the inventory.

A task that was near completion. All he had left on the premises was the one Deere front-loader out back. And the backhoe attachment, which he'd already sold.

He returned to his desk at the front of the building. Shuster and Sons never had much of an office, just the desk, a small refrigerator, a computer, phone, fax, and a TV set mounted on the wall. Off to the right of the desk, walled off behind a partition, were a toilet and sink.

Dale sat down on the ancient swivel chair and stared at the clock. Some things he couldn't tidy up by being methodical. Like the weather. He picked up the remote and thumbed on the TV. He'd been tuned in to the Weather Channel exclusively for the last week.

Rain was bad for the equipment business.

He waited through a commercial and then watched Heather Tesch stand in front of a map of the United States. Behind her, a straggling green amoeba of precipitation crept across North Dakota, Minnesota, and into Wisconsin. Low pressure squatted on the Midwest, fed by a warm front coming from the Gulf.

The Gulf air drove the jet stream into a coil up and into the North, disrupting the normal pattern. Where the hot Gulf air and cool stuff from Canada collided it was raining like hell. In the wake of the storms, the fields were green sponges.

At least the thunderstorms had moved on through Minnesota and Wisconsin and were petering out along Lake Michigan. It caused delays. Even the biggest crawlers were stymied by mud.

But he'd used up all his waiting sitting behind this desk, sifting through these files. When he started working for his dad he'd had an electric typewriter and a rotary phone. Dad never really trusted him on the big iron; that was Ace's job, running the machines. Dad put Dale in the office. When he started he'd filled legal pads with his crisp penmanship—Palmer Method—drilled into him at Langdon Elementary in the second grade by flat-chested Miss Heidi Klunder, with skin like oatmeal and skinny blond hair.

Not like Ginny Weller.

That was ten years ago and he could still hear Ginny's voice like it was right now, like in an echo chamber; still feel the tease of her lips, her moist warm breath against his ear. *"C'mon Dale baby, we're all alone, just you and me. Just be a minute and I'll give you a feel . . ."*

He dropped his eyes to the computer screen, clicked through the invoices. He tried to avoid looking at the clock on the wall. But in the right-hand corner of the blue bar at the bottom of the screen the digital time stared at him.

Once he had endured time like everybody else. Now he felt it gushing like a Niagara of digital code through his chest. He tried to get his mind around numbers; tried to imagine a million people going about their lives, all of them taking time for granted. None of them knowing for sure how many days, minutes, hours, seconds . . .

He laughed. Christ, there weren't a million people in all of North Dakota.

Then, vividly, he pictured the tape hidden in the kitchen pantry, in a box of Fruit Loops. He moved the tape every day to a different hidey-hole.

Thinking about the tape stopped his breath. He almost gasped. The tumescent squirm of anticipation was like the petals of a flower opening deep inside. Gave him shivers.

For years, down in his basement apartment, alone, he'd fantasized the image of Ginny Weller down on her knees, begging him not to punish her for what she'd—

The bell on the front door jingled and Gordy Riker strolled in looking very pleased with himself. The image of Ginny vanished. Gordy had an elbow raised and was conspicuously sucking on the knuckles of his right hand.

"Hey, Needle-Dick, we gotta talk." Gordy bouncy, full of himself, jerked his thick neck back across the road.

"Don't call me that," Dale said calmly.

Gordy mugged surprise at Dale's controlled response. It only slowed him for a few beats. "Okay, sure, I'm sorry. Don't mean to offend. But the thing is, you gotta talk to Ace."

"I heard about the woman, and I just saw you hit that guy."

"You see me put him on his ass with one punch? He's bigger'n me, too."

"Who is he?" Dale said.

"Bitch's husband, *she* says." Gordy furrowed his brow.

"What do you mean, 'she says'?" Dale said.

"Kinda coincidental, don't you think? She shows up in a bar hardly nobody goes to, on a highway hardly nobody who ain't local uses," Gordy said.

"So?"

"And she's traveling with the only lesbian ever seen north of Grand Forks."

Dale perked up, went to the window, and stared across the highway at the bar. "A lesbian? Here? No shit." *Now that would be something.*

"What I'm saying is, it's too coincidental. Nobody comes to Langdon except . . ."

"Yeah, yeah, for weddings, funerals, or unless their job sends them here," Dale said. He smiled at Gordy's consternation. "So you think she's working, huh?" If Gordy was worried, it could only be about one thing. "Some kind of snitch? Cop maybe?"

Gordy shrugged. "Maybe the Canadian excise people are bitching about the whiskey again."

Dale's smile broadened, enjoying Gordy's discomfort. "Ace don't ship that much. It's the meth has everybody riled. More likely she's after *you*."

Gordy was not amused. "Ha ha. But that ain't the point. Ace's thinking with his pecker. I mean, c'mon, at the very least she's a lush. And he's drinking."

"Think of that: the two of them shacked up in the back room. They'll drink up the inventory."

"I'm serious here. They catch him driving and drinking one more time, he'll be eating takeout pizza in county. Walking the halls for exercise, on one cigarette a day."

Dale shrugged fatalistically. "It's because of Darlene and the kids leaving. The divorce." He made a sympathetic assay with his flat blue eyes. But behind his expression he hid a swell of satisfaction. Ace was finally falling back to earth in flaming, whiskey-soaked pieces, spiraling so low he was almost taking orders from this piece of shit, Gordy, who'd had a D average, who had to go to summer school to graduate. Who had to get special permission from the principal to go on the Senior Trip.

"So what do you say? Have a talk with him."

Dale nodded without enthusiasm. "He don't listen to me, you know."

"At least try."

"Okay. I'll talk to him."

Gordy nodded, looked around. "So, ah, where's our favorite funny fucking Indian?"

Dale settled back into his desk chair and took his time reaching into the refrigerator, taking out a Coke, popping the top. Gordy called Joe Reed the "funny fucking Indian" because Joe had this very un-Indian habit, according to Gordy, anyway, of always being strictly on time.

So that's why he's here. He wants Joe back. Dale jerked his head north. "Went over the border yesterday. Don't know why. He don't exactly leave detailed trip tickets. Guy like Joe, I don't really want to know."

"I hear you. Well, when he gets his sneaky blanket ass back here, tell him to drop by and talk to me," Gordy said.

"You ain't got the balls to say that to his face," Dale said.

They stared each other down. Gordy broke first, laughed, and said, "You're absolutely right. But like I said, *ask him* polite to drop by."

"I don't think he's into running your dope across the border anymore, Gordy," Dale said.

"Yeah, right. He's got such a future here, huh?"

"Hey." Dale brightened. "I just sold off two of my last three machines, Irv Fuller bought 'em. He's in the big time now. Got that construction outfit outside the Twin Cities, just won the bid on a big job."

"Irv Fuller." Gordy made a face.

"Yeah, Irv Fuller," Dale said. Irv had been Homecoming King. And Ginny Weller had been Homecoming Queen.

"Did Irv pay you?"

"Put some money down," Dale said.

"That's Irv. Be twenty years getting the balance."

Dale shrugged. "Oh, I don't know. I gotta feeling this deal is going to work out for me."

"Yeah, right. So whattaya say, talk to Ace, will you?"

"I told you. I'll try."

"Good. So, ah, what are you going to do?"

"Sell off the last machine and lock the door. You know anybody needs a cheap 644 front-end loader?"

"That one?" Gordy pointed to the big yellow tractor sitting deeper in the shed. "The wheels are bald."

"That's why it's so cheap."

Gordy shook his head. "Then what? Go down to Florida with your dad?"

Dale grinned broadly. "Probably."

"Well, good luck, Needle-Dick."

Dale stood up and placed his hands on his hips. "Don't call me that ever again."

Gordy laughed and held out his hands and wiggled his fingers in a mock fright. "Oooh."

"I mean it, I'm giving you fair warning," Dale said calmly.

"Needle-Dick." Gordy grinned, flipped Dale the bird, and walked out of the office. Dale watched him swagger back across the road, go up the porch, and disappear into the Missile Park.

Dale held his fists tight against his chest. Ten years Gordy had been picking on him.

He had lost his focus and now he had to get it back.

He took a couple of cold Cokes from the small refrigerator and tossed them in his backpack. People used to ride him about the pack. Just a tiny thing in his huge hands, the seams parting, yellow with a little blue butterfly on the flap. It had been his schoolbag in elementary school. Just room for two Cokes and a sandwich.

Methodically, he shut off the lights, locked the door, and walked to his ancient Grand Prix. Getting in, his boots poked around, stirring through a compost of hamburger wrappers on the floorboards.

The windshield was clouded with grime. Dale paid no mind. He started the car and drove north along the grid of roads through wind-rippled fields that were mostly empty. Here and there he saw a huge-wheeled tractor. The skeletal rails of a hay wagon. They were waiting on the crop to ripen. Waiting on the custom combiners to come through.

He poked the radio and KNDK came on with the weather for the Drayton, Walhalla, and Langdon area: cloudy and humid, ninety-two degrees. Legion baseball tonight, Langdon at Grafton. First pitch at 5:45, weather permitting. Dale turned it off when the *Successful Farmers' Radio Magazine* theme music started up.

He thought of the deserted homes that dotted the fields. *Successful farmers, my ass!* The houses were just hulks, long since abandoned; the farm families who used to live in them had been torpedoed by consolidation and had sunk out of sight beyond the sea of wheat.

Finally he pulled into an overgrown driveway. He shut off the motor and listened to the buzz of the cicadas. The damp ferment of sodden crops rolled over him as he looked up the drive at the house. He had fields of his own in his chest. He could feel the waves of sadness rippling off to the horizon.

He heaved out and walked toward the peeling farmhouse. Every year it looked more tiny and more run-down. The wind had finally stove in the north end of the barn and now it sagged in on the foundation. The once vibrant red lumber had faded to gray splinters. The old pasture and truck garden were long since plowed up and put into wheat.

He heard a rasp of steel—sheets of rusty tin that had come loose on the Quonset shed in back of the house. A death rattle in the wind.

Hard to believe a family of five had lived in this tiny place. Two bedrooms upstairs, an alcove downstairs with a curtain on a runner for his sister. The old Fisher woodstove.

He stopped and stared at the blister packs of Sudafed torn open and littered on the steps. Rage stirred in his chest as he kicked through the wrappers that dotted the steps and the mud porch. *Fuckers. They snuck in here and cooked meth.*

He trudged up the stairs and into the room he'd shared with his brother until he was seven. The springs from his old bed lay in a rusted tangle next to the window. The springs creaked as he lowered his weight down on them.

Funny how he remembered this cramped house feeling so clean. Hell, the wind would sift the dust right through the walls. No way to keep the dirt out of the kitchen. But field dirt was different from town dirt. Dad used to say dirt with sweat in it wasn't really dirty. Dale's chest fluttered. Last time he remembered being happy was sitting here, looking out the window facing east, watching the sun rise over the fields.

During the time of the missiles.

His eyes fixed on an irregularity in the wheat two hundred yards away. He could barely make out the square of chain link and barbed wire. Once the power lived there, a hundred feet beneath his father's field. A silo with a Minuteman II. Like his own scary genie.

Sixteen-year-old Ace would say to six-year-old Dale: "Enough power in our field to blow up half of Russia. Just in our field alone."

There was bad mixed in with the good, like when he would wake up at night convinced he heard the remote controls snapping and hissing under the ground and he just knew the field was going to explode. That fire was going to fall from the sky.

He woke up screaming from the image of the cows and pigs burning up, the rabbits, the geese, the chickens.

Stubby, his cat. Shaggy, his dog.

Never people, though. He never saw people burning. Only animals.

The nightmares changed and he'd just wake up and sneak out and walk across the field and stand at the edge of the mowed grass belt around the wire and hold up his hands, palms out, and try to feel the power radiating out from the silo. Not too close, because they had remote sensors and the air-basers would come by helicopter to check. Little by little he overcame his fear and made friends with it and soon the dreams went away.

All that harnessed energy poised and quiet, down deep in the earth. Dale thought he could actually feel the power in the crops that pushed up out of the earth in the spring. Feel it brood beneath the winter snow. Hear it howl in the blizzard wind.

He'd watch the trucks come in when the air-basers checked the wire and the sensors. In the summer they came and mowed the offset perimeter grass around the wire. Sometimes he'd stand on the road and wave to them.

In the end, Army engineers came with explosives to implode the empty silos. Joe Reed, whom Gordy wanted back working for him, explained how they did it. Joe knew about explosives. He was an Ojibwa from the Turtle Mountain rez and he'd worked in the oil fields up in Alberta. Some folks called him Pinto Joe because of the patchy way his face healed after an oil well blew up on him.

So they blew them in on themselves and filled them with dirt and strung barbed wire around the sites so they looked like little grave-yards dotting the wheat. Something about verification, like the empty silos left open for the ABM sites south on State 1, at Nekoma.

He looked up. Little empty graveyards, so the Russian satellites could count them.

Dale drew up his legs and hugged his arms to his chest. Some-times he felt like a buried atomic bomb they'd missed when they'd pulled out the Minutemen and the Spartans and the Sprints. The missile fields had all gone to seed and fallow. But what if they missed one? What if buried deep under the wheat there was one last cone of latent power?

Poised.

Dale shut his eyes and imagined his gross body swept away in the launch flames. Then they'd see him for who he really was, a moment of beautiful fire and grace exploding into the sky.

The moment passed.

He clambered off the old springs and walked down the stairs, running his finger along the wall like he'd done every day of his childhood. He trudged through the rooms littered with wrappers and plastic bottles and went outside. He looked up at the heavy, roiling clouds, gravid with rain. Far to the west a shiver of lightning.

Dale looked up at the relentless clouds that combined and came apart against each other. The constant gray churn could be the gears of history up there, meshing, grinding out fate.

The future.

He went around back of the house and stood for a long time staring at a pile of meth trash. There were discarded coffee filters gummy with pink and white residue; plastic funnels; a cracked blender; aluminum foil boxes; discolored Pyrex dishes; plastic jugs; and a scorched twenty-pound propane cylinder.

Furious, Dale kicked at the heap of refuse. Then he walked to the Quonset, dug around in the debris, and found an old leaf rake, a regular rake, and a shovel. He returned to the pile. Methodically, he cleared away the drug-cooking garbage until he revealed a square of railroad ties buried in the weeds.

The sand was damp from the rain and it was easy to spade up the thistles and burdock. Then he raked them in a pile and flung them away.

Sweating now, breathing heavy, he spaded over the sand, ran the rake through it until he had excavated several strata of buried refuse: old pop bottle caps, a spoon, one of his sister's Barbie dolls.

He snatched up the brown plastic figurine and slowly snapped off the arms, then the legs, and finally the head. He hurled the pieces away.

Then he sat down on the ties and removed his boots and mismatched socks and stuck his bare feet in the clean raked sand. He wiggled his toes.

Dad had built the sandbox for him when he was four.

Slowly Dale shaped two squat castle towers in the sand. The

damp sand set up well as he carefully smoothed off the tops, making them round and symmetrical. He took a can of Coke from his pack, opened it, and sat hunched forward, staring at the sand castles and sipping the Coke.

When he finished the soda, he threw the empty can toward the pile of crud he'd raked from the sandbox. Then he reached into his pack and took out a small yellow precision-die-cast replica of a John Deere front-loader.

Not like the toys he'd owned as a kid, a collector's item from Dad's dealership—the same dealership whose demise he was presiding over. The tiny tractor had sat on a shelf at home.

In the basement, where Dale lived.

He bent over on all fours and ran the small vehicle back and forth in the clean sand. Then, in a sudden burst of rage he slammed the replica into the towers, smashing them.

"Kashuusshhewww!" he shouted, making explosive sounds as he grabbed double handfuls of sand and threw them into the air.

"*Ka-boom.*"

Chapter Sixteen

"Aw, God, what an asshole. You all right?" Nina raised her hand gingerly to Ace's cheek, which was a little red where Broker had hit him.

"I'm fine. Good thing his hand was hurt. You see the bandage?"

Nina improvised. "Nailgun, slipped on him. He was putting new planks on the deck for Gull's Retreat. That's what we call Cabin Six."

"Lucky me," Ace said. "Otherwise he would have coldcocked me. I *did not* see that punch coming."

"Ah, that one punch was all he had in him, 'cause I put him down pretty quick," Gordy said triumphantly.

Ace eyed Gordy like he wasn't real sure about that. He turned to Nina and said, "What was it you said your old man did?"

"*Ex*–old man." Nina arched her back.

"Yeah, yeah, I know, but what does he *do*?" Ace said.

"What the fucker did was change on me. He was nice enough when we were getting to know each other, then I got pregnant, and we got married, and . . . ah, shit." She waved a hand in disgust.

"No, I got that part. I mean what he does for a living. He don't look like a guy who hangs in an office," Ace said.

"That's for sure. He gets a bad stomach in an office. He likes being outside. So he's got this landscape gig besides the cabins." An old reflex of protectiveness crept into her language, distancing, wary.

"What about before that?" Ace said, narrowing his eyes.

"Well . . ." Her eyes hardened up a bit. "There was some stuff he was into before I knew him. Just stories I heard, because he don't really talk about it." It came out tone perfect, sounding rehearsed in a way Ace and Gordy would understand. Couched lines used to answer questions that maybe cops had asked.

They were sitting at the bar. Ace and Gordy were drinking coffee. Nina rotated a tumbler in both hands. It was a seven-and-seven she'd poured herself, but about 95 percent ginger ale.

"What kind of stories?" Ace said.

"He used to say the government had no business interfering with people's rights to smoke a little grass and own a few guns."

Gordy pounded his palm on the bar. "Hear, hear. For the grass part."

Ace stared at Gordy, then turned to Nina. "Gordy here thinks the Canucks are going to legalize marijuana. He thinks when that happens it's going to be like Prohibition again up here."

"How's that?" Nina played into their talk.

Gordy grinned. "During Prohibition there was stills lined up along all four thousand miles of the border on the Canadian side. This time it's going to be one long field of hydroponic weed from Maine to Washington State. Box-loaders kicking out hundred-pound bails of the stuff, whole hay wagons chock-full coming through Mulberry Crossing . . ."

Nina shrugged, curled her lips a tad, nodded her head back and forth. Gave a knowing smile. The two men leaned forward, almost like dogs sniffing for some common ground. "Phil would dig that. You might say he dabbled in the grass business," she said.

"He still peddling a little on the side?" Ace asked.

Nina went sour, irritable. "Nah, that was years ago. Christ, I guess what happened was all these heavily armed . . . *black* . . . guys showed up in Minnesota and took over the drug trade on the streets . . . He decided to head north and reinvent himself."

Gordy smiled. "Don't need to mind your language around us. We got nothing against niggers. Ain't any up here. What we got is Indians. Like that Pinto Joe Reed; now, there's one ugly son of a bitch."

Ace smiled. "But you'd take him back in a minute working for you if you could get him away from my brother."

Gordy shrugged. They dropped the subject.

"So . . . Phil," Ace said. "That's his name, your husband?"

"Yeah. Phil Broker."

"So Phil got out of organic pharmaceuticals?"

Nina nodded. "He made a little money and bought some shore-front up north on Lake Superior, fixed up these old cabins, and now we've got the resort."

Ace and Gordy looked at each other. Ace gave this nodding gesture, something like permission. Gordy shrugged. Then Ace turned his attention back to Nina, pointed at the travel bag Broker had left, and said, "You're still in your pajamas. Think maybe it's time to put on some clothes."

"Got a point," Nina said, feeling the tension thicken in the room. She started to slide off the stool.

Then Gordy reached for her purse that was sitting on the counter, tipped it over, and slid out her wallet. Flipped it open— "Your last name is Pryce on your driver's license. How come his name is different?"

"He could have changed his name to Pryce if he wanted," Nina said, poised, hands on the bar.

"Uh-huh." Gordy continued to stare at her as she pushed off the bar, picked up her bag. As she started toward the stairs he snaked out a hairy arm and flattened his palm against her stomach, feeling around there. As she recoiled, he said. "Not upstairs. Pick some clothes out of your bag and put them on, right here."

"Strip for you? Over my dead body," Nina said in a steady voice.

"It could be arranged," Gordy said softly, coming up off his stool. Nina saw Gordy was serious, and Ace was letting it happen. A ripple of goose bumps raised on her bare arms. She instinctively reached over and gripped her glass off the bar, holding it like a hand hatchet as her eyes measured the distance to the door.

"Slow down," Ace said. "It's just that Gordy has a suspicious mind."

"You see, we got a bet," Gordy said.

Nina narrowed her eyes.

Ace smiled. "Gordy bet me a hundred bucks you're a cop. He thinks maybe you're wired."

"You mean wearing a tape recorder under *this*?" She plucked at the flimsy shirt.

"Ah, yeah."

"You're joking, right?" Nina said.

"'Fraid not," Ace said.

"Show and tell time, honey," Gordy said.

Nina set the glass down, eased back two steps, lowered the bag, zipped it open, and searched around. She found a pair of shorts and a tank top.

"Okay, I'll play your silly game." She walked up to Gordy, dropped the shorts and top on the floor, reached down, crossed her arms, grabbed the hem of the shirt and peeled it up and off as she executed a pirouette. With her back to them, wearing nothing but the low-cut panties from Victoria's Secret—thank you, Janey—she tossed the shirt accurately over her shoulder. It draped Gordy's face as she stepped into the shorts, pulled on the tank top, and turned to face them.

Clearly pissed, she said, "Just what makes you guys think you *rate* a cop, anyway?"

Ace clapped and started to laugh. Gordy removed the shirt and folded his arms, scowling. "You think it's funny. Well, it ain't funny."

"C'mon, man, it *is* funny," Ace said.

Gordy slid off his stool, stooped, and emptied the contents of Nina's bag, immediately retreating as if propelled by a natural aversion to the volume of strange items a woman could stuff into a bag. He returned to poke through the mess for a few seconds, then stepped back once more.

"Gordy," Ace said firmly.

Grunting, Gordy squatted and pushed the clothes back in. He planted his hands on his knees, stood up, and, far less hostile now, faced Nina. "Um, is Phil the kind of guy who's going to go brood about what happened out there? And come back on us with a 12-gauge at one in the morning?"

Nina shook her head. "He just turned forty-eight. He don't bounce so good anymore. I suspect what he'll do is take Kit back home. His parents are there to help out."

Gordy threw up his hands in mild disgust, spun on his heel and stomped across the barren barroom, threw open the front door, and continued across the highway. Ace and Nina craned their necks and watched Gordy enter the barnlike Quonset with the rusted Bobcat and windmill out front.

Nina turned to Ace. "He don't like women. I could tell the way he looked at me."

Ace shook his head. "He don't like women like *you*. Taller than him, lean, smart. He likes 'em about seventeen, no neck, big in front, and stoned." He made a gesture with both hands cupped before his chest. Then he pointed to his head. "And small up here."

"So you think I'm a cop?" Nina asked, pretending to be flattered. And confident, because she could cross her heart and hope to die and swear she was not a *cop*.

"Don't know what you are," Ace said, Then he ran his hand

along the bar and felt the leather grain and distinctive scale pattern of her wallet. "Don't know for sure what this is either."

"Ostrich. Phil's got a buddy who raises them for the meat and makes leather goods from the hides."

"Really." Ace kneaded the leather. "Tell me something."

Nina threw a wary glance out the front window toward the corrugated tin building where Gordy had disappeared. "Depends."

"You think ostriches could run with buffalo? After the bar's gone I was thinking of going out further west, maybe try to raise some buffalo."

Nina got stuck, once again blindsided by this easygoing, mostly sad, but definitely hard-to-read man. It wasn't easy to locate the danger in him. But it was there. She had to catch her breath and restart her act.

"It's okay," he said.

"What's okay?" Nina said, letting herself drift, letting the color come into her cheeks.

Ace winked. "That you like me. C'mon, let's take a ride. I want to show you something."

In the Tahoe, heading west. "So why would I be a cop?" Nina asked.

"One reason is whiskey. Most of the bars up around the border backdoor a little extra inventory into Canada. Bottle of booze costs fourteen bucks here, sells for thirty-eight up there. Hell of a markup. So there's money to be made. Same's true for cigarettes."

"Give me another reason."

Ace pointed out the window, at a grain elevator. "See those tanks?"

A big one looked like a giant white sausage to Nina; half a dozen smaller ones sat on wheeled carriages.

Ace went on: "Anhydrous ammonia. Basic fertilizer, used throughout the state. Also an ingredient in making methamphetamine. Meth freaks driving through here from the West Coast are struck dumb by all this stuff just sitting out here, like fat white cows waiting to be milked. They think they've died and gone to heaven. Just have to pull over by the side of the road and cook up a batch."

He turned to look at her. "I've sold some whiskey to Canadians from time to time. But I've never taken it across the border myself. And I got nothing to do with that meth shit. So if you're some kind of fancy ATF agent slumming, you gonna have to wait around a long time to get something on me."

"Give it a rest," Nina said. Then she stared straight ahead, scanning the straightedge of Highway 5 heading west. After a few minutes Ace slowed and turned left off the road. An overgrown gravel drive led up to a chain-link fence that surrounded a square empty plot. A big white sign with black letters: A7.

"What's this?" Nina said.

"Where we keep the invisible monsters."

"I don't get it," she said. Then she thought about it and maybe she did.

"They trucked the missiles off to Montana and imploded the silos. They keep the fences up and numbered so Russian satellites can verify that they're empty. My brother Dale insists they ain't empty. He says we got these cages all over the county, looks like nothing in them. Dale says they're still in there, pacing back and forth. Wanting to get out. We just can't see 'em."

"Kind of creepy," Nina said.

"For sure. That's Dale's sense of humor. He was the only kid who had trouble with the missiles. Only one I know about. Most of us just took it in stride. We had two silos on our farm. One next to the barn, and one like this, in our wheat field a couple hundred yards from the house. And Dale, he'd have these bad nightmares. Fire falling from the sky, burning up all the animals, stuff like that. Twenty years ago we were still on the farm. I was seventeen, Dale was about eight. I heard this shooting and I ran down to the barn and there was Dale with the .22 rifle. He had shot two cows, some chickens, a pig. He was reloading the gun when I took it away from him.

"And he was crying. Real shook. So I ask him just what the hell he was doing, and he said he didn't want the animals to suffer in the fire that was going to fall from the sky." Ace shook his head. "Well, Dad was gonna be pissed for sure, so I went in the house, got out the whiskey, and started drinking. When Dad came in from work he found me shit-faced, shooting pigeons in the barn with that .22. I took the heat for Dale and had to get an extra job to make enough money to replace the stock."

He looked over at Nina and winked. "That's when I started drinking." He slowly turned the Tahoe around and pulled back on the highway. "That's a true story," he said. After that they rode in silence for a while. Ace came to an intersection and turned east on State 20.

"So how's life look today? What you gonna do?" Ace asked.

"Not what I been doing, which was what other people wanted me to do."

"I can relate to that. The trick is to find what you want to do."

"Easier said."

"Amen."

"So, are you doing what you want to do?" Nina asked.

"I'm driving you, aren't I?"

"I guess."

Nina caught herself unconsciously touching at her hair. She put her hand in her lap. Then she reached in her purse, took out an American Spirit, and lit it. "So, *you* ever have any nightmares?" she asked.

"Lots. Only one real good one, though," Ace said. He flung his hand at the surrounding fields. "Our people came out here, hell, before practically anybody else. Early 1850s. Lived in one of those sod houses. We found these letters they wrote, and they said one time they got stuck in that house for two days straight while the buffalo came through."

Nina shook her head.

Ace explained. "Herd of buffalo so big it took two days to pass. And so close-packed my ancestors couldn't open the door to get to the well."

"And that's your dream?"

"Sort of. I dreamed I was up on the border running a dozer, knocking down some bankrupt farmer's house, and that herd of buffalo came through again. Me trapped on the bulldozer and the buffalo coming forever."

"Is Ace your real name?"

"Nickname. Name's Asa. That was my grandfather's name. Grandfather helped organize the Nonpartisan League after World War One. You ever hear of that?"

Nina cautiously shook her head.

Ace smiled. "Grandpa used to say if you took a railroad man from St. Paul, a mill owner from Minneapolis, and a banker from New York and you stuffed them all in a pickle barrel and rolled the barrel down the hill, there'd always be a son of a bitch on top."

"Sounds like your grandpa wasn't a Republican."

"You got that right. When he had a few beers in him he used to say there's nothing more dangerous than a bunch of angry farmers with rifles. Was how America started, he'd say."

Nina sat up a little straighter, attentive. "Sounds like militia talk."

"Ah, I met some of those guys—just weekend beer bellies, like to dress up in camo. Not real serious folks for the most part."

Definitely more attentive. "What's serious?"

"Changing something. Fixing something." Ace shrugged. "Hey, I'm not much for politics. But I do know that if one guy shoots the banker it's murder. If twenty guys lynch him it's a mob; but if the whole county takes him out and strings him up it's a change of administration. That's kinda what they did here in the teens and twenties, took over the state, wrote new laws, created the state mill and the state bank. Back then they called them Socialists."

Ace shook his head and laughed. "Then we become the launch site for all the missiles aimed at Communist Russia. Which made us into a big target. Kinda like payback for what the Nonpartisan League did to the fat cats, maybe."

Nina eyed him carefully. "You have this habit of surprising people, you know?"

Ace smiled wryly, and Nina thought he could probably do that for a few more years, but once the tiny wrinkles around his mouth came up sharper it'd be sad all the way. He said, "I used to play ball. That's a game where you stand around a lot. But then if something happens, you got to be on top of it. Got to be ready for surprises, I guess." His eyes lingered on her when he said that, searching.

She held his gaze. "So what is it you're going to show me?"

"Just a place where something happened."

Nina looked away and watched the wind stream through a long row of trees. "What kind of trees are those?"

"Poplars. Immigrants used to plant them. Put 'em in cemeteries when somebody died. Instead of headstones. More windrows to cut down on the wind. Notice how they all kind of bow to the east. That's the wind." He grinned and gave her a sidelong glance. "You know why the wind blows in North Dakota?"

She knew that one. "Yeah, yeah. Because Minnesota sucks."

They laughed and Nina got comfortable, curling her legs under her in the bucket seat, something she hadn't done in a car with a man since high school.

More dead straight road, fields of wheat and oats and occasional pools of flax that seemed to float against the green like wisps of mirage.

Then a tall gray grain elevator loomed up on the left side of the highway. Ace slowed and turned left. The red sign by the road said STARKWEATHER.

"Quaint name for a town," Nina said.

"Got an echo to it, that's for sure," Ace said. They drove past an abandoned grocery, a shack with a gas pump, and a post office that maybe was still functioning. Ace parked across from a run-down tavern with a big Pabst Blue Ribbon sign hanging over the door. He zipped down the window, fingered a Camel out of his chest pocket, lit it, exhaled, and said, "How many chances you think people get?"

"Not sure. Sometimes I think some people never *had* a chance."

"Well, I did. Nineteen eighty-three I graduated high school. Had a good year in Legion ball, batted eight hundred and change. Coach compiled my stats, pulled a few strings, and I got letters from the Twins and the Reds. So I went down to the Twin's tryout." He leaned back, smiled. "Knocked two home runs out of the old Met Stadium. Got it on film. That was before video was big. Made the cut the first day.

"Then come the second morning and I'm there warming up and . . ." He paused and his eyes got stuck remembering. He raised his right knee, moved it in a slow circle. "You could hear the pop clear across the field in the stands."

"ACL tendon?"

"Big time. They told me where to go to get the best treatment and I went and they give me all this physical therapy. Said it would be six months to heal up. Maybe an operation.

"And I started the program, but I came back here . . ." His eyes drifted out he window. "Started driving the big stuff for Irv Fuller's dad. Then, what the hell, I thought I'd try farming. Took over my dad's place. He'd moved into town by then. Had the Deere dealership and the bar.

"I got in trouble with the bank and tried to cut costs and didn't pay for crop insurance, and between the hail and the rain and the bugs, that ended my farming career."

He pointed across the street at the run-down bar.

"Was right in there on a Friday night. I had a little too much to drink and this fool named Bobby Pease, who was just a big bag of wind and a bully and a real mean drunk—well, Bobby decided he was going to throw me out of the bar, and he came at me with a beer bottle and I was not in the best mood, having just lost the farm . . ." He held up his right hand, studied it. "So I hit him. Just once."

Ace sighed. "Well, some who were there said it was the fall that broke his neck but I heard it crack when I hit him. He must have been way off balance." He sucked his teeth and his voice turned wistful. "And I always did hit pretty good. There was more than a few bankrupt farmers on the jury and I'd been working for Fuller, plowing under farmhouses to make more room for the big twelve-bottom plows." Ace shook his head. "They gave me manslaughter. Reckless endangerment. Cost me a year at Jamestown, the state farm."

Nina didn't know what to say.

"But you know what they say about silver linings." Ace grinned, starting up the Tahoe. "That's where I got started reading."

Chapter Seventeen

His cameo role completed, Broker limped back to town in the Explorer. Walking funny, nursing his swollen eye, he came back into the Motor Inn, ignored the scrutiny of the elderly lady behind the desk, went up the stairs, and rapped on Jane's door.

The door opened. The sound of the Road Runner was muted in the motel room. Now Kit was up on the bed, doing the chicken dance opposite Holly.

I don't wanna be a chicken
I don't wanna be a duck
So I'll shake my butt . . .

Broker stared at the hoary Delta full bird shaking his bony ass. Barrel of laughs, these guys.

"So? I ain't *all* snake eater," Holly protested as he stepped off the bed and studied Broker's face. "I got grandkids."

"You don't look so hot," Jane said.

"You got a black eye, Daddy," Kit said.

"I got too involved, I overacted. Took a swing at Shuster. With my bad hand," Broker said. "His helper stepped in and pasted me." He pointed to his left eye.

"Hey, great touch," Holly said. "I'll go get some ice." He grabbed the ice container off the dresser and disappeared into the hall.

"Bravo," Jane said, "let's have a look." She went to her equipment bag, took out a first-aid bag, and motioned Broker to the sink. Holly returned, wrapped some ice cubes in a washcloth, and handed it to Broker, who held it against his cheek.

Broker flinched as Jane peeled up the edge of the adhesive strips holding the bandage in place over his infected palm. Kit and Holly moved in to watch.

Jane said, "You're an old-fashioned macho tough guy like Holly, right?" Before Broker could respond she yanked the tape off. Broker winced and gritted his teeth.

"Ex–macho tough guy," Jane said.

"Yuk," Kit said, screwing up her face but peering intently. The wound was going purple in the center and draining pus. An area the size of a silver dollar was bright red. "You want to know something?" Kit said. "In Africa they put maggots on infections to eat the bad germs."

Broker remembered something Nina's dad had said about *his* daughter. About how he knew he had his hands full when she was five and went out and poked her finger into some day-old roadkill.

A certain kind of curious.

"This is going to sting," Jane said.

"That's what the doctor says when it's *really* going to hurt a lot," Kit said.

"Thanks, honey," Broker said.

Jane pointed to the injured hand. "Move your little finger."
Broker did.

"Looks like you've got full function. How about numb?"

"Sore as hell, not numb."

"Looks like your ulna nerve is all right," Jane said.

"I *been* to the doctor," Broker said.

Jane pressed some gauze into the wound, making Broker wince.

"He tell you to change the dressing every day and not go hitting people?" She swabbed the wound—which hurt—then poured on some Betadine and wiped it down. She reached in her bag and took out a brown tube. "This is Bag Balm. Topical antibiotic. Vets use it on distressed udders. Good for infection." She daubed on the salve, then wrapped on a clean bandage, and taped it in place.

Then Jane turned to Kit and handed her the tape, three bandages, the disinfectant, and the veterinary salve. "Make sure he changes the bandage every day, got it?"

Kit accepted the medical supplies and nodded solemnly. "Got it."

Jane turned on the tap and scrubbed her hands. "So how'd it go?"

"Can't tell for sure. Maybe they buy it, maybe they don't. You guys are flying by the seat of your pants, that's how it went," Broker said.

"We don't need the executive summary. A simple Sit Rep will do," Holly said.

Broker exhaled. "Jealous husband delivers suitcase, gives possessive ultimatum, gets pummeled by local rubes." He removed the slip of paper Nina had given him from his pocket with his good hand. "Nina says check out this guy. Him and Ace have something going down."

"Wonderful." Holly seized the note. Scrutinized it. "Khari, that ain't no white-bread wheat farmer."

"Could be Syrian or Lebanese," Jane said offhand.

"We'll get right on it." Holly pressed his open palms together. "Well, that's it. Shake it up, Janey. We're outta here."

"You gonna leave her on her own?" Broker asked.

Holly narrowed his eyes. "She's a one-sixty. They don't come any better."

Broker studied the older man's blank eyes, then shook his head and looked away. Christ. This Holly was a case of early dementia, lost in his elite bullshit. *One-sixty. Jesus!* It was an in-group term that got thrown around in MACV-SOG during Vietnam. It referred to a Pentagon study on combat effectiveness compiled in the Second World War. According to the study, the average infantryman became ineffective after 155 days of combat.

"One-sixties" were people who adapted to the unadaptable and continued to function. Lots of people in SOG were logging two and three tours in the war zone.

People like Broker.

Broker scowled. "I'd watch the way you're throwing terms around, considering you guys haven't been in a war that lasted more than a month for the last twenty-five years."

Holly sighed. "Okay. Go on. You've earned the right to sound off, I guess."

"Guess is right! They call it undercover work for a reason. *Cover* being the operative word. A commodity there ain't a lot of around here. Like, say, back in the city a lot of people buy dope, so it's easy to slip a UC into the revolving door. Penetrating a tight organization is more problematic and takes a long time to build up street credentials. You can't just fall off the turnip truck and do it over the weekend." Broker was grim.

Holly nodded. "Sure. That's the conventional wisdom. And if we come up empty we'll go to the locals, the state, the feds. But then we lose the element of surprise. When those Washington goons gear up their egos and intramural politics it's like a herd of touchy elephants getting organized."

Jane's face tightened up. "That's why *we're* here, not the people who are hung up on procedure and protocol, like the FBI."

Holly was less sanguine. He held up a hand to calm Jane and said, "We know this is a serious reach. We talked it over and decided we gotta give it a try," Holly said.

Then, in a spooky divot of speech, Holly and Jane both turned and looked at Kit and said, at exactly the same time, "Too much is at stake . . ."

• • •

Kit was perplexed. The three grown-ups in the room had abruptly stopped talking, and remained silent for almost half a minute.

Jane broke the silence, and her first words came out naked and vulnerable. It took her a full sentence to get back to the disciplined meter of her language: "And we figured having Kit on the scene would provide a touch of realism—plus make you show up. Now it's up to her." Jane rushed past the unprotected moment by furiously packing her go-bag.

Slam-bam. Efficient. Hu-ah.

"Aw," Kit whined a little as Jane packed her fancy laptop.

"Sorry, honey. No more computer games. This has to go with me." She picked a hefty book off the bureau and handed it to Broker.

"*Harry Potter and the Sorcerer's Stone?*" Broker read the title slowly, wondering out loud.

"You got some catching up to do, muggle," Jane said. Then she knelt and hugged Kit. "Okay, Little Bit. Uncle Holly and Auntie Jane have to go. And so do you and your dad. We talked about this with your mom, remember?"

Kit nodded and chewed the inside of her lower lip. Broker didn't especially like the way she was *handling it.* The way she nodded, stoic, and said, "We'll all get together on the other side."

Seven was too young to have a game face.

Holly's knees creaked when he kneeled down and said goodbye to Kit. When he got up, his pale ghost-eyes cut Broker fast. "We'll be close, but not in the town."

"How close?" Broker asked.

Again, the fast, cool eyes. Impatient with being challenged by a civilian, Holly said firmly, "We got it in hand, okay? Now, I advise you two to get out of here, pronto."

Yeah, bullshit you got it in hand, Broker thought. But he nodded as Holly and Jane went into motion, lugging their go-bags out the door.

Special ops. The manner of their leaving made a New York minute seem like overtime.

Broker sat on the bed and held his daughter in his lap. Sensing his anxiety, she made an effort to reassure him. He listened, amazed as she flipped roles with him:

"In Italy, when the dads went away, the kids and the moms just sit and wait. Like now."

Broker noticed she was chewing at the corner of her thumbnail as she spoke. He moved her fingers away from her mouth and saw that several fingers were worried almost raw.

Kit went on. "When a dad doesn't come back, the mom gets a flag. And, um, the chaplain comes and talks."

"Chaplain?"

Kit furrowed her brow. "You know. They talk about God. How when something bad happens, it's his will."

Broker cocked his head at his daughter as a thought occurred. "Did you and Mom ever go to church over there?"

Kit shook her head. "Nah. Mom told me you said if God was really there, he wouldn't live inside a house. He'd live outside."

"Your mom said that, huh?"

Kit nodded. Then she sniffed—chlorine from the pool, or allergies maybe. Not tears. She rubbed her nose with her forearm. Scrunched her forehead, thinking. "Sometimes I go outside and look up."

"We never talked a whole lot about God, did we?" Broker said.

"Mom says we did but I was little so she'd remind me."

"So what'd you come up with?"

"I don't know. Some kids believe in Santa Claus and some kids believe in Jesus. In America, you get to believe what you want. That's Mom's job."

"What?"

"You know, keeping it so people can believe what they want."

Broker stared at his child.

After a moment, she said, "So now we gotta go home and wait?"

Broker continued to stare. He pictured them traveling back to Minnesota, to the house on the point overlooking Lake Superior. Saw himself pacing. Making breakfast, lunch, dinner. Waiting for Nina to walk down the road to Broker's Beach.

Or the chaplain with a flag.

When Broker didn't answer right away, Kit chose her next words carefully, "I can't stay, can I?"

"No. You're going back to Grandma and Grandpa tomorrow."

"Are we gonna drive?"

"You're going to fly. They've got an airport here, I drove past it. I'm going to call Grandma and arrange for a plane."

She considered this for several seconds. Broker could almost hear the thoughts churning behind her broad forehead. She kept the tears out of her eyes but not entirely out of her voice.

"Dad, are we gonna leave Mom here all alone?"

"No."

He swabbed some of the Bag Balm on Kit's chewed fingers and ordered her to keep them out of her mouth. Then he called his mother. Two hours of phone tag followed, with Daffy Duck and Bugs Bunny for accompaniment on the TV. Finally they arranged to have a reliable local pilot, Doc Harris, fly in with Lyle Torgeson, a Cook County deputy, and pick up Kit at the Langdon airstrip. Torgeson's wife, Lottie, ran a preschool back home that Kit had attended three years ago. Kit would be comfortable traveling with

Uncle Lyle. The Torgesons were extended family. They just had to nail down the time. As he waited for the call with an ETA for tomorrow, he took Kit on a walk around the corner from the motel and down the main street.

After window-shopping, they went into a store and bought a locally sewn quilt. Kit picked it out, calling the tight pattern of grays, maroons, and blues "Grandma's colors."

Irene Broker, who dabbled in astrology and melancholia, was Norwegian.

They went back on the street. Looking up, Broker saw that the clouds matched the brooding colors of the quilt. The barometric pressure throbbed in his wounded hand like mercury, marking heavy time.

They had an early supper at a restaurant next to City Hall. Kit had macaroni and cheese. In elliptical snatches, mixed in with a forced game of "I Spy," she told him about going to first grade at the military school on the Aviano Air Base. Then about Ria, her tutor in Lucca.

Lucca was a town out of a history book, located in Tuscany, between Pisa and Florence. "It's got a big wall around it. You could walk or ride your bike," Kit said.

Broker nodded along with her conversation, chewing his rib-eye (hold the potato, double veggies). After hot fudge sundaes—strictly a no no for the Atkins Aware—Kit said she wanted to swing. She explained that Jane had taken her to a playground near the swimming pool, so they took the quilt back to their room and then walked toward the city park.

They passed by old houses double shaded by trees and the solid clouds. The late-afternoon breeze heaved, thick with humidity, slow tidal air pressing in. Holding Kit's hand, sensitive to the gentle pressure of the pulse in her moist palm, Broker was nudged by eddies of foreboding.

He accepted clinical depression as a condition for other people, but not for himself. He had never been incapacitated by his dark thoughts. But he had never been free of them, either. They ran non-stop in the back of his mind like a cable TV package of channels from Hell.

Knowing they were there didn't mean he had to watch them.

He was watching them now.

So he tried his tricks. Broker was adept at walling off his life into compartments, only allowing enough fear and doubt to percolate to the surface to add a streak of afterburner to his adrenaline. Everything else he kept strictly locked up.

Repressed? You bet.

They came to the elementary school and Kit dashed through the gate for the playground equipment. Broker hung back, dug in the hip pocket of his jeans for a Backwoods Sweet cigar. He took out one of the rough wraps, put it in his mouth, and flicked his plastic lighter.

Smoking was another trick, a method of fear management.

He walked down the block, not wanting the smoke to drift into the playground, and came to the corner of the school.

Down the street the Spartan missile stood against the gray sky like a stark black-and-white exclamation point.

He glanced back at the playground, where Kit and a boy her age were monkey-walking up the slide, holding on to the sides. They were still intact, he realized: forty years of Cold War reflexes. Clenched guts, every day, as whole populations went to work, loved, hated, propagated, and always they carried in their hearts the same blank fear when they looked up at the threat suspended in the sky.

Is this the day our children will burn up in fire?

Did we really think we'd drawn a pass because one government collapsed? Because a wall had come down?

A lot of that shit was still out there.

Some of it came in suitcases.

Kit and her playmate were at the swings now, yelling, exhorting each other to pump higher. Their seven-year-old minds incapable of imagining the images and feelings churning in his—

"Dad! Da-dee. Do an underdog. *DA-DEE . . .*"

Broker shredded his cigar, tossed it, joined Kit at the swings, and pushed her with his strong right hand, straight arm over his head as he ran under her. Kit swung higher.

"Again," she squealed.

Again.

As he pushed her on the swing he felt the dizzy spin of Nina's, Holly's, and Jane's frantic intensity. And all his compartments came to nothing, and all his daddy fears washed through him.

How much time—what kind of time—would his daughter have in this new century?

After he was gone.

Who would protect her?

Broker watched Kit arc up toward the gray clouds, and the persistent shadows moved right into his chest. He had the fleeting thought—

What if I never see the sun again?

Chapter Eighteen

Joe Reed came down from Winnipeg just before dawn, drove through Mulberry Crossing with his headlights switched off, continued on into Langdon, and pulled into the lot in front of Shuster's equipment just as the sun came up. He unlocked the door, unfolded the surplus cot Dale kept behind the desk, lay down, and was asleep in minutes.

An hour later, Dale Shuster had his usual breakfast of a double stack of blueberry pancakes at Gracie's Café. Coming back to the shed, he saw Joe's beat-up, brown Chevy van parked in front. Dale opened the door and found Joe napping in his underwear on the cot next to the desk. A fan wobbled back and forth on the floor, stirring the dampness. The second the door eased open Joe rolled up, his good hand coming up from under his pillow with the Browning nine automatic.

"Just me," Dale said. Once you knew Joe for a while you expected him to go armed and you didn't ask him how many times he'd used it. That big pistol was the main reason Gordy Riker wanted Joe back in his employ, to help increase market share with the rough-cut biker gangs up north.

Joe grunted, slipped his pistol into a leather gym bag under the cot, and sat up. He rubbed at his patchy brush cut with his right hand. People rarely tried to make conversation with him. For starters, it just wasn't easy to look at Joe straight on.

Joe's face looked like a Klingon special-effects mask-in-progress from *Star Trek*. Ridges of grafted skin had healed unevenly and there was a suggestion of fine belly hair on his cheek and forehead where they'd taken the grafts from his abdomen. The stitch marks looked like wrinkles stretched the wrong way.

And then there was his voice. He'd swallowed fire and the sound that came from his throat was somewhere between a grunt and a hoarse whisper. He'd scarred his vocal cords.

The little finger was totally missing from his left hand, along with the first joint of his ring finger. Snakeskin ridges mapped his arms and his neck. His black hair grew in streaks between furrows of scar tissue. He limped.

But he was something to watch. He'd been handsome once. Athletic. Now he was like a photo of his former self that had been ripped longways and sideways and then pasted back together. None of his edges quite lined up. Yet the injuries had the effect of making him heal stronger. Joe could come up on people real quiet.

Joe showed up one night last winter to pick up a load of whiskey at the Missile Park. He was driving an old border runner, a muddy, rusted-out truck without license plates. And that's how Dale came to meet him, when Gordy Riker put him to work hauling contraband: whiskey and tobacco going north into Canada, meth precursor coming south.

Joe was the ideal driver. A Turtle Mountain Ojibwa, his treaty card gave him privileges crossing the border. Once he was known to local customs, they usually just waved him through. Dale understood vaguely this had to do with the Jay Treaty of 1794, which excused Indians crossing the border from paying duties on "their own proper goods and effects of whatever nature."

But Joe didn't fool much with formal ports of entry. He knew all the prairie roads in four counties.

And locally, people who were put off by Dale and Joe as solitary misfits approved of them as a pair. Maybe it was just that now that they had each other to talk to, it cut down the talking load on normal people. People said that Joe and Dale sort of *found* each other.

They found each other, all right. Meeting Joe turned out to be the most significant event in Dale Shuster's life.

Next thing, Dale had stolen Joe away from Gordy to work for him. Gordy was still pissed about that. And now Joe and Dale had become something of a team.

Joe gestured vaguely with his good hand, cleared his throat, spit, and said in his feathery voice, "So how'd it go?"

"The rental haulers arrived on time. Irv took possession yesterday afternoon," Dale said.

"In the fucking rain," Joe said.

"In the fucking rain," Dale repeated.

Joe shook his head. "He give you a check?"

"Sent partial payment. Called me and said one of the loaders ran a little stiff. He's using that as an excuse to hold back on the balance."

"Uh-huh. Just like we figured. And you told him what?" Joe asked.

"That I'd be happy to make a special trip to check it out. Him being such a good buddy and all," Dale said.

"Good." Joe inclined his head and carefully studied Dale's bland face. "Okay. I got all your stuff. And the Minnesota plates. Some cash." He reached under the cot and pulled out a briefcase. "There's more coming later." Joe gave a twisted smile and looked up almost deferentially at Dale. Then he pushed the briefcase forward across the concrete.

Dale reached down and picked up the case and hugged it to his chest. It was a pretty decent leather briefcase with a brand-new smell that was intoxicating, that new car fragrance.

Dale controlled his excitement. It was important to him to always appear absolutely in control in front of Joe. Casually he placed the leather case on the desk and said, "Gordy's come asking again. Wants you back for something. And, uh, he got in a fight."

Expressionless, Joe said, "Word travels. Was it about the woman who showed up?"

They stared at each other until finally Dale said, "Maybe."

Joe blinked several times and scrubbed at his head with the knuckles of his right hand. He got off the cot and crossed the floor to the window over the desk, favoring his bad left leg, and stared across the highway at the Missile Park. After a moment, he said, "We should go have a look at her."

"Okay, first we gotta load that digger attachment for Eddie Solce. After that, we'll go have a look."

Joe nodded and put on his jeans and boots. A minute later, a rumble and cloud of smoke filled the back end of the shed as Joe started up the solitary old Deere 644C loader that needed new tires. Dale had three 644's and had given it his best try to get Irv in Minnesota to take them all. But Irv didn't want to deal with putting a new set of tires on this one. And Dale wanted to sell it as is. So the deal went down for the other two. Dale hadn't been able to peddle this beast at any price and was resigned to let it sit here for scrap.

Dale pushed open the tall sliding door at the back of the shed. While Joe maneuvered the loader through the open door, Dale collected two heavy lengths of chain.

The backhoe boom sat in the weeds along the side of the shed like a leg joint plucked off a giant yellow crab. Fortunately the ground around the shed was well drained, because the bald tires on the old loader would get zero traction in mud.

Gingerly, as Joe raised the wide bucket, Dale attached the chains to the bucket, then looped them down from the control tower on the boom and around the elbow joint by the bucket. Then they played with the tension, Joe raising the bucket ever so gently as

Dale made sure the chain didn't pinch any of the hydraulic lines on the tower. Satisfied, he gave Joe a thumbs-up and slowly the arm was hoisted in the air.

Carefully, Joe drove it around the shed to the apron of trap rock out front, where he lowered it, leaving just enough tension on the chains to keep the boom upright.

A few minutes later Eddie Solce showed up with a twenty-ton lowboy off the back of his Chevy dually. Nice trailer. Eddie welded the frame himself. Dale gave Eddie a good deal on the digger arm because Eddie had done some difficult custom metalwork for him on fairly short notice.

Eddie was a vinegar shrivel of a man with a silver mustache and a silver Trautman farm hook where his left hand had been. He'd lost the hand down around Oakes, working on his brother's farm, when he reached in to clear the corn picker one too many times. Doing metalwork around loud machines all his life had taken most of his hearing, and he had a habit of shouting when he spoke.

The customary joking ensued, Eddie giving Dale his usual loud shit about leaving town, moving to Florida. They raised the arm and placed it level on the trailer bed, loosed the chains, and proceeded to ratchet it in place with chain-link tie-downs.

Joe remained in the cab of the loader, just a shadow in the dirty window glass. Eddie waved at him once in perfunctory greeting. Eddie found it hard to look directly at Joe. He had a thing about blown-up Indians, Dale figured.

Whatever.

"You sure you don't need this old Deere?" Dale asked one last time.

"Sorry, Dale. Hell, my wife finds out I'm bringing this boom on the place she'll skull me with the frying pan."

"Shit, don't see why. You're getting it practically for nothing. Now, for a few more bucks you can have . . ."

Eddie waved Dale away with his hand and his hook. No.

They shook hands. Joe climbed down from the loader and they watched Eddie get in his truck and haul the boom away.

Joe came around from in back of the shed where he'd parked the Deere. He said he was going to get some breakfast. He'd be back in an hour to check out Ace's new lady friend.

As Dale walked Joe out to his van, a green Ford Explorer with Minnesota plates pulled off the highway and into his parking lot. A man and a little girl got out. The guy was six foot, outdoor lean, but not a farmer. Carpenter maybe. The kid was six or seven, with coppery hair done back in a pony. She wore denim shorts, a green T-shirt, and scuffed tennies.

Looking closer, Dale saw that the guy had a fresh bandage on his left hand and the makings of a shiner on his left cheek under his eye. Then he placed him.

"That's the guy Gordy knocked on his ass in front of the bar yesterday," Dale said in a low voice to Joe. "Supposed to be that woman's husband, come to take her back home. Guess he didn't get very far."

"Still here though," Joe said slowly. "Maybe he's gonna give it another try."

"Or maybe he's shopping for big iron. Tell you what. He can get a hell of a deal on an old Deere 644."

"An hour," Joe said. Then he got in his van and drove away.

Dale walked up to the stranger with the black eye and the little girl. He extended his hand. "Dale Shuster. You need some help?" They shook hands.

"Phil Broker," the guy said. "We're just passing through on our way back home. Heard in town you were clearing out your stock. I got this little landscape operation on the side. Thought maybe I'd take a look."

"Damn near all gone." Dale motioned for Broker to follow him into the shed. Then he pointed at the Deere sitting just outside the open door at the far end. "All I got left is that loader. She's got a few miles on her, so you could practically name your price."

"Kinda looking for something in a backhoe."

Dale smiled. "'Backhoe in every garage' was my old man's motto. Sorry. No backhoes left."

"I was looking at this Jap rig back home, a Komatsu . . ."

"Nah, don't do it. They might be cheaper up front, but the repair and the replacement will kill you. That's where they make their money. Stay American. Get you a Cat or a Deere."

"I'll remember that," Broker said. He pointed to the loader. "Mind if I take a look?"

"Go on. Go ahead, start her up if you want." He paused and pointed to the ground. "Ah, kinda muddy out there. Probably more than her footwear can handle."

Broker nodded and stooped to his daughter. "Kit, I'm going to look at that machine there. You stay right here where I can see you. I'll never be out of sight, okay?"

"Okay," she said.

"She be all right here?" Broker asked.

"Sure," Dale said. "I'll find some cartoons on the TV."

Arms folded defensively across her chest, Kit nodded warily.

Dale went and thumbed the remote off the weather channel, finally found Nickelodeon. "How's that?"

"Thanks."

Then Dale opened the refrigerator. "Would you like a Coke?"

The girl, arms still crossed, looked at him, wary, smart, judgmental. "That's just sugar-water and acid. It rots your teeth and makes you fat."

"Oh-kaaay . . ." Dale studied her and felt a slow rise in his mood. She was a pretty kid, healthy, athletic, nurtured. Smart little bitch would never be fat or unpopular.

"I'd like a water, please," she said, pointing at several clear plastic bottles on the shelf next to the ranks of red cans in the open refrigerator.

"Sorry," Dale said blandly. "I don't have any water." He watched her young face jerk, trying to make the evidence of her eyes and the message of his words link up. He shut the ice-box door. "Where you from?" he asked, sitting down in his desk chair. He was starting to enjoy himself.

She shifted her feet, uneasy. Glanced out toward her dad, then back again. "Devil's Rock, Minnesota."

He glanced toward the back of the building where Broker was walking around the loader, inspecting the worn-out tires. He stayed in sight, like he told his kid, but he was ducking around back there, definitely snooping. Dale swiveled his chair back toward the girl, composed himself with his hands folded in his lap. "You like stories?" he asked.

"Sure."

"Well. I know a guy named Ole, and he went over to Thief River Falls in Minnesota and he bought this cow."

"Uh-huh," she said.

"Well. He got this cow home and he went out to milk it. You know how to milk a cow, don't you?"

She nodded her head. "I been on a farm. You squeeze the things and the milk squirts out."

"Right. The things are called tits, just like your mom's got. Course she's only got one on each side. Cow has four."

The kid narrowed her eyes, alert but not quite sure what she was supposed to be wary about. She took a step back to put distance between herself and something in Dale's manner.

Dale said, "So this guy yanks on the tits and the cow farts."

The girl made a self-conscious face, but a fast lick of humor darted in her green eyes. The old bathroom humor connection.

"So the guy went and got his neighbor and brought him over and he says, 'This is the damnest thing. I bought this cow and I go to milk it and I grab hold of the tit, and when I squeeze, the cow goes and farts.'

"And his neighbor says, 'You got this cow in Minnesota, didn't you?'

"And the guy says, 'How'd you know that?'

"And the neighbor says, ''Cause I got my wife in Minnesota.'"

Dale laughed at his joke, and at the girl's discomfort and confusion. She went to the edge of the concrete pad and called to her dad. "Dad, I need to use the bathroom."

Is there a bathroom she can use?" Broker called.

"Sure, it's right in here," Dale pointed to the doorway in the partition. "Sometimes you got to flush it twice."

She nodded and went through the door and shut it behind her. Almost immediately Dale heard her playing with the toilet, flushing it twice. Then after a few moments, she flushed it again.

By the time she had finished in the bathroom and was back out standing by the desk, Broker came back.

Dale watched him closely. The guy was trying to act interested in machinery but what he was really doing was scoping out the Missile Park across the road. Looking for signs of his runaway old lady.

If that's what she really was. Jeeez—if the wife could be a cop, *this guy* could be a cop too.

"Well, thanks for letting me look around," Broker said.

"Any time. Like I said. There's not much left. I'm about to the pull the plug."

They said goodbye to the heavyset, moonfaced guy and walked out to the Explorer. Kit looked up at her dad and said, "That guy's weird."

"Why do you say that?" Broker said.

"Well, he told me this story about cows and farts."

"Yeah?" A little more alert, Broker looked at the thickset man standing in the doorway.

"And when I went to the bathroom . . ."

"He didn't do anything weird *then*, honey. I was watching him. He was sitting at the desk the whole time."

"No, it was something that was *in* the bathroom. The toilet wasn't flushed."

Broker nodded in vague sympathy.

"*No, Dad.* There was this blue poop in the toilet."

Broker grinned. "That's probably Lysol bowl cleaner, you squirt it around the edge to clean—"

"No, Dad." Kit stamped her foot and folded her arms across her chest. Peeved, she continued. "You're *not listening*. There was this blue poop floating in the water. It was yucky."

"If you say so."

Kit turned away, hugged herself tight around the chest, and raised her chin in a haughty display of disapproval. "*Dad.* You are *not* taking me seriously."

"Okay. I don't know about blue poop. But I do know that when little girls crank their stuck-up noses in the air, they gotta watch out so birds don't drop white poop on them."

Kit glowered and kicked at the trap rock in the driveway.

"Sometimes you're not a very nice daddy."

"C'mon, honey," Broker said. "Time's getting close."

Exactly an hour after he left, Joe Reed drove up and parked his van. He came into the shed wearing fresh jeans, a clean oatmeal-colored Carhartt T-shirt, and all his scars washed. Musta taken one of his cat baths in his van. He saw the loader. "No sale, huh?"

"She's a boat anchor. Leave it for scrap."

Joe looked up suddenly and cocked his head. Nothing wrong with his hearing. If anything, his other disabilities had made it more acute. Because Dale heard stuff just fine, and he didn't hear it until seconds later.

"Plane coming in," Joe said.

Chapter Nineteen

Nina woke up alone—not just in Ace's bed, but in an empty apartment over an empty bar. No smiling Ace handing her coffee. In fact, no coffee.

She had spent a second chaste night in Ace's bed and he had slept on the couch. They had gone to dinner yesterday and to a movie at the refurbished Roxy Theater in town. *Signs*, with Mel Gibson. Then they'd gone out for a single beer afterwards at the bowling alley and talked about the movie. Like a date. She had been willing to kiss him at the conclusion to the evening, but he had stepped away.

Not yet, he'd said with less of his usual gallantry than tangible distraction. Was he losing interest? Was he coming around to Gordy's suspicious way of thinking? Did it matter? She was getting antsy, too. She assumed that Holly was checking this Khari guy five different ways. So something might roll out tonight. Which was fine, because her game with Ace and Gordy was running out of steam. She'd just have to ride out the day. Later this morning she would call Broker to see how things went with Kit. Right now she wanted a cup of coffee.

She showered fast, threw on a summer shift, and went downstairs just as Gordy came in through the front door carrying a bag of groceries. Seeing her, a malevolent smile smeared his hairy lips. His beady eyes darted around the room and Nina could practically read the thought bubble over his head.

They were alone.

She ignored him, went into the office, saw the can of Folgers on the sideboard sink, and started pouring water into the Mr. Coffee machine. Gordy followed her, set down his bag, came over, and stood beside her. She had never been this close to him and he smelled like stick deodorant aged in old sweat.

"I'm still here," she said, deciding to take the offensive. He was wearing that Velcro back brace. She wondered if he slept in it.

"You ain't the only one. Green Explorer, Minnesota plates, parked at the Motor Inn."

"Shit," Nina said. *All right!*

"Yeah, he's hanging around. Here. Let me do that." Gordy took the can of Folgers from her and started measuring out the coffee. "Ace likes it strong."

"Where is he?"

"Run off with the most popular chick in town." Gordy grinned and held his hand palm down about waist level. "'Bout this tall. She ain't got legs or arms but she got these great lips, and her head is flat on top, just right for setting down a beer can."

"Old joke," Nina said and fixed a bored expression on her face.

"Ace went into court to fight a speeding ticket. He'll be back pretty soon." Gordy shrugged and removed a six-pack of Coke from the bag, and a cardboard box of assorted doughnuts.

"Breakfast of Champions, huh?" Nina said.

Gordy put the Cokes in the refrigerator, all but one can. He popped the top, took a sip, and opened the bakery box. "Want one?" he asked. As he held the pastries up he stepped closer, too close, so his arm grazed her arm.

Nina threw a warning glance. Gordy just smiled and selected a jelly doughnut, took a bite, then leered at her, with a gob of goo caught in his mustache. His tongue darted out, snapped up the goo. Then he started to make his move. "So, where did he sleep last night. On the couch or on you?"

Nina extended the middle finger of her right hand.

"You give it up yet?" Gordy said, staring at her hips. "You satisfy his *curiosity*?" The leer accelerated and his breath came faster, working up to something ugly, and his eyes started to go fast, like two little caged rats.

"Back off, Gordy. I mean it." Nina started for the door.

Gordy blocked her path, looming. Almost touching her as he whispered in her ear with his sugar breath, "It's like this—you could leave under your own power, or you could disappear. It'd be easy . . ."

Nina, an inch taller, dropped her eyes to focus on the lump of Adam's apple nestled in Gordy's hairy throat. *Go on, asshole, touch me. Crush his larnyx in about two seconds . . .*

She moved past him and then the knife came out.

He drew it from his back pocket: a standard folding Buck Hunter with a fat, almost four-inch, stainless-steel blade. Gordy whipped it open with a smooth practiced flick of his thumb. He raised the knife in his right hand, menacing the blade back and forth. Catching the light. Not exactly threatening her directly with it, more like showing off and working up to something . . .

Broker had always told her how a lot of the assholes out there weren't that smart. How sometimes they just *did* things before they thought . . . Okay, so, a knife—she prepared herself to fight. Gordy puckered his lips, blew a kiss, took a half-step toward her, still swinging the blade off to the side.

Instinctively Nina's hands came up and she stepped back. What happened next was so strange and fast that she found herself in the middle, missing the beginning:

The voice rasped: "Leave her alone, Gordy. I mean it."

Nina watched, stunned. *Where'd he come from?* A swarthy

man about five-ten, in jeans, a gray T-shirt, and boots. He had jet-black hair and the corded arms of a circus roustabout. His face was all wrong, rippled with uneven pigment. Scars showed even through his short hair. He approached silently, moving with a graceful limp, favoring his left leg. He carried his left hand protectively close to his hip, not swinging naturally and Nina immediately saw the nubs of the two missing fingers. She'd seen his kind of face before, in VA hospital burn wards; guys who'd been blown up, their skin grafted. But this guy was very focused, his quiet eyes checking the blind angles, the back doorway by the stairs.

Her response was visceral. One player sensing another player coming onto the field.

Gordy immediately put the knife away, stepped back. "Hey—just kidding, Joe," he said.

If push came to shove, Ace and Gordy were country tough. Basically they were muddling along in a local tradition of smuggling whiskey and petty crime. Not this guy. Nina was sure. He was a trained man. For the first time since this project got under way, Nina knew she was close to something scary.

The guy stopped and probed Nina fast with cold brown eyes so intense she could almost feel her bones glow. Then he turned to Gordy and said, "We got nothing else to talk about, you and me. You understand?"

"Sure, Joe."

"Where's Ace?"

"He ain't here," Gordy said.

"Tell him George says it's tonight, at the old remote missile bunker east of town."

"Jesus, Joe." Gordy rolled his eyes at Nina, alarmed.

Joe's eyes stayed fixed on Gordy but his voice turned contemptuous. "Since when are we scared of women?" He inclined his damaged face toward Gordy for emphasis, then, "You tell Ace."

Gordy stepped back, eyes wide; trying to make the best of things. "Yeah, sure, Joe."

Then Joe continued on past the stairs and went out through the storeroom. Gordy, minus most of the color in his face, grinned nervously at Nina. "Just joking around, right?"

"Yeah, sure, Gordy. Ha ha. Who was that?"

"Joe Reed," Gordy said, clearly agitated. He shook his head. "I don't get what's going on anymore. It wasn't like this when Ace's dad ran things."

Nina folded her arms across her chest and watched him go into the office. Then she went to the table, where Ace's morning newspaper was spread out. As she sat down she released a delayed shudder.

The Indian's presence lingered in the room like a cool shadow. Tonight, he said. George, he said. She was with Gordy, thinking, *Why was this guy putting it on front street? What the hell's going on?*

Gordy reinvented himself fast, coming out of the office, smiling, bringing her a cup of coffee, and holding up two fingers in a V peace signal. Ace came in a few minutes later and set a still-warm Dairy Queen breakfast bag next to her.

"You're still here," he said with a wry smile.

Gordy watched her carefully from the bar to see if she'd let on about their confrontation. She didn't and he occupied himself with his clipboard.

Ace said, "I had to leave early to go to court. Overslept, didn't even have time to make coffee."

"No problem," Nina said airily. "Good old Gordy whipped up a pot."

"Anywhere, anytime," Gordy said.

Ace observed the touchy back-and-forth, filed it away. Gordy joined him, walked him to the stairs, and lowered his voice. "Joe was by, playing hard-ass. George sent him. George says it's on for tonight. He'll meet you at the old RLS site east on 5. Didn't give a time."

Ace nodded, stared at Nina's back for a long moment, then went upstairs. The phone on the bar rang, Gordy crossed the room and picked it up. Nina opened the Dairy Queen bag. It contained an egg muffin.

Gordy talked for a moment, put down the phone, then said to her, "That was Dale across the road. Your husband was over there this morning. Thought you should know."

Nina lowered her eyes, picked up her coffee cup in both hands, and took a sip.

Dale really wanted to get a closer look at this woman who had come to spy on his brother. He wanted to so bad he kept putting it off just to build up the anticipation. He had Gordy's request to intervene with Ace as an excuse to mask his curiosity.

Woman comes all this way just to see Ace. *Well, isn't she in for a surprise.*

It was an accepted fact that some new floosy blowing into town would be attracted to his brother. This had always been the case, all his life. And that's why he found this woman so tantalizing.

Just showing up, kind of mysterious.

So he puttered around in the office, brooding, periodically glancing across the road. He'd glimpsed her twice now. First in that clingy tank top, then wearing one of Ace's T-shirts. Tallish, lean. Short red hair. His eyes drifted up to the windows over the bar. He remembered playing there as a child, when his dad had an office there. Now Ace was probably sticking it to the woman up there—maybe right where he'd put his Tinker Toys together.

He peered out the window and finally he saw Ace's Tahoe pull in and park in back. He picked up the phone and called. Gordy answered.

"Is he there?" Dale asked.

"Yeah. He just got back."

"That guy you hit was here this morning with a little kid. He pretended he wanted to look at machinery."

"I'll pass it on."

"Okay. Maybe I'll come over in a little while," Dale said. He hung up, then stuck his head out the door. "Give me about five minutes to clean up," he said to Joe. "Then we'll go across."

Joe nodded, raised his good hand and pointed. Across the highway, toward town, a small, single-engine plane took off, banked, and headed east.

Dale shut the front door and went into the small bathroom next to the office and inspected the toilet to see if the smart-ass little kid had left any unpleasant messes. She hadn't. So he washed his face and brushed his teeth and gargled with Scope. Then he took a moment to study his reflection in the mirror. His teeth were normal and healthy but his gums were slightly oversized and made his choppers look slightly like lingering baby teeth.

At rest, Dale was plain. In motion, he tended to look deliberate, the power in him deep, hard to see. Clothes never meant much to him. But he wore a heavy leather belt; keeping himself real tucked in and tightly cinched. If you had stuff you had to keep inside, every little bit helped.

The way his life had worked out he wound up uncomfortable with his body. He had always suffered from a debilitating shyness, and now he went to great lengths to avoid looking at himself disrobed. If he used a public restroom on the highway he made sure the door locked. Then he'd turn out the lights and do his business in the dark.

Dale was a big man with a layer of fat on the outside. But he was solid on the inside. Years spent working around the big iron had given him a hefty core of muscle.

Sometimes he snuck looks at his brother, Ace, and had the impression that there had been a screw-up. Ace, with all his flaws, should have this awkward tub of guts. *He* should have Ace's body.

As it was, he was just over six feet tall and weighed 240 pounds, with sloping shoulders and a longish neck. His skin was smooth and white. He wore wide-brimmed hats and long-sleeved shirts. This habit struck people as odd in a farming community. "Dale, he avoids the sun," people said.

That wasn't it. Dale was hiding his body. Even from himself.

Everywhere he looked he was reminded of his grossness. The images of little-bitty tanned bodies shrieked at him from magazines, TV commercials, and especially the hours of "paid commercial programming" on cable—all those bikini babes demonstrating exercise equipment.

His face was the polar opposite of his older brother's; as if Ace's handsome face had been turned inside out. Where Ace's cheeks were smooth and defined, Dale's were lumpy with moguls of persistent acne. Where Ace's nose was straight, Dale's was thick.

Being plain and naturally reticent, his quiet voice had grown softer and softer over the years.

His hair was dirty blond, unruly even when short, as it was now. It sprouted from his scalp like a neglected lawn taken over by weeds. His eyes were pale blue and flat, without sparkle.

And now he was ready. So he stepped out into ninety-two muggy degrees wearing distressed Levis, steel-toed work shoes, and a long-sleeved blue cotton shirt buttoned to the neck and to the wrists. A broad straw Stetson perched at an angle on his head.

He looked to the east, at the ambiguous sky. According to the Weather Channel the rain had finally tapered off in Minnesota. But the solid cover of clouds remained.

He locked the door to the office and motioned to Joe, who pushed upright in the lawn chair on the concrete apron in front of the office.

"Let's go have a look," Dale said.

Joe squinted and said, "I just was over there. I don't think this is a good idea."

"C'mon," Dale cajoled and Joe grunted, reluctantly heaving to his feet. And so they walked across Highway 5. When Dale was little, the Missile Park had smelled like a saloon early in the morning. Sawdust and soap covering a deep underscent of alcohol and tobacco smoke. He remembered the morning sun catching fire in all those bottles behind the bar. Now the bottles were gone. Now it just smelled musty, like what it had become, an empty warehouse.

They stepped inside and saw the woman sitting at Ace's table at the back of the room, next to the pinball machine.

Gordy was standing at the front window, sipping on a Coke. Without turning, he said, "Christ. Here come both of them." Then he spun on his heel and went past her up the stairs.

She heard them before she saw them; heavy footfalls on the porch. Then the creak of the screen door, the two men coming into the bar. The big one came in first—a Yogi Bear ramble of a walk, heavy in the middle, a long neck. Grinning. This would be Dale, Ace's odd brother. She was prepared for him being a little off. But not the way he wore his shirt buttoned up to his neck and down to his wrists on such a humid hot day. At the moment, however, she was more interested in the Indian, Joe Reed.

He took her in as his eyes swept the room; dark eyes doing that cold burn. They shot a fast dagger thrust. Quick, sharp, and deep. Too quick to read, but Nina thought she felt contempt in his eyes, maybe even hatred.

She didn't know a whole lot about the social range of disfigured Indians. She'd only had one acquaintance with a Native American for any length of time: Ranger Sergeant Norby Hightower, a Cheyenne from Wyoming. Nina worked with Norby in Bosnia. Strong as a bear, Norby's handshake was child-soft, a dissimulation of his true strength. His whole style had been probing, cautious, indirect.

Not point-blank and icy, like this guy's.

Joe peeled off, walked behind the bar, opened a cooler, and took out a can of Mountain Dew. He popped the top, shrugged at Dale, and walked out the front door.

It bothered Dale deeply that she was more interested in watching Joe than him. But he brushed the slight aside for the moment.

She was pretty.

Maybe not as pretty as Ginny Weller had been—she was older and she'd had a kid. But still pretty.

As Dale walked down the length of the barroom toward the table, she looked up. When he felt her eyes he knew she was acting. The lazy, slightly vague, expression on her face was a mask. Behind that pretend mask she was watching Joe go around the bar, get a can of pop.

Dale swallowed and stared. He could hear Gordy and Ace talking upstairs. Joe got his look and now he walked back out. They were alone.

He was close enough to smell her now; a clean, rain-in-the-forest scent, distinct in the musty air. He knew he should look away, look down, be humble, or at least polite, but he stared. Starting at the top of her head, where her short red hair was carelessly combed by her fingers, then her face.

Her coloring, freckles, the strong cheekbones, the shamrock eyes. The red of her lipstick, hair, and freckles brought to mind images of a lake trout—smooth and supple, but also spiny with fins and stinging to the touch.

She crossed her legs and, staring at the flash of thigh, he had the powerful recollection of holding a struggling fish, feeling its life squirm against his encircling palm, peering into the red spasm of the gills.

As this sensation shuddered inside his bulk his gaze dripped down over her body like greasy water, gathering in her hollows, racing over her curves, marking every detail. Her strong body promised a lot of struggle.

She oozed confidence, like she wouldn't bat an eye at the dirtiest joke. Like she'd seen it all before. She watched him walk up with a neutral expression in her eyes. She smelled like the Herbal Essence shampoo Ace kept in the upstairs bathroom.

She had this body that clothes always looked good on, lean and long-legged, but sinewy too. She was wearing a casual cotton-print dress with a green-and-amber pattern creasing down into her lap. The rounded neckline dipped low and he could see a only a sugges-tion of the firmness of her breasts, but what he saw looked more taut than soft. As Dale's eyes drifted up, he mentally diagramed the apart-ment upstairs, all the rooms she had moved through, until he came to the bathroom shower stall. He imagined her naked up there, drawing a sponge across her stomach. "Hi," he said, inhaling her.

Joe continued on across the road, finishing the soda in several long gulps. As he tossed the can, he noticed the green Ford Explorer was back, parked next to his van. He walked directly to it, tried the door. Locked. But the window was open a crack. Joe went to his van, rummaged in back, came back with a coat hanger, straightened it, hooked one end, slipped it through the crack, rotated it, and pressed the straightened end down on the lock button. He opened the door, ducked low, checked the glove compartment, the front seat. Almost immediately he found a holstered .45 under the driver's seat with a Minnesota deputy sheriff's badge. He took the pistol and badge, shut the door, got in his van, tossed them into the back. He started the van, pulled onto the highway, and removed a satellite phone from the glove compartment. He activated the phone and pressed in a number. When he had the connection, he said, "I delivered the message, but I'm not so sure about this."

• • •

"Hi yourself," Nina said.

Dale realized he was holding his breath and she was looking at him, taking in his appearance, assessing him, and being patient with him. *She knows I'm Ace's brother, and all the rest. She's patronizing me.* Finally in a burst of released air he said, "I'll bet you went to the prom, didn't you?"

She cocked her head and laughed, a feminine laugh that was pleasant to hear, like she was spontaneously amused.

"See," Dale said, "I made you laugh."

"I guess you did."

"And you did go to the prom."

"Guilty as charged."

"Were you the best-looking girl there?"

She shook a cigarette out of a pack on the table, lit it with a blue plastic lighter, and blew a stream of smoke at the ceiling. Then she tilted her head as if to let her mind roll backward. "Actually, I was about third or fourth in line for looks. I was on the skinny side." She brightened. "But I'll bet I was the smartest."

Dale thought, but did not say, *Oh yeah? Then what are you doing in this nowhere place?* He studied her intently for several heavy heartbeats. He had no idea what a woman cop would really look like. All he'd seen were the ones on TV and in the movies, and they all had bigger chests.

He just nodded. "It's good to be smart. But it helps to be pretty, too."

She diplomatically didn't answer that. She just shrugged her shoulders.

Dale smiled and said, "When Ace breaks your heart, I'll take you out. I'll be real nice to you."

That amused her, too, because again she smiled a big smile, parting her teeth. She had good even teeth. And a hearty laugh. "I'll tell him to keep an eye out for the competition."

"Oh, I ain't the competition. In fact I don't mind being the last in line. I don't mind sloppy lasts." He broadened his grin, showing his gums, as she adjusted to the remark. Drew herself up. Tensed. Like she could bound right out the chair and pound him through the floor with kung fu or something. He imagined what it would be like to have all that vitality under his control.

"Dale? That's your name?" she said in a measured, no nonsense voice that gave away the lie of her act, the way it presumed to arrange life in straight lines, like she knew all the rules. He nodded his head, his smile oblivious to the warning in her tone.

"Dale, that crack was pretty obnoxious."

He shrugged. "Just want you to know I'll never lie to you." He stared at her hard, marking her with his eyes.

"I guess we just ran out of things to talk about. So why don't you move it on down the line."

Dale wiggled his fingers. "Bye." He walked past her and went up the stairs. As he went up, Gordy came down the stairs, smiled tightly, and went into the office.

Nina lowered her eyes and stared at the twist of smoke coming off her cigarette. *Jesus, what's cooking with these guys?* Joe Reed was scary and Dale was creepy. Gordy was barely under control. And Ace—he was rowing across an ocean of booze, striving to maintain an even strain between mania and depression.

Dale walked into the apartment and said, "I seen your new girl."

"Nina?"

"Uh-huh. Her husband came by the shed this morning pretending to look at my old Deere. You fuck her yet?"

"Nah, it ain't like that. She's going through a bad time breaking up. We're just sort of fellow travelers." *The husband*, he thought, moving toward the front window.

"Losing your touch?" Dale said.

Ace stopped and regarded his brother with gentle eyes. He had never allowed himself to be angry with Dale, regardless of what he said. "What's on your mind, Dale?"

"Gordy come and talked to me about her."

"Yeah?"

"He's nervous, thinks she's here to snoop."

"What do you think?'

"I think Gordy has reason to be nervous. More than you. That's what I think."

Ace clapped his brother on the shoulder. "So he's got a reason to be nervous, huh?"

"Yep. Joe says Gordy's running too much dope; Pseudoephedrine in bulk down from Winnepeg, some coke, and that hydroponic grass they got. Joe says he's attracting sharks." Dale pointed down the stairway. "Maybe federal sharks."

"A fed, huh? I ain't so sure. She just don't strike me as a cop."

"Has she been asking around, kinda snooping after something?"

"Mainly she's been pissed from the minute she walked through that door. At her husband mostly, but I get the feeling she's pissed at the world in general."

"Still, you gotta be careful, brother. You gotta do something about Gordy."

"Christ, Dale, Gordy does all the work around here, he keeps the books. How am I going to replace him?"

Dale shrugged. "Hell, I can keep books, you know that."

Ace shook his head. "Nah, I don't want you mixed up in this. You sell off the last of the junk across the road, padlock the door, and go to Florida."

"I wanna help. What if I could get him to quit running dope. How about that?" Dale said. "You always looked out for me, except when you were in jail that time. Just fair I do something to help."

Another sore point. Ace's easy smile masked a swell of remorse. Would it have made a difference if he'd been around during the end of Dale's senior year, when he turned funny, inward, a little weird? Probably not.

"Sure. Talk to Gordy if you think it'll help. But don't take any shit. If he gets antsy, you tell me." Ace continued to the front window, eased the curtain aside with his finger.

Dale smiled. "I'll give him a talking-to he won't forget."

"You do that," Ace said, facing away, looking out the window. *Hello. What's this?* Across the road he saw Broker walking next to Deputy Jimmy Yeager. Broker got in a green Explorer that was parked in front of the Shuster shed. Yeager got in his cruiser on the road. Then Broker followed Yeager east toward town.

What do you suppose they're up to?

Dale nodded and left him, went down the stairs, ignored Nina, who was still sitting at Ace's table, smoking, drinking coffee, and reading the *Grand Forks Herald*. He walked up to the office door.

"Guess Joe's pissed at me, huh?" Gordy said, looking up from the desk.

Dale said, "I can fill you in on where he's coming from—say, later tonight. You got anything going on?"

"Maybe."

"Mind if I come along?"

Gordy shot a wary look at Nina in the other room, took a pen from his chest pocket, and wrote "*9 P.M., here*" on a notepad. Then he tore the paper in half, then in quarters, and tossed it in the trash can behind the bar.

Dale nodded and started for the door. As he left the bar he sang out, "Be seeing you, Nina . . ."

Chapter Twenty

"She calls herself Nina Pryce. Red hair, mid-thirties, and she's competent. I don't think she's a cop. More like government. Maybe military."

"How can you tell?" the Mole said into the telephone receiver.

"The way she watches things, the way she moves. Trust me on this. And then there's her alleged husband . . ."

"Forget the husband, there are already too many distractions."

"I'm just saying—"

"No, stay on plan, you understand?"

"Okay. But this is taking a funny bounce, the way she's coming on to Ace, pretending to have drinking problem, marriage problems. Point is, they are definitely here."

As the Mole listened, his eyes traveled across the deserted truck stop and fixed on the word CLOSED written in soap on the empty diner windows. Closed. Out of business. The end. Now *they* would be out of business if he didn't act.

"We'll see how it goes tonight," the Mole said.

"You're taking a big risk, cousin."

"We're after a big jackpot. You just get our friend out of there."

"It won't be easy. We've created some kind of monster. He's getting harder to control. We might have to put him down and let it all go."

"No. We're almost there. Stick to the plan. We'll get rid of him when it's all over," the Mole said. The calmness of his voice was at odds with the violence with which he slammed the phone down on the hook. Immediately he regretted the show of anger. The man he'd been talking to was family, a distant cousin who handled the Canadian end of the smuggling network. Now his cousin was having doubts, and the moment he decided the plan was losing its wheels, he would likely disappear back to Canada.

Shit. The Mole clenched his fists. He'd been too long out of play. His method of recruiting the American had been flawed, and now it had backfired.

Damn, it had all been so perfect.

At first, he had just agreed to smuggle Rashid's shipment and had brought in his cousin for extra security. They'd met with Rashid to finalize the deal and lingered over coffee. Rashid revealed the depth of his background check. He knew that twenty years earlier the Mole had trained with the group that went on to hit the Marine barracks in Beirut. That he had been diverted from the front lines for this lonely work in America.

Rashid politely wondered if years spent living in the suburbs quietly smuggling drugs to finance Hamas and Hezbollah might have eroded his commitment to killing Americans.

"Try me," the Mole said.

Some testing back and forth ensued. It was established that the Mole had been trained in the bombmaker's art and that the contraband being negotiated was explosives. Not long after that, and after he'd made reference to jihad three times, Rashid confided that, yes, he was associated with Al Qaeda. But he was no zealot, he insisted. And being a practical man, he was willing to contract out work; especially in the current security environment.

Which was fine, because while the Mole and his cousin paid lip service to the Cause, basically their background was rooted in the criminal underbelly of the movement in the Bekáa Valley. They preferred their politics heavily flavored with money.

Then they returned to North Dakota to case the specific smuggling route for Rashid's Semtex. That's when they were found out by the strange American. The easy solution would have been to kill him on the spot. Instead they let him talk. In the man's desperate babble the Mole discerned the essence of a plan that could dwarf the 9/11 attack.

The American understood he was in dangerous company. Instead of being intimidated, this fact encouraged him to talk freely, ultimately revealing his secret desires. It was, the Mole perceived, a marriage made in hell. In the end, they agreed to an exchange of favors. The American wanted to kill three people. But the Mole figured that three million dollars deposited in a Danish bank would be a fair price for the project he now envisioned. After thinking it through, he'd traveled to Detroit and sat down for coffee with Rashid a second time.

He told Rashid: "Your organization is under a lot of stress right now. It's gotta be difficult to mount a large operation in the States. I, however, can offer you one-stop shopping."

Rashid said, "Explain one-stop shopping."

"None of your people would be involved," the Mole began. "Just give me the ton of explosives you have in Canada. I'll build the weapon and position it and execute the attack. If I succeed, you pay me three million dollars."

"That's a lot of money. What do you intend to attack?" Rashid asked.

The Mole explained the kind of target he had in mind, but not the specific location.

Rashid's coffee cup trembled slightly in his fingers and he leaned closer. "What exactly is the weapon?"

The Mole briefed him with the aid of some photos and several pages of detailed diagrams.

Rashid licked his lips. "But how would you get inside?"

So the Mole told him.

Rashid leaned closer, thought for a moment, then whispered, "God in heaven. This could work."

Eventually someone in a cave on the Afghan-Pakistan border thought so, too, and the deal was struck. Now, after a lot of work and a bit of luck, the weapon was in place. The Mole had his passport in his pocket, along with an airline ticket to Copenhagen.

He looked up into the clouds with a pained expression as a sprinkle of raindrops dotted his windshield. *Please, no more rain.* Forget the rain. He had other things to worry about. Like their "friend." They had set him up for his first kill, thinking that by taping the crime they could always blackmail him if they sensed him slipping outside their control. The opposite proved true. He couldn't get enough of the tape. Now he wanted more.

But first they had to get through tonight.

Chapter Twenty-one

Broker and Kit watched the blue single-engine Piper Saratoga II HP cruise the Langdon strip at 500 feet then go into a standard landing pattern: flying counterclockwise, making a series of left turns around the strip, and finally lining up on approach and setting down. When the prop stopped moving, two men emerged: Doc Harris, the pilot, and Lyle Torgeson, a Cook County deputy. They greeted Kit and shook hands with Broker.

Harris, a tanned, well-preserved seventy, a retired general surgeon, asked Broker about his hand. Broker lied and said it was no problem. Lyle said, "I don't suppose you'll tell me what's going on here? Your mom had us lined up to pick up Kit before you called."

Broker just smiled, clapped Lyle on the shoulder, and said, "I really appreciate this."

Lyle said, "I figured that's about all you'd say. Watch yourself."

Kit, still in a huff from their minor tiff leaving Shuster's equipment shed, remained distant and stoic. Broker wondered if she'd acquired the old army trick of picking a fight with loved ones before shipping out, to make the parting easier. But climbing into the small door aft of the wing, she turned and grabbed him in a bear hug and he had to pry her arms from around his neck as she shouted, "I want you and Mommy to come home *together*."

Then she climbed into the plane, pressed her face up against a passenger window, and nagged him with her teared-up eyes. The prop revved up but the engine noise didn't quite drown out the echo of her words.

Broker's marching orders were getting more complicated.

Then the plane taxied down the strip and flew away. Kit's face, framed in an aircraft window, faded into a blur as Doc climbed and banked east.

Broker stood awhile watching the plane disappear. He reminded himself that the Saratoga was a first-class high-performance aircraft. And that Doc Harris was a veteran pilot. But as he walked back to the Ford he was mindful of the moody clouds hanging overhead. And that JFK Jr. had taken his last flight in a Piper Saratoga.

He got in the Ford, pulled up to the highway, and looked right and then left. The entry road to the airstrip was about 300 yards from the bar and the equipment shed. He could just make out Dale Shuster and another guy walking across the highway and going into the bar.

Broker had dismissed Kit's strange comment about Dale Shuster's toilet, but he'd noticed something else at the shed that got him thinking. So he decided to pay another visit. Making no attempt to hide his approach, he drove down the highway and pulled into the weedy lot in front of the shed. There were two vehicles in the lot, both pretty beat up—a Grand Prix with a filthy windshield and a brown Chevy van.

Okay, he thought as he got out of his truck, *so I'm being a little obvious.* He threw a glance across the road at the bar's brick facade. Maybe he wouldn't mind a rematch with that Gordy guy.

Broker walked around the back of the shed to where the lone piece of earth-moving equipment was parked. Something about the Deere had caught his attention: on the left rear end, one of the counterweights was missing. A solid hunk of yellow cast iron two feet square, six inches deep, and weighing perhaps 500 pounds, a counterweight was the ultimate blunt object. Huge bolts held it to the machine's frame. Its purpose was to offset the load in the bucket. It was not something that got damaged under normal use.

Broker cocked his ear when he heard a motor start. He peeked around the edge of the shed and saw the brown van pull onto the highway, caught a glimpse of the driver—the scarred-up dude he'd seen with Dale Shuster this morning. The van accelerated back toward town. He waited a few moments, heard nothing else, and moved off ten yards into the damp weeds along the side of the shed. Looked around to get his bearings. Right about here he'd seen a flash of yellow on his first visit. The ground was disturbed, dug up and refilled. Okay. He moved deeper in the weeds and found it. A corner of yellow cast iron peeked from the ground. The rain had washed away the top layer of dirt.

Broker stooped and rapped his knuckle against the dense iron. Now who in the hell would bury a counterweight? He got up, walked back to the Deere front-loader, and began to study it like a puzzle.

"Morning," a voice said behind him.

Broker turned and saw the husky deputy—Jim Yeager—watching him. Yeager was in uniform, tan over brown.

"Hi," Broker said.

"What's up?" Yeager asked.

Broker held up a red Bic lighter. "Was by here earlier looking at this Deere. Dropped my lighter. Just found it."

"Uh-huh," Yeager said. "Mr. Broker, would you mind following me into town?" Polite but firm.

"I could do that," Broker said. He walked back to his truck, pressed the lock remote, opened the door, and got in. As he turned the key in the ignition, he instinctively checked under the seat with his left hand.

Shit. After a fast inspection he noticed his window open a crack. And now the badge and gun were missing. Yeager? The brown van? Okay, so it was getting tricky.

Broker decided not to mention the missing pistol and badge as he followed Yeager back to town. He'd just watch and see if Yeager gave anything away. He pulled into the parking area in front of the motel, next to Yeager's Crown Vic. Yeager got out and leaned against the cruiser's front fender, hatless, smoking a Marlboro Light that looked like a white straw in his thick fingers. He could have got those arms lifting free weights, but you don't lift iron for hours on end. Throwing hay bales, more likely.

"It's Yeager, right?" Broker said.

"Yeah." Yeager took a drag, exhaled. The steady breeze bled the smoke from his nose and mouth. "Kinda figured you'd be on that plane that took off." Inhale, hold, exhale. "Guess not."

Broker did his best to look attentive. He pointed to the Explorer and said, "I'll be driving."

"When?" Yeager asked.

Broker mugged a tight smile, looked away.

Yeager was mellow, totally relaxed. He was, after all, completely in control here. He raised his chin inquiringly. "So how's the hand? Heard you tagged Ace Shuster with a left. Musta smarted some."

"Some."

"Uh-huh. And I noticed that you and the little girl dropped in on Dale Shuster this morning. I don't think he's going to sell that old Deere, do you?"

"Not likely," Broker said.

Yeager looked away for several seconds. "You know, there's this Air Force radar base east of town. Real sophisticated stuff. Tracks all the space junk, is what they say. Can spot a beer can at eight hundred miles."

"Really."

"Really. Got private security, though. Local guys man the gate. They stay on orange alert there. The rest of the country is on yellow. But they know what's going on, and one of them tells me this helicopter showed up last night. One of those Black Hawks, like in that movie that just come out." Yeager paused and watched Broker's face for a reaction.

"No shit," Broker said.

"No shit. The story is, the chopper was en route to Grand Forks on a routine flight and had to stop for minor mechanical repairs. Six guys plus the crew. 'Cept they all wear civilian clothes and keep strictly to themselves. This guy told me four of them are, like, in real good shape. Regular animals. The other two are kinda nerdy looking. Just hanging out, playing basketball next to the hanger. Thought you might be interested."

"Well, maybe they just had minor mechanical trouble."

"Yeah, probably. Another thing . . . Your wife? Nina?

"Yeah . . ."

Yeager watched him come forward through his cool act, alert.

"Yeah, well, thing is . . . Her and that Jane Singer"—Yeager hooked his fingers, making air quotes—"the overt lesbian? Army doesn't know anything about them. Where they are. What they're doing in North Dakota. Said they'll get back to us."

Broker smiled his unhappy smile.

Yeager went on talking in a steady, friendly voice. "And the old guy in the beach shirt who was hanging around the swimming pool when you showed up?"

"You been following me, Deputy Yeager?"

Yeager shrugged and smiled. "Not me."

"Somebody else maybe?"

"Maybe. Well, after Jane checked out of the Motor Inn yesterday, the old dude drove out of town behind her. Just take a wild-ass guess where they spent last night."

Broker stared at him.

Yeager smiled. "My buddy the security guard at the radar site heard that Jane has a mean hook shot."

Broker saw that Yeager wasn't going away. So, effectively agreeing to dance, he said as much. "You ain't going away, are you, Yeager?"

"Hey, Broker, I live here. See—after the spooks and the black helicopters and the feds finish creepy-crawling around and have their moment, then they'll leave." Yeager studied the coal of his cigarette, put it back between his lips, and calmly placed his hands on his hips. "Then, well . . . I'm still here in this county. Me and, basically, three other guys."

Broker withdrew the tinfoil pouch of Sweets from his back pocket, dug out one of the rough wraps, put it in his mouth, and waited while Yeager took out an old-fashioned Zippo and thumbed the wheel.

Broker puffed until he was lit and then pointed at the lighter. Yeager handed it to him. The case was nicked and rubbed smooth. Ditto the brass eagle, anchor, and globe on the side. Under the Marine insignia there were just two engraved words, one almost faded away, one newer:

IWO

BEIRUT

Yeager said, "My dad gave it to me when I went into the crotch. I had it in the 'Ruit in '83."

"The barracks?" Broker handed the Zippo back.

"I was on detail, hauling ash and trash, about a mile away when it blew. Three other guys in my room—they never found enough to fill one body bag." Yeager paused, thumbed his smoke, set his jaw. "Nineteen years old. I handled a whole lot of dead bodies the next couple days. How many dead people you touched in your life, Broker?"

Broker looked past Yeager, scanning the scrolls of clouds that filled the sky, as if he'd find a list of instructions spelled out. *Damn.*

Yeager, ever patient, watched the wheels revolving in Broker's eyes. "Okay. Tell you what. Instead of just standing around looking out of place, why don't you hop in my cruiser and let me show you around. I'll do all the talking. You just listen. Then, later, if you want to talk or get ahold of me—like, if something were to happen . . ." Yeager heaved his shoulders, let them drop.

"What the hell," Broker said. The more he saw of Yeager, the more sure he was that it was the guy, the one in the van, who broke into his truck. Deal with that later.

"Get in. Your Ford'll be just fine here."

Broker got in, looked around. "No computer."

"Nope, we got us a time warp going here when it comes to budget. So it's old-style. Just the radar and the radio."

They were easing east on 5 and came up to the flashing red stop. Yeager hung a left, looked across the seat. "So when's the last time you worked patrol?"

"Jesus. Hadda be the eighties."

"Goddamn. And I thought I was old. Things have changed, huh?" He paused. "Not here, maybe."

Broker wished he still had Kit because the fields started to roll out like a scene from the *Wizard of Oz*, all green and yellow. Swirls of blue. Dizzy with the heat. But no contour to the crops. Flat.

"Yeah," he said, "things have changed. The new breed of cops are a lot smarter than I was."

Yeager grinned. "Got to be smart to drive, talk on the radio, type on a computer, answer your cell phone, and ding out messages on your Palm Pilot all at the same time."

"Way too smart to rush into things the way we did," Broker said.

Yeager leaned back and rubbed his chin with the knuckles of his right hand. "Something to be said for rushing in. I watched that Columbine thing live on TV. Those Colorado boys sure didn't do any rushing in on that one." He cut Broker with a frank look. "Just my opinion—but my gut read was if there would have been more dead cops, there would have been less dead kids." After making his point, Yeager swung his eyes back on the road. Then he said, "Your wife and her army pals are old-style, when it comes to rushing in . . ."

Broker didn't take the bait and so Yeager drove in silence. They passed two deserted farmhouses in as many miles, the driveways filled up with weeds, the white paint on the wood siding peeled back to gray pith. Stark as rib cages left to molder in the wheat.

"Looks like the real estate market is kinda depressed," Broker said.

Yeager shrugged. "Some of it's consolidation. Big ones eat the little ones. Cheaper to just plant around the abandoned houses than tear them down. But some of it's just changing times. That last house, they still farm but they moved into town. When I grew up we had animals, an orchard, a big truck garden—enough stuff to keep a family busy. And a cushion to fall back on during a bad year." Yeager twisted his lips in a cynical smile. "In addition to durum, we used to grow more of a certain kind of kid out here. Yeah, well—couple years ago they closed down the Future Farmers of America program at the high school."

Yeager slowed as they came up to a long capsule-shaped white tanker on a wheeled gurney parked next to the road. He pointed to the hose coming off a coupling. "This is a dumb shit, leaving his hoses on the tank."

"I don't follow," Broker said.

"You're out of touch, Broker. These white tankers you see all over. It's anhydrous. Liquid fertilizer. There can be enough ammonia left in the hoses to cook a batch of meth. A gallon of anhydrous is worth less than half a buck to a fertilizer dealer. But it converts to two ounces of meth, worth a thousand bucks on the street in Grand Forks, Fargo . . . Minneapolis."

They lost the asphalt and were driving on gravel now.

Yeager jerked his thumb over his shoulder. "Those deserted houses we went by? Perfect sites for Beavis and Butt Head meth labs. Little assholes come up from Fargo, Bismarck. Road-trip around, assembling their cook kit, then come up here for the free anhydrous sitting all over the place. Then they find a deserted house to cook in."

Broker nodded. "It's just starting to hit Minnesota. Since they regulated the ephedrine, it's harder to cook it down from commercial cold medications, like Sudafed. Can only buy two packs a pop."

"Yeah," Yeager said. "They have to cover a lot of territory to come up with quantity. Mostly it's kids making it for their personal use. The real problem is the border."

Broker saw a cluster of buildings. A flutter that could be flags.

"Maida," Yeager said. "Port of entry." He turned left on a less maintained gravel road. They bumped along in silence for a couple miles and then Yeager turned right into a rutted path. Just two tire tracks running off into the green, empty, treeless horizon. But they were well-worn tracks, no grass growing in them. Yeager drove slower now, the weeds swishing up to the windows of the cruiser. Finally he stopped the car. "Let's get out, stretch our legs."

They walked down the path. Yeager pointed to the ground that was damp enough to clearly show fresh tire treads. "Mulberry Crossing. Active." They continued walking. A hundred yards further and the path turned and paralleled a slight road embankment. A yellow sign was set in the ground next to the tire tracks that climbed the embankment. It said: ILLEGAL BORDER CROSSING.

"See how easy it is," Yeager said.

Broker nodded. "This is Canada."

"Yep. And in good weather this prairie road will support a tractor-trailer. Pick a no-moon night. Turn off your lights. From here to the road we came up on," Yeager pointed back toward his cruiser. "Maybe twenty seconds and you're across. Like we were talking before, less and less people living out here now. And them that do, hell, they all shop in Canada, because the dollar buys more. They see somebody coming through here at night, it could be their neigh-

bor buying fertilizer at a forty-percent savings. Just come across, go
east, in an hour you're on the interstate.

"So," Yeager went on, "ephedrine is still easy to get in bulk in
Canada. Say, a case of seventy-five thousand pills might go for eighteen thousand bucks. Makes about eight pounds of meth that
wholesales for around forty-eight thou. Figure a hundred cases of
pills in a trailer. Adds up to serious money."

Broker squinted back toward the customs station. "What about
the border patrol?"

Yeager smiled. "They say they got sensors, but I don't hear any
alarms going off, do you? They started sending more bodies up
after 9/11. Guys mostly with names like Martinez, from Texas.
Right after they started showing up, that first October, it was about
thirty-eight degrees out and I noticed them all out in front of the
Motor Inn plugging in the tank heater on their shiny new Tahoes.
So I go over and ask, 'What's up?' 'Getting cold,' they said." Yeager
shook his head. "They come and go in thirty-day rotations, like
R&R. Hell, I understand they need a break, they got some hairy
duty down south. But the point is, they don't stay long enough to
know the ground. And they don't patrol, anyway. They sit on the
official crossings."

Broker shifted from foot to foot. Thought of starting another
cigar to keep his hands occupied. Clearly Yeager was laying foundation, leading up to something. Gamely, Broker tried to hold up his
end of the conversation. "They just watch the crossings?"

"Yeah. Used to be, when the customs shut down the border and
went home from ten P.M. to six A.M. they'd put orange plastic cones
across the road. Of course, after 9/11 they geared up for heavy-duty
action and built these little steel gates. Border patrol, they watch the
gate. And, sure, there's a few aircraft overhead from time to time."

Broker decided to start that cigar. Yeager popped his Zippo,
giving him a light.

"So," Yeager said.

"So," Broker said.

"Point is, the border patrol's number-one priority up here ain't to stop our meth problem. Not now. Like, say, take our friendly smuggler who usually drives a load of ephedrine pills, or kitchen cabinets, or flush toilets."

"Toilets?"

"Yeah, we had a run on full-capacity flush toilets a while back. You know, we got all these environmentally correct toilets now that use less water—you gotta flush two, three times. They were bringing truckloads of the big five-gallon jobs down, some of them right through where we're standing. Any rate, point is, one night our driver hauls a different cargo. Maybe he don't even know what's in his trailer."

Yeager squinted down the rutted track back toward his cruiser. "Like, say, a full load of Stinger missiles. Or those Russian SA-18s. That'd play some hell with the air traffic pattern."

"So you guys been brainstorming scenarios, huh?" Broker said.

"You bet. Your wife's caper has a terrorism angle all over it. And we wouldn't have had a clue if she wouldn't have used your kid as a prop. I don't know if that was brilliant or just plain cold—but once your sheriff buddy called and asked us to get tight on the kid, we got onto you, and then we started getting pieces of the whole picture."

"Look, Yeager. Nina and her crew are cowboying, way out ahead of something. I got a feeling the big-footed feds will roll into your shop any day with the official word."

"I don't think you're hearing me, Broker. What good is some fancy helicopter full of commandos gonna do? Hell, they don't know what it's like out here on these prairie roads at night. Me and the boys grew up here. We can keep track of Ace and Gordy. It ain't like they're going to do anything with Nina along. Or didn't she think it through that far?"

Broker thought about it. Yeager was right. But so was Holly.

Once the words *nuclear device* were put into the mix there was no telling how even steady-looking dudes like Yeager would bounce.

"Yeager, I just came up here to get my kid." Broker didn't sound convinced and Yeager sure wasn't.

Sensing that Broker was weakening, Yeager remained patient. "Okay, come on. Back in the car. We got one more stop."

They got in the cruiser and backed out of the trail and drove the roads on the American side. For Broker the empty monotony of these fields now took on a sinister sweep. There was just no way to stop a simple suitcase coming across.

After a mostly silent ten-minute ride, Yeager wheeled his cruiser into a weed-thick driveway and drove up to yet another deserted farmhouse. A windmill tower stood beside the house with just the gears up top, no blades. A collapsing barn leaned off to the side, and a rundown Quonset hut out back. This house had a narrow front and a high-pitched roof, its two upstairs windows empty of glass and the front door, torn away, looked like gaping eyes and a mouth.

Yeager leaned back in his seat and lit another Marlboro.

"This is where Ace Shuster lived when he was a kid." He pointed south. "Our house was about two miles that way, and it's in worse shape than this place."

"What are we doing?" Broker asked.

"Figured I'd bring you up to speed on Ace, since he's become the object of all this intense interest."

Broker had to grin at Yeager's style—laid back but relentless.

"What? You got something better to do?" Yeager grinned back.

"So you're going to take your time, give me the county tour. Spend half the day out in the tullies and maybe my cell phone will ring and I'll have to go somewhere and you'll just have to take me there."

"Hey, Broker, you got a suspicious mind. You should be a cop."

"I already met Ace."

"What'd you think?"

Broker thought about it. "At first he seemed like this aging hell raiser, and then . . ."

"Yeah?"

"His eyes. His eyes were . . . sad."

Yeager nodded. "The whole family is just a little bit"—Yeager gently waffled his hand—"off center. His sister, Dorsey, was the one who showed it most. And then, I guess, the kid brother, Dale. The dad, Gene, he was crazy but disciplined. Always cooking these wild schemes to get rich, but always worked like hell. Now, Gene's dad, Asa—he had the outlaw gene. A regular bomb thrower, back in the days of the Nonpartisan League . . ."

The term *bomb thrower* got Broker's attention. He'd been sitting back, hands crossed in his lap. He came forward, opened his arms, draped one back on the rear seat. Put the other hand on the dash. More attentive now, he said, "Sounds like some family."

"Yeah. I think their mom, Sarah, she just checked out and went on automatic pilot. Like one of those women you read about back in the old days: too much work, too much prairie. The wind gets to some people. The winters . . ." Yeager chewed at the inside of his cheek, looked off across the fields. "Ace, he was the oldest kid. Thing I respect about Ace is the way he fights to keep that outlaw gene at bay. Gets up every morning and has to choose twenty-four hours of not breaking the law. That's a tough one. Another thing, he pretty much looks after everybody."

"You saying Ace has *real* psychological hang-ups?"

Yeager shrugged. "Hard to tell with German farm stock. Everybody keeps it in. Then they get behind with the bank, have a couple bad years, and we get a call from an anxious wife with supper cold on the table. Sometimes find the guy's body out in the corner of a field with his shotgun next to him. Ace? He ain't exactly your Prozac kind of guy, so he maintains with alcohol."

The question was on his face so Broker went ahead and said it: "Not the bomb-throwing type?"

"Ace? Is that what they think?"

Broker decided to take the chance that Yeager was waiting for. "Okay, here we go . . ."

Now Yeager was sitting forward. "Yeah?"

"They got a picture of Ace standing near McVeigh at Waco."

Yeager rolled his eyes. "They're basing this whole circus on a fucking *picture*?"

"I didn't say that. But they have a picture."

"Hey, man, these people gotta do their homework," Yeager said, getting more animated. "Remember I mentioned his sister, Dorsey? Well, she was wild as hell in high school and then did one of those come-to-Jesus flip turns. She started chasing religious cults. Word got back she was hanging out in this wacko compound in Texas. Turned out to be Koresh's operation. So Ace went down there, just about the time the ATF did their famous ninja walk in their pretty little black suits."

Broker braced himself. "So?"

"Once Ace got down there, he found out that Dorsey had been there but split a month before. Ace eventually found her in Seattle, working in a Starbucks coffee bar. Married some guy and is still there, as far as I know. A happy ending." Yeager squinted at Broker. "If I was *you*, I'd put a little more faith in what people say over coffee at Gracie's diner and less in the people who breeze around in black helicopters."

"Okay, maybe he doesn't want to blow up federal buildings— could he be the kind of guy who would run *anything* across the border for money?"

Yeager kind of sidled closer, on the scent. "Anything? Like something real dangerous?"

"C'mon, Yeager . . ."

Yeager wagged his finger in Broker's face. "No. Ace wouldn't do that. But that little creep Gordy Riker would. In a fucking heartbeat."

"Why you so sure Ace wouldn't?"

"'Cause I've known him all my life. Look, we played Legion ball together. Jesus, could he hit. He was eighteen and people were saying he was another Maris. He had a shot at the majors, hurt his knee in a tryout camp, and never went back. Just bad luck. That's the story of Ace's life. Nothing ever worked out right for him." Yeager shook his head.

"He killed a guy in a bar fight."

"More bad luck. Goddamn loudmouth Bobby Pease down in Starkweather. Came at Ace with a beer bottle, and Bobby musta been loosey goosey flatfooted when Ace hit him. Broke his neck. Ace did eleven months on the state farm for involuntary manslaughter."

"What about Dale, the equipment dealer?"

Yeager shook his head. "Jeez, I don't know. Parts to that guy are missing. Like, the key to the ignition. Guy is gonna live and die in his folks' basement. He's gonna follow them to Florida."

"And Gordy?"

"Cunning little fucker. And greedy. I been trying to catch him running meth precursor for over a year. He has grandiose dreams of being a big dope dealer."

"Violent?"

Yeager grinned and eyed Broker. "You tell me. Story going round is he knocked you on your ass." He paused, still grinning, then said, "That's how we know you're in on this thing. We figure it was for show. No way in hell a guy like you's going to let a Gordy Riker put you on the ground, shot hand or not."

As Broker was composing his comeback, the car radio squawked: *"Two-forty, where are you?"*

Yeager keyed his mike. *"Six north."*

"Your ten-seventeen just showed up at the SO."

"Ten-four."

Yeager quickly wrote his cell phone number on the back of a card and handed it to Broker. Then he put the cruiser in reverse and backed out of the driveway. "We'll have to finish saving the world later," he said. "My wife just dropped my son off at the office. I gotta coach T-ball."

Chapter Twenty-two

Ace came down the stairs two at a time; edgy, snapping his fingers, shaking it out. Gordy assessed him. Uh-huh. So much for mellow. Ace's serotonin was definitely headed south. It was not a coffee day.

He tossed the cup of coffee he'd prepared and set a bottle of Wild Turkey on the bar with a glass. As Ace sat down and poured his breakfast, Gordy pointed to the *Grand Forks Herald.*

"Inside section. They're scaling back the search for Ginny Weller," he said.

"Ginny was your basic land shark, but she didn't deserve this," Ace said, taking a drink. He produced a Camel from his chest pocket in a snappy display of dexterity, lit it, and inhaled. He pushed the newspaper aside, blew out the smoke, and looked around. "Okay, where'd she go?"

"Out front. On her cell," Gordy said.

Ace took his glass to the window and saw her pacing on the trap rock with her head cocked over in the New American Silhouette: neck straining to cup a cell phone. Ace thought how a whole lot of orthopedic surgeons were going to make out in twenty, thirty years, when all the crook-necked cell-phone casualties came walking into their offices bent over funny.

He took a long, slow swallow and felt the whiskey burn down his throat and rush out to the tiny capillaries in his fingers and toes. He watched the humid prairie breeze catch the summer dress and wash it up around her thighs and hips. A ripple of maroon and green. Alive against her body like a flutter of moths. Or a flag, maybe. A flag just for a woman. It wasn't that she had smallish hips, just tidy and tight, like everything else about her—efficient, traveling light, no padding. And her shoulders were broad.

Those legs and that back. *I bet she swam butterfly in school,* he thought.

Probably had her kid by C-section, with those hips.

If so, there'd be a halfmoon scar under her belly button.

Just over her bush.

So am I gonna get to see that scar, or what?

Gordy came up beside him. "One way or another she's going to fuck us up."

Ace kept his eyes on her and thought, *Aw shit, Gordy is probably right.* So much for believing life could move like a soft, easy dance. Course, she was far from soft and easy. He was tired of slow dancing. It was time to make a call. "Don't doubt it for a second," he said. "Like you said, she don't add up." He cuffed Gordy on the shoulder. "She'll be gone before dark."

"'Bout time."

"Yeah. Now, look, something's going on. I don't know what you all were doing downstairs but I just saw her husband meeting with Jimmy Yeager across the road." He reached out, clamped his hand on Gordy's shoulder, and pulled him in closer. "Tonight, you work your jigsaw extra special to see if you got a tail. I'll do the same. If we got company we'll run 'em through an old-fashioned snipe hunt." Ace winked. "Let's have some fun out on the gravel."

"Awright, boss—*awright!*" Gordy smiled.

Finally.

"It's me, I want to talk," Nina said.

"So talk," Broker said. He had been pacing in the motel room, watching the Weather Channel, mulling over his drive with Yeager and his missing pistol. Hearing her voice, he admitted to himself he had been waiting for the cell to ring, and now it had.

"Face-to-face," she said.

"You had lunch?"

"No."

"There's a restaurant a block from the motel. Gracie's. It's right on the highway."

"I'll be there in fifteen minutes. Did Kit get off home?"

"Lyle Torgeson and Doc Harris flew in and picked her up this morning. She'll be with my folks later today. You should give her a call."

"Not a good idea right now."

"Right, I forgot. Mission over men."

His remark killed conversation for several seconds. He imagined her mind maneuvering in the silence.

"Fifteen minutes," she said finally in her clipped, hard voice.

Broker found himself sitting up, leaning forward, hovering over the tiny phone. "You need a ride?" But the connection had ended.

Broker heaved up off the bed, stripped off his clothes, peeled the bandage from his hand, walked into the bathroom, and ran the shower to revive himself after the long, hot ride along the border. All the shower did was concentrate the humidity into liquid jets. He stood under the needles of water, eyes shut. Then he held his injured hand up to the shower and let the spray irrigate the ragged flesh.

Jane's salve worked. The swelling and redness were going down. He got stuck, went blank, and then realized he was staring at a

Barbie Doll, naked flesh-colored plastic, awkward jointed hips and arms, sitting on the soap tray like a crumb left behind by his daughter, part of a trail leading into the forest of his marriage. He picked up the toy and observed that Kit had cut the doll's red hair short.

So it looked like Nina, or perhaps Jane. He put the doll with his toilet articles so he wouldn't forget it.

One towel. Two. Trying to get dry. Then, gingerly, he tested the smaller, but still red, fan of infection radiating from the wound. Still tender. He applied the Bag Balm and taped on a clean dressing. As he took two of the Vicodin, it occurred to him that ten years earlier he'd have ignored the wound; it wouldn't have slowed him down. He felt every one of his forty-eight years as a specific weight dragging on his body.

He shook his head and swore softly as he pulled on a pair of jeans, cross trainers, a T-shirt. The idea of finally sitting down with Nina brought on a snap of resentment—at finding himself caught up in another of her projects.

They had not planned on getting married. But, then, they had not planned on getting pregnant. Maybe she thought, given her chosen line of work, it would be the only shot she'd have at a child. Maybe he thought that having a kid would nudge her out of the Army. No, not maybe.

She thought he *wanted* her to get pregnant, his assigned role in the male plot to boot her out of the service.

No, Nina, I just think Mama, Papa, and baby belong under one roof.

So, you can come to Europe.

Or, you can come home.

So you can stick me in the kitchen with a kid and an apron.

Broker shook his head. Ten minutes after he'd met her he told her straight out she had a chip on her shoulder. And she fired right back:

That's no chip. Those are captain's bars, mister.

The fact was, she was a disaster in the kitchen.

He looked one last time at the Weather Channel, how the green mass of precipitation was finally moving out of the upper Midwest. The local report said scattered showers. He eyed his rain parka and decided to leave it. Then he clicked off the TV and left the room.

He grabbed a Styrofoam cup of motel coffee in the lobby and went outside, lounged against the hood of Milt Dane's Explorer, and lit a another cigar. He assumed she'd come walking into town from that bar. Or maybe Shuster would give her a lift.

Ace.

Carefully he mulled the all-too-ready image of Nina waking up in bed with . . .

He dragged on the cigar a little too hard and got some smoke down his throat and coughed.

Shit. So here he was dead in the water, waiting for her to come down the highway. The Missile Park was about a mile west down Highway 5.

Broker remembered back to the beginning. He should have picked up on the clues when he visited her apartment in Ann Arbor—when he met her she was on academic leave from the Army, finishing up her master's in business administration at the University of Michigan.

Her place looked like somewhere Dracula slept between night shifts. Spare and functional. TV dinners and beefed-up vitamin shakes in the refrigerator.

No houseplants. No cat. No paintings on the wall. The only personal item sat on her desk. A trophy from the national military competition pistol shoot at Camp Perry. Second place in the fifty-yard offhand with a .45.

Make a note. Never marry a woman who can outshoot you with a handgun.

When Nina barged into his life he had been dating a woman named Linda who worked at a nursery north of Stillwater, Minnesota. Linda had long black hair she pinned up with a turquoise clasp and always managed to look like she'd just stepped out of a grove sacred to Demeter. Always had her hands plunged in potting soil and wood chips. Good old Linda. Always listening to Minnesota Public Radio. Ripe as a D. H. Lawrence love scene.

C'mon, Broker, tell the truth. Linda would have bored you stiff after a while.

Never bored with Nina. Never once.

Broker spotted her. A stride of color coming at a brisk step down the gravel shoulder. He got up. Check it out. See. It was impossible to be bored and mad at the same time.

Okay.

The watery light licked her bare arms and legs. She wore this meager sleeveless summery dress that came down to mid-thigh and gave her the look of an R-rated Monet in motion. Red-painted toenails in Chaco sandals. And, naturally, she'd never worn a dress like that for him. Strictly jeans and shorts and working duds. Or a goddamn Army uniform. Seven years of married life and they'd been together less than three.

As he waited and sipped his coffee, his eyes swung up and down the highway, out of habit. He spotted Yeager leaning against the side of the county office building across the street. Ostensibly taking a smoke break. A moment later Yeager was joined by another cop in different uniform, a darker shade of brown on top, gray striped trousers below. The state patrol guy. Cute. Both of them playing cop face, affecting sunglasses on a sunless day so they could watch without showing their eyes. A boy, seven or eight came out of the building and talked to Yeager. They all went inside together.

A few minutes later she walked up and they stared at each other.

Broker drifted his eyes across the street to the county building. "We're in a goddamn fishbowl here. They're real suspicious about you over there."

Nina scrunched her lips. "Yeah, so is the guy I'm with."

"With," Broker said.

They locked eyes. Let it sputter between them.

"Yeah," Nina said. "Gordy bet Ace I'm a cop."

"Great," Broker said. He turned and they fell in step, walking east toward the restaurant.

"He's a strange guy, Ace Shuster," Nina said. "Not what you'd expect."

"I hadn't thought about it," Broker said.

"Bullshit. You've thought about it in great detail. Just like I thought about it when you told me about your fling with Jolene Somer."

Snap and hiss in the close space between them. Like a live high-tension wire that got loose.

"Yeah, what about your Ranger captain in Bosnia—Jeremy," Broker shot back.

"I *necked* with Jeremy once. You *fucked* that tramp Jolene."

"So this is what? Payback?"

Nina smiled briefly. "Ace hasn't even tried to touch me." She paused for effect and bored a look into his eyes. "Yet."

They went into the restaurant. Nonsmoking booths on the left, counter front, tables and more booths to the right. They sat in an open booth to the right.

A waitress in tight toreador pants and a deeply tanned face brought them water and a coffeepot. Broker ordered a late breakfast: ham, eggs, no toast, no potatoes, oatmeal on the side. Nina ordered an omelette. She raised an eyebrow.

"Oatmeal *and* eggs? I thought you were strictly oatmeal. That's all Kit will eat for breakfast since you brainwashed her."

Broker shrugged. "Maybe that Atkins guy has a point. I'm checking it out."

Nina grinned. "You had a birthday last week. The old waistline creeping up on you?"

"I'm doing fine."

"I don't think so." In a completely disarming move she leaned across the table and laid the inside of her cool wrist along his forehead. "You're running a fever and I'll bet that hand is infected."

The day heaved when she did that. Broker almost wanted to stayed glued to her arm, but it moved away. *She's fucking that guy, I know she is and she'll never admit it. Never should have told her about Jolene. Never.*

Their orders arrived and Nina was all business. Broker struggled to give her his full attention, but between his smoldering anger, the mild fever, and the painkillers, the edges on things got blunted. Nina looked faintly screened, distant.

"Get in touch with Jane and Holly," she said. She took a pen and a business card from her purse and wrote on the back. "Here are their cells"

She slid the card across the table. Broker turned it over and saw the pine-tree logo of his resort: Broker's Beach.

Nina started to say, "They're staying—"

Broker cut her off. "I know. One of the local cops told me. They're at an Air Force radar site east of town. Along with some rough trade in a Black Hawk."

"Aw shit."

Broker pressed on. "Remember the famous Shuster-McVeigh photo op? Well, it's total bullshit. Pure coincidence. Shuster was at Waco looking for his nutzy sister, who was reported to be in the compound. She wasn't. He found her in Seattle."

"You know this how?"

"One of the locals told me this morning."

Nina stiffened slightly when the highway patrolman entered the café and started toward their table. He was snappy-looking in his uniform, duty belt, and Smoky Bear hat.

He passed their table smartly and inclined his head in a deferential nod, just as polite as can be. "Broker. *Major* Pryce." He continued on and sat down at the counter, his back to them.

Nina sagged and stared at Broker.

"I tried to tell you. You're wrong for this kind of work. All you guys are. Once Jeff back home heard our kid was stranded in North Dakota he called the local sheriff. Asked him to keep an eye out for her. That raised a flag. It is definitely not SOP for abandoned children to have sheriffs in other states immediately start calling and asking personal favors. It suggests I'm connected. So, Wales, the local sheriff, did some checking around with the Minnesota AG's office and got an earful about me and then about you. The Vietnam trip in '95. The rumors about the gold. And you being a big Army celebrity after the Gulf."

Broker leaned forward. "You have a reputation. Some terms got thrown around."

Nina's glower was frayed at the edges. She was exhausted. Playing barfly with Ace was eating up her reserves of control.

Broker raised his eyebrows, questioning. "So the sheriff asked me what the Purple Platoon is."

"There is no Purple Platoon."

"Of course there isn't. How can there be? It's part of Delta and Delta doesn't exist."

"Are you through?"

Broker shrugged. "Just saying, you should have gone to these guys, they probably have some real undercover resources—this being their turf and all."

Nina shook her head and looked out the window. "If we don't run out this grounder, there could be . . ." Her voice petered out, exhausted.

It struck Broker that he had not taken the time to really study her face in minute detail since he'd hit town. He did so now and saw that she had acquired the streamline of sheer necessity; hollow, driven, almost like a haggard statue of a woman who had been pretty in real life. But now her human touches did not survive the translation into metal. Not his wife anymore. Not a mother. She'd turned into this fucking iron mask of . . . courage, duty, sacrifice . . .

Broker had seen that look on people's faces before. People who were getting ready to die for something. It made him furious.

"So there it is," Nina said.

Jesus, Broker, get ahold of yourself. This was serious, he told himself. Not personal. He tried. "So what do you want me to do?"

"Tell Holly something's staging up with this George guy tonight." She shivered, hugged herself. "But it's weird because this Indian guy named Joe Reed made a point of letting me know Ace and George are going to meet at some old missile sight east of town. This Indian is all screwed up—missing fingers, face burned to hell . . ."

Broker nodded. "I saw him at the equipment dealer across the road from the bar this morning." *And I'm pretty sure he made off with my .45. But I ain't telling you that.*

"He's real bad news. I get the feeling he's been . . . trained. Then there's Ace's weird brother, Dale. God knows what he's into. Gordy's easy, he's just a minor thug with delusions of grandeur. Holly needs to check them all out. There's something about them as a group that doesn't track," Nina said.

It was crazy. Broker watched his rising frustration appear like some brain-dead clown dancing in front of his eyes. He couldn't throttle it. Couldn't find a way to tell her he was worried sick about her.

He smiled tightly and pointed at the broad back of the highway patrolman, up at the counter. "If I was you I'd ask him to check out your Indian. Probably knows him by his first name."

Nina scowled. "I can do this, goddammit."

Broker narrowed his eyes and it jumped up between them—their marriage, their personalities, the whole rolling ball of wax jammed full of razor blades . . . "No, you can't. You're going to screw up. C'mon, Nina. Admit it. You're not a soldier. Not really. Armies are human systems that depend on cooperation. You've always been a prima donna. A lone wolf."

"Oh, right, and when did you turn into Mr. Cooperation! You spent so long out in the cold that half the cops in Minnesota think you migrated to the other side."

It was coming apart at lunch, in front of maybe a dozen farmers and one state highway cop.

"Just saying, you should listen to me on this one." Broker lowered his voice. But it was too late. She was frayed, nothing but bare wires.

She stood up and jammed her finger. "Stop trying to tell me what to do."

Heads turned in the restaurant as Nina walked out. An older guy in a feed-store cap removed the filter cigarette from between his teeth and said, "Now, that girl was ticked."

Broker stared at the egg yolk on his plate. When he raised his eyes he saw that the state patrol cop had swiveled in his counter chair and was watching him. Patient, like Yeager. Waiting.

Broker looked out the window, saw Nina striding back up the road. He looked down at the numbers she'd written on the back of the business card. She could easily have made the calls.

But you want me in the middle of this thing.

Chapter Twenty-three

"This is Jane."

"How you liking that Air Force chow? As I recall, the zoomies always did have the best clubs . . ."

"Who is this?" Then. "Broker? Where the hell are you?"

"What a bummer. I know where you are. You don't know where I am. What kind of show you guys running, anyway?"

He was pacing in front of the TV in his motel room hunched over with his cell tucked in the crook of his neck. On the Weather Channel, the green glob of precipitation was breaking up to the east over Minnesota and Wisconsin, still spotty over the Dakotas. Northern Minnesota, Kit's destination, looked clear. Good flying weather. He clicked the picture off.

"I say again: Where the fuck are you?"

"On the job at the old Motor Inn, girlfriend." Upbeat Broker. A tad raunchy, ramping up for it.

"This is not good. Where's Kit?"

"Some friends flew in and collected her this morning. She should be home by now."

"And you decided to stick around? This is not in the plan. You're cluttering up the board."

"Be advised, your plan is made out of Kleenex." Broker walked to the end of the room, pulled the drape aside, and watched the raindrops start to splatter below, on the asphalt. "And, if you listen carefully, you'll notice that it's starting to rain." He reflected that Jim Yeager's T-ball game might be rained out.

After an interval of silence, Jane said, "So what do you want?"

"I just had a talk with Nina. She says to tell you it's getting sticky, like something's going to happen tonight between Ace and some guy named George. She also wants you guys to take a look at this Indian dude, Joe Reed."

"Why am I getting this from *you*? *She* should call me."

"But then I wouldn't be in the loop, huh?"

"Aw, man, look—her Indian will have to wait. We're more interested in Ace and George Khari. What else?""

"I want a meet with Holly. Face-to-face."

"Holly's busy."

"I can imagine. Smoothing things out with the front office, huh?" No response.

"You'll do, then," he said. He could practically hear her hackles snap to attention.

"Why should I?"

"'Cause I just went on a scenic tour with one of the indigenous personnel. And he ticked off some items. Like you and Holly hanging at the radar station down the road. And this Black Hawk landing there with a gang of knuckle walkers and some nerdy tech types. Oh, yeah, and he hears there's this hoop by the hangar and you got a fair hook shot."

"Shit."

"Why are you surprised? It's their turf. And there's more, girlfriend."

"Don't call me that. More what?"

"Let's meet."

"Shit. Where?"

"Somewhere midway on the road's fine. You still driving the Volvo?"

"The Volvo's been seen in town. I'll go for a run. I'll be coming west down 5, toward town."

"In the rain?"

"I won't melt."

"I'm leaving now. I'll keep an eye out for a moving cloud of steam."

"Fuck you, Broker."

"I don't think so. Your heart'd give out."

Broker grinned as she abruptly ended the connection. He was getting past the deadlock in the café with Nina. *Which was what she wanted.* Uh-huh. Because he'd do the ground work with the locals. Goddamn her, anyway—playing coach, getting him warmed up and in play.

Broker pushed the Explorer through the light rain, east down Highway 5. The geography had become a fixture: the wall-to-wall slab of sky, the perspective of two-lane blacktop shooting a plumb line through the green flat, thinning down to nothing. The most common things that grew over four feet tall were the telephone poles, power lines, and cell-phone towers.

He was leaning forward over the steering wheel, juices starting to stir. Past his initial frustration, he guessed why Nina wanted him to stay on here. She knew he'd naturally find an in with the locals.

And he could feel the same frenzy to do something that gripped Nina, Holly, and Jane. But doing *something* does not mean doing *anything*. If their tip was real, they would have only one chance.

And it wasn't Ace Shuster or Gordy Riker they were after. It was the people who were picking up from Shuster and Gordy. This George maybe? The Indian?

And Nina'd only have one chance, if they showed themselves.

And if that happened, he wanted in.

Like Yeager did. And his buddies.

He saw her motion before he got her outline. A flicker of white and gray, and brown skin. Smooth energy pulsing down the shoulder, on the right side of the road. He pulled over, put it in neutral, and waited. The rain moderated, then slowed to a few drips and he watched the cloudburst trundle away in the flat gray sky, trailing dark tatters.

As Jane ran closer, Broker compared her to Nina. Younger of course, and . . . he searched for a word and settled on Nina's— *trained.* She had learned that smooth stride to eliminate excess motion. Jane didn't seem to come by it innately, unlike Nina, who had these lazy fluid kinetics. Nina made everything look so easy. Almost slow, you thought, and then she was on top of you in your face, or past you and it was too late.

Broker suspected that nothing had ever been easy for Jane, and most likely men were the reason why. Not a trifling insight for a man who had a daughter.

She came in close now and he saw she was wearing a scissored-up white T-shirt with *Cancun* printed across the front, dark shorts, and worn New Balance shoes. She also had a fanny pack slung around her waist on thick webbing, sturdy enough to keep it from bouncing. Big enough to accommodate a cell phone, and probably a Beretta nine. As she yanked open the door and hopped in, he noticed she wore no metal. Just raindrops today. The ear piercings, the nose stud, the ax thing around her neck. Gone.

He handed her several of the motel towels from the backseat and waited while she scrubbed some of the rain from her face, neck, and shoulders. In that moment, as she leaned forward, arms raised, chasing the rain from her short hair with the towel, she looked disarmingly feminine and unguarded.

"Why'd you stay?"

"You guys need all the help you can get."

She glared at him.

"I was asked," Broker said simply.

Jane narrowed her eyes, then slowly nodded her head. "Nina. When you delivered the suitcase at the bar and got knocked on your butt."

"There it is."

"So what do you have in mind?"

Broker said, "If something is on for tonight, you need the local cops. They know every stalk of wheat in the fucking county."

"No way. The locals hear what we've got, they'll shit their pants." She paused and gave him an intense stare. "They haven't *heard*, have they?"

"They didn't have to. They already figured it out."

Jane slumped back in the seat.

Broker pointed across the road, north. "I been up there. I seen the border. It'll break your heart."

Jane pushed forward, plopped her elbows on her carved knees, and stared into the middle distance. "Holly's in deep shit. The pogues in Homeland Security are bitching to Special Ops at Bragg. Justice and Homeland Security are involved. They say we've exceeded our mandate. Fuckers. We weren't supposed to have a mandate. We're supposed to be totally in the black."

"How long have we got?"

She held his eyes for a few beats and said, "We, huh?"

"Yeah, we. How long?"

"Holly's arguing that right now. They want to pull our backup. But we might have something with this Khari guy. He's Syrian-Lebanese, out of Grand Forks. Owns a warehouse and a chain of liquor stores in the Dakotas. Turns out there's a lot of Lebanese around here, especially in South Dakota . . ."

Broker nodded. "Ex-senator Abourezk."

"Who? Never mind—this Khari guy was Ace's dad's liquor supplier. He's an immigrant, born in Beirut. His father was active in the Popular Front for the Liberation of Palestine. Khari came here at nineteen, after his parents were killed in the civil war. He was raised by the mother's brother in the Maronite Catholic Church. He's not a Muslim. In fact, Lebanese Christians don't even consider themselves Arabs. Just Lebanese. We got a team on him with a parabolic mike, trying to monitor his phone conversations." She made a face. "It's pretty thin. But it's our only chance. Except now some honcho from Homeland Security is on his way to keep an eye on us."

"If tonight involves something coming across that border, you better bring one of the locals," Broker said.

"And you already got somebody lined up, huh?" Jane said.

"Just a cell phone call away. Deputy named Yeager. Because you guys won't be able to find your butt up there in the dark."

"What else did Nina say?"

"That the gig with Ace is pretty much up. It's turned into a game. Gordy and Ace have a bet. Gordy bet Nina's a cop. Ace took the bet. So he's playing along for the drama."

Broker smiled one of his non-smiles and continued:

"Sometimes undercover work is like the flip side of being a cop. The target knows you're undercover, but he can't prove it. Knowing how to play out that tension can be the trick that produces results. They're playing a game, all right. A game of chicken."

"You said that. I didn't." Jane folded her arms across her chest. Her arms came away sopping wet. Broker handed her a third towel. She draped the towel over her shirt, unzipped her fanny pack, and fingered out a Marlboro filter and a lighter. She lowered the window and lit the cigarette. After she blew a stream of smoke into the sodden air, she turned to Broker. "Doesn't it bother you? What she's doing?"

"Sure."

With a burst of pique or frustration, Jane came forward in her seat. "Nina talked about you. How you screwed around when you did your UC stuff as a cop. How it destroyed your first marriage."

Broker held up his hands. "*Chieu hoi.*"

Jane screwed up her face. "Holly says that. I don't know what it means."

"It means 'I surrender.'"

"*Ana la takakalum Vietnameaziah.*"

"Come again?"

Jane smiled. "Means 'I don't speak Vietnamese.' I'm the closest thing to an Arab-speaker in the group." She squinted, poked her cigarette out the window. "Is that the sun?"

"No, just a lighter shade of gray. But it's clearing."

"Yes it is." She opened the door and got out of the car. Broker opened his door, came around, and joined her. She puffed on her cigarette and stared across the flat green. "So do it," she said. "Bring in the locals for tonight."

"Just one."

Then she turned to him and said, "Three days ago we were in Detroit with the hottest tip in the world. Now look at us. In the middle of nowhere with some suit on his way to pull the plug."

Broker shook his head. "Not so. There's a reason Shuster's name came up. You gotta run it out. And there's another thing. You only think you're in the middle of nowhere."

"Oh yeah?"

"Yeah. The fact is, right now you're standing in the absolute center of things. Like the North American continent."

"No shit?"

"No shit. That's why they put all the missiles here."

Chapter Twenty-four

Nina needed the walk back to the bar to get herself back under control and stop swearing. Goddamn marriage like a goddamn broken jukebox—get every goddamn song in the box at once.

All of them variations on him always trying to lord it over me.

At moments like this she had to take the time to center herself back in her job. She always used the same image: a room full of Kits—Kit at two, at three, at four, and five. A couple dozen Kits. That's what that day-care center in New Jersey was like the night of 9/11. She wasn't positive the story was for real, but it had gone around the teams so regularly it had acquired the force of truth. According to the story the staff became so distracted with shock that nobody really told the kids why most of their parents wouldn't be coming home from the Towers.

She saw those kids waiting, caged in the seconds and minutes and hours, until slowly they started to cry. Maybe one of those kids would have taken it upon herself to go beyond her own fear and doubt to stand up, go over and help the other ones, comfort them.

That kid would be the dummy, the one saddled with the frontline preselection factor, the one who felt the need to take care of the others. There were always a few dummies who felt the duty to go up front. Like that day at the Towers, tens of thousands coming out, hundreds going in.

Dummies like her.

And, goddammit, like Broker.

The thing gnawed at her. It was the knot cinched tight at the center of her marriage: Did two people like her and Broker belong together? They each knew all about going in first, and nothing at all about backing off.

And what a wonderful mom I've turned out to be—taking my kid on her first op at seven.

She kicked at the gravel along the side of the road. Ouch. Not a good idea in sandals.

God, where the hell did they get so much sky? The clouds grew right up out of the earth. Piles and piles of gray clouds stacked in the fields and going up and arching overhead like a Sistine Chapel of clouds forever.

Then it started to rain and she ran the last hundred yards and came back in the bar with mud spattered up her calves. Ace was not reading the newspaper. He stood behind the bar twirling his finger around the rim of a tumbler half full of whiskey. "So how'd it go?" he asked. She noted that the passive repose had departed his manner. Now his eyes were moody, hot, sulking; they measured her in a certain way, undressing her.

"Fuck him." Nina sank into a chair at the table.

"You already did that," Ace said over his raised glass. "Maybe you should try fucking someone else who appreciates you."

Uh-oh. First there was Dr. Phil. Now comes the direct approach.

She made a face, stood up, and went into the bathroom and washed the mud from her legs. Twenty-four hours ago she would have been willing to go to bed with him, if there was no other way of getting the fix on a target. Now they had a fix.

When she came out of the john, the rain shower had stopped.

Ace came around the bar, antsier than he'd been, but still attractive. The way a guy in a beer commercial is attractive.

She gave him an honest, tired, thirty-five-year-old-woman look: On top of everything else, do I have to put out—*now*?

But she was still mad at Broker, no faking that. And Ace picked up on it. The natural rebounder, he would catch her in midair, coming off her fight with Broker.

And she saw how it could happen. A revenge fuck.

In the line of duty.

Ace grinned at her quandary, put his empty glass on the bar, and said, "C'mon, let's go for a drive."

Nina slumped in the passenger seat while Ace pushed the Tahoe down South 1. He listened to a crop report, turned off the radio, flung his hand at the fields. "Right at the saturation point, three days of water's about all the grain can stand. Don't start drying soon, it's all gonna turn to green mush."

They passed a deserted crossroads: empty store, gas station, the remnants of a miniature golf course, and this phone booth sitting out all alone. Nina leaned forward in her seat. In the distance, across the highway, a huge concrete pyramid started to rise out of the ground, four, five stories high, with a circular facing on it, like a bull's-eye.

"What the hell?" she said.

"Our local ruins. Nekoma. That's the radar for the old ABM system, the Spartans, like that picture I showed you. Never was used. They negotiated Salt II and they shut 'er down." He winked at her. "In high school, senior year, I knew this girl named Sally Solce. We used to come here to make out."

"I was beginning to think you weren't interested in sex. Just family counseling."

Ace grinned, pulled to the side of the road, turned off the engine, and said, "Sally was a great believer in pyramids. Said they gathered energy . . ."

Nina eyed him sidelong across the suddenly charged distance between them. She felt the color creep up her throat. She squirmed on the seat and the rustle of her tight thighs against light cotton on the leather upholstery generated a zip of static electricity.

". . . And not just any old kind of energy," he said, smoothly turning, getting closer.

Okay. Here it comes.

But their lips just bumped. His opening move came to grief on bucket seats. They were separated by the shift console, a storage compartment, a travel cup in its plastic socket.

Nina realized her hand had come up to her throat. What was this coy act? Was she starved for attention? *How long since I've been kissed seriously?* She didn't even know how to backtrack into the subject. Was she even the kind of woman who gets kissed seriously anymore?

Ace grinned and laughed. "Thing about high school and Sally was, I had this old Chevy, three on the tree. The seat was more, ah . . ."

"Friendly toward gathering energy," Nina said tartly. "That was then. This is now. I'm too old to fool around in cars, or fields."

Ace mouthed a silent laugh. "You're right. That's for kids." Abruptly he cranked the key, put the car in gear, and started to drive.

The uses of silence. In the quiet refuge of her thoughts, she concocted sexual scenarios. Starts, stalled middles, and no finish. Just couldn't make it work.

But the flush clung to her cheeks. Her freckles must look like copper rivets. But she could only allow herself so much indulgence. The lapse ran its course.

Now they passed through the town's one flashing red light and were going the opposite direction, north. Not casual. He was very deliberate today. Like he was working through stations.

More forever fields to go with the forever sky. Add desolate deserted houses. They pulled into an overgrown driveway. Now what?

Ace got out, fingered a cigarette from his chest pocket, carefully not revealing the pack. Broker had told her about that one. Old yardbird reflex—hide your smokes from the other cons. He lit it with a plastic Bic, then stood smoking and staring at the gray wood siding and broken windows and the weeds. The collapsing barn. A rusted Quonset.

He marched forward and she followed him until they stood on the cracked concrete next to the side entrance to a mud porch.

Ace pointed at a rusted twenty-pound propane tank that lay on its side on the steps. The kind used in gas grills. It was surrounded by other trash—Pyrex two-quart measuring cups, Mason jars, rectangular Corning dishes, worn-out plastic funnels, discarded rubber gloves.

"Tell me what you see," he said.

Nina shrugged. "Lots of junk. Somebody's old grill tank."

He studied her face. "Why's it stained blue all around the brass valve?"

"What is this, twenty questions?"

"Only two so far," Ace said. He turned and walked to the back of the house.

"Where are we?" she asked.

"I grew up here. Tried farming here. Place has been abandoned for years."

"Somebody's been here. Look." She pointed to the carefully raked sand in a frame of weathered railroad ties. "The sandbox is clean."

Ace squatted on his haunches and trailed his fingers through the rain-pocked sand. He reached over and picked up a tiny yellow tractor with a shovel on the front. The detail on it was too exact for a toy. It was the kind of replica some men keep on their desks. He put it back down where it had been, next to two half-destroyed sandcastle towers. More ruins, eroded by the rain.

"Dale, probably. He comes out here. Sometime he brings a sleeping bag and stays up there. In our old room." He pointed to the broken window on the second story.

"That's pretty sad."

"Oh, I don't know. Dale's smart enough. He functions fine. He's just socially . . ."—Ace scrunched his eyebrows looking for a word—"remote. Like, he got to this threshold and decided not to come out and play. I don't think it's a limitation. I think it's a choice he made."

"How about friends?" Nina made it sound like a logical question. Just talking along.

"Not really, except for Joe Reed. They been hanging out together the last couple of months."

Her voice speeded up. "The guy with the burns and the bad hand?"

Ace nodded. "Pinto Joe. Got burned up in the Alberta oil fields. Well got away on him. Caught fire."

"Where's he from?"

"Don't know for sure. He don't say. Turtle Mountain, I guess." Ace said. His hand floated up and touched her lightly on the cheekbone, under her eye. "You got to work on your eyes, Nina. When something catches your attention it's like shark fins turning on a dime in there."

"What's that supposed to mean?"

"Means, you want to know about Joe, you better go ask Joe." He walked past her, toward the Tahoe.

Driving again. Back to town. Mile by mile, she felt the tension building. She almost had to laugh at the extra freight the female soldier was obligated to carry. If captured, she could expect to be raped. And, like they drummed into you, her whole body was a weapon—to include, apparently, what nature put between her legs.

If war was an extension of diplomacy by other means, was sex, too, an extension of war?

She did laugh.

"What?" Ace asked.

"Nothing," she said. She had been through Airborne and Ranger school. She had been to Escape and Evasion. She had shot pistol on the Marksmanship Unit. Eleven years ago she gunned down two Iraqi Republican Guards close enough to see their eyes react to her bullets. That was hot-blooded killing. Now she was looking straight at cold-blooded sex in the line of duty.

She made practical calculations. Six days since her period. Probably should insist on a condom. Get some health history. *And get a hold of yourself. Stop acting like a piece of driftwood coming in with the tide.*

Do your job, goddammit. Afterwards he might open up and talk. That was the idea, wasn't it?

They spoke hardly at all on the drive back to the Missile Park. Some of it had to do with a shift in the air; here and there patches of sun collapsed the cloud chapel, dappling the fields with light.

He parked in back of the bar, got out, and opened the back door. She followed him inside, through the storeroom into the main bar. The lights were out. Gordy was nowhere in sight.

Ace walked to the bar, sat on a stool, and stared at his reflection in the mirror. She sat on the stool next to him.

"So what are you going to do?" he said staring straight ahead, talking to her reflection.

"What do you think I should do?" she said to his reflection. She thought about how mirrors work. They throw back reversed images, right? Like little lies.

"Okay, then." He heaved off the stool, walked to the stairway, and went up to the apartment.

Nina stood up, squared her shoulders, and climbed the darkened stairs.

He was waiting in the small living room. There was a bottle of Seagrams on the kitchen table. He got two glasses from the draining board and poured two short drinks. He handed her a glass. She sipped the whiskey then set it on the desk. He tossed down his drink, put the glass back on the counter.

Then he stood, hands at his sides. Not gloating or even expecting much. More like, just very much present, as if he knew the few things he was good at. He was a player who knew how to make a play. He knew how to touch a woman.

And as if borne by a swell, she drifted up to him. He put his arms around her and kissed her. She let herself go, melting into him.

Ace was obviously a good time. But, holding him, she could feel the hollowness. Could almost smell the doubt filter through the whiskey on his breath, taste it pump in and out of his lungs. She knew that a strong enough wind would blow him and his party-time erection away.

But she managed a reasonably wanton kiss, part nostalgia for things missed, part exploration, but with not too much tongue. Just enough to jolt his circuits. Then she drew back and looked at him. "So what is it you think you know?"

His blue eyes were half wary, half joking. But honest. "The only thing I know for sure is when some other man's wife wants something she ain't getting at home."

"Like now?"

"We'll see." His practiced hand moved up her butt and followed the seam of the zipper at the back of the flimsy, outrageously expensive dress Janey had picked out for her. Like a bead of cool mercury, the zipper ran down her back. Then Ace stepped back to watch.

Nina kicked off the sandals. Then she wiggled her shoulders in an instinctual move. As the cotton slipped over her shoulders and down her arms, she watched his melancholy eyes as they studied the ripple of light and shadow play down the front of her body.

Not desire so much as curiosity. And this sense of waiting for something.

And then she realized she was doing it wrong. The thing she always did wrong with men. There was something they always expected from her at times like this. Something she wouldn't give them. Since junior high she had been training herself to never show fear. Or anything remotely like it. Broker was the only man she'd ever met who seemed to understand. Barefoot naked or with a fifty-pound ruck on her back and muddy boots, she always looked the same:

Ready.

"This isn't a strip show," she said defensively as the top of the dress fell past her breasts. She wasn't wearing a bra and her breasts were nothing special—tidy and functional, with a faint webbing of stretch marks.

She reached down and firmly took hold of the elastic on her panties. With a little shift from foot to foot she peeled them down below her navel.

Ace said, "There *is* a scar."

"What?"

He pointed at the faint cesarean incision peeking from the reddish hair just above the rolled waistband of her panties. "I figured you had a C-section. The narrow hips . . ." Then he said, in a different tone, "*Wait.*"

A drop of nervous sweat streaked down the puckered flesh on her belly. A squirm of nerves, gooseflesh.

"What happened there?" he said.

He was pointing at the deep-purple dent on her left hip. The entry. His hand moved around her hip, smooth across her ass, and felt the bumpy slick whorl of scar tissue where the Republican Guard's Kalashnikov round blew a chip of pelvis out through her glutes.

"That's a gunshot wound," he said.

"I can explain," she said.

The self-deprecating joke came stronger into his eyes. He raised a hand to quiet her. "It's okay. I just had to find out how far you'd go. You would have gone all the way, right?"

"I don't get it. What are we talking about? This? I told you, I can . . ." Indignant, she pointed at the bullet hole.

Ace shook his head. "I'm sure you can explain it. And the cut ear. And I'd probably believe you. That ain't it. Every woman I ever been with in my life except working whores and country-club land sharks—they're always a little bit vulnerable when they takes their clothes off, at least at first. You're not exactly comfortable, but you're miles from vulnerable, girl. You ain't afraid one bit."

Nina curled her lip, played it tough, and shot back, "So this is what happens after all the talk? You're not even gonna fuck me? Just talk some more?" She shifted her stance, not sure what to do with her hands or the rest of her. So she reached for the whiskey on the desk.

And he said, "You probably don't drink in your real life, do you?"

That brought her around sharp. *Too fast, Nina, too fast.*

Ace smiled. But his sad smile was gone. This was a cold smile. Cold struggling not to turn into mean. "I wanted to believe we met for a reason. And I guess we did. The reason is you're working." Then his expression hardened. "Cover up your ass. And get your things. We're through here. Take a walk. Back to your husband. If he is your husband."

Chapter Twenty-five

Dale had a few errands. First, he stopped at the Alco Discount and bought several sets of heavy bungees. Then he bought some blank videotapes. He spent a few minutes looking at the digital gear. He would definitely have to upgrade, but later. He didn't have time now to install a new TV, DVD player, and figure them all out.

He drove south, to the ruins of Camp's Corners and parked in back of the buildings. The old gas station had a garage and he pushed open the rear door of the mechanic's bay and went in. An eighteen-foot 2001 Dodge Roadtrek camper van was parked in the bay. He'd purchased it a month ago in Grafton.

He walked up to the boxy vehicle and inspected the new paint job. When he bought it, it still had the scorch marks around the windows from the propane fire that had gutted the inside. So he got it cheap. A body shop in Grafton fixed up the outside and finished it off with a new coat of light blue.

Then he gave it to Eddie Solce, who refurbished the inside and put in a cheap chemical toilet. Dale didn't need a sink or refrigerator; a cooler with ice would do—he wouldn't have the vehicle that long. He did have Eddie put new carpet down in the rear compartment, and Dale had set up his old wooden twin bed there.

Nowhere near as fancy as when it was new. But functional. Just a curtain behind the buckets seats now. And the bed, freestanding next to a makeshift closet with shelves. A TV and videocassette player that would run off the battery. Various other items were strewn around.

He placed the bungees and the blank tapes on the front seat. Then he opened the briefcase Joe had brought and sorted through the contents. An envelope containing cash. And two Minnesota license plates. He selected the license plates, went out, took a screw driver from a toolbox on a worktable, and removed the blue-and-gold buffalo-motif North Dakota plates. Then he screwed on the pale-white-and-blue Minnesota plates.

He got back in behind the wheel and started it up. Sounded good. And a full tank of gas. Joe had topped it off from two five-gallon cans now sitting empty in the corner of the shed.

He turned off the engine and took a tackle box from the floor under the passenger seat. It contained a number of different containers, several were plastic prescription drugs. One was written in German. Others were glass vials with rubber stopper tops for the insertion of a hypodermic needle. They contained a clear liquid. Dale held one of them up to the light coming in through the dirty windows, read the label, and smiled.

Ketamine.

Joe had acquired a cache of the stuff. Before Joe, Dale had broken into a veterinarian's office in Cavalier to get the drug.

A dozen fat yellow plastic pens were stacked with the pills. Another of Joe's innovations. They were Epipens, prescription dispensers for epinephrine, first-aid injectors for people susceptible to anaphylactic shock. Joe had some people in Winnipeg remove the original contents and refill them with 100 mg doses of the ketamine.

Dale hefted one of the pens in his closed hand like a dagger. You just twisted the top. A sturdy needle extended from the bottom and you jammed it in a muscle group. The spring-loaded mechanism in the pen delivered the dose. When used as a general anesthetic during surgery, it was fed directly into a vein through an IV. The intramuscular route was slower and let you feel the effects come on over a period of minutes. Ketamine totally paralyzed people for a short time. And for some people, it simulated the peculiar out-of-body sensation of dying.

He selected one of the Epipens and slipped it in his chest pocket. Then he looked around one last time, walked out, and closed the door. As he got back in his car, he felt a ray of sunlight poke through the clouds and warm his face.

It was a good sign. Joe was getting anxious to get on the road, was questioning some of Dale's ideas. But Dale had zero doubts. It was gonna work out just fine.

He started up the Grand Prix and drove back to town. When he got into Langdon, he took a fast swing past the high school to get a little edge going. In twenty-four hours he would be on his way to a whole new life.

Outta here.

The Shusters had lived in a comfortable four-bedroom prairie rambler on the east end of town. The house sat on three lots, and Dale had always cut the lawn—his dad expected it since Dale had converted the basement into an apartment for himself.

Dale Shuster. Never been on his own, people said.

Now, with his folks two weeks gone to Florida, and all the rain, the grass was creeping up the post of the FOR SALE sign in the front yard. Dale had not cut the lawn since his folks left, and now it was so high it flipped over on top like a pompadour.

He parked in the garage and went inside. The main floor and up-stairs were empty, just furniture runners on the floors that the movers had left. The kitchen table remained, and two chairs. The sink was full of dirty dishes.

His mother had left notes taped to the refrigerator and the cup-boards about when to thaw and eat each meal she'd left stacked in plastic containers in the freezer. He opened the fridge, which con-tained nothing but Coca-Cola, twenty cans of it.

He snapped the flip top on a can of Coke. Took another along for backup, and went down the stairs into the basement.

The basement was stripped.

Dale had not so much packed as given everything away to the Lutheran church his mom had gone to, mostly alone, for the last thirty years. Except for his computer, which he'd smashed into a pulp and dropped in Devil's Lake. All that remained was a desk, an arm chair, and hassock in front of the TV.

He still had the VCR set up. It was so old nobody would want one like that anymore. Just leave it when he . . .

No. He did not intend to *move*. He was going to *change*. Reappear as a totally new person. But first he had to do this favor for Ace. More of a favor than Ace had ever done for him.

Gordy. Dale smirked. Gordy had mocked and bullied him all his life. Well, Gordy was about to get his heads-up.

His barren desk set against the wall under an old *Star Wars* poster. Barren except for his high school yearbook. Dale sat down and flipped the pages to the senior pictures until he came to the picture of a younger, smiling Gordy Riker, looking like a toothy, hairy werewolf zit.

With a deliberateness of ceremony, Dale reached up to his chest pocket, moved the stubby Epipen aside, and grabbed the thick-nib Sharpie. His breathing came more rapidly, and a squeezy bubbly sensation started in his chest as he methodically blacked out Gordy's eyes with the pen.

Then he turned forward a few pages and studied Ginny Weller's picture. Her eyes, too, were blacked out.

Not so pretty now—huh, bitch?

Real funny. Ha ha. It was supposed to be a joke. For their senior trip, the whole class went for the weekend to a hotel in Bismarck. To see a play. He should have figured it out. How come the prettiest girl in the class all of a sudden started seeking him out, sitting next to him? Paying him attention.

It happened the second night, late; Ginny had dared him to go skinny-dipping with her in the hotel pool, which was closed for the night but she knew a way to get in.

Just the two of them. The naughty taunt in her voice.

"Come on, you scared? Don't you want to see me naked?"

At this point in his life Dale was considered shy; quiet but not that weird. He had a B-plus average. Played linebacker on the football team. Kept his turmoil carefully tucked away inside. Kept a certain distance from people, especially girls. He had this notion that if you kissed a girl—one of those open-mouth, slurpy French kisses—she might be able to see down your throat, right inside, all the way down to all your secrets.

Everybody left Dale alone because he was Ace's brother. But halfway through senior year, Ace hit Bobby Pease, over in the bar at Starkweather. Ace spent the next year hoeing beans down in Jamestown.

So why was Ginny Weller flirting with him? He knew it had to be some kind of a game. Maybe she was trying to make Irv Fuller mad. When her talk didn't work, she maneuvered him into a corner in the lobby and planted one of those French jobs on him, sticking her tongue between his teeth.

After that he couldn't resist. Though he was scared plenty, because the farthest he'd been with a girl was messy hand jobs with dumpy Margie Block up in her dad's hayloft.

He had to give it a try.

They met in the hall, at midnight. She showed him how she'd put tape on the lock to the door in the ladies' room that led to the pool. Taped it on vertical, up the inside edge of the door, keeping the lock bolt from engaging.

They slipped into the darkened bathroom. Ginny told him to go on in and undress. She'd meet him in a second and they'd go skinny-dipping.

"For starters," she'd said.

A chance like this would never come again. So Dale went in, stripped off his clothes, and waited in the darkness. There were little lights along the bottom of the pool that cast wavy shadows on the ceiling. It felt humid and smelled of chlorine. The longer he waited, the more excited he got.

And when he had become real excited, and no Ginny yet—that's when the lights exploded on.

And there was Ginny standing by the door with Irv and Gordy Riker. They pointed their fingers and rocked with laughter.

"Boy," Irv sang out, "that's what I call real hard."

"And real small," Gordy chimed in, moving forward and extending his hand. He wasn't just pointing. He had a squirt gun and proceeded to squirt Dale in the crotch. Dale covered up and ran to the other side of the pool, to where they kept the towels, but there weren't any towels.

To his chagrin, Dale discovered that Gordy's squirt gun had been filled with cheap perfume. And for the rest of the trip, and all during the bus ride home, people kept saying: "You smell anything? I sure smell something."

The nickname "Needle-Dick" became common usage.

Dale smiled, took the videotape from his desk, and fed it into the VCR. He pushed the play button on the VCR remote. As the screen flickered into focus, he settled down into his chair, raised his hips slightly, and unbuttoned his jeans.

Chapter Twenty-six

"This is Jane."

"Game over. Ace just gave me the boot," Nina said.

"Not to worry. You got all your stuff?"

"Yeah, I'm doing my famous walking-down-the-highway-to-town."

"Did you keep your legs crossed?"

"Turns out he wasn't that kind of guy."

"Nina, they're all that kind of guy."

"Well, what have we got?"

"We got movement on your tip. Khari, the liquor dealer in Grand Forks, is planning a road trip tonight. Bugs got a parabolic mike on his house. Overheard a call to Shuster about the special pickup. It tracks with what you told Broker. Distinctly heard him say they'd meet at the RLS on 5. That's missile talk for the deserted Remote Launch Site east of Langdon. So Bugs will be tailing him. Holly is standing by with the bird if we need him. We'll follow Ace, in case the meet on the highway is a diversion."

After her awful scene with Ace, Janey's upbeat voice was a blast of relief. Nina's knees trembled, a little weak. "Great," she said, "where do you want me? I'm out here all alone, walking down a country road half-dressed."

"Hey, I thought you liked that dress. And I got a feeling you won't be walking alone for long."

Before Nina could ask Janey where she was, the call ended. Nina kept walking, looked back once. Okay. A deserted pole barn and some trees broke the line of sight to the Missile Park. If Ace was watching her she'd be lost in the roadside clutter now. She was almost to the airport. From Janey's remark, she figured they were close. But where? She squinted down the road: patches of sunlight alternated with muggy afternoon shadows.

Then she caught movement to the right, a figure stepping from a grove of trees, an arm whipping in a tight circle. About forty yards off the highway, standing in the thick stuff behind an abandoned Quonset. Hand signal: *Rally on me.* She hefted her travel bag and started up the rutted trap rock driveway. When she came closer and entered the trees, she saw it was Janey.

"What's going on?" Nina said.

Janey stood casually in jeans and a dark pullover, one hip thrust out, a cigarette hanging from the corner of her mouth, like a B-movie moll. She said, "Watching Ace. He's talking on the phone, to George. Like I said. I doubt he can see out the window and through this building. On the other hand, if you climb up top this Quonset you can get a fair view in through the living room window. With these." She held up a pair of binoculars. "Quite a little striptease going on for a while there." She handed over the smoke. Nina took a drag and handed it back.

"How long you been here?" Nina grimaced.

"We been here all afternoon. Since you and Ace rolled back in."

"We?"

Janey yanked her thumb over her shoulder and said, "This way, darling. We is now a *combined task force.* Ad hoc, mind you."

"Ad hoc, huh?" Nina glowered, then said, "Sounds like . . ."

Broker was standing deeper in the brush, spraying mosquito repellent on his arms and face. He handed the cannister to a husky
man with short-cropped brown hair. He was wearing jeans, boots,
and a long-sleeved shirt over a T-shirt. The shirt did not quite hide
the dull twinkle of a pistol holstered on his belt. Broker's truck was
parked in the tall clump of Russian thistle.

As she approached, Broker softly clapped his hands in a lewd
take-it-off rhythm. Jane left them and scrambled up a makeshift
ladder made of several old air conditioners stacked together. She
leaned over the top of the building next to the boxy capola of an ex-
haust fan and trained her glasses on the Missile Park.

Down on the ground, the guy standing next to Broker extended
his hand. "Deputy Jim Yeager, Cavalier County Sheriff's Department. It's a real pleasure to see special ops in action."

Nina dropped her bag and shook his hand. Broker took a step
closer and said, "We concluded the man is very fast, considering the
brief amount of time elapsed from when you first showed some skin
to when he booted you out the door," Broker said with a straight
face.

"Fast on his feet, as it were," Yeager said.

"Right, strictly a vertical encounter. No reclining going on that
we could see," Broker added.

Nina's glare was wasted in the shadows. Broker and Yeager, however, were like two Cheshire cats, gleaming teeth floating in the
gloom.

Broker handed Nina her go-bag, which Nina snatched from his
hands. "Assholes. How about you turn around."

"You'll need this." Broker handed her the can of OFF!. To their
credit, Broker and Yeager let the ribbing die and turned around.
Nina quickly sprayed a chemical bath, slipped out of the dress, and
flung it at Broker's back. It draped over his head. He raised the ma-
terial in one hand and sniffed it, but said nothing.

Nina opened her bag, pulled on a pair of loose jeans, a sports bra, a baggy gray T-shirt, and a pair of black cross trainers. As she strapped on her pistol belt, she took a deep breath and let it out. Beneath the raunchy banter and her gruff reaction she felt a palpable aura of relief. She was in and out unscathed, and something was up.

And she and her husband were finally doing something together. She smiled as she checked her .45 auto in the hideout holster, made sure that it was on safe. Not exactly dinner for two and theater tickets, but what the hell . . .

She swatted at the bugs. "Damn critters are out in force."

"All the rain," Yeager said. "If you got a long-sleeve shirt in that bag, I suggest you put it on."

Nina, stooped to her bag and pulled out a slipover and put it on. The mosquitoes hovered in close, probing, like little pin pricks of anxiety.

"So," she said, "does your boss know what you're doing, Yeager?"

"Let's say I'm staying flexible," Yeager said.

"He's flying by the seat of his pants, like you," Broker said.

"Anybody ever check out that Indian guy?" Nina asked.

"I called the BIA police at Turtle Mountain," Yeager said. "They got a Joe Reed on the tribal roll. But nobody's been in contact with him for two years, since he went up to work the oil fields in Alberta. Story is he got burned in an oil-rig fire."

Nina shook her head. "Those scars on him are a lot more than two years old."

"You got a point," Yeager said.

"So now what?" she said.

Broker toed the ground. "We wait."

Chapter Twenty-seven

Dale ran the tape over and over until the light in the small basement windows went from gray to black and then he watched it one more time in the dark.

Then he went upstairs and microwaved one of Mom's frozen suppers. Lasagna. A favorite. After his meal, he stacked his dirty plate in the sink, went into the garage, and took his bike off the hooks on the wall.

It had been a while since he'd been on a bike, but his plan for tonight made it necessary. He rode a little shakily through town and took a side street that paralleled the highway, following a roundabout route to the Missile Park. Just as he was approaching the intersection with State 5, he saw Ace's Tahoe going east, toward town. He strained his eyes to see if she was in there with him, but the light was already too faint and he couldn't tell.

He continued on around back of the bar and saw Gordy's Ford F-150, then Gordy, girded in his back brace, standing in a cone of light and swarming bugs under the utility bulb over the loading dock door. Gordy spotted him, eased off trundling the four cases of whiskey on his dolly, and laughed.

"What's so funny?" Dale said.

"You on a bike." Gordy squinted. "Where's your car?"

Dale shrugged as he got off the bike, dropped the kickstand, and parked it next to the truck. "Little exercise can't hurt."

"You shoulda thought of that starting about ten years ago," Gordy said.

Dale gave him the finger, looked around. "So where'd Ace go just now?"

Gordy grinned. "Working, for a change."

"Where's the woman?"

"Gone. He kicked her out."

Dale shook his head. *Uh-uh. That can't be.* He fidgeted from foot to foot. Not part of his plan. She was supposed to still be here. "Maybe he took her along," he said hopefully as he trudged up the steps to the dock. The woman had to be there at the end of the night; without her, it was gonna be a long couple days of terrible work. No play. Damn.

"Don't think so." Gordy paused, yanked a red bandana from his hip pocket, and mopped sweat from his forehead. "We had this bet. I got a hundred says she's a cop. At first Ace wasn't sure. But don'tcha know it, I was right."

Dale shook his head, struggling to disguise his disappointment. "How did you find out?"

"It's not like she told me, man. All I know is she's gone."

She'd be back, Dale was sure. He changed the subject. "So what are you sending to Canada tonight?"

"The last forty cases in the basement, most of it Jack Daniels. I appreciate the help, but I figured you got more than being a helping hand on your mind."

Dale took the dolly from Gordy, went into the storeroom, worked the dolly under a stack of cases, tipped the cases back, and wheeled them outside. "Well," he said, "I did talk to Ace, and he ain't real pleased about the meth traffic. Especially if there's cops snooping around. Maybe you could hold off till we're outta here."

"For sure. The guys up north say there's some kind of squeeze going on. And Ace says I got to be extra careful tonight. Play some hide-and-seek, keep the lights out," Gordy said.

Dale forced a grin. "Like in high school, drinking beer. Dodging the sheriff." He wheeled the load into the truck and eased it off the dolly.

They worked in silence as they finished up the load. Gordy pulled a tarp and a cargo net over the cases, fastened it down, and then they sat on the loading dock and waited as the real dark inked over the fields. Dale watched the lights come on brighter in town, peered at every car that went by.

"So, they could be watching us?" he said.

"Yeah, and *they* could be anybody—deputies, state guys, who knows? But we'll lose them in the dark." He cuffed Dale on the shoulder. "Be fun, huh?"

"Yeah," Dale said, trying to cover how bummed he was inside. What if she was really gone? He had trouble seeing his way through what lay ahead without taking her along.

The traffic quieted down, and after nothing went by for fifteen minutes, Gordy decided it was time to go. "It ain't like we're breaking any laws," he said. "Just unloading this stuff in Phil Lute's old garage, on the U.S. side."

Dale insisted on taking his bike, so he hooked it in the back of the truck, in the webbing of the net. Then they drove slowly across the highway and headed north until the lights of the town receded and they were the only set of beams poking through the fields.

The way ahead was all black except for two faint farmyard lights. Gordy aimed at the solid blackness between them. When his tires left the asphalt and hit gravel he pulled over, killed his headlights, and parked. The smell of damp, ripening wheat and canola rolled in through the open windows.

"Fuckin' mosquitoes," Gordy said, swatting his cheek. He leaned over, popped the glove compartment, took out a can of insect spray, and gassed the interior of the cab.

Dale held his breath and didn't protest. He'd grown up with this, sitting by his dad. They needed to keep the windows open to listen.

They waited and listened for half an hour. When nothing unusual happened, Gordy eased the truck over the gravel road—no lights, methodically working off tenths of miles on his odometer. Then he finally turned and followed the skeletal gravel trace of a prairie road into the wheat. He had whole sections of the road grid memorized, and he counted as he drove—". . . eight-one-thousand, nine-one-thousand, bang. There it is, right up there."

Dale got out and helped Gordy back up. He could just make out the mass of Lute's swayback garage, backlit by a trickle of moonlight—all that remained of the old farmstead. They were sitting in the middle of a field, within fifty yards of the border. The Canadian pickup crew would creep down from the north along the same prairie road and load the booze later that night.

Gordy came around from the cab and dropped his tailgate, then suddenly hissed,"Don't move . . . freeze." But Dale was already still, motionless. He saw the headlights knife the dark. But a good two miles away.

"Cops?" Dale said.

"Don't know." They waited until the lights went out. Then, ten minutes later, the lights came on again, this time headed back toward town.

"Probably somebody just shopping in Canada," Gordy said. He opened the garage door.

Dale took a step inside, feeling his way, and knocked into a pile of light cardboard boxes. "Hey, what's this?"

Gordy flashed a tiny pencil light. "Boxes," he said.

Unmarked boxes. Dale hefted one. Light. A rattle of cellophane and tinfoil.

"Okay. So it's cold medicine. Ephedra," Gordy said. "C'mon, ten measly boxes."

"This could get us all sent to jail."

"Get off it. Everybody from here on down through Montana to Idaho is cooking meth. Home brew, private use. A few boxes. C'mon, it'll just take me a minute to stash it."

"Where you gonna put it?"

"I thought maybe Irv's old house."

Dale grinned. He liked that idea a lot.

They worked quickly, Gordy handing down the whiskey, Dale stacking it. Then Dale passed up the flimsy cardboard boxes. They were light, practically empty, but Dale began to gush sweat. The night smothered him in green humidity rising off the dewy field.

It was nerves made him sweat so bad, so he unbuttoned his shirt, took it off, carefully folded it, set it aside, and worked bare-belly in the dark.

"You all right?" Gordy asked, a little alarmed to see the normally modest Dale throwing around his beefy white gut.

"Fine," Dale wheezed, using his hand to mop sweat off his face and sodden chest. Swat the bugs.

When they'd tossed the flimsy boxes in the back of the truck, they waited and listened again. Dale put his shirt back on, making sure his Epipen was still secure in the pocket. Then they got back in the truck and drove slowly in the dark till they came to an intersection. Gordy cruised blind for a few minutes, then he pulled up a driveway.

Dale began to smile, and with the smile came a flash of hesitation. He was remembering how, back during the missile time, they played here as kids. He pointed to a thick apple tree in the front yard. "Remember we used to climb that sucker, hide in the upper branches from Irv's mother?"

"Back when you could still climb, huh, Needle-Dick?" Gordy said, jabbing Dale in the side.

You could always count on Gordy to say the wrong thing at the wrong time. His smart-ass remark wiped away the last quiver of doubt. Dale patted the Epipen in his pocket and stared at Gordy. "I told you, asshole."

"Yeah, yeah. C'mon, we'll throw them in the root cellar."

They each grabbed two of the bulky cartons and walked toward the house. Gordy had a battery-powered light bar hooked over his thumb. He put down his boxes, opened the slanted door to the root cellar, and peered in.

"What?" Dale said.

"Stinks."

"Probably gonna get worse, too," Dale said. He reached in his pocket and slid out a pair of Latex surgical gloves, slipped them on.

Gordy went into the musty cellar. Horror-show cobwebs; wiring in the joists dating back to 1910. He poked around and stamped his feet in the sediment. He rested the light bar on a ledge in the uneven stone wall. Then, energetically, he put together a rough platform out of rock debris and old lumber, so the boxes would sit up off the damp floor. Then he waved a hand at Dale.

"Dale?" he wondered aloud. "How come you're wearing gloves?"

Dale ignored the question and handed one of the boxes to Gordy, then paused and selected a board from a pile of loose lumber stacked on the rickety stairs next to the fieldstone foundation.

"Lookit this old piece of oak. Bet this is a hundred years old."

"Yeah, yeah, gimme another box."

Dale turned the board in the pale light. "Got a big-ass spike in here. But it's bent." Dale studied the problem then hooked the bent spike on a ledge of rock and grabbed a piece of debris that had fallen from the wall. Holding the rock like a hand hatchet, he banged down on the top of the board.

"What the fuck are you doing?"

"Straightening out this nail."

"Very cool, Dale, except that ain't no nail. That's a pole-barn spike. How about you hand me the boxes."

"Coming right up." Dale whacked the board again and inspected the result: the rusty nine-inch spike was mostly perpendicular to the board. While Gordy shook his head, Dale set the board aside and picked up one of the boxes and passed it down.

"By the way, what's got Joe all pissed off?" Gordy asked.

Dale smiled. "He's done with you. Especially after that Sioux City business."

"Ah shit, I'll make it up to him," Gordy said. But he looked glum. "Sioux City was a bummer."

"Whole trailer packed with crates of full-capacity toilets down from Winnipeg. He runs the border, drives like crazy down to outside Sioux City. And then nobody's there to unload them. He has to unload them himself and hide them in a barn. Not the ideal job for an eight-fingered Indian. Those toilets are heavy . . ."

"Yeah, yeah. I owe him."

"Ah, I don't know. You were right about Joe being sneaky. I did catch him in a lie once."

"Fuckin' Indian, don't surprise me."

"Yeah," Dale said as he turned away and removed the Epipen from his pocket. He twisted the top, felt the needle engage, tucked it in his cupped hand, and turned back around. "Last April, Joe was loading cases in the storeroom at the Missile Park. He didn't hear me come up on the dock. Thought he was all alone. He's in a hurry and he tips the dolly and dumps these cases on his foot . . ."

"Dale, c'mon."

". . . Starts swearing like I never heard. Whole string of words, only a couple I could remember. One I sounded out: *nik-o-mack.* Another was *zarba.*"

"*Nikomak*? Sounds kinda Indian," Gordy said.

"I thought so too, so, for kicks, I checked around on the Internet, and you know what?"

"What?"

"This was a surprise to me. I couldn't find anything on Ojibwa, but I did get into a site about a Cree dialect that's close to Ojibwa, and you know what? They got no cuss words. Got about twenty words for fuckin' snow. But no profanity."

Gordy stared at Dale, clearly exasperated.

"Took me all night surfing all these websites about swearing in foreign languages, but I finally found *nikomak*." Dale grinned slowly, his whole face lighting up.

"Good for you," Gordy said, starting up the steps to get the other boxes.

Dale turned, sweeping his hand forward at mid-thigh level and jabbed the injector into Gordy's thigh. "Fuck your mother," Dale said contemptuously as he tossed the used injector in the dirt between them.

"Oh shit!" Gordy grabbed at his punctured thigh, shook his head. "What the—?" He stared at the fat yellow dispenser lying at his feet. Anger came fast after surprise, and he swatted at Dale. Tried to grab him.

But Dale fended off Gordy's hand. "Fuck your mother—that's what *nikomak* means. Don't you wanna know in what language?"

"I about had it with you. What'd you stick me with—some nail?" Gordy, angry now, balled his fists.

"One question at a time. Get this: it was *Arabic*," Dale said.

Gordy blinked, stared. His knees wobbled slightly and he began to sweat.

"You ever notice how Joe never hangs out with other Indians? That's 'cause they could tell he was a fake. See, Joe was born in Beirut. He ain't no Indian. In fact, his mom was Italian. He grew up watching reruns of American TV westerns. He said the Indians in them were always played by Italians. So he figured he could pass for an Indian. Then his folks sent him to stay with relatives in Detroit, 'cause of all the fighting over there. He graduated high school here, in the States. That's why his English is so good. But he went back over there, was in the Syrian army for a while, but mainly he got into the family business, which was growing dope and hating Jews. The downside to messing with Jews over there is, they come back on you, big time. At some point, they shot him up pretty good."

Gordy shook his head, took several breaths, staggered back against the wall. Suddenly it felt like this bag of ice cubes was leaking through his chest. And his fingers were falling asleep. He tried to focus on this new information coming from weird Dale. Then the cellar started a slow spin, like a scary carnival ride.

Dale extended his thick arm, placed the flat of his hand on Gordy's chest, and shoved him hard against the wall. "You gotta pay attention. There's two Joes, okay? Joe *Reed* was some Indian guy from Turtle Mountain. Our Joe, who ain't the real Joe—his real name is Joseph Khari . . ."

Gordy put out his hand on the wall for support, squinted. "That's George's . . ."

"Yeah, they're relatives. He ripped off some Indian's identity, up in Alberta. I guess they kinda looked alike. Any rate, he killed the guy, had new ID made. He knows people that do all that shit in Winnipeg—false IDs, counterfeiting, this incredible computer shit," Dale said, cocking his head to the side. "The thing about Joe and George is, they kill people if they have to. Hell, they almost killed me 'cause I heard Joe cussing in Arab."

"I don't feel so hot," Gordy said. For the first time his voice caught in his throat. He had a sensation that something very big now loomed over him, and he could almost hear the crack of fear start to break his night apart. His arms weighed a ton each. Couldn't lift them.

"Woulda killed me, too, if I hadn't pointed out a few things." Dale drew himself up and tucked in his shirt, which had been hanging out since they unloaded the whiskey at Lute's garage. He smoothed his hand down his sloping chest and stomach. "They say killing the first one is the hardest. The second one is easier, they say. You think that's true?"

"Please," Gordy mouthed weakly as his eyes rolled up, showing a lot of white.

"Man, you're sad. Ginny, at least she put up a fight," Dale said. And then he kicked one of the boxes and sent it flying into Gordy's face. It bounced away in the dark. "They been using us. You, Ace, me. Before us my dad. To study the border." Dale slipped the board under his arm and smiled. "George has been doing a huge business in meth precursor. Joe handles the Canadian side . . . and the people they're in with are way heavier than the biker clubs up north. Shit, man, they're running dope to finance those suicide bombers over there."

Gordy pitched forward and dropped to his knees and Dale saw he was losing his audience. He talked faster to get it all in.

"But then they met me and now they're onto something a lot bigger than boxes full of cold pills. Oh, yeah, and *zarba*—that means shit. Just thought you should know."

Dale could see the wheels turning slower and slower in Gordy's mind. See him struggling to connect the dots.

"He's an . . . *Arab*?" Gordy was drooling all over his chest as the ketamine really hit him. He fell forward on all fours. Blinking and shivering like a dog, he watched Dale lean over and pick up the yellow thing . . .

Dale weighed the Epipen in his palm. "I stuck you with ketamine. It's slowly paralyzing you. Some people say it feels like dying. Any comments?"

Dale yanked the board up off the wall, wrapped his big hands around it, planted his stance, and drew it back.

"Shit," Dale said, "you'd think I'd be good at baseball, since Ace had such a good swing. But I always struck out."

Putting all his bulk into the move, he swung the heavy board like a Louisville Slugger. Gordy, bent over on his hands and knees, stared straight ahead through dull, uncomprehending, heavy-lidded eyes. Didn't even see the pole-barn spike before it hit him in the center of his forehead.

The spasm erupted out of Gordy's head, an electric jolt that Dale felt momentarily in his own hands. Dale expected more blood than just the red masklike pool around the one eye that was filming over. The breath a deep rattle. The ketamine probably eased the pain a bit. Merciful almost.

Dale squatted and held the light bar close to Gordy's trembling face and studied the life growing dimmer in his eyes. "Told you. Shouldn't call me Needle-Dick. But you wouldn't listen." He took a handful of Gordy's hair and tipped his head back and up. With his other hand, he scooped up a fistful of the loamy sediment from the floor of the root cellar. Slowly he released his fingers so a stream of the sandy soil filled both of Gordy's nostrils. Some involuntary reflex forced a deep cough, his tongue protruded as he struggled for breath.

Handful after handful, Dale slowly poured sand down Gordy's gagging throat until his entire mouth was full and his chest eventually became massively still.

Dale took off the rubber gloves, reached down, peeled up one of Gordy's eyelids, exposing the opaque iris. Touched it. Made a face. It felt like a grape. "In case you haven't noticed, asshole, I've changed."

Dale stood up, dusted off his jeans, marched up the stairs, and closed the door to the cellar. He stood, taking deep breaths of the thick night air. *Damn. I'm getting good at this.* This was the first one he'd done all by himself.

He went to Gordy's truck, took out his bike, and then drove the truck into the empty barn behind the house. He closed that door, too. Then he got on his bike and pedaled slowly down the empty road, the long fields ticking with cicadas on either side. The orange dome of light glowing against the horizon guided him.

And lots and lots of stars above. That meant the clouds were finally clearing out.

Half an hour later he pumped up the driveway to his folks'

house, and there was Joe's brown van. Joe was sitting on the front porch steps, smoking one of those French cigarettes.

"Where you been? George is out there risking his neck for you, to throw them off," Joe said, getting to his feet. Dale could see he was pissed, but holding it in.

"I been looking for that woman," Dale said. No need to tell Joe about Gordy.

"She ain't at the bar, I just came from there. Look, we got to get on the road. And you have to call Irv Fuller. Remember? He has to arrange for a security clearance and a time. It's not like you can just walk in unannounced."

"Too late to call Irv, I'll call him in the morning. And I ain't going without her."

"Listen, there's other . . . women," Joe said.

Dale pointed his finger. "No, you listen. It's *this* woman. I gave you this idea. I showed you how to do it. Without me you'd still be wandering around on the fucking prairie with a ton of explosives. *I'm* making this happen."

Joseph Khari studied Dale Shuster in the dark. Many things passed through his mind; mainly the irony of how a great event could emerge from such a disgusting piece of shit.

"Nothing goes boom without me," Dale reminded him.

If it was up to him, Joe would shoot him and leave him in the driveway. But, in the end, practicality won out. The fat fool was right.

Chapter Twenty-eight

George Khari, driving north from Grand Forks, was thinking numbers. When he looked up, the night sky sparkled with numbers instead of stars. Endless random numbers. It was like a big lottery, see, because, George was thinking, out there in the darkness, millions of people were touching numbers at this very moment. Pressing buttons on wireless telephones, sending signals to towers. Connecting.

Why had he listened to Joe and wired the blasting caps to telephone pagers? Didn't he have enough problems?

The American agents were virtually on top of Dale and Joe. So close yet so blind, because they'd focused on Ace as a target. So George had told Joe to make a point of mentioning his meet with Ace in front of the female agent. He would draw the agents toward himself. He doubted they'd be interested in tonight's petty contraband. If his plan worked, he'd be off the hook. It might even collapse their operation.

George smiled. It was like the weapon itself; sometimes it was best to hide in plain sight.

He'd know pretty soon. The van he'd spotted in his neighborhood and around his store was following him right now, at a discreet distance.

George grinned and shook his head. As a youth he had commanded respect in the Bekáa Valley. Now he was down to running two killers, both difficult to control. He hunched forward and tightened his grip on the steering wheel.

I can do this thing.

The lights, traffic, and general clutter of Grand Forks had faded behind him, and now he was alone with the huge sky and the empty ribbon of road. For more than two decades he had dwelled among these spoiled children; envying and despising them as they ignored the suffering of Arab peoples. Watching them as they busied themselves watching O.J. and Monica, eating bigger portions, driving bigger cars with bigger gas tanks.

But 9/11 got their attention. Though they still didn't really understand. That now it was their turn. For decades they had channel-surfed over mass graves filled with Rwandans, Bosnians, Chechens. A million Afghans. Now viewers in the Middle East would get to recline in *their* living rooms and watch Americans fester and die slowly on satellite TV for a change. Just like the children in the camps. Or burn fast, like his parents, like his own baby and his wife, who met their end in the Israeli napalm . . . manufactured in Midland, Michigan, U.S.A.

It wasn't just about the money.

He turned left off the interstate onto State 5, the road to Langdon. An expanse of night sky now showed through the tattered clouds.

The wind streamlined the clouds and gave the exposed heavens the appearance of a long, ragged black flag dotted with thousands of stars and a haunting crescent moon.

He had never believed.

Allah and Jesus were just two more storybook characters for the instruction of children and fanatics, like the people in the caves along the Afghan-Pakistani border. Or Mr. Ashcroft in his marble cavern at the Justice Department. Their faith reminded him of the Solomon Islanders who formed the cargo cults, who still believed building fires on their jungle mountaintops they could summon the jet airliners down from the stratosphere to land in their midst and deliver wondrous presents.

The jihadists, for their part, believed that if they started a big enough fire in America, it would bring back the Middle Ages. In the end, they would fail. And when they failed, people would want rational answers again, and men like himself—like George Khari— would come back into style. Until then, he would watch for opportunities to make himself useful.

If the price was right. Without the incentive of a payday, he wouldn't be traveling this road. He wondered who would be there. FBI? Local police? Maybe the military? The woman Joe had mentioned, the one Dale coveted—would she be there?

Getting closer; less than half an hour. George shook his head. He hoped Joe was getting Dale out of town. Dale. The brilliant, invaluable fool. He had picked the target. Anyone remotely Middle Eastern could never gain this sort of access.

Parts of Dale were clearly missing. George believed that he was the real fundamentalist, the way he took Holy Writ literally and quoted the Koran to them: *So what's the difference if I kill one person or a million? Huh?*

Dale came up with the idea to put the explosives in one of his machines.

At first the task had seemed impossible, how to make it work? Specifically—how to design the explosives? The answer was in the big tires. They didn't inflate with air. They were injected with antipuncture foam that hardened. It didn't go in an air nipple, like on a car tire, but in a large valve, about five inches across.

So when Dale bought the machine at auction in Winnipeg he also bought a new set of tires. Because they were cheaper in Canada. The tires were empty when they came off the shelf.

It had been one bitch of a job that took them most of a week, working in a rented garage in Winnipeg. The charges had to be configured in a symmetrical pattern. They'd used cheap garden hose, slit it down the middle and opened it up. Then they stuffed it with the Semtex in a continuous chain, taped up the hose, connected the pagers and blasting caps, and fed it in with this big glob of epoxy on the end so it'd stay anchored to the wheel hub. Then they'd jack up a tire, spin it on the hub, and reel the hose inside. They did that four times. Then they programmed the pagers, inflated the tires with foam, and capped them up.

Eventually there were six separate charges, placed to avoid detection. All rigged to detonate simultaneously.

He looked up at the sky. And the crazy sensation came back: that he was trapped inside the biggest slot machine in the world. Spinning round and round with millions of numbers.

Those six separate pagers would be activated by a single group number he had committed to memory.

He just had to laugh. He was a ruthlessly pragmatic man hoist on the petard of the thing he most dreaded: chance.

The pagers were in place, activated, awaiting his call. All he had to do was press seven digits into his satellite phone. But not until the weapon was in position.

And it wasn't in position.

What were the chances of some fool out in the big American night accidently tapping in the wrong number?

His number.

The weapon would detonate prematurely. In which case, there would be no grand reward. No triumphant story attached to his name. He would just be a nobody again, a nobody who had failed.

So he had to hurry this thing along. He had to take Dale in hand himself and make it happen. George stepped on the gas.

Chapter Twenty-nine

They were taking one-hour shifts, perched on top of the pile of air conditioners, keeping watch on the Missile Park. Gordy's blue F-150 arrived at the bar and parked around back. Nina and Broker marked time, sitting side by side in a mist of mosquito repellent. She lit a cigarette to discourage the bugs. He got out his rough wraps.

"When did you start smoking again?" he asked.

"About the time this thing picked up speed." She put out her hand in the graying light and squashed a mosquito on his cheek. It left a small dot of blood. Then she patted his waist. "So, where's your club?"

Personal joke. He was at best a competent shot with a handgun, and usually packed a .45 for its utility as a hefty "tamer," for close-in thumping. "Don't say anything," he said softly, "but I think your Indian lifted it from under the front seat when I was parked across from the bar."

She laid her palm along his cheek. "Broker, Broker."

"Yeager brought an extra shotgun, in the back," he said.

"You won't need it. Holly's crew will handle any rough stuff." She leaned back, then said, "So, did Kit get home okay?"

Broker grimaced. "You know, I never called once this rolled out."

Nina nodded. "We'll call tonight, if it's not too late."

Just ordinary talk, like little building blocks. Repair work. Due diligence. Broker nibbled lightly on his cigar. After several false starts, he said softly, "I'm glad you're all right."

She turned away, almost nervous to be close to him after so long. What if he really did see her in the window with Ace? She turned, faced him. *Jesus, Broker.* Impulsively she reached over and squeezed his hand.

"Ouch." He drew back.

She cringed. Wrong hand. *Story of my life,* she thought.

"You were never one for hand jobs," he quipped.

"Not like Jolene, huh?" she came right back.

"Jolene, as I recall, had three hands."

They moved closer to each other so their legs and shoulders touched.

Yeager passed around water bottles and energy bars from Jane's bag. They ate, they smoked, they were bitten by mosquitoes as the light faded to dusk and then to darkness.

Then Jane's urgent whisper cut through the bug-spray stink: "He's on the move."

She hopped down from her perch and said, "Okay, I'll drive. Yeager rides shotgun. Nina and Broker can neck in the backseat." They walked swiftly to Broker's Explorer that was parked in the tall weeds a few yards away. As they got in they could see the headlights on Ace's Tahoe swing as he turned onto the highway.

Yeager said, "Give him a hundred-yard lead, then pull on the road. No lights."

"What's the deal?" Nina asked.

"Yeager is guide. He knows the roads," Broker said.

"But how do we follow a guy in the dark on a deserted road without being seen?"

"Trust me," Yeager said. "Let's go."

Jane put them on onto the road, following the tiny red dots of Ace's running lights. Then he hit his break lights and turned left just before he came to the town limits. North.

"Keep going, past where he turned," Yeager said.

"We'll lose him," Nina said.

"We keep going," Jane said.

"I don't know about this," Nina said. They drove for minutes, too long. Ace was gone.

"Take the next left," Yeager said.

They swung left and accelerated down a two-lane blacktop. Yeager pointed to the left. "We'll parallel him. See? Those are his headlights." A mile away across the black fields they saw his beams cut the night.

Nina looked around, noticed they were losing the light from town, headed into total blackness. "He's speeding up. We can't keep pace with our lights off," she said.

Jane reached down. "How soon you forget. Remember? We own the fucking night." She reached for a set of night-vision goggles on a webbed elastic headband. In a fast, practiced move, she yanked them over her head and adjusted them to her eyes. Broker made out her profile in the dim spill light from the dashboard—part insect, part unicorn.

Yeager said, "That's what I need, a pair of those . . ."

Then Jane dialed the dash lights down to a bare flicker, stepped down hard on the gas.

"*Ohhhhh shit!*" Broker and Yeager reached for the handholds above their doors as the Explorer bucked, hurtling forward through the rushing darkness. No road in front of the car. No center line. No shoulder. No control. Lots of stars, though.

Jane glanced to the side, her head and the protruding goggles grotesque and alien in the faint glow of the dash. "How we doing, Yeager? Better than lights and sirens?"

Yeager, his feet braced, leaned back and grinned through clenched teeth, enjoying the carnival ride of his life. The headlights to the left fell off behind as they pulled well ahead.

Oh, Jeez. Broker didn't like this. There were going sixty, maybe faster. Maybe seventy. Three, four minutes of it, more . . .

"In about two miles we take a left. We should be able to beat him to Richmond Corners. There's a tree line we can pull into. When he goes by, we'll fall in behind," Yeager said.

"He won't see us?" Nina said.

"Don't think so," Yeager said. "He'll kill his lights when he hits the gravel. What they usually do is creep up to their pickup point. Since there's hardly any moon, he can't spot landmarks, so he'll be going by his odometer. He won't be scared off by anything but headlights."

"Not bad," Nina said. Yeager knew his stuff. Never could've done this on their own. And if they'd gone through channels, there'd be a mob of cops and feds out here cluttering up the road. But this, so far, was just right. She reached over, found Broker's good hand in the dark this time, and squeezed it.

"What do you want?" he feigned wariness.

"Hold your hand, asshole," she said.

He returned the squeeze. Felt good, too. After all this time. Then Jane stabbed the gas and Broker tensed, pressed back in his seat by imaginary G-forces.

Jane, her augmented eyes fixed on the road, had an adrenaline frog in her throat as she shouted over her shoulder: "Don't get your hopes up, Nina. Holly ran this Khari guy through all the databases. His dad was with the Popular Front for the Liberation of Palestine. But that was twenty years ago. Khari immigrated here to live with his uncle after his folks died in 1982. He comes off pretty clean. And his uncle was a decorated Korean War vet."

"We'll see," Nina said.

"It gets worse. Homeland Security sent a honcho in to watch

over us tonight. One of those serious prayer-breakfast types. Same old same old. He wants to shut Holly down for exceeding his authority."

"Aw, Christ," Nina said. "It's Afghanistan all over again."

"You got it," Jane said.

"What happened in Afghanistan?" Broker asked.

"Holly and some of his regular Army pals tried to commit a couple U.S. battalions on the Pakistani border to seal the routes out of Tora Bora. Washington was afraid of taking U.S. casualties on the ground. They nixed the plan and relied on the B-52s and the Afghan warlords. Holly got in a lot of trouble and bin Laden got away," Nina said.

"That's our Holly—fighting a two-front war against terrorism *and* Washington. Then there's the hawk," Jane said.

"The hawk?" Broker asked.

"The Black Hawk at the radar base," Nina explained. "The people trying to shut us down are saying Holly stole it."

Hearing this, Broker smiled in the dark. *I'm starting to like this Holly guy . . .*

"Wait a minute," Yeager said nervously. "You guys *stole* a helicopter?"

"Whoa, hold on," Nina said. "It's this gray area. Justice and the FBI want to arrest people and charge them with civil crimes, right? But if these guys are the real thing tonight, we're going to snatch them as enemy combatants. Naturally, they're a bit more sticky about procedure. We didn't ask permission, we just took the bird and went."

"Uh-huh," Yeager said, sounding unconvinced. He turned in the front seat. "What do you think, Broker?"

"I think they probably *borrowed* the helicopter . . ."

"Yeah, borrowed. Along with a Delta team and an NBC response tech," Jane said.

"NBC?" Yeager said. "Christ, we got televison in on this?"

"That's a nuclear, biological, and chemical responder from Department of Defense," Jane said with a twist of humor in her voice.

"Oh shit!" Yeager said.

"Yeah, see? Now you know who you're running with? No wonder they're so strung out," Broker said.

"Hey, people. Turn should be coming up," Yeager said.

Jane slowed the Explorer, pulling up hard on a gravel road. They completed the turn and she accelerated again. Off to the left the headlights were almost a mile away.

Several minutes passed. The headlights drew closer. "You should see a clump of trees on your right, and the road intersection," Yeager said.

"Got 'em," Jane said.

"There's a shallow shoulder and a dip, just ride it into the trees and stop," Yeager said.

Jane didn't respond, intent on driving. The tires left gravel, then bit into dirt and vegetation. Weeds and shrubs snapped against the chassis, whipped in the dark through the open windows. Broker still couldn't see anything but an orange glow back toward Langdon. A big clump of brush hit the door. Milt's Ford was going to need a visit to the body shop.

"Good . . . stop," Yeager said.

They stopped, killed the motor, and held their breath as the night air turned loud with insect buzz and the cooling ticks of the engine. The headlights came closer and they only caught the barest flicker of a vehicle a hundred yards away as it passed. Then Ace turned off his lights.

"It's him all right—a new Tahoe," Jane said.

"Okay, give him another hundred yards," Yeager said. Jane did. "Now get on the road." She drove to the intersection, turned right. Much closer now. "Okay, when he turns off, you turn off into the fields, but the minute he stops you stop. And kill the motor. We play dead. He'll probably shut down, too, and listen before he does the pickup."

"Christ, this is like a submarine movie," Broker said.

They all giggled to break the tension.

"Oh shit," Janey said. "He just turned again."

"We're cool, he's just turned on a prairie road that runs toward the border. Get ready. Won't be long now," Yeager said.

Jane followed the Tahoe through one last turn and they all breathed in sharp when she cranked the wheel and drove into the waist-high field. Damp splatters pelted the sides of the Ford and a heavy, pungent scent came in through the open windows. Tiny wet blossoms tickled Broker's face.

"Canola," Yeager said. Then: "Kill it, *now!*"

They jerked to a halt and the motor stopped. Dead quiet. Just the oily reek of the crushed canola, the engine ticking down, and the whir of mosquitoes.

Jane leaned out her open window, straining her body into the night.

"He's out, he walking. Walking . . . Barely see him, more'n a hundred yards. Shit, now he's walking around in a circle, like he's lost. Ah, wait. Okay. He stopped. Oh boy, he's bent over and he's dragging something heavy, dragging it back to the truck."

"All right," Nina said. Sitting next to her, Broker could feel her shift gears as a wave of exhausted tension drained out of her. And the adrenaline afterburners kicked in.

"That's it, he popped the hatch and he's manhandling it into the back. He's done. Hatch is down," Jane said.

"I thought it would be more of a load," Yeager said.

"There's some small packages that pack a hell of wallop," Nina said slowly.

"Jesus—NBC, huh?" Yeager said.

"Yeah," Nina said.

They all saw his brake lights as he backed up.

"What do we do?" Janey said.

"Give him some room. We know where he's going, don't we?" Yeager said.

"Fine with me." Jane flopped back in her seat and took a few deep breaths. Then she got on her cell. "Holly, this is Jane. We have a confirmed pickup." That's all. She put the phone down.

"Let's take a minute to work out the ground rules," Nina said, her voice exploring the darkness in Yeager's direction.

"The way I explained it to Yeager, he wants in, he accepts that the rules are pretty fluid," Broker said.

"Yeager," Nina said, "you got your badge and gun on you?"

"Yes, ma'am."

"And this place they're planning to meet, it's in your county?"

"Yep."

"You aren't thinking of like—*arresting* anybody, are you?" Janey asked.

"How far would I get?" Yeager's voice was respectful but with just an edge of testing.

Broker joined in. "There'll be other people where we're going, people who work with Jane and Nina. I got a feeling that Jane and Nina, they're the nice ones."

"What? You're saying I could disappear?" Yeager said evenly.

No one answered.

"Okay, at least tell me what I'm not a part of here." Yeager said. "Is Ace Shuster meeting some terrorists? 'Cause that's what you're putting out between the lines."

"This is just my gut read on him," Nina said, "but I don't think he knows if he is. I don't think he has any idea what he just dragged into his car."

"So what did he just drag to his car?" Yeager said.

"They can't say," Broker said, "'cause they ain't here, are they? But *I* can speculate . . ."

"Like, you mean, just you and me talking," Yeager said.

"Just you and me talking."

"And?"

"They have some pretty good intelligence it could involve a tactical nuclear device."

Another interval of silence.

Then Nina said, "Yeager, if you or me disappear, well, that's not cool. But if a big chunk of Chicago or Kansas City disappears . . ."

"Start the car," Yeager said, his voice trembling with excitement.

Chapter Thirty

After a tense half hour sneaking around out on the gravel, Ace was relaxing, leaning back, one arm draped over the steering wheel of the Tahoe. He cruised east on Highway 5 with the windows open, enjoying the rush of the summer night in his hair and listening to Linda Ronstadt singing what could be the story of his life—"Desperado," on KNDK. His other hand came up and he sipped from a bottle of Moosehead Ale. He wondered if Gordy had encountered any hassles. It had been dead quiet on his end.

The easy pickup and a day of drinking had hammered down his spikes and he was sinking back toward mellow. Another day, another dollar; rolling the old boulder up the hill. Ole Camus said we must imagine Sisyphus happy. Ace wasn't sure about happy, but he did have a moderate buzz going, enough to be charitable—like, maybe they'd been wrong about Nina. Maybe she was just another woman coming up hard on forty in a marriage that didn't fit.

Woulda been nice to roll Nina Pryce up the hill just once, find out who she really was. Ah well . . . fact is, she was already starting to fade . . .

He raised up off the seat slightly, turned on the dome light, and looked over his shoulder at the old-fashioned footlocker in the backseat. Didn't even weigh much, maybe sixty pounds. He didn't know a whole lot about George, his dad's crony. Mostly, Dad and George had played it legal, then every once in a while George would come up with volume he had to move fast, off the books, no questions asked. And everybody made a lot of money.

Sometimes there were small favors, like tonight. Again, no questions asked.

He pushed in the lighter and took out a Camel. When the lighter popped, he lit up. Three drags into the Camel his high beams reached out and caught the crisscross of the chain-link fence that surrounded the old site. He slowed and saw George's new silver Lexus parked in the driveway. Old George did all right for himself.

"Hey Bugs, Nina. How's it going?" Nina was on her cell.

"We're following Khari. He's in a Lexus RX300, driving west on 5. He's all alone, no passengers, no other cars."

"Good. Our guy made his pickup and is driving east on 5 out of Langdon. ETA about five, six minutes to that old base."

"Okay. We got people in position on site. Holly is standing by with the Hawk. We all roll in when the smoke clears."

"Let's hope there's no smoke." Nina flashed on a pile of Bosnian corpses and saw Ace Shuster sandwiched in the middle of them. Eyes open, smiling that smile. She remembered the .38 in his desk. She hoped he'd left it there.

"Ah, roger that."

Nina ended the call. "No need to rush," she said to Yeager. "From here on in we just watch. They belong to the Hardy Boys now."

"Hardy Boys?" Yeager said.

"Delta slang for a tactical team in position at the meeting spot," Jane said as she eased off the gas. They lagged far behind Ace now, driving the speed limit with their lights on. In a few minutes it would all converge on Highway 5 in the dark.

Broker suddenly became aware of his throbbing left hand. He held it up and placed it on his head. Seeing his awkward posture, Nina laughed, this happy release of nerves. "Hey," Broker protested, "it gets the blood out of . . ."

"I know, silly," Nina said. "Like when we met."

"When *you* crashed *my* undercover scene."

"Yeah, and that mean redneck almost bit off your thumb and we drove up north with you holding your hand up like that . . ."

"Hey, cut the lovebird crap," Jane said. "Situational awareness, remember? Nina, how many in the car coming to meet Ace?" she asked.

"Just Khari, driving a Lexus SUV."

"Just one guy?" Jane made a face. "Nobody else with him? Or on the road?"

"Nope, just him."

"Too easy," Jane said.

"You sound disappointed," Broker said.

Jane did not answer. Nina turned back to Broker and then to Yeager and said, "Whatever it is, it's on the rails."

Ace slowed, made the turn, and parked to the rear of the Lexus. He left his lights on so they could see to make the transfer. He got out and so did George.

"How you doing, George?" Ace said.

George Khari slapped his solid middle. "Too much baklava. Need to get back in shape." They shook hands.

Ace had known George from a distance, ever since Dad got the bar. That's how long George Khari had been selling whiskey and beer to the Shusters.

"Quiet night," Ace said.

George raised his chin slightly and asked, "Anybody in back of you?"

Ace looked back down the road he'd just driven and shook his head. "Not even a deer crossing the road, just me out there."

"Good," George said. He was a muscular man of medium height with a strong square face. Another hairy guy, like Gordy, with a perpetual five-o'clock shadow on his chin and cheeks. The headlights gave his olive skin a yellow cast and pocketed his brown eyes in shadow. His thick black hair was carefully groomed, and there was more hair on his forearms. And, like Gordy, he liked to show off the chest, leaving the top two buttons of his short-sleeved shirt open. Ace remembered him wearing gold chains. Not tonight, though. Tonight this little silver medal glinted now and then in Ace's headlights. A religious medallion, like Catholics wear. "I appreciate this, Ace. Just an extra touch, you know, a favor for my regular customers." He had a soft voice with the barest foreign tug to the syllables. Born in the old country.

"This is the last time we do this, George. We pretty much cleaned everything out."

"You going to Florida with your dad?"

"Nah, Dale probably is. I thought maybe Montana, look into raising buffalo." He cocked his head, heard engine noise to the south, a helicopter maybe, over by the PAR site. Something taking off.

"It's funny," George said, looking at the fenced compound. "This place is deserted but they still come in and cut the grass."

"That's the government for you. Pop your hatch and I'll load up this beast."

George raised a hand. "In a minute. I just want to look around first."

Ace shrugged, stretched, and took a drag on his cigarette. "Go ahead but there's nothing left here but stories." He gestured with his cigarette toward the ditch on either side of the driveway. "Like, they built this control bunker in a peat field. Dug a couple stories down into it, ran the cable out to the remote sites. One night this air-baser who worked here was walking the perimeter, having a smoke, and he flips the butt into the ditch." Ace paused, then said, "Next morning they smell smoke."

"No kidding."

"Yeah, set the damn peat to burning. Well, they tried everything to put it out. Nothing worked. Sucker burned down, way underground, for two years, got under and around the control bunker, the electrical conduit. This site controlled ten Minutemen! Can you imagine if a peat fire short-circuited everything and launched a fucking ICBM at Russia."

"But it never happened, huh?"

"Nope, but no thanks to our high-tech . . ." Ace took a last drag on the Camel, then bent back his index finger against his thumb and shot the butt in an arc of sparks into the weeds along the ditch. "What the hell . . . let's see if we can set her going again . . ."

Holy shit!

The cigarette came streaking back from the darkness. Along with this real loud no bullshit voice:

"NOBODYFUCKINGMOVE!"

The night puckered up tight. Real tight. Real fast.

They rose out of the ditch, four shooters in black watch caps, black vests, blackened faces. They pointed stubby M-4 carbines and moved with strobelike intensity, hyperalert to the slightest movement.

Fingers on triggers. For real.

"What the . . ." George's hands started to ball into fists.

"I think you better get your hands up where they can see them, George," Ace said slowly, doing the same himself, showing they were empty. Already bending his knees. Going down. He knew the position.

"Down on the ground. Hands on your head." The men approached in a stylized walk, hunched over their weapons.

Like in the movies.

Ace and George dropped to the ground. Rough hands moved over them, frisking them for weapons. Off to the right Ace heard this whole new order of sound and motion. Turned his head.

"Don't fucking move!"

Ace froze, cheek on the gravel. George raised his head, "What's that?"

Ace saw it materialize out of the dark: snout-nosed and hump backed, it was lowering to the highway with praying-mantis menace. Shit, that was one of those Black Hawks.

Cops didn't rate shit like this.

The helicopter settled down under the loud fan of its rotors and landed on Highway 5. The prop wash beat down the crop on either side of the road, bent over the taller shrubs. Three guys jumped from the helicopter. Unlike the shooters, they wore regular clothes. And, okay, uh-huh—Ace recognized the older one, with the white hair. The guy with the lifer eyes who'd been in the bar when Nina showed up. A second guy carried some kind of recorder thing, with a mike on a cord. The third looked wildly out of place in a white shirt, a tie, flak jacket, and a face like a hunk of raw beef. They ran toward the parked cars. Now other cars showed up—a van from the east and a Ford Explorer from the west.

Whoa!

The guy with the recorder thing went right for the back of Ace's Tahoe, like he knew. He opened the hatch and ran the mike all around the foot locker inside. Through all the commotion, Ace heard the ticking sound. Not a mike.

"What the fuck's going on?" George shouted. He was one of those ballsy short guys. Feisty when riled.

"Shut up," shouted one of the shooters holding a rifle trained on them.

"It's clean," said the guy with the Geiger counter.

The other cars stopped, the doors flung open. Ace saw Nina pile out. Jim Yeager, out of uniform. That Broker guy. Jane.

Ace started to laugh.

"I said *shut the fuck up*," snarled the shooter.

Ace tried to stifle his laugh as he watched a black dude get out of the van with another guy. Nobody wearing uniforms, but that had to be a military helicopter. Ace smiled into the gravel. *I was right. She wasn't a cop. Gordy owes me. A soldier girl!*

Dumb shits. Now whatta you suppose they thought was in George's foot locker?

"Open it," the guy with the flak jacket ordered. One of the shooters shouldered his rifle and went to the foot locker which now, in addition to the dome light, had several intense flashlights trained on it.

The locker was secured with several bands of duct tape. The shooter took out a Randall knife and cut the tape. As he peeled it away, the others crowded forward, like holding their breath as he snapped the hasps up and lifted the lid.

Pure stunned silence.

Flak Jacket turned on the older white-haired guy and snarled. "Colonel Wood, you better be able to explain this."

"Check it. Take everything out and check it," Holly said in a tight voice.

Ace started laughing again. No one moved to stop him this time. He watched them remove the tightly packed wooden containers and stack them to either side of the foot locker. Open one.

"That's it?" Nina said in a strangled voice. *"CIGARS? I took my fucking clothes off for a box full of cigars?"*

"Not just any old cigars," Broker said, trying to hold down his rising mirth. "Those are Cohibas, honey."

"Not just any old Cohibas, either," Holly said in a weary voice.

"Looks like forty-two ring, seven inches. Those are Lanceros. What Castro used to smoke."

The shooters slung their rifles and motioned for Ace and George to get up. Ace turned to George and said, "Better let me do the talking." Seeing the small catlike smile play across George's lips, he said firmly, "George, hey man, this isn't funny."

George Khari immediately sobered.

The shooters moved off with Nina, Jane, Broker, and the two guys from the van. They all joined the white-haired guy and the guy with the Geiger counter. They stood in a little semicircle. Flak Jacket was doing all the talking, in a controlled shout. He waved his hands in tight circles. The guy was pissed. Ace heard the word *circus* several times.

Jim Yeager stood back from the harangue and then moved smoothly into the power vacuum. Hands on his hips, faintly smiling, he said, "Okay, Ace. Why don'tcha explain what's going on here. Like, who's this guy?" Yeager pointed at George, who was now furious, trying to dust the gravel stains off his shirt and shorts.

"Assholes!" George yelled. "They put oil on the gravel, or something. Look—brand new, from Cabela's, fucking ruined." He shook his fist at the coven of military types and shouted. "You pussies. You got nothing better to do? Is this because I come from Lebanon? I pay taxes, you know, goddammit, and so does my uncle. He was in Korea. First fucking Marines. He walked from Chosen to the coast with shrapnel in his knee, and you fucking Girl Scouts have fought—who, the fucking Panamanians? The Grenadians? The dipshit Iraqis? Some losers in Afghanistan?"

"George, calm down," Ace said. He turned to Yeager. "He's George Khari, an old friend of the family. He's a liquor distributer from Grand Forks. We kind of run into each other on the road."

"Uh-huh," Yeager said. "And what about that?" He pointed to the foot locker.

Ace smiled, enjoying himself. "Well, we were trying to figure out what to do about that. I found it just sitting there on the gravel north of town." Ace paused, relishing the moment. "Fact is . . . *I* didn't open it, Jimmy. *You* did."

"Who are those fuckers?" George demanded, pointing at Holly and company. "I want all their names and their jobs. I want to talk to my lawyer!"

Yeager said, "C'mon, figure it out. They're people from the air base across the road. You're on government property here. They probably scrambled to see why you're creeping around the site. Like back during the missile time."

"Yeah, right. Protecting the gophers who live here, huh?" Ace grinned. "You know what I think? I think you should get your ass out there and write a ticket to that fuckin' helicopter. Looks to me like it's blocking traffic."

"Watch your mouth, Ace," Yeager warned.

Broker gathered that the troubleshooter who'd flown in from the Office of Homeland Security was willing to break the rules for a nuclear event. But not for a box of smuggled cigars. They had nothing on George Khari—who was a *Christian*, for heaven's sake, the guy said with a whiff of born-again indignance—not some Muslim fundamentalist crazy. And nothing really on Ace Shuster for possession of the cigars that a good lawyer couldn't get thrown out of court. Jane and Nina were right. The guy was after Holly's scalp. He used the words *irresponsible, renegade,* and *rogue.*

"You got till tomorrow morning to clean up this mess. Then I want everybody en route to Bragg by noon. Figure out a way to make it so that this didn't happen. End of story." The Washington bureaucrat took off his flak jacket, dropped it at Holly's feet, and stalked back to the helicopter.

"Dry fucking hole," Holly said, kicking at the dirt. "Rashid fed us a line of crap." He circled his fist and pumped it. The guy with the Geiger counter and the four shooters trotted back to the helicopter. It lifted off and droned away to the south. The black guy and his partner got back in their van and drove off to the east. Holly gestured to Yeager to come over and talk. That left Broker, Jane, and a very pissed off Nina standing on the side of the road, illuminated by the lights from the Tahoe, looking at Ace and George.

"So this is your real life, huh? Some kinda soldier?" Ace called out to Nina.

"Ace, you know what's good for you, you'll shut your hole," Yeager yelled. Then he went back to conferring with Holly. After a few moments, Holly motioned to Nina, Jane, and Broker. When they were huddled around him, he shook his head. "You heard the asshole from D.C. We're outta here."

"You mean just let them go?" Jane pushed out her chin and planted her hands on her hips.

"No choice. What'd they do?" Holly said.

"I can take Ace in for possession of contraband," said Yeager, "but he has a point. It was a classified Army unit opened that box. If we charge him, that could bring this whole operation into court. A good attorney would try to subpoena you guys, take depositions, make you testify in court . . ."

"You heard the man," Holly said and jerked his head in the direction of the fading helicopter rotors. Then he turned to Yeager. "Can you make it go away?"

Yeager heaved his shoulders. "I'll try." He walked over to Ace and George. Broker, Nina, Jane, and Holly followed.

"Okay, Ace, we're going to offer you and George a deal, and if you're smart, you'll take it." Yeager took out his cell. "I can call the

SO, get a man out here in a cruiser and arrest you two on suspicion of smuggling . . ."

"Am I under arrest?" George asked, jaw thrust forward, truculent.

"Not at the moment, but I never want to see you in my county again," Yeager said. "You understand, you little asshole?"

"Fuck this. I'm calling my lawyer," George hissed.

"Wait a sec, George, let's hear him out," Ace said.

"Or," Yeager said, "we do this little trade. Real simple. You forget what *you* saw here. We forget what *we* saw."

"Who gets the cigars?" George stepped forward and narrowed his eyes.

"What cigars?" Yeager turned and faced the highway.

Broker smiled and said, "Maybe you could spare a few, for sweetener."

George's scowl evaporated the more he thought about it. "Sounds good," he said quickly. He immediately started loading the cigar boxes into the foot locker. Ace helped him load it in the back of the Lexus. Then George shut the hatch and handed two boxes to Broker. "Best fuckin' cigars in the world." He turned to Ace, shook his hand, and said, "Say hello to your dad when you see him." Then George Khari got in his Lexus and drove east, toward the interstate.

As the taillights receded down the highway, Ace turned to the people standing in his high beams and said, "So what's out here that calls for military helicopters and guys in ninja suits? Do I get an explanation?"

Nina and Jane exchanged glances. "Sorry, Ace," Nina said.

Ace set his jaw. "I deserve an explanation."

"Just take off, and keep your mouth shut," Yeager said. "I'll be keeping an eye on you. I mean it."

Ace decided not to push it. He ambled back to his Tahoe, got in, and drove west toward town. Soon he was laughing, shaking his head, and pounding the steering wheel. What a night. *Sonofabitch! I almost got me some Green Beret pussy!*

• • •

Holly walked off alone and stood staring down the highway at something in the dark. Probably his imminent retirement. Broker figured it was not the best time to talk, so he joined Nina, who sat on the ground where Ace's Tahoe had been parked, arms drooped between her knees. She shook her head. "That Rashid guy back in Detroit just shined us down the road. And we went for it."

"We had no choice. Had to check it out. Had to be something going on up here for him to come up with a name, a place," Jane said, sitting beside her.

"If there was, we missed it," Nina said.

"Hey, cut yourself some slack," Broker said "You ran a fast, tight operation. Just didn't pan out. Human systems are like that. Flawed . . . Pretty goddamn funny, though, you got to admit. Delta commandos popping out of ditches. Locking and loading on Communist cigars." He was chuckling as he opened one of the wooden boxes and extended it to Yeager. They selected cigars, nibbled off the plugs, and sat down alongside the women.

A lighter flared as they lit the Cubans. The smoke rose in aromatic billows and sent the mosquitoes pinwheeling off in drunken circles.

Broker continued to laugh softly.

"I don't see what's so damn funny," Nina said.

"I'll tell you what's funny," Yeager said, moving in deftly. "They built this bunker in a peat field, and one night an Air Force guy was having a smoke and he flips his cigarette butt into the ditch and . . ."

Ace pulled up to the Missile Park, turned off the engine, and got out. No sign of Gordy.

Okay. Just me and about five cases of booze left in this empty building tonight.

After what just happened, I can handle that.

As he started up the steps he sensed them before he saw them, two figures standing in the dark, back against the building, on either side of the porch.

"Hey," he called out, putting a hard challenge in his voice.

"Take it easy," Dale said, coming forward. "Just me and Joe."

"What are you two doing, lurking?" Ace asked.

"Just talking," Joe said. "Say . . . you ever meet up with George?"

"Oh, yeah."

"And?"

"Worked out just fine. Tell you about it sometime," Ace said, pushing past them, getting out his keys. "But not tonight. I ain't in the mood."

"What about that redhead, Nina?" Dale asked.

Ace was feeling around in the dark, fitting the key in the lock. He laughed and said over his shoulder, "She's gone, brother. So gone you could say she was never really here."

Broker watched Northern Route come apart on a deserted North Dakota highway just as fast as it had been put together. And the .45 he had on loan from his buddy J. T. Merryweather was missing. He'd talk to Yeager about it. But not now. In the morning.

The Cohibas were the only good thing about the whole night.

Well, not entirely. Here he was again, reunited with one really worn out, pissed off redhead. Nina's adrenaline crash left her numb, and he was careful not to indulge in any more sarcasm. When she hung her head, he put out his arm and she nestled into that cranny in his shoulder where she'd always seemed to fit so well. Amid the wreckage, a rapprochement of sorts was taking shape.

Holly told Nina and Jane to take a down day and rest. The backup team was flying east tonight with the suit from Homeland Security. The helicopter was slated to fly back to North Carolina tomorrow.

Broker drove Janey and Holly to the Air Force radar base across the highway and dropped them at the gate. Nina stayed in the car and they drove Yeager back to his house in town. Then they made a U-turn and drove to the motel.

"I should call Kit," Nina said when they were in the room.

"It's too late. Do it in the morning."

The bed was suddenly irresistible and Nina lowered herself to it and rolled over and propped her head up with pillows.

"We should talk," she said in a fading zombie voice.

"Yeah, we should," Broker said. He was sitting at the small table in the corner, taking off his shoes. When he looked up, she was sound asleep.

As he gently removed her pistol belt, her shoes, and clothing, a lot of thoughts passed through his mind. They all came under a simple heading:

Married Life.

Chapter Thirty-one

Nina jerked awake as her cell phone buzzed on the table next to her head. Broker bolted upright on pure reflexes, eyes wide open but still asleep. "Wha?" he said.

"Go back to sleep," she said, checking her phone display, "it's Janey."

"Hmph," he muttered and flopped back down.

"Morning," Nina said to the phone.

"How you doing?" Jane said.

"The sleep helps. Otherwise . . . it sucks."

"I hear you. How you and Broker getting on?"

Nina studied him briefly. In less than five seconds he had started to snore. She leaned over and gave him an elbow in the shoulder blade. He grumbled, rearranged himself, and proceeded to breathe normally. Then she turned back to the phone and checked the time on the display: 7:39. Jesus. She'd slept for nearly nine hours.

"Don't know. I crashed the minute I saw the bed. Now I'm up and he's out cold."

"I was thinking we could get some breakfast."

"I'm for that. But I think I'll let him sleep. Where are you?"

"On the highway east of town, in our trusty Volvo."

"Give me a few minutes and I'll meet you in front."

Nina put the phone down, got up, and headed for the bathroom. After taking her first carefree pee in a week, she got in the shower. The jets of hot water were a good start, but it would take days for the booze and amphetamines to work out of her system.

And for what?

Don't think about it.

She shampooed her short hair, worked in conditioner, and decided not to shave her legs. Janey was waiting. She rinsed off, toweled, and thoroughly enjoyed brushing her teeth.

She dug through her go-bag, found a pair of loose-fitting shorts, a tank top, and Chacos. Out of habit her hand went to her pistol belt.

Nah. Clothes were all wrong. And anyway . . .

Then she took a moment to study Broker, who was strangled in a twisted sheet, spread out, hogging the bed, as usual. And she remembered how, asleep, all the care lifted off his face. Except for the bushy eyebrows, he looked like a young boy. She smiled. A rough young boy who'd read too much Robert Louis Stevenson . . .

We *will* have to talk, she reminded herself. She kissed the tip of her finger and touched him on the forehead. She wrote a note and left it on the table. *"Went out for coffee with Janey. Be back soon."* Quietly, she started to slip out the door. Then, on impulse she returned, dug in her cosmetic bag, found the lipstick, and applied it. She went back to the note and blotted her lips, leaving a full, open-mouth impression of a kiss.

That'll mess with his mind.

She grabbed her purse, eased out the door, gently closed it behind her, and walked down the stairs, through the lobby, and outside. Whoa. She squinted her eyes and took a step back.

After living for a week in half-shadow, the sun was doing double time and had turned the sky into one vast blue flame. She looked around. No Janey yet. So she ducked back in the lobby, flipped open her cell, and called Broker's folks in Minnesota. His dad, Mike, picked up.

"Hi, Mike, it's Nina."

"Hey, kiddo, how you doing?"

Nina scrubbed her knuckles in her hair, blinked several times. "Looks like I'll have some leave. I wanted to tell Kit I'll be coming home."

"Home?" Mike Broker said.

"Yeah. Is Kit there?"

"Irene took her down to the beach to pick cobbles. They're set up to paint them. If you wait . . ."

"No, let 'em go. I'll call back after breakfast."

"Okay. Ah, Nina—what's *my kid* up to?"

Nina thought about it and said, "Tell Kit her dad and I will be coming home together."

After a moment of thoughtful silence, Mike said quietly, "We look forward to seeing you both."

Nina ended the call and went back outside as Janey pulled the Volvo in front, looking like someone hiding a hangover behind Ray-Bans. Nina came around and got in. Janey wore an old baggy *Take Back The Night* T-shirt, gray shorts, and sandals.

"Where'd you get the shirt?" Nina said.

"I found it in the trunk, washed and folded in a Goodwill bag. So I figured, what the hell, goes with the car."

Nina fished a pack of American Spirit filters from her purse. "I gotta start working on quitting," she said, reaching for the lighter in the dashboard.

"Why? You thinking of taking up a different line of work?"

"I thought maybe counterterrorism analyst for Fox or CNN," Nina said.

"Not housewife?" Janey looked pointedly at the motel.

"Hey, fuck you." Nina gave her the finger.

"I wish. But then you'd never go back to him," Janey said with a coy smile. "Okay," she said, shifting back to work mode. "There's the place by City Hall or the one back down the road."

Nina blew a stream of smoke. The taste of nicotine reminded her of something. On impulse, she said, "I'm going back to the bar. Just for a second. I need to tell Ace something."

"Not smart."

"C'mon. Two minutes."

"You sure?" Janey said.

Nina nodded her head. "Look, you don't have to come. I'll drop you off, you order breakfast. I'll be back in ten minutes."

Jane put the car in gear, steered onto the highway, and headed west. "No way. I go along to keep you out of trouble."

Dale's eyes were red from lack of sleep as he stood in the office of Shuster and Sons and kept looking out the window, across the street at the Missile Park. He could feel Joe's equally tired eyes burning a hole in his back. They had passed a fitful night in the office, grabbing snatches of sleep punctuated by arguments. Joe had been on his cell regularly to George. George had started out pleased as could be over last night's successful diversion. His self-congratulations fizzled, however, when Dale refused to budge from Langdon. Now George was stuck at the abandoned gas station at Camp's Crossing. He'd waited there all night. And George didn't like waiting. Dale didn't care how pissed they were; he'd made up his mind: he wasn't leaving without her.

He turned to glance at Joe, then returned to the window. Joe and his gun didn't scare him that much anymore. Not after Gordy. He continued to stare across the road. *Where was she?*

"Hey," Joe said, shoving the phone in Dale's face for the third time in as many hours, "talk to George."

Dale took the phone. As usual, George remained calm; even

without his morning coffee. "She's gone, Dale. I saw her last night. They all got in a helicopter and flew away."

Dale didn't believe that. He could just tell. He knew things. So he told George, "I'm going to give it another hour."

"Okay. An hour." Patient George, teacher, mentor, puppet master. He chided gently, "Did you make the follow-up call to Irv Fuller? It's very important to make that call."

"I know, give him my Social Security number," Dale said. "I'll call him when we're through talking."

"Good," George said. "An hour."

Dale got off with George, then dutifully reached Irv Fuller, on his cell.

"Yeah?" Irv said, guarded.

Dale smiled. Old Irv was nervous, worried that Dale would harass him for the balance owed on the machines. Instead Dale said, "Just checking if that Deere is giving you any trouble."

"Well, one of the boys says that loader is riding kind of hard."

"Tell you what," Dale said reasonably, "I'm passing your way later today, thought I might drop by and give her a look. Maybe see the job. Say around four or five this afternoon."

"No problem," Irv said, sounding relieved that Dale didn't mention money. "Just need your Social Security number. They'll run a quick background check to get you by the gate."

"Sure thing," Dale said. He gave Irv his Social Security number and said goodbye. He turned to Joe. "See. Easy."

Joe seemed a bit relieved. He thrust out his hands, palms up, fingers spread in a plea.

Dale stood his ground and continued staring across the road.

"Forget it," Joe said. "Like Ace told you last night. She's gone."

Gone. Dale shook his head. He had not told Joe about Gordy and the information was a source of power. But he wasn't strong enough to get what he wanted alone, not just yet. He needed Joe and his gun. "Just before the sun came up we took a drive through town and saw her husband's car at the motel, remember? She could be there," Dale said.

Joe was adamant. He shook his head. "Even if she's at the motel, there's too many people around. Can't be done. Let it go. Dale, we're too close. Let's not fuck it up."

Dale stared at him hard. Joe was different from him. Joe's gifts were practical, tactical. He was not inspired. Dale, who was inspired, couldn't let it go. He'd prepared a place for her. It was meant to be. He knew it.

And then he knew it for sure.

"Look! Look!" he shouted, bouncing on the balls of his feet. Joe rushed to the window and actually slapped his hand to his forehead. How had they allowed themselves to become so dependent on this nutcase?

The answer came easily. For the money. For the access.

So Joe watched it come together like a swarming nightmare he was powerless to escape. He watched the red Volvo pull off the highway and come to a stop in front of the bar. He watched the woman with the red hair get out from the passenger side. The one Dale wanted. He watched her walk to the front door of the bar.

"Now we're cooking with gas!" Dale shouted as he went toward the door.

Joe watched his spreading nightmare crowd out the day as Dale grabbed his yellow backpack—that little kid's pack with the butterfly on it—and headed out the door.

Joe shifted from foot to foot at the window as Dale strode confidently across the road. "There goes my life," he said, shaking his head. "My whole fucking life . . ." He had no choice. He was chained to the nightmare rails and could only follow and make Dale's fantasy come true. Everything depended on it.

"Zarba."

He grabbed the compact gym bag at his feet and walked stiffly out the door.

Chapter Thirty-two

Jane stayed in the car as Nina went to the front door and tried the doorknob. Locked. So she banged on it. Once, twice, three times. Nothing happened. She turned to Jane and shrugged. But then, as she was starting to think about going around the back and trying the warehouse entrance, she heard someone cough inside, then a shuffle of feet. The doorknob turned.

The Ace Shuster who opened the door was badly in need of a shave; eyes red, his breath smelled like a whiskey blowtorch. He stared at her without expression, blinked, looked up and down the empty highway, and then said, "Don't know where Gordy is. That's why the door was locked." He raised his hand to shield his eyes from the sun and managed a wasted wolfish grin.

"What?" she said.

"Never had a look at you in real daylight, as it were," he said.

God, she thought, even now, the guy can't help trying to connect. "Look. I'll make this quick," she said. "I can't give you an explanation. You'll have to draw your own conclusions. But this whole mess could have been a lot uglier. The other thing is, some of what you said made a difference."

"Oh yeah?" He cocked his head.

"Yeah. I'll be going back to spend some time with Broker and Kit."

Nina stopped talking when she saw Ace's eyes move off her face and look behind her. She turned as he asked, "Now what do they want?"

At the same time Jane picked them up in her rearview mirror: two men, one big and sloppy but moving at a fast shuffle, the other darker, his face all wrong, and he walked with a slight limp. The way they moved got her attention. Her hand snapped to her face and tossed off the sunglasses. So much for a leisurely morning. They were coming across the road into the parking lot at a brisk pace. The big one carried some kind of yellow backpack, but tiny. The darker one had a gym bag in his hand. That would be Ace's brother and the brother's sidekick, the Indian, Joe Reed, the guy Nina had noticed.

Dale climbed the porch steps. Ace moved to block him and said firmly. "Can't this wait? I'm busy."

"You seen Gordy?" Dale asked with a broad smile. Then, not waiting for an answer, he said, "Aw, fuck Gordy, he was just one of the little people." He grinned at Nina. "See? I knew you'd be back. I just knew." He shouldered on past Ace, went through the door and into the dark interior of the bar.

Ace had never seen his brother so positive, so happy, so pushy and sure of himself. A little amazed and curious, he was dragged into Dale's gravity field and followed him inside. Nina, too, was swept along. She had been interrupted and was not quite finished. Jane was out of the car now, fully alert. And irritated. She'd thought that this drive-by farewell was a lapse of common sense on Nina's part, and now it was getting complicated. At first she picked up no hostile vibes off Joe; he just stood at the door, shifting from foot to foot, waiting. But when she came closer she felt his cold eyes.

I'm gonna watch you, fella, Jane thought as she went through the door and stepped to the side so her back was to the wall. Her right hand shook out, just in case. A Beretta nine in a breakaway hideout holster lay across the small of her back, under her shirt. But Joe stayed out on the porch. She moved deeper into the room, where her back was secure and she could monitor him through the window. Her eyes tracked from Joe on the porch to the awkward scene percolating between Ace, Nina, and Dale.

Finally Ace said, gently, "Whatever it is, Dale, this is not the time."

Dale's round face was swelling up, about to burst, like a kid at the Christmas pageant getting set to deliver his one big line. "Ain't it funny, Ace? My whole life, people always notice you and never me." He bared his teeth to his handsome brother.

"What the hell are you talking about?" Ace said, his patience worn hangover-thin.

"What I'm talking about is—*It's me!*"

Ace stared at Dale, slowly shaking his head.

Dale went on triumphantly. *"She didn't come to town to look for you, she came for me."* He was speaking to Ace, but he was looking at Nina.

And Nina saw enough resentment and malevolence surface in Dale's eyes to kill a whole high school. Along with a leer of sheer physical lust that made her skin crawl. But then she realized that Dale wasn't speaking in some kind of sibling code to his brother . . .

Jesus. That means . . .

Oh shit!

And she got caught in one of those expanding fractions of a second that inform enlightenment—except this was gonna be very bad.

Like Broker, she was a natural fighter. Physically and psychologically, she adapted to conflict. The Pentagon spent a lot of time and money trying to train people to acquire the sort of reflexes she had naturally. She could anticipate a threat and move to disrupt it, step inside other people's physical time, second-guess their intentions. She did this without thinking.

"Janey." Her voice rose to a dangerous treble.

"I'm here, girl," Janey said, tensed forward, her right hand sweeping behind her back, her left hand reaching out, sensing like a rangefinder. Then she spun to check the porch, to locate Joe. Her Beretta coming up, her free hand meeting it to form a two-handed brace on the grip.

"What the hell?" Ace said, starting to react himself. And Dale just went on grinning except now his hand was reaching into his foolish little pack.

And that's when Nina got stuck on the slo-mo glide path. Powerless, all she could do was watch. A fraction of a second stretched out long like a colonnade, pillars going on and on, endless. She distinctly saw her .45 in its holster—on the table in the motel room where Broker lay peacefully sleeping. The note next to it with her lipstick smear . . .

She was moving now, toward Dale. Good. Janey bringing the Beretta up as she came around from looking out the window.

Then not so good.

Janey's eyes ran wild because Joe Reed appeared at the other end of the room, in the doorway to the stairs, the one that led to the rear entry. And she was still coming around in the turn.

Fucker came in through the back.

Came in hot with a big Browning held rigid in a professional two-handed grip, arms extended, on target, taking small quartering steps. Both eyes open. Not aiming like an amateur. Pointing like a pro.

Jesus! Rashid had not lied.

They had gone after the wrong Shuster.

Nina stretched out for Dale, pushing past Ace, who had jumped in front of her, his arms spread protectively. Had to stop Dale's hand in the pack. If she got her hands on him she could disable him. Bet on it. And if Janey could . . .

But it was like competitive swimming. Hundredths of a second decided . . .

Joe squeezed the trigger while Janey was still cementing her grip around the nine and—*crack crack*—Joe Reed shot her twice in the chest at a distance of ten yards. Janey Singer went down and Joe came on another two steps—*crack*—and put that one in her head.

Nina saw Janey jerk with each impact but all that registered in the moment was the need to dive across the floor and get her hands on Janey's gun. As she hit the floor, seizing the pistol from Janey's motionless hand and rolling over, Joe Reed wheeled the Browning on her.

"No!" Dale yelled. "She's mine!"

But Joe was on automatic, operating on pure survival reflexes as his pistol centered on Nina's chest.

Ace was in midair. And Nina would have occasion to remember his remark about playing ball: *You stand around a lot, but then sometimes you gotta move fast to make a play.*

Like now.

He dived as Joe fired and put his body between the bullets and Nina's heart and took two in the back. She felt his body collide with her, still alive, bounce once, and what he'd lived in flopped on top of her in a messy lifeless embrace.

Dale's boot stomped down on Nina's right hand and she lost the Beretta. His hand came around, held something—yellow, a knife? No, more like a stubby pen. There was a needle in the end. He plunged it into her thigh.

Calmer now, more in control, Joe came forward, covering her as Dale grabbed the body of his brother by a limp arm and dragged it aside. "Now look what you went and did," Dale said. Not to Joe, but to the corpse. And Nina, who felt the first lift of a rearing narcotic wave, noted the homicidal marker of not owning the motivation of one's violence, of assigning it to others.

She was being swept away. Out of herself completely. She'd mourn Ace and Janey later. *Right now gotta work on having a later.*

Deadly efficient, Joe covered her.

"No need," Dale said. "She going in the K-hole. Be a couple minutes."

Nina going slack, shook words from the fog enveloping her: "Not Ojibwa . . ." Joe just smiled. She tried again. "Where did you train?"

The smile broadened. He shrugged. "In the Bekáa Valley."

"Not Afghanistan?"

"Fuck Afghanistan and their religious bullshit," Joe said.

That was all. The last thing she saw was the contempt in Joe's chilly eyes. And blood, Ace's blood, on her chest. Then Dale roughly grabbed her hair and jerked her head back in a gesture of acquisition.

The thought that she'd never see her daughter again . . .

Her eyes rolled up. A soft nothing rose up on a flutter of euphoric wings and banished the dread.

Chapter Thirty-three

Joe stood at the window talking on his cell to George as he nervously kept checking the road and motioning with his free hand for Dale to be quiet. But Dale had a very different reaction to the shootings, and the capture of Nina. He couldn't keep still. Stepping in the blood, tracking it around. "Look," he said, "it's okay. Nobody heard. We can just leave the bodies. We plan to disappear, right? We won't be coming back."

Joe spun furiously, yanked the pistol from his waistband, and waved it in Dale's face, then at the floor. "Just shut up, okay? And clean up your shoes and the tracks on the floor." He turned back to the window and the phone.

Dale didn't care for that, Joe pointing a gun at him. But he removed his work shoes and washed them thoroughly in the bathroom sink. Then he took Gordy's mop and pail from the closet and removed all trace of his footprints. Dale was thinking as he worked, and the more he thought about it, the more he decided Joe should be punished for sticking a gun in his face. Uh-huh.

By the time Joe ended his phone conversation and approached Dale, stepping carefully around the bodies and the remaining blood on the floor, he'd settled down. "George and I think it's best to change the plan. After this, what happened here."

Dale shrugged. He didn't care. He had the woman to be with all the way to Florida. "Sure," he said.

"Good, so I'll get you over to Camp's Corner to hook up with George. Then I'll split back over the border. George will go with you to the target."

"Fine," Dale said, "let's get going."

While Joe went across the road to the equipment shed for his van, Dale dragged Nina's unconscious body to the back storeroom and lay her down next to the door. He returned to the barroom and picked up her purse. It did not particularly surprise him that he could look at the dark-haired woman's body and Ace's without feeling anything, other than a certain satisfaction that he was finally succeeding in life, despite all the obstacles he had to overcome— while Ace, who was gifted from birth in every way, who had always squandered his potential, had failed.

"You lose, asshole," Dale said.

He stooped down and rubbed Nina's purse in the pool of blood that spread around Janey Singer's torso. Then he came back and studied Nina, watched her labored breathing. But he wasn't real worried. He'd given her 100 mg. Usually enough to put even him into a K-hole for an hour. And he outweighed Nina by almost a hundred pounds.

He couldn't resist removing her wallet from the purse and carefully fingering out the Minnesota driver's license. Holding it by the edge, he took the Sharpie from his chest pocket and blackened out the eyes on the photo. Then he inserted the ID back in the wallet and put the wallet back in the purse.

He heard Joe's van pulling around the building. "Asshole," he said under his breath. "Pointing a gun at *me* . . ." Like Gordy, trying to boss him.

Joe backed up to the loading dock, got out, and then checked to make sure there were no cars on the highway, no one in the fields. Then they lifted her off the dock and put her on the cargo floor in the back of the van. Dale folded her arms across her stomach and put her purse on her chest. He stayed with her, in the back, out of sight, as Joe drove west on Highway 5, took a turn to the south.

Right through town. That took some balls.

Yeah, well, so does this.

Dale hunkered down behind the driver's seat so Joe couldn't see him in the rearview. Okay. He removed his pocketknife and studied his open left hand. The crisscross lines in his palm were supposed to predict things about his life. Damned if he knew what.

What the hell.

Keeping his hands low, he drew the sharp blade along the heel of his left hand and watched the blood drip onto the floor of the van. He flexed his hand so the blood made a small pool in his palm and then he grabbed at the spare tire mount, then the back door latch, leaving a red spongy pattern of his hand and fingerprints. He searched in his back pack, took out some Kleenex and a surgical glove. He wadded the tissue over the cut, applied pressure. Not the greatest, but it would do for now. Then he pulled on the Latex glove, one he'd worn last night.

With Gordy.

"How you doing?" Joe called back.

"Fine. Just drive."

"We're really going to do this," Joe said.

"Drive," Dale said as he sat back and watched Nina's chest rise and fall. Later, when they were alone together, she'd be awake and he could watch her eyes when he told her what he was going to do. Watch her think about it.

He looked up, at the back of Joe's head. Joe was relieved to think he would soon be free of Dale. He'd head north, cross into Canada. Joe Reed would vanish. He'd be Joseph Khari again. Smiling all the way, a rich man. A big man in Winnipeg.

They came to Camp's Corner. Immediately one of the doors on the garage bay opened and George stepped out and waved them in. Dale got out, looked around, saw nothing but flat green and the anomalous bulge of the Nekoma pyramid floating in a blur of ground thermal.

George looked haggard, dressed in a dirty shirt and shorts, unshaven, and blinking in the sun. He and Joe made quite a pair, both looking so grim and nervous. Joe shifted from his good foot to his bad foot and licked at the scars around his lips. Dale wasn't sweating drop one. They were just foot soldiers in a war, same as Nina. He felt more like Truman—cool, calling the shots.

Hiroshima? Fuck it. Just drop that sucker.

"We gotta do this fast," George said as he looked searchingly at Joe and Dale. Dale made his face stolid and obedient. Like George would expect.

"No one saw us. We're good," Joe said.

"We have to do this fast," George repeated. Dale saw he was antsy now, so near the end. And keyed up about all the things that could still go wrong.

The Roadtrek was parked in the baked shadows, gassed up, with the new Minnesota plates Joe had stolen off a car in long-term parking at the Winnipeg International Airport. Hopefully they wouldn't be missed for the next few days. Dale planned to ditch the camper and be in Florida by then.

If the prevailing wind patterns didn't change.

George and Joe averted their eyes as Dale carried Nina from the back of the van into the Roadtrek and placed her on the bed that filled the rear compartment. The bungee cords were waiting, laid out on the sheets with a pliers. He used the cords to secure her wrists and ankles to the bed's side boards. He used the pliers to crimp the hooks together. Just a formality. Ketamine would control her.

And Dale had lots of ketamine.

He checked the compartment to make sure he'd removed everything that could be used either as a weapon or a tool. Just a TV and VCR on a wall shelf overlooking the bed. Where she could see it. His own video camera, a tripod, and remote hookup were stacked in the corner. He shook his head. *Focus.*

"Dale," George yelled. "C'mon out here."

Keeping his injured left hand well down by his side, he shook hands with Joe, clapped him on the shoulder. "Good luck," Dale said. "You gonna take Mulberry?"

Joe shook his head. "Richmond Crossing. Not as active."

"Smart," Dale said.

George embraced Joe and said, "Look for us tonight on CNN."

"*Inshallah,*" Joe said, with a twist of irony in his torn smile.

"But you don't believe in God," Dale said, and they all laughed.

Joe got in the van, pulled out on the road, and turned north. George immediately handed Dale two maps: North Dakota and Minnesota. He'd written his cell-phone number prominently on them and traced a route in orange Magic Marker.

"We'll keep in contact by cell. I'll lead, you follow, but not too close. Halfway, we'll stop. I have something to show you."

"The pictures?" Dale asked, smiling.

George nodded, pointed to a circled town on the Minnesota map. He was bouncing slightly on the balls of his feet, fingering the medallion around his neck. "Here, in Fergus Falls."

"What if I gotta stop to take a leak?"

"Signal with your lights for the next rest stop. But we gotta hurry, get back on the road. Okay."

"Hey, calm down, George. We got time. I told Irv I'd be there by five P.M."

George didn't calm down. He talked faster. "We drop down to Highway 2, take it to Grand Forks, then drop south on 29, pick up 94 . . ."

Dale grinned, "I got it. C'mon. Let's go."

Solemnly, George shook Dale's hand and stared into his eyes.

Dale figured George was in danger of trading his dope-smuggler cool for a bunch of holy-warrior bullshit. Whatever. Then George turned and got into his Lexus. Dale shut the door, got in the Roadtrek, checked Nina in the back. She was still in the K-hole. He pulled the big camper outside, went back, shut the garage door, got back in, and put it in gear. As he pulled on the road, he watched the sun glint on the back of George's silver Lexus.

Imagine that, cool old George getting flustered, and me getting cooler and cooler. Like now . . .

Dale grabbed his cell phone off the passenger seat. First he held his breath, then he started panting as fast as he could until he was gasping. When he sounded like he was hyperventilating, he punched in 911. Funny about numbers, wasn't it? Nine-one-one. Nine-eleven.

Dale thought for a moment. Okay . . . Karen Fremuth would be on duty at the SO. Dale had gone to school with her older sister. Hopefully she would recognize his voice.

"Nine-one-one."

He held the phone close to his chest, rasping in a loud whisper. "Help. Oh shit it hurts. He shot Ace. You gotta help. And this girl . . ."

"Calm down who is this where are you who was shot!!!"

Dale grinned. Karen's starting to sound like old George. Now she's the one who had to calm down. "It's me, Dale. Dale Shuster. Joe Reed, that fucking Indian went crazy, he shot Ace . . . at the bar."

"Dale? Your brother Ace? You have to talk louder, I can't hear you."

"I can't. I'm *in the back of his van* on a cell, me and that women Ace was with. Shit, he's taking us . . . going north on Richmond . . ."

"You mean Pinto Joe?"

"Pinto Joe, a brown GM van. Oh shit, no, no . . ."

Dale ended the call. That'd teach Joe to point guns at him. They knew Joe's van at the sheriff's office.

All hell was about to break loose!

Chapter Thirty-four

Barry Sauer was sitting three miles east of Langdon, parked on the side of Highway 5 watching the cherry-red 'Cuda grumble off the shoulder. He glanced at the file on his MDT screen. He'd just tagged Kyle Shriver doing seventy-five in a fifty-five. Fifteen years ago he'd given Kyle's old man about the same ticket for about the same margin over the . . .

"Jimmy, Barry, Lyle: Dale Shuster just called." Dispatch at the SO came on the radio yelling, so blown-away excited she skipped the ten codes, *". . . and was he freaked. Said Joe Reed shot his brother Ace and maybe some woman at the Missile Park and sounds like Joe kidnaped Dale . . . maybe shot him, too. EMT is started . . ."*

The voice on the radio changed. Norm Wales had taken over the mike. *"Where is everybody?"*

"Yeager. Two north."

"Lyle. On Main. Headed for the bar."

"Sauer. Three east," Sauer croaked as the adrenaline thickened his throat. He whipped the cruiser around, tires fliging gravel, then hammered the gas as he headed into town. Pins and needles played

hopscotch up and down his spine—the déjà vu running with the acceleration.

Last week. Really cranking, lights and sirens to an accident, and this deer . . .

Doing sixty now, sixty-five . . .

His skid marks were still carved into the road surface headed toward the Pembina Gorge, panic hieroglyphics about what happens when an 02 Crown Victoria with a Interceptor package and a 351 Cleveland engine with high-performance fuel injection and two-hundred-dollar Eagle GT tires doing 120 miles an hour . . .

. . . mature running whitetail, weighing 200 pounds . . .

The nylon air bag was in his face like an air fist. Everything went steam white from the hot blast of nitrogen that powered the inflation; add the cornstarch coating from the bag, which wound up in his teeth. Damn deer drove in the grill and the radiator and pushed them back into the engine. Crammed the bumper back into the left front wheel . . .

Coming up on town . . . driving his sergeant's car today. *Shit!*

Gotta make a decision here. In his trunk, tucked in with his emergency gear, he carried an M-14 semiautomatic rifle with a twenty-round magazine. If he stopped to take it out, how much time would he lose? He glanced at his speedometer. Already going seventy.

No M-14, he decided. He loosed the safety strap on the holster that held his .45. The radio squawked:

"Joe driving that brown metallic van?"

"Where is he?"

"Bet he's headed for the rez."

"Don't figure. He can't outrun us on the flat."

"If he just shot Ace, he's probably not thinking real clear."

Then they got a break from a local game warden.

"Norm, this is Phil Lutes. Monitored your traffic. I'm out on Richmond just off 5 and the sumbitch just turned off the highway,

heading north . . . I got him. I got him. Just turn onto Richmond Road going north. That's him, brown GM van, kinda metal-flake brown."

"Hey, people, you got that? He's heading for the border. I'm calling customs to get the Canadians up. But remember—no pursuit into Canada."

"We got it."

Then a transmission stepped on the others, persisting through the static. *"Norm, it's Lyle."* Lyle was out of breath, shouting. *"I'm at the bar. Ace and a woman are down, shot."*

"Lyle. Secure the scene for EMT."

"They don't need no ambulance. They're dead, Norm."

"You monitor out there?"

Sauer put his foot on the floor, picked up his radio mike, called it in to the state net. *"Milton Tower, two-five-nine. Langdon nine-one-one has a double shooting, two confirmed dead, suspect running north on Richmond Road in a brown Chevy van. Am in pursuit. Request backup."*

"Milton ten-four."

Sauer switched to his shoulder mike. *And I got the fastest car.*

Two miles north of town, closer in than Sauer, Jimmy Yeager did not step on the gas first thing. Thinking Joe probably had a shotgun in his van, or maybe a deer rifle, he popped the trunk, jumped out of his cruiser, and unclipped his M-14 from the inside roof of the trunk. He inserted a twenty-round mag of 7.62 NATO rounds, advanced one to the chamber, set the safe, and stashed the big rifle in the passenger foot well.

Don't want to get outgunned.

Yeager got back in, put the cruiser in gear, locked his seat belt, and stamped on the gas.

Roaring past the city limits, Sauer was thinking it might be smarter not to go to noise yet. Play it stealthy. But he was coming up on the four-way stop on north 1, and he was already doing seventy-

five, eighty. So as he blew past the line of brand-new Border Patrol
Tahoes parked at the Motor Inn, he hit the lights and the siren.

The whoop of the siren brought Broker up to an instant sitting position. He reached over and felt the empty bed next to him. He saw
the gun belt on the table, got up, read the note. As the siren receded
in the distance he got a real bad feeling. He grabbed for his clothes.

Sauer made his second decision. He'd shot past the Richmond turn
and was beginning to brake to catch the next road. *"Where is everybody?"* he yelled in the radio.

Sheriff Wales answered first: *"In back of you, coming outta
town."*

"I'm going to parallel west. Try an' get ahead of him."

"I'll come up Richmond. Get on his tail."

Sauer tightened both hands on the wheel and manhandled
through a skid. Turning, rear end sliding out. Caught a piece of the
far ditch and threw clods of dirt. *Oh shit. Shit. Gonna flip.* Amazingly, he didn't. Got her stable and back on the road, rattling along.
"Jimmy?"

"Parallel east of Richmond and I think I see him."

"Okay." Sauer blinked sweat. *Goddamn, I hope nobody's on this
road ahead of me. "I'm going to try to get ahead of him."* He
glanced at the speed. *Holy shit, does that 140 mean 140?* Nothing
under the accelerator but fuckin' floorboards now.

As Broker pulled on his jeans and stepped into his shoes he heard a
second siren start to wail. Coming out the motel front door he saw

the familiar boxy green shape of an ambulance, flashers revolving, heading west on 5. He ran for the Explorer, got in, started up, and took off after the ambulance.

On his way out of town Broker heard and caught the barest glimpse of a red flasher whipping over the fields to the north. Then the lights were gone. Just the sirens ahead of him and to the north. The whole town seemed to echo with sirens.

And he caught some of the old frenzied feeling in his chest. Car chase. Then the adrenaline jag solidified into a dull thump when he saw the ambulance pull into the parking lot of the Missile Park bar . . .

. . . and stop next to the dusty red Volvo with the Minnesota plates and the Wellstone bumper sticker. He parked behind the ambulance and got out.

One cop car. A stout county deputy stood on the porch talking to a female EMT. The other EMT hunched over the wheel of the ambulance, absorbing the staccato radio traffic.

The EMT slouched, empty hands hanging at her sides. Her bag sat on the porch. The body language didn't look good, none of that pit-bull intensity of a medic starting in on a casualty. She was waiting.

For a crime lab and a coroner.

Broker came abreast of the Volvo. The window was open on the driver's side, and he saw the blue pack of American Spirits lying on the dash. The brand Nina smoked. He approached the porch and stopped at the steps. He took a breath, held it for a moment, then let it out. "Who's down?" he said.

The deputy and the EMT studied him, put their heads together, and conferred. Then the deputy said, "You're Broker, right? We all heard how Jimmy Yeager went out with you last night."

Broker nodded, still edging toward the door.

"Okay, it's like this. I'm Deputy Vinson. And, Mr. Broker, you can't go in there. We have to keep it sterile for the lab guys."

The EMT stepped forward. She had a short strawberry-blond

shag, a face dusted with freckles, and vivid blue eyes. She paused. "There's two women that were in town, soldiers . . ."

Broker's knees started to buckle, the edges of his vision occluded, and he had trouble breathing. He forced the words out: "I'm married to the redhead."

"She's not in there," the EMT said crisply. Broker could see a weight lift from her face. "It's a young woman with very short black hair. And Ace Shuster."

"What happened?" Broker said.

"They think it was a guy named Joe Reed. That's who they're after," the deputy said. Broker toed the gravel, hitched up his belt. "I'd be out there, 'cept the sheriff told me to wait here."

"My wife was with Jane, the dark-haired woman." He pointed to the building. "They went out for breakfast . . ."

"We don't know much, yet," Vinson said.

Where's Nina? Broker's hands started shaking and he turned and walked back to the Volvo, reached in through the open window, took the pack of cigarettes, removed one, and put it in his lips.

He didn't have his lighter.

Vinson came off the porch and popped a Bic. Broker inhaled the comforting poison. Exhaled.

The ambulance driver yelled, "They got him! They're closing in."

They waited, all probably holding their breath. Half a minute passed. Another fifteen seconds. They all looked up to the north at the same time. A sound like sheets ripping in the wind.

"Thunder?" the EMT wondered, looking into the fierce blue sky.

Broker and Vinson locked eyes and shook their heads.

Sauer had pulled ahead of Joe's van, but a half-mile of barley separated them. He spotted Yeager coming in a little behind and to the right. First he just saw Yeager's lights, a red streak against the green fields, then the lights erupted in a cloud of dust as Yeager left the pavement and hit the gravel.

"He ain't working no jigsaw to double back west for the rez," Yeager shouted on the radio.

"No shit. He's headed for the border," Sauer shouted into his shoulder mike.

"Richmond Crossing."

And Richmond Crossing was coming up fast as the brown-green field to the right changed to bright yellow and the Crown Vic hit the gravel and started to shimmy and slide. Sauer gripped the wheel and felt his forearms load up with the road tension. He had to make another decision. Unless Yeager intercepted and rammed the van, they would lose him.

The solution was visceral: high ground dry, low ground still wet.

Old man Kreuger's field fanned out with ripe canola. He had hunted whitetails on it for years. One of the few parcels with some roll and height to it west of Pembina. Little work road skirted the slight rise, running in just about *here* . . .

Ooohhhh shittt!!!! He took his foot off the gas, tapped the brake, and swerved into the chest-high blossoms at 110 mph.

Joseph Khari fixed his eyes 200 yards ahead, where the gravel road ended in a rutted two-lane path with a strip of grass growing up the middle. He had driven this route dozens of times in the dead of night. Canada was less than a minute away. He knew the American cops could not pursue across the border. He figured someone had seen him leave the bar. But he was too disciplined to waste energy wondering why the police were chasing him. He kept his focus on driving, on feeling the gravel under his wheels at high speed. A mile beyond the border he had another truck hidden in a copse of trees. Get to it. Destroy the Joe Reed ID. Wait for dark.

He had always been practical and unflappable. It would be close but he could make it. The cop on the left had no access across the field; had, in fact, dropped out of sight. The one on the right would be too late to stop him. They might have radioed to the Canadians, but it was happening so fast. A plane or a helicopter would be a problem.

But he saw no activity out ahead of him. He could do it.

Then he saw the steak of white shoot through the yellow field to his left, plowing down a slight rise. A police car coming almost out of control. Oily with crushed plants, flattening them like a wave. On a collision course.

The American fool cut through the field and was going to crash into him.

Reflex and instinct dictated that Joseph swerve right to avoid the onrushing car. But the moment he drove off the trail his wheels slipped into a muddy depression. He lost traction. Had to turn back to the trail . . .

But the American stopped abruptly just shy of the trail. He'd hit something. The air bag inflated in the police car. Yes, he'd crashed into something.

Joseph mashed his foot on the gas. It only spun his wheels and dug him in deeper. The van shook and then stalled. Instantly he jumped out the door. Wading through the muck—all right then. For a split second he'd considered reaching back for Broker's pistol. No time. All he needed was the Browning in his hand. He kicked open the door, hit the ground in a lopsided run. The police car was heeled over, at an angle. The policeman was clawing at the air with his hands, wrestling the air bag aside, wiping something from his eyes. The Browning swept up. So Joseph would run the last thirty yards to Canada on his bad leg—but first he would kill himself an American.

● ● ●

Jimmy Yeager saw it happening. He slammed on the breaks and skidded off the road, aiming for a slight knoll in the field. He saw the van jerk to a halt. Saw Sauer block the crossing.

Three hundred yards and closing. Gotta stop now. No time. Two hundred was what he wanted but this would have to do. Timing the lurch of his vehicle so as not to lose time opening the door, he pushed the door and exited, dragging the M-14 by its skinny barrel and heavy flash suppressor. *Shit! Can't see! Fucking fold in the land.* Immediately he hopped on the hood and then clambered onto the roof.

Now he could see. It was Joe, all right. Out of the van, running toward the State Patrol cruiser, his right arm extended.

The crack and snap of shots.

Jesus. Shaking, breathing all wrong; Yeager swung up the M-14. His old Corps dad made him learn to shoot offhand at 200 yards.

If you can't shoot offhand you ain't shit!

Joe running with his arm straight out, windows blowing apart in the state cruiser making it hard to see, to tell . . . All these shots and then Yeager squeezed off three of his own.

It wasn't fair. They had so much. So much space, this lush yellow-and-green emptiness, the tilt-a-whirl blue sky. Joseph spun like a bad dancer, shredded. He smelled the raw sewage of the camps, saw the bloated corpses again at Sabra and Shatila. The tiny children with flies crawling on them. Cholera, typhoid, diseases that never touch these fat Americans.

Not fair.

He collapsed deeper into a million little yellow flowers. Moist like pollen, smelling like medicine, buzzing of insects. Footfalls coming from in back. Where was the Browning? But all feeling was draining from his arms. Then gone. George and Dale would have to kill the Americans. He, Joseph, was through with them.

Losing pieces of the sky and sound he thought he saw a broad white face loom over him. Lonely now. Leaving. Not sure why, he rasped his goodbye.

"*Ma'assalama . . .*"

Yeager stooped to hear Joe's last words. All he got was a rattle of breath. He placed two fingers along Joe's throat and felt for a pulse. There was none. Yeager hoisted himself up slowly. He was gasping, and starting to shake.

Joe was pitched on his side so Yeager could see his back and front were both a mess. They got him coming and going. Sauer's .45 sure tore some holes coming out.

Sauer.

Yeager jogged the last fifteen yards to the State Patrol cruiser. Barry Sauer was sprawled forward across the front seat. His hair and grimacing teeth were covered in white powder. His arms still extended out the shattered passenger-door window. Gently, Yeager pried the .45 from the death grip of Sauer's clamped hands. Yeager gritted his teeth, seeing the blood at Sauer's throat, thick above his shirt collar. On his cheeks, his nose.

"Man," Sauer gasped, "I am . . . sure . . . fucking glad . . . my . . . wife . . . made . . . me . . . wear . . . *this.*"

With his left hand, Sauer ripped at the top buttons of his uniform shirt, tearing the cloth away to show the two deep impact impressions on his Kevlar.

"You're bleeding!" Yeager said, his voice too loud.

Sauer shook his head. "Just cuts. Glass. Whole lot of stuff flying around for a minute there."

Yeager helped Sauer out of the car and supported him as they walked up to Joe's body. Cars with flashing lights were converging. Norm's Silverado. Cops from Towner.

"I yelled for him to drop it but there was no way," Sauer said. Then more urgent. "The van?"

"I went by it. No sign of Dale. Was in a hurry. Then when I got to him he said something, couldn't make it out. Sounded strange. Indian maybe."

Sauer grimaced and said, "Now we got some people missing."

Yeager nodded.

"Damn," Sauer said. This time he pointed at his cruiser. "Old Man Kreuger probably only had one sleeper rock in his field and I had to hit it." He shook his head, dripping blood. "Totaled another state car. That's the second air bag I kissed in seven days."

Yeager grinned. "Three more and they gotta make you an ace. Don't sweat it, road dog, we're gonna be all right."

"How's that?"

Yeager pointed at the cloud of dust kicked up by four new Border Parol Tahoes coming in a tight convoy. "The cavalry's here."

Chapter Thirty-five

Face into the wave.

Numb, her teeth fuzzy. Hard to breathe. Nina tried to spit the taste of decay from her mouth, but she was too dry. *Memory jabbed.* Some drug he used.

Moving. Patterns of light and shadow dappled a wall of knotty pine veneer.

The morning's shark attack all came back to her. Jane. Ace . . .

Not now. Focus on the present. She tried to move.

Spreadeagled on a bed.

Not good.

Resistance at her wrists and ankles. Little strength. She could move her head and she saw that her wrists were secured with double-tied bungee cords. The same for her wrists. The hooks had been crimped together tight. She strained against the cords with her wrists and legs. Some give. They were makeshift. Maybe she could defeat them. Given time, she figured, she could. But not if he kept giving her that drug.

He. Dale. The other Shuster.

Her mind churned, scurrying. *Not okay yet. Process.*

Automatically, she confronted the fear. She had been trained to convert it into a manageable image. So it became a wave building in the distance. An instructor in survival training explained that extreme fear was like the ocean. Too big to get your mind around, too fast to outrun. You had to navigate it. *Great, so now I'm in the fucking Navy.* You had to turn into it, meet it head on, ride it out. If you froze up or ran away, it would roll you up and take you down.

Orient yourself. Face into the wave.

She was lashed down on a bed in the rear of a van or camper. From some calm center in her brain she recalled that Broker had ingrained in her a suspicion of vans. She twisted around to get a better look. Not the kind of bed that was built into this kind of vehicle. This was an ordinary twin bed, wooden head and footboard, sideboard, slats and springs and mattress. The interior of the vehicle had been gutted and the bed brought in. The bedroom was partitioned from the front seat by a curtain. Dale. Up there driving. Maybe that other dude, too. Just ten, twelve feet away.

A screened window over the bed was partly open, letting in patches of light and shadow. She heard the thrum of tires, road sounds. Traffic passing.

She tried to look around the compartment. She could see where a sink, counter, and partitions had been removed. It had been stripped and now just contained a TV bolted to a shelf over the bed, a VCR stacked on top. A small chemical toilet sat next to the curtain. Then her eyes stopped on the video camera set on a tripod in the corner with a cable looped around it. The cable ended in some kind of remote device.

The vehicle went over a bump. The video camera jiggled, came to life. The cheap tripod legs rattled on the floor, taking baby robot steps. Toward the bed. And her intuition made a few fast leaps.

Nina understood that the camera was for her.

● ● ●

No preparation for this. But she found it familiar. Down deep, she had been braced for something like this all her life. Every woman carried the nightmare in her blood salts: you wake up bound, powerless in the hands of a disturbed, angry man. Usually it happens to other people and you read about it in the newspaper. You see it on TV.

Not this time.

Furious, she reared against the restraints, and succeeded only in bruising her wrists. She collapsed back on the bed.

As best she was able to determine her clothing had not been torn, didn't seem to have been removed. The smear of blood on her chest was dry and flaking around the edges, still damp in the center. Some time had passed.

The only pain she felt was in her right hand, and she carefully—selectively—worked back. Dale Shuster had stepped on her hand when she went after Jane's pistol.

She had hardened herself to accept rape as part of capture, like a beating. In theory. But this was more. She was lashed down to something in motion. She swallowed and tried to get her breathing under control.

She was caught up in the mechanics of the thing she had been looking for. Taken. For a reason.

Not by Wahhabi fanatics out of the Afghan camps. But by Dale Shuster. And Gordy's "funny fucking Indian," Pinto Joe.

Then the road noise lessened and she could feel the vehicle slowing, the tires hitting gravel. Turning. The sunlight coming in through the window dappled down to shade.

Motion ceased. The sound of traffic had disappeared. She could almost hear the heat buzzing on the green griddle of fields. Birdsong. The idling motor vibrated under her, a warm steel kitten. She heard a body moving beyond the curtain. Voices.

"Goddammit, Dale, not now!" An impatient voice she could not place.

"Take it easy, we got lots of time," Dale said. Then a hand swept the material aside and Dale entered the compartment. His bulk made the space where she was smaller, stole the light. He held a twenty-ounce plastic bottle of Coke in one hand and the remnants of a doughnut in the other. Nina could see grains of sugar on his thick lips, see his tongue dart out and lick them off.

He smiled. "How about I show you a movie?"

Chapter Thirty-six

Broker stood next to the ambulance, listening to the radio traffic wind down. The fields were quiet again, the sirens stilled. Joe Reed had resisted arrest and had been killed in a shootout on the border. He watched the EMT's face go from mortal anxiety to relief as she talked on the radio. They assured her the state cop was all right.

"Her husband," Vinson told Broker.

A second deputy arrived at the Missile Park in a Toyota Tundra. He'd obviously been summoned in a hurry because he wore a uniform shirt tucked into his jeans. He huddled briefly with the regular deputy and the EMTs. Then he introduced himself to Broker as Marly Druer, part-time help called in special for today.

Druer was brief: "Sheriff says you were a cop so there's no need to baby around with you. There was a nine-one-one call from Dale Shuster, he said Joe Reed shot the two in there. Then it gets confusing. Maybe Dale was taken hostage. They been going over the tape and it sounds like Dale said another woman was involved. That could be your wife. So, first off, where was your wife this morning?"

"She left a note at the motel that she was going out for coffee with Jane." Almost ashamed, Broker added, "I was asleep." He pointed to the bar's desolate brick facade. "I think Jane's in there."

"It's Jane," said Vinson. "I met her when they came to town."

"Neither of them were in Joe's van when they caught up with him," Druer said. "Could be your wife is missing in this. So the sheriff wants to talk to you. Leave your truck here. You can ride with me."

Okay . . . I'll take missing. Better than dead.

A few moments later, Broker realized he had thought *Okay* when he'd meant to say it. Gears weren't meshing, switches failed. What good is language at a time like this?

"Okay," he said finally. He took a drag of the cigarette as he armored himself with control. The shock whirled his guts to the brink of nausea, edged back. "But I need a minute to call my folks in Minnesota. I sent my kid back there and she's expecting her mother to call her this morning."

"Ah, jeez. Yeah, sure," Druer said.

Broker walked off a few paces and took out his cell phone, pulled the card with Holly's number from his wallet. Punched it in and hit send.

"Colonel Woods."

"Holly?"

"Yeah, who's this?"

"Broker."

"C'mon, I don't need any more shit. I'm up to my ass in alligators here . . ."

"You sure are. Jane's dead and Nina is missing. It ain't over, Holly."

"Goddamn . . . How?"

"Shootout in that bar. Ace Shuster is dead. This Indian dude who worked for his brother is the prime suspect. It's possible he took Nina and Ace's brother with him when he made a run for it. They mouse-trapped him, killed him in a gunfight trying to run the border. And Nina and the brother are nowhere in sight. Listen. The local cops are all over me. I'd stay out of sight if I were you. I'll call you as soon as I can."

"Broker."

"Yeah, Holly."

"She's as tough as they come. If there's any . . ."

Broker ended the call, cutting Holly off. He didn't need coaching about what was going on. He put his cell away, got in Druer's truck, and worked hard at resisting gravity. Let it float. He stared straight ahead, tried to slip the first wave of shock as if it were a punch.

Ain't over till it's over.

But the jolt was maybe just what he needed to knock him a little off kilter. To see this morning's events and everything that had happened from a slightly skewed angle. So he stared right into it. All of it. He stared and he stared.

And sonofabitch! There it was.

They parked in back of the county building and went to the sheriff's office, buzzed in through dispatch, and waited. A few minutes later, Sheriff Wales came in, flushed. Dark patches of sweat staining the underarms of his uniform. From the knees down he was damp and smeared with crushed, tiny yellow flowers that smelled faintly like last night's canola fields.

He motioned Broker through the corridors to his office, where they faced off. "You gonna help me on this, Broker?" Wales said. "Now that we got dead people lying all around."

"You know about the fiasco last night?"

Wales nodded. "It's all over town. But I can't figure why they'd go after Ace."

"Five days ago Nina's bunch cracked an Al Qaeda finance officer in Detroit. He gave up a smuggling operation. He suggested they were bringing a nuclear device in through your county and, that they were dealing with an American named Shuster."

Wales took it like a body blow, narrowing his eyes, incredulous. "Ace had some kinda bomb?"

"Don't know."

Wales recovered quick. "Yeah, well, you seen what Ace was smuggling last night." Then he pointed his finger at Broker. "Don't play games. We haven't had a murder in this town for twenty years. Now I got three people shot to death in an hour's time. And two missing, kidnapped . . ."

How do you know they're kidnapped?" Broker said.

"Dale called in to nine-one-one that—"

Broker cut in, "The Qaeda guy in Detroit said they were working with a Shuster. You got one dead Shuster and another one telling you something on a phone . . ."

Wales chewed at the inside of his cheek, cocked his head. "You mean . . . Dale . . . ," he said slowly.

"Yeah, Dale. What if that distress call was misdirection?" Broker ventured.

Wales headed out the door, motioning to Broker to follow. "C'mon."

"Where we going?"

"To the Shuster house, for starters."

Wales paused at dispatch to put instructions over the radio. "Lyle, stay at the bar and keep an eye on the ME. And when the crime lab people get in from Bismarck, thank them for assisting but make it clear we want the jurisdiction. Break. Yeager, get Barry to the hospital, then stand by at the SO." He turned to the dispatcher. "Karen, where are we?"

"Bismarck is started. They got the crime lab on the way and two investigators."

"Okay. Who we got up at the border?"

"The Border Patrol. Hal Cotter from Pembina, Jack Lambert from Towner, and Gerry Kruse from the state."

"Ask real polite for the BP to secure the scene. Kruse has the most training as an investigator out of that bunch. Ask him to meet me at the Shuster house."

"Gotcha. Anything else?"

"Tell anybody who inquires we're gathering the facts and trying to figure out what happened. No names."

They went out the door, got in Wales' Silverado, and drove to the east end of town, where a row of large ranch-style homes sat off separated from the other houses by sizable landscaped yards. Wales pulled up a driveway. There was a FOR SALE sign. The grass needed cutting.

They studied the front door, which was pretty sturdy. Next they went around to the side. "Should really have a warrant," Wales said.

"Right. In Minneapolis, before 9/11, Coleen Rowley tried to get a warrant on that Moussaoui guy's computer and FBI headquarters turned her down," Broker said.

Wales grunted, stooped, pulled a brick from the edging of the side garden, and smacked the pane of glass on the side door. "It's called reasonable suspicion." He started in.

"Wait a minute, you smell something?" Broker, sniffing, lifted his head.

"Yeah, around back."

They went around to the backyard, where a fifty-five-gallon garbage drum was smoldering. Wales kicked it over. Stacks of computer printout paper and magazines spilled on the patio. Like they'd been pitched into a fire in a hurry, in thick stacks and only the edges were burned.

Druer, the part-timer, drove into the driveway. Wales asked him to poke around in the burn-barrel debris. Then he and Broker entered the empty house and did a fast walk-through, careful not to disturb anything.

"Not much here," Broker said.

Ace's mom and dad left over two weeks ago for down south. Dale was living here until the place sold."

Druer stuck his head in the door. "Norm? You better get out here," he yelled.

They hurried out the side door and around the back. Druer raced ahead and squatted on his haunches, poking a thick scorched pile of bound, laminated pages with a pen.

"Cover's gone. But this is a high school yearbook from ten years ago," Druer said. He tapped the pen on one of the charred pages. "And look here."

Broker stared at a burned page. A girl's picture was circled. Wales swept his palm over it, ignoring the sparks and ashes, bringing it up cleaner. "Look at the eyes."

The eyes had been blacked out.

"Holy shit. It's Ginny Weller. She went missing in Grand Forks last month. Was never found," Wales said.

Carefully, Druer started working through the pages, flipping them one by one with the pen. They came to another circle. Another picture with the eyes blacked out. This time it was a boy. Even at ten years' remove, Broker recognized the hairy face of Gordy Riker.

Wales bent to the radio mike clipped to his shoulder. "Karen, check around on the whereabouts of Gordy Riker. We ran into something weird at Dale's house. Somebody's been blacking out eyes in his high school yearbook. Like Ginny Weller's eyes. And Riker's. So call the other dispatchers. Get 'em on the phones. Where's Jimmy?"

"With Sauer, at the hospital."

"No I ain't," Yeager's voice cut in on the radio. "I'm on my way to the Shuster house. I heard you on the yearbook pictures. You got Broker there?'

"Yeah, he's here," Wales said.

"Ask him if he's missing a .45, and a Washington County shield. We found them in Joe's van," Yeager said.

Wales turned to Broker who shrugged, held up his hands. "Was lifted out of my car yesterday."

"I also found his wife's purse," Yeager said.

Broker did not shrug this time. Wales touched his shoulder and said, "Just wait till he gets here."

Then Kruse, the state cop, pulled in, and Wales asked him to search the house. Jimmy Yeager arrived a few minutes later. His cruiser was caked with mud and rattled like half the undercarriage was about to drop off.

Yeager got out of the car, immediately walked up to Broker and checked his face, his eyes. "What I got ain't good," he said.

"Show me," Broker said.

Yeager held up a plastic evidence bag. Broker recognized Nina's purse. The gray quill-patterned ostrich-hide saddlebag he'd given her for Christmas three years ago. The bag was messy red around the edges. He took a sharp breath. Messy red from coagulating blood.

Carefully, Yeager put the plastic bag down on the hood of his cruiser and worked the purse out. With a pen he nudged the wallet open, then eased out the Minnesota driver's license.

Nina's picture ID on the license had the eyes blacked out.

Chapter Thirty-seven

Name, rank, serial number.

Something to brace on. Get ready. Sound went in and out. Light rippled on the wall, the wind slipping through leaves outside. Dale had parked off the road, in the shade of some trees. Her mind played tricks, defaulting to bad trips . . .

Seven years ago she'd been forced down on another bed by Virgil Fret, who tried to rape her. She had mocked his manhood and driven him into a fury of violence. He burned her with cigarettes, kicked her, and then punched her with his fists. His brother, Bevode, who was a lot scarier than Virgil, cut off part of her ear and gave it to Broker as a present.

But Virgil didn't bind her hands because he liked the back-and-forth of physical contact, the feeling of knocking her around. She'd used that to stay alive minute by minute until Broker . . .

She forced away the image. Nothing personal, not now. Not Broker, not Jane . . .

This was different from Virgil.

· · ·

Unlike at the bar, now she got nothing overtly sexual off Dale Shuster, who stood in the compartment, bland and white as the Pillsbury Doughboy. It was hot in this tight space, but still Dale wore a long-sleeve blue Carhartt work shirt buttoned down to the wrists and up to his neck. The bloodless white of his skin was something you see on the inside of a seashell.

Hard to gauge reactions and focus. She thought she knew her body. Always counted on hemorrhages of adrenaline. But that old surge had turned on her, had congealed into a cold, heavy coil that pressed down on her chest. Hard to breathe with Dale studying her. His flat, patient eyes were teaching her stuff she didn't want to know. Like how fear was a fast surface blast of pins and needles. Fear was fight or flight. Fear helped you survive. She'd swept right past fear into something deeper. More permanent. This was dread.

Dread was no way out, looking down into darkness. Getting ready to die.

To hold dread at bay she reached deep for hate. With difficulty, she forced a breath into her lungs. Let it out.

Face into the wave. *Easy for you to say.*

Still, she had to know.

She forced herself to look directly into Dale's eyes and said, "What was that you gave me?"

"Ketamine. It's a general anesthetic. Makes you paralyzed. I hit you in a large muscle group, so it came on slow. Like, say, when you have to use the bathroom. I'll give you half a dose and you'll be like a puppy. Easy to handle."

Nina couldn't help making a face.

Dale shrugged. "I have this problem with women. Ketamine helps me get over it. You didn't eat any breakfast this morning, did you?" he asked blandly.

Nina shook off the weird question, gritted her teeth, and said, "Do you know who I am?"

He nodded. "You're the government. You came looking for me

because a Saudi named Rashid was arrested in Detroit earlier this week. He talked."

That stunned her, and though she was still trippy from the drug, she had to know. She pushed up against the restraints. "Dale, is there a bomb?"

"Oh yes. Maybe you'll get to see the windows rattle when it goes off. From a safe distance, of course." Dale pushed the last bite of his doughnut into his mouth, and she noticed the milky flesh under his fingernails. A sign of a congestive heart. His blood was probably white too. Clots in his veins like maggots.

He chewed, took a final gulp of Coke, and set the can on the carpet. Then he lowered his bulk to the side of the bed. His weight depressed the mattress and she shifted toward him. Their hips touched. Almost blushing, he shyly moved away.

Nina started to tremble. It wasn't his casual talk about a bomb that undercut her nerve. It was his creepy fit of shyness. The weird things he said.

You didn't eat breakfast this morning?

After several false starts, she managed to say, "Rashid used the word *nuclear*."

"Yes. There is a nuclear component," Dale said.

"How"—she shook her head, concentrated, then continued—"did they get it in?"

"They?" Dale drew himself up. "*They* didn't. *I* did. It's my bomb. Well, actually, George and Joe made it, but it was my idea first." His smile, though modest, showed half an inch of gum.

"*George?*" her voice rose.

"Yeah. You met him last night. He faked you guys out, huh?" Dale jerked his thumb at the rear of the van. "He's right outside, parked in back. Probably smoking one of his cigars. We're on our way to blow it up."

She wasn't processing this. She was losing it to the shakes. Her hip and left leg started to charley-horse, and out of reflex she stretched against the cords, causing her to arch her back, raise her hips to flex the cramped muscles. Dale averted his eyes and immediately rose from the bed.

"Don't do that," he said.

Nina couldn't stop blinking, as if rapid eyelid movement could clarify the confusion. *On their way* . . . then a spasm circled her spine and she fought off a deep tremor, afraid her bladder and sphincter would let go. She had lost control and now she would lose her dignity. She would be reduced to mere fluids: sweat, tears, piss, shit, and blood. She knew if she allowed herself to think of her daughter right now she would cry.

Suddenly, enveloped in shivers, she got it. He wasn't your ordinary sexual predator. He wasn't some high-prairie militia whack job. They figured how to use him because . . .

He was crazy.

Dale edged around the bed, went to a small wicker basket by the toilet, and removed a folded sheet. Methodically he opened it, shook it out, and held it at arm's length. It was as white as his face. He returned to the side of the bed and carefully spread it over her, pulling it up to her neck. "That's better," he said.

Then he reached up and closed the window and pulled the curtain shut so it was dark in the compartment.

"Movie time," he said.

Chapter Thirty-eight

It was turning into the kind of hot July day when you want to stay inside, draw the blinds, and turn up the A/C. Broker lit another of the cigarettes from Nina's pack. As he smoked, he continued to hold the pack in his hand, like it was a link to her. He felt the remaining cigarettes in it, resisting the urge to actually count them. About half left. In the back of his mind a scared little kid made up a game.

As long as I have her cigarettes, she'll be all right.

As they drove in Wales' truck, Broker wondered if these cops had been waiting for this ever since they swore an oath and strapped on a gun—a killing in their town. Now it was on them; three people shot dead in less than an hour. One of them by their hand.

Barry Sauer was in the hospital ER getting his face stitched. The Border Patrol was in charge of the site where Joe Reed had been stopped. Kruse was searching the Shuster home. Druer, the part-time deputy, was now helping Fire and Rescue organize a search party to comb through the fields and ditches along Joe Reed's escape route. Looking for Nina and Dale. They were covering all the bases.

Norm Wales drove up in front of the Missile Park and parked next to the county car. Deputy Vinson ushered them into the bar with a stern proprietary admonition: "Now, nobody touch nothin'."

The older men glared at him. He glared back. "I mean it, I been keeping this site *clean.*"

Ace and Jane lay about three feet apart. Ace was facedown, curled slightly, compact, his arms tucked under his chest. Two red rosettes had spread no more than three inches wide in the back of his T-shirt, between his shoulder blades. Jane's position was more dynamic—pitched on her right side, her right arm outstretched. A 9-mm Beretta lay on the pine floorboards about six inches from her spread fingers. He couldn't see Ace's eyes, but he could see Jane's. They were open but had become things, mere organic matter, no longer human. Hardly any blood was evident on her broad forehead, but her chest was still soggy with it. A wet copper stench hung in the musty room.

"There's five ejected cartridge casings by the rear doorway," Vinson said.

Broker took a deep breath, let it out. You can get used to being around the dead but you never get used to the questions they pose.

"Broker, you been around some shootings?" Norm Wales said.

"A few," Broker said.

"What do you see?" Wales said.

Broker studied the way Jane was sprawled. She had been trying to fight, had been chopped down in the act of trying to aim her weapon. He looked at the doorway at the other end of the room, where the empty brass lay. He said, "Not much bleeding. They died fast. That guy Joe could shoot."

"Yeah," Yeager said. "He hit Barry twice in the Kevlar at a dead run over broken ground—from more'n twenty-five yards on the first one."

"I'm assuming Jane was no slouch with a handgun. But she took two in a two-inch group in the chest. Pretty fancy shooting under a lot of pressure for a blown-up Indian from Turtle Mountain," Wales said.

"Nina told me to watch out for him," Broker said. "Said he looked trained."

"Trained," Wales repeated. Like it was an especially potent word.

"She meant it as a backhanded compliment, as in trained like an operator. Like her. A peer. Maybe she was right," Broker said. "Maybe she found exactly what she was looking for."

Wales took a step closer and stared hard at Broker. "She's your wife. Where you at with this thing?"

Broker had to explain something. They'd all been watching closely as he cycled, by turns intense and cool, burning an icy hole in the day. "It's like this—Nina and I have had a few moments like this, and we made a pact that if the shit hits the fan—like now—we focus on working the problem until we know something for sure."

"For sure," Wales repeated.

"Yeah. Like until there's a body." They continued to stare at him. So he said, "Bottom line? Let's say Dale Shuster is a bad guy. If she's still breathing and he's dumb enough to take her along, he better watch out."

Wales nodded, he turned to Yeager. "Nuff said. Okay. What about Ace? Taking two in the back?"

"Don't figure," Yeager said. "Ace never ran from anything in his life."

Wales shook his head. "'Cept maybe success." He turned to Vinson. "You're doing it right. Keep everybody out till the state crime guys get here." Broker and Yeager followed him outside. He stood in silence for a few moments on the porch, staring at the equipment shed across the road. "Shuster and Sons," he said under his breath. "I'm going to have to call Gene Shuster, tell him about his boys. Question is, tell him what, exactly?" He collected himself and faced the other men. "Okay. We plan along two tracks. Until someone convinces me otherwise I'm treating Dale's nine-one-one call like what it appears. A murder-kidnap. So I got search parties started to go over every inch of ground on Joe's route." He looked directly at Broker. "You understand."

Broker nodded. "If they're dead, he had to dump the bodies."

"At the same time we'll give your misdirection theory some play. We'll dig up a photo of Dale, put out an all-points, and fax out the picture of Nina off her military ID."

Wales turned to Broker. "Okay, you come up with any bright ideas, you let me know. I'll let Jimmy spend some time with you. There's a couple carloads of people on their way from Bismarck and other counties, so it's not like I'll be hurting for help. All I ask is you two stay out of their way."

"You going to tell the state guys who Jane was?" Broker said.

Wales folded his arms across his chest. "Not right off. "'Cause all I got is hearsay, right? Nobody's going to confirm her, or Nina. And there's this—we haven't had a shooting in this county for a long time. This here's news. There'll be reporters coming. Loose talk about Army Delta and black helicopters could get real nuts real fast. Get way out of hand." Then he squinted at Yeager. "Jimmy, now you've got a taste for this weird shit, how you going to go back to writing speeding tickets and counseling domestics?"

Yeager shifted from foot to foot. "Norm, what about a shooting board? Do I turn in my sidearm and go off the clock?"

"And reduce my full-time staff by thirty percent? Anyway—you fire that Colt on your hip?"

"Nope."

"Then turn in the rifle. We'll start the paperwork. Everything going on, it'll probably be a week before we have a sit-down." He pointed his finger. "Don't do anything to antagonize the state guys."

Broker and Yeager nodded.

Wales started for his car. "I'll be at the SO, *coordinating*," he said, cranking some irony and awe into the remark.

As soon as Wales pulled away, Broker reached for his cell and called Holly.

They agreed to meet in the parking lot of Shuster and Sons Equipment, across from the bar. Holly drove up in his undercover rig, the dust-blasted gray Chevy truck with the Arizona plates. With his pale eyes and shaggy hair he projected an aura of a spooky wind blowing off the Superstition Mountains. He wore faded jeans, cracked dirt-whitened leather boots, and a colorless T-shirt frayed from too much sweat and too many washings that bore a small line of type over the heart: John McCain for President.

"Holly, you remember Yeager. He dropped the guy they think killed Jane." Holly and Yeager shook hands.

Holly studied the deputy. "We met out on the highway last night."

"Sorta. You arrived in the helicopter," Yeager said. He nodded across the road. "State crime agency is on the way to process the scene. You want to identify her?"

Holly shook his head and gazed across the road to where Vinson was stringing yellow crime scene tape. "I go in there, the forensic investigators'll want to know who I am, and I can't tell them." He paused, then said softly, "SOP. If it was me in there, Jane would say the same." He cleared his throat and planted his hands on his hips. "So I got one down and one missing." He swung his pale blue eyes on the deputy, waited a couple of heartbeats. "So . . . with us here— are there any rules?"

"Whatever you cook up, I go along. How's that for rules?" Yeager said.

"And if I don't like it?" Holly asked.

"Then I take you in for questioning."

"Well, then I guess I agree." He turned to Broker. "Whatta you think?"

"I think Dale and Reed were your smugglers. I don't know if Ace was involved. Somehow Nina and Jane bumped into them this morning and they panicked. If we find Dale, we might find what you came looking for," Broker said.

"Great," Holly said. "My crew is gone, my assets are gone. Any minute now, my chopper will be gone, too. I spent all morning getting chewed out on the telephone for running a cowboy operation. Now I've got casualties. And this ain't exactly my turf. So where do we start?"

"Right here." Broker pointed to the equipment shed, then turned to Yeager. "I saw something yesterday I want to show you. C'mon, it's out in the back."

Holly and Yeager followed Broker around the large shed. The weeds were chest high and still wet in the shadow of the building, and the dew drenched their trouser legs and footwear. They picked through a rusty junkyard: cast-off machinery parts, orange and flaking with rust, weeds growing in and around them. They came to a disturbed area, the dirt churned up and gouged by huge tire treads. The weeds in the dirt were dwarfs compared to the other weeds. Recent growth.

"He had a big loader in here," Yeager said.

Broker pointed to a slick of yellow metal among the churned dirt. "I'd stepped out the back door and just looked around, and I caught this flash of yellow. See that? I was wondering why he'd bury something like that."

Yeager stooped, scooped dirt away, and uncovered the top of a thick slab of yellow iron about two feet long and six inches deep. He moved closer, going down on his knees, and started to paw away the sand and dirt. "We need something to dig with."

Immediately they spread out and started searching around the large pole barn and its outbuildings. Yeager went to a nearby utility shed, kicked in the door, and returned with two dusty old shovels. He gave one to Broker and they began to clear away the soil.

After a few shovelfuls Yeager was panting and sweating profusely. He staggered and leaned on his shovel. "Don't know what's wrong."

Holly took his shovel, drove it into the dirt. "Delayed stress," he said quietly. "You ever kill a man before?"

Yeager shook his head, mopped sweat from his face.

"Kind of weight you pick up and never put down. Takes some getting used to. Hello . . ." His shovel twanged on hollow metal.

They looked at each other. "That ain't right," Yeager said. "It's a fucking counterweight, it's solid iron."

They went back to work and got it exposed. The weight was squared off on top and a slightly wider trapezoid on the bottom. Three large bolt holes were drilled into it, and an oblong opening through the side and out the top, like a handhold.

"What kind of weight?" Holly asked.

"Counterweight for a Deere loader. A 644C. Common enough machine around here," Yeager said.

Broker curled his hand around the opening in the top and yanked. It heaved slightly. "Jesus, what's it weigh?"

"Yeager squinted. "Something's wrong. You shouldn't be able to move that thing. Sucker should weigh over four hundred pounds."

"Why bury it? It's not like they wear out, like tires," Holly said. Real curious now, his shaggy white eyebrows drew closer together, his forehead wrinkled. Broker cleared away more dirt, tossed the shovel aside. With Holly, he squatted, grabbed handholds, and together they upended the weight.

"No shit, lookit that," Holly said.

The three of them explored the cast-iron slab with their fingers. More than a third of its volume had been cleanly machined to create a cylindrical cavity, open on one end.

"A hollow counterweight?" Broker said as he and Holly turned to Yeager.

"See here," Yeager said. He pointed to one end of the cavity, where the edge of the weight had been thinned down to less than a quarter-inch. It had cracked and shattered. "If it was bolted on the machine, with another weight in back of it, you could never see it was drilled out. But they screwed up milling out that thin edge to the hole and it cracked. Woulda gave it away, so he tossed it."

"Dale Shuster is sounding more and more like a tricky guy," Broker said. "What do you suppose he had in mind to put inside this thing?"

Yeager squatted, ran his thick fingers over the steel. "I seen a lot of smuggling tricks—false bottoms in gas tanks, compartments in trucks. But this is way too much work to get on and off a machine unless it was for something real special." He looked at Holly. "Would what you're looking for fit in here?"

Holly shook his head, tapped his teeth together. "Not sure."

"Still, it'd be one hell of a chore to get the weight on and off. You'd need a hoist, air wrenches for the bolts. And only one fella around here has the gear to do millwork like this," Yeager said. He looked at Broker, then at Holly. "Eddie Solce. He's done a lot of repair work for the Shusters, going way back."

On the ride out, Yeager explained how Eddie Solce lived south of town. He'd failed farming and had sold off half his land and had the rest in the Crop Rotation Program. He's always been the local guy to repair farm equipment in his metal shop. "And he's only got one hand. Lost his left hand in a corn picker, 'bout twenty years ago. Got him one of those old-fashioned Trautman farm hooks—just this clamp, but he can practically pick his nose with it."

Yeager wheeled into a long driveway leading up to a white

foursquare farmhouse in need of a paint job. Pointing toward a green F-150, he said, "He's home, there's his truck. Another thing, Solce always liked Ace. He was a little disappointed Ace didn't marry his oldest daughter, Sally. They dated pretty heavy during high school."

At the front door, Eddie Solce came out to meet them in blue jeans and a Chambray work shirt. Lean and rawboned, he'd shriveled into one mean nest of wrinkles after sixty and now it was impossible to tell his age. But he still looked strong, especially his right hand—as if the loss of his left hand had pumped twice the strength into the right. Broker thought he looked garrulous and he was.

"I already heard. Goddamn shame. Ace got himself shot by that goddamn Joe Reed. And some woman, too. Ace always did follow his pecker into trouble. Damn Joe anyway. Dale should'a never taken that buck on." Eddie paused, squinted, nodded toward Broker and Holly. "Who the hell are *these* two? Ain't from around here, that's for sure."

Yeager took Eddie by the shoulder, walked him off a few paces. "You don't want to know who these boys are, believe me."

Eddie flexed his jaw and sucked in his cheek on one side as he snatched a look over Yeager's shoulder. "That one dusty white-haired fucker—he looks like he came outta a goddamn *movie*."

"Eddie." Yeager said it like an admonition, like a command to come back to his senses and get serious.

"Yeah, Jimmy," he said, more collected.

"C'mon, let's take a walk."

"Am I in trouble?" Sober now, his voice slower. "Where we going?"

"Your shop. Something I wanted to talk to you about. We found it over at Shuster's shed. But the thing is, it's too big to carry around."

Solce set his jaw in resignation when Yeager said that. Like he knew where this was heading. They started toward the barn and the pole barn alongside. Broker and Holly fell in behind, listening to the conversation.

They went into the shop, which was an orderly rectangular work space with a long metal fabrication bench in the middle. A stick welder, along with tanks of acetylene and oxygen, sat off to the side. Racks of mixed plain and diamond-plate chromed steel sheets lined the wall. Yeager walked up to a machine at the end of the shop. It stood six feet tall, had a complicated drill head and a video console on an arm off to the side.

"Bridgeport mill," Broker said.

"Yep," Holly said, "That'd be the thing."

They settled back and watched.

Yeager put his hand on the mill and looked at Solce. "Well, Eddie?

"I got nothing to do with what happened at that bar. I been here all morning, ask Margo and the grandkids," Eddie said. He began to scratch at the steel hook with his right hand.

"But you did some unusual work for Dale this summer, didn't you?" Yeager said.

Eddie ground his teeth, tapped them together a few times. "A job's a job."

"But this job was pretty strange, you gotta admit . . ."

Eddie swallowed and said very respectfully, "Am I in trouble, Jimmy?" He scratched at his hook faster, like it really itched.

"I'm thinking no, but if you don't tell me straight about drilling a channel in a five-hundred-pound Deere counterweight I'll sure as hell figure out a way to put you ass deep in something," Yeager said.

Eddie sagged and sat on his metal bench. "Wasn't just one. Was five of the fuckers."

Broker and Holly came forward, their eyes getting wide. "How the hell did you get five of those things in here?" Broker said.

Eddie shrugged. "Joe Reed brought 'em over on a lowboy. Had a hoist and jacks. He was good at stuff like that. We brought them in one by one on a forklift."

"When was this?" Yeager said.

"Beginning of June. Took me two weeks to do the four on the loader. Then one of them cracked and I had to do another one."

"Jesus Christ, Eddie," Yeager said. "Did it occur to you to wonder what the hell Dale wanted with bored-out weights on a 644C?"

"Well, it was different. And Dale, he just said, like—'I know this looks weird but it's a joke I'm playing on Irv Fuller.' See, he was getting set to sell the loader to Irv, in Minnesota."

Broker and Holly were squinting slightly, leaning forward, listening carefully. They shot quick looks at Yeager.

"One hell of a lot of work for a practical joke," Yeager said.

"I know, Jimmy. But those two families have a history of shorting each other way back. And there's the stuff from high school. Remember? Irv was behind that stunt they pulled on Dale."

Yeager narrowed his eyes, folded his arms across his chest, and said quietly, "Along with Ginny Weller."

"They ever find her in Grand Forks?" Eddie asked.

"No," Yeager said. He glanced at Broker and Holly.

Broker took Holly aside and explained about the burned yearbook, Nina's license. Then he stepped forward, raised his hand to calm Eddie, who instinctively edged back. "Give us a diagram of the job, how you milled out those weights."

Eddie's eyes flitted to Yeager, who nodded his assent. Eddie got up from the bench, went to a counter next to the mill, and took out a pad of paper and a pen. He held the pad in place with his hook and sketched an angled channel running through two weights from the side view. He looked up. "Big enough to stick your arm in, except it don't go through and through. The channel on the rearmost weight was open on one end and to within an eighth of an inch on the other end. That's why one cracked, 'cause it was such a close tolerance. But the other weight, the channel was only halfway through, so when you put the weights back on the machine you can't tell they been milled."

"The same on both sides?" Broker asked.

"Yeah, but they wanted them angled kinda. So they run continuous together." Eddie raised his hands and pulled them in tight to his chest in an inverted V. "Like the two channels come to a point." He licked his lips, swallowed. "Kinda," he said, his nerves kicking out an extra word.

Yeager clapped Eddie on the shoulder. "Take it easy, Eddie, You did good. I'll be in touch."

They left Eddie Solce sitting on his bench staring at the concrete floor of his workshop. On the swift walk back to Yeager's cruiser, Holly said, "Angled channels converging, steel plug in the back, paper thin in front. What's that sound like to you?"

"Like a funnel for a shaped explosive charge," Broker said.

"Well, technically, more like a directional charge. Man, we gotta find that machine," Holly said.

"I'm working on it," Yeager said, flipping open his cell.

Chapter Thirty-nine

As Yeager drove back to town, Broker worked at shoring up his compartments. He lit another of Nina's cigarettes. He tore open the pack and counted; nine remaining.

He stared straight ahead, fixed on the dead-straight two-lane narrowing down to a vanishing point. He avoided the image that waited one mental partition away—of Nina lying dead in a North Dakota ditch.

He refocused on the present. At least he had blundered into a good fit with these guys. Especially Holly, who had migrated past tough, scary, and super-elite, achieving now the cool intensity of a ghost. He was utterly without affect, like he was already spending his weekends on the other side.

Yeager was smart enough to know he was running with the big time. But he was proud and grounded and suspicious enough not to take it all too seriously until he had proof.

And they had none of the macho posturing that afflicted some cops, feds, and soldiers. Usually the ones with the peacock-strut were the guys who'd only shot their weapons at stationery targets under the watchful eyes of a range officer.

As the grain elevators and water towers of Langdon came into sight, Yeager finally reached his wife.

"Pam, find me a phone number on Irv Fuller in the Cities. Somebody's gotta be in touch with him. And it's urgent." He ended the call, put down the phone, and turned to Broker in the passenger seat.

"Irv Fuller's dad had a construction business in town. Irv's dad and Ace's dad always got in these pissing contests back and forth over equipment. But the thing that got me thinking is—Irv and Dale were in the same class in school. Along with Ginny Weller and Gordy Riker. And those three really stuck it to Dale senior year.

"Then Irv and Ginny got married when Irv took over his dad's business. Ginny wanted to leave town, Irv wanted to stay. Ginny left him and took up with an attorney in Grand Forks.

"After Ginny left him, Irv migrated to the Cities about seven years ago and remarried a gal whose dad had a construction outfit. Irv's dad and father-in-law threw in together and word is, now he's got this big operation."

Yeager turned to Holly, "Except Ginny went missing and Dale Shuster blacked out her eyes in his yearbook."

"That yearbook. Somebody should take a look at Fuller's picture," Broker said.

"You got it," Yeager said. "And I want to go back to the shed and look at that loader. It's the same model as the one Dale sold to Irv. Maybe we look at it we can get more of a picture on those channels." Then he picked up his mike and called dispatch. "Anyone get a line on Gordy Riker?"

"Nobody seen him since yesterday morning. He bought some doughnuts at Linder's bakery."

Yeager looked at Broker. "You ain't missing after just twenty-four hours. He could be down at Devil's Lake fishing."

"Still," Broker said.

"Yeah," Yeager said. He keyed the mike again. "Kruse, you monitor?"

"*I'm here, Jimmy.*"

"Could you check that yearbook they found. Look for Irv Fuller in the senior pictures. Tell me if there's anything weird about the picture."

"*Ten-four.*"

Three minutes later they were pulling in at Shuster's shed when Kruse called back: "*No Fuller. In fact no names starting with F.*"

"Burned?" Broker asked.

"*Missing. Just ragged paper curled against the binding. Page has been ripped out.*"

"Thanks," Yeager said and hung up the mike. Broker, Yeager, and Holly exchanged apprehensive looks and got out of the car. Across the highway Lyle waved. Yeager called to him. "Where's the crime lab?"

"On the way. Probably another half-hour."

While the two cops traded information, Broker felt the first delayed panic attack flap through his chest. He looked up into the blazing sun, shivered, lit another of Nina's cigarettes.

Eight.

They tried the front office door, found it locked and walked around back. The rear entrance was a tall, wooden, barn-type sliding door. Only rusty wheels on a rail resisted them. They pushed the door open and went inside.

The John Deere 644C front-loader sat in veils of heat and shadow like a giant yellow steel-and-rubber Sphinx. It stood ten feet tall to the roof of the cab and weighed fifteen tons. The bucket rested on the ground at the end of the lowered hydraulic boom and cylinder. Motionless, it mocked them like a deceptive, sleeping beast of burden with long yellow steel muscles and fat, four-foot-high Michelin tires.

A spray of white dots speckled the cab, the motor assembly, the huge wheels, and the bucket. Pinpoints coming in through birdshot punctures in the tin roof.

Broker imagined Ace or even Dale: country kids with their dad's shotgun, knocking down pigeons.

The left rear counterweight was missing from the chassis.

Holly leaned forward and rested his right palm against the hot metal where the missing weight should be. He closed his eyes— Spock in a Vulcan mind-meld. Abruptly he turned, walked from the pole barn, and went around to the right, into the weeds, generally in the direction of the buried counterweight.

Broker and Yeager walked around the machine, trying to puzzle out Dale Shuster's strange millwork. Then they wandered up toward the office area, which had been stripped clean. No phone. No computer. Just the chair, a desk, and the small refrigerator, un-plugged, empty, with the door open. Yeager's eyes traveled around the empty structure, then his cell rang. He answered. It was his wife. He hunched the phone to the crook of his neck, took a notepad and a pen from his chest pocket, and jotted something down. Thanked her and hung up.

"We got Irv Fuller. He lives in Lake Elmo, Minnesota," Yeager said. "Just a sec, I gotta take a leak." He went into the bathroom as Holly came back in the shed. Yeager flushed the toilet. Came out. He called to Holly. "We got a location on Irv Fuller."

Holly nodded, walked faster.

But something had Broker thinking. "I only met Dale once," he said. "Yesterday morning. With Kit."

"Yeah," Yeager said, momentarily distracted, yawning in the heat.

"Kit said he was weird. She used the bathroom and she said it was creepy because when she went in there she found blue poop in the toilet . . ."

"What?" Holly came alert, pale eyes zeroing in as he moved closer. "She said what?"

"Something about blue poop. I thought she meant that some toilet-bowl cleaner—"

"No." Holly bit off the syllable. "I spent five days with Kit." He waved his hands for quiet as he came closer, then he jabbed his finger. "She never made anything up. She was not suggestible at all. Not easily influenced. She was always very precise. If she said blue poop, she saw blue poop."

"Holly, man; slow down," Broker said.

"Slow down, my ass. Blue poop *does not normally occur in nature.* Blue poop is one of the side effects of ingesting ferric hexacyanoferrate II, a mineral compound commonly known as the paint pigment Prussian blue. It was invented in Berlin around 1704." He took a step forward and tapped Broker on the chest. "Guys. Prussian blue has other uses. It's an antidote to radiation poisoning. It absorbs thallium and cesium 137 in the intestines. Then the radioactive isotopes are excreted."

Broker and Yeager stared at him.

Holly went on, "Blue shit in Dale Shuster's toilet means he could have been working around something radioactive and taking precautions."

"Jesus. And he's drilling big hidey holes in construction machinery," Broker said.

"I think we gotta locate that machine fast," Holly said.

Yeager referred to his notepad and punched numbers in his cell. They huddled around him. His lips jerked in a disappointed expression. "Got an answering machine."

"Wait. Don't leave a message. End the call. If Dale's got Nina . . ." Broker said. "What if he's in contact with Dale? It would telegraph we're onto him." He asked Yeager, "Would people in town call Irv about the shooting and Dale disappearing?"

Yeager shrugged. "Possibly, but he's been gone quite a while."

"Broker's right," Holly said. "We want to talk to Fuller face-to-face. So where is he?"

"Lake Elmo, Minnesota." They looked at Broker.

"Little town east of the Twin Cities, just south of where I was working last week," Broker said. "I could call the county sheriff's department, they could track down Fuller."

Holly shook his head. "Same problem, might signal we're coming. We have to hit him cold. Just us." Holly was moving toward the door, reaching for his cell phone. "C'mon, Yeager, we need a ride to the PAR radar site."

They piled into the cruiser and Yeager wheeled onto the highway. Holly started talking fast into his cell. "Screw what they say. Northern Route is active again. So get the bird ready, file a flight plan to Lake Elmo, Minnesota . . . Okay, it's a direct order, I take full responsibility. Just get the bird ready. Lay on some ground transportation, location to come." Holly ended the call and smiled, back in the game.

"You borrowing another helicopter?" Broker asked.

"Step on it. We gotta get in the air before the pilots start having qualms," Holly said, leaned over the seat. "And, Yeager, you have to come with us."

Yeager's eyes went wide. "Where? To Minnesota? In a stolen Army helicopter. You're shitting me."

"He's right," Broker said. "You know Fuller. We don't."

Yeager reached for his radio handset. Holly leaned over the seat and stayed Yeager's hand. "Don't call. Just go. Trust me."

"Jesus," Yeager said. "Gotta tell 'em something." He called dispatch. "Karen, this is Jimmy. Ah, I'm going to be outta the car for a few hours. Personal time."

Broker said, "The sheriff said he had enough bodies to handle the scene here. He told you to keep an eye on us, right?"

"If it's nothing, you'll be back in a couple of hours," Holly said.

Shaking his head, sweating profusely, Yeager drove the speed limit through town. He cast a pained expression at the county office building. "Norm ain't gonna like this."

"C'mon, punch it," Holly said.

Fifteen minutes later they hurried through the security check-point at the radar base and drove to the helipad. Following Holly's instructions, Yeager parked his cruiser in a hangar out of sight. Without consulting with anyone, they jogged across the strip and got in the waiting Sikorsky UH-60 Black Hawk.

Chapter Forty

Dale crossed to the TV/VCR, pushed in a tape, and picked up a remote.

"Electrics hooked into battery system. Shouldn't be a problem long as she's idling. Ah, I'm new at this, so the quality is uneven. Ours will be better. I just wanted you to see . . ."

Under the sheet, Nina took advantage of the darkness to test the slack in her bonds. She had to get control of her breathing, she had to gather her strength. She had to begin to resist.

The screen filled with scrambled gray static, then Nina was looking at a black-and-white photo of a young blond woman, pert, attractive. The length and cut of her hair appeared a bit dated. With a chill she remembered Dale's odd question when they met. *I'll bet you went to the prom, didn't you?* When the camera panned, she saw she was looking at pictures from a high school yearbook. The camera zoomed in close enough to read the block of type:

> *GINNY WELLER*
> *Student Council 4*
> *Cheerleading 1, 2, 3, 4*

G.A.A. 1, 2, 3, 4
National Honor Society 2, 3, 4

Back to the jerky static, then to green. Too much lawn for a yard. It was a park, the trees not quite fully leafed out. White letters and numbers punched the date into the bottom of the screen: June 11.

Last month.

The camera picked up a running figure. A woman in brief running shorts, a sports top, and a Walkman: blond, in shape, tanned. The video was framed in black, some kind of window. Then it moved, unevenly panning across seats, a dashboard, a rearview mirror, and a windshield. The camera was shooting from inside a van.

Now the woman was closer, the camera picking her up out the passenger window as she jogged on a path. The path wound along a wall of shrubs.

A man Nina recognized as Joe Reed stepped from the bushes in front of the jogger. Powerful. Confident, his arms wrapped her up as he quickly stabbed an object into her thigh. Not a knife. One of those needles Dale stabbed her with.

Dale hit the pause button and explained in the patient tone of a tour guide who liked his job, "Epipen. Same thing I hit you with at the bar." His patient profile was sidelit by the flickering screen. "Joe took out the epinephrine and replaced it with ketamine."

Nina went back over the struggle in the Missile Park. How long had it taken the drug to take effect after he jabbed her thigh? Several minutes to put her completely out.

Dale hit a button. "Play," he said in a dreamy voice as the tape resumed and showed Joe hauling the woman back into the shrubs. Quick, efficient. The snatch had taken less than five seconds.

The camera went to static, then focused again. This time on a box of Coco Puffs cereal, a used bowl, a milk spill on a tabletop, and the front page of a newspaper. As the camera panned, it caught a sweep of sunlight and shadow and a feel of kitchen windows open to a summer morning. The sound of a lawn mower. Now the paper came into focus. The *Grand Forks Herald.* It zoomed in on a color photo below the fold. LOCAL WOMAN MISSING.

Some of the sharpness had mellowed on the face but it was the same girl in the yearbook picture. Older now. A grown woman. Nina braced for nausea.

All this time Dale stood next to the bed, his left arm folded across his chest, and his right arm cocked up so he rested his chin in the palm of his right hand. In his left hand was the remote. Dale was absorbed.

The static blipped away. The video came on.

At first it was a confused jumble. The camera swinging over a bare mattress on a filthy floor. The light bouncing off blue cinderblock walls.

Ginny Weller startled up from the darkness, squinting, hands up defensively, starting to scream. She had backed herself into the corner. Her tank top was soiled, as were her arms and legs. An advancing shadow fell across her face, blacking out her image. Joe Reed's cold, clipped voice gave direction in the background:

"Go on, Dale. Show her who's boss. Don't take any shit."

Ginny put up a fight and Dale had to wrap her in his thick arms and smother her down. He jabbed her with one of those pens. The picture ended.

Dale turned and spoke in a bland voice, "I couldn't stand to touch her when she was all squirmy and sweaty and dirty. The thing was, she wasn't ready for me. So, the way it worked out, I had to prepare her."

Prior to 9/11, Nina traveled back and forth between her posting in Lucca and the Joint Special Ops Task Force in Sarajevo. JSOTF targeted Serbs wanted by The Hague, and some of the pickup raids required covert female operators. During these operations she became acquainted with a Ranger captain named Jeremy Stahl. They had in common that both were the same age and both were going through career-related strife in their marriages. They were alone and attempting not to be lonely. Their flirtation was chaste and did not go beyond a few good-night kisses.

One early fall evening they went to a bar in Measle Alley. The street took its nickname from the Bosnian practice of commemorating their dead by painting red dots the size of large dinner plates on the street or sidewalk where they had died from shell or sniper fire. It was hard to walk a straight line anywhere down Measle Alley without stepping on a dot.

They drank beer in a bombed tavern that was missing most of its roof. They could watch the stars come out as they ate bad Bosnian pizza.

Jeremy was a beautiful man, much as Nina imagined Broker must have been when he was young, still in uniform, and standing in the close shadow of death.

Shawing more bravado than good sense, they drank and discussed the worst things in the world. What had she said? Something about never seeing her daughter again.

Christ. What good were words or thoughts? Nothing got you ready for this.

Ginny Weller lay on a white sheet that spread like a puddle of clean snow in the grubby basement. Her chest rose and fell softly. Drugged. Except now she was nude. She had been washed clean of dirt. The white bikini patches of her breasts and crotch gleamed against her smooth tan.

Dale's shadow preceded him as he approached the mattress. He performed an awkward shuffle, some personal dance of discovery and joy in his nakedness.

He knelt, then got on all fours. Nina watched the limp spiral of

Ginny's arms and legs as Dale tried to position her beneath him.

Nina forced herself to watch everything. He might reveal a pattern, a weakness. The flicker from the screen clubbed her steady eyes. After his second toadlike orgasm, Dale crawled beside the still figure and experimented with touching. Caresses. A kiss.

Helpless, Nina found herself sinking into a corner of perfect grief and hatred. No escaping the single thought that smashed her again and again:

Kit. Kit. Kit.

Seven years old. She didn't know things like this waited out in the world, in the shadows. Just that single thought crashing down like a bludgeon, over and over.

Dale paused the video and explained: "I must've got the dosage wrong, or maybe she had a lot to eat before we took her. Because she aspirated—that's what they call it—threw up and choked her airway. Got a little snuffy there toward the end." He hit the play button.

His last robotic climax was complicated by the onset of his victim's rigor mortis. When it was over, Dale rewound the tape and opened the curtains. Just as the daylight flooded in, a fist slammed the side of the camper, echoing deep through Nina's body.

"C'mon, for Christ sake," George Khari yelled. "Finish up in there."

Like they were working. Like they had taken a break.

"Yeah, yeah," Dale yelled back. Then he turned to Nina and grinned. "I'm going to be real careful with you, so you last all the way to Florida."

"C'mon, Dale, we gotta get on the road," George yelled again.

"Coming," Dale said, moving forward. He stopped as he pulled the curtain aside, turned, threw her a last exultant grin, and held up his right hand, like in a Boy Scout salute—thumb to little finger, three fingers extended. "You see that? Three times. I bet even Ace couldn't do it three times in a row."

Chapter Forty-one

Point to point, the distance from Langdon to Lake Elmo stretched the outside limits for the Black Hawk's fuel range, even adding in its emergency thirty-minute reserve. The pilots arranged for a refueling stop at the Minnesota National Guard training ground at Camp Ripley, just outside of Brainerd.

The flight plan took them over the Red River Valley, then south toward the Twin Cities. Estimated flight time: two and a half hours. That would put them on the ground in Minnesota between 3:30 and 4:00 in the afternoon.

Broker had never flown in the Black Hawk. Times had changed. As soon as he climbed in, he saw that this bird was special. None of the old noise, or death-on-the-highway reek of av gas, or exposed raw electrical circuits that he remembered from the bare-bones Vietnam Hueys. The cabin was carpeted and lined with two rows of bucket seats that faced in, like a conference room. There were even pockets for drinks in the chairs. Fabric dressed the walls to cover the soundproofing. The pilot and copilot were screened off behind a cockpit door. The crew chief tried his best to make himself invisible, squirreled back in a forward nook.

After they were airborne, Holly talked briefly on a headset, then pulled it down around his neck. "The crew is not happy, but they'll get us there." He leaned on his elbows over a complex communications console and rubbed his eyes.

"This is all pretty fancy," Broker said.

"It's the MDW." Holly allowed himself a grin. "Military District of Washington model. Got the VIP package. Everything but a shower. Probably one of the reasons they're pissed at me. Technically, this bird is a little over my pay grade, but I took it anyway."

Yeager pointed to the radio. "Who can you talk to on that?"

"Anyone in the world," Holly said. "But we ain't breaking radio silence, because if we do, somebody is going to tell us to like, ah, land immediately." Then he pointed to the cell phone on Yeager's hip. "Keep trying to reach Fuller."

Yeager tried again, got the machine. They settled in and waited. Broker realized that with the doors closed, they could carry on a normal conversation. But right now nobody felt like talking. An hour went by that way. Off to the northeast Broker spotted the triple puddle of Leech Lake, Cass Lake, and Lake Winnibigoshish.

Should he call his folks and tell them about Nina's disappearance? Should they discuss the tactics and timing of telling Kit that her mommy was missing?

Another part of his mind counseled that this pursuit of Dale Shuster was pure denial. According to this part of his mind, he should be getting ready to identify a corpse and make funeral arrangements.

Yeager tried the Fuller number again, with the same result. The machine. He tried directory assistance for construction firms in the Minneapolis–St. Paul area with "Fuller" in their name. No luck. They sat and stared. The steady whack of the rotors torqued up the tension. Holly especially seemed to be getting wound tighter and tighter.

"Pretty smart," Holly finally said. "Using a piece of construction equipment as a delivery system. Hell, we're used to seeing them sitting all over the place. Drive right by, never give it a second thought."

"We gotta wait and see," Broker cautioned.

"Bullshit. Why go to all the trouble to mill out solid cast iron?" Holly's voice trailed off as his eyes drifted out the windows. "I just worry we'll be too late."

Yeager sat calmly and listened. He had the look of an A student playing hookey; amazed pressure was building in his wide eyes.

Broker realized he'd been holding the pack of cigarettes since they took off. Holly reached down, produced an ashtray, asked for a smoke. Then Yeager put out his hand. "Left mine in the car."

They lit up. Broker stared at the crumpled blue pack. Five left.

When Mille Lacs Lake was a shimmer in the distance, the pilot contacted the tower at Camp Ripley. They dropped to treetop level and eased down on the landing strip, topped off their tanks, and were airborne again.

Half an hour later they were over the silver ribbon of the St. Croix River, where it winds toward its juncture with the Mississippi. They banked and began a gradual descent southward along the river, then turned west. Holly was on his cell. Then he went forward and conferred with the pilot. Looking out the window, Broker saw a sight from twenty-six years ago. A red smoke grenade popped in an empty field next to a rural intersection. The Hawk swooped down and landed next to the smoke.

Seeing Broker eyeball the smoke, Holly grinned. "Like old times, huh?"

A gray government Chevy Nova waited for them next to the dissipating red smoke. Holly told the pilots to stand by, and then he, Broker, and Yeager ran to the waiting car.

The ground contact Holly had been talking to was a young, black Army MP sergeant from Fort Snelling. He had a Hudson's map open, with the route to the Fuller address indicated in yellow Magic Marker. He was in uniform and he was wearing a sidearm.

"Let's go," Holly said.

Irv Fuller lived less than three minutes away on four wooded acres. A sign next to the address announced PRIVATE DRIVE. House numbers had been chiseled into a large granite boulder.

"Ole Irv looks like he's doing all right," Yeager said as they drove up a long asphalt drive screened by evergreens. The house was deceptive on approach, showing a limestone-faced Tudor, casement windows, and cedar shake in the front. But it was built into a hill with a third-story walkout on the back slope over a swimming pool. A large Morton building sat off the driveway apron. The doors to the Morton building and the three-bay garage were closed.

They got out and snooped the house. A gray-and-white cat stared at Broker from a window; otherwise, it looked like no one was home. The MP sergeant sat in his car reading an Easy Rawlins paperback while Broker, Holly, and Yeager continued to nose around.

"So, what do you think?" Broker asked.

"I see an office in there," Holly said, pointing through a window. "Maybe there's business cards, stationery, invoices . . ."

They had walked a circuit around the back, looking for a likely window, when a horn beeped out front.

Then they heard the purr of an engine coming down the drive as they jogged around front and saw a Mercedes sedan pull up to the Chevy. The MP was out talking to a blond woman dressed in gym-rat Spandex, sweatband, sport top, and cross trainers. The woman was tapping her foot and had her arms folded across her chest.

As they walked up, Yeager speculated, "Irv's first wife, Ginny Weller, was better from the waist up. I'd say Irv's generally moving south in his life. This one's better on the bottom."

She was attractive enough but Broker thought she'd better back off on the tanning booth unless she was working on donating her skin for a crocodile purse. She was uncertain, seeing an Army uniform and gun belt and then Yeager's uniform in her driveway.

"Is something wrong?" She asked.

"Mrs. Fuller?" Yeager asked.

"Yes. Sydney Fuller."

"I'm deputy Jim Yeager, Cavalier County Sheriff's Department in Langdon—where Irv's from. We know each other."

"Yes . . ." She shook her head. "He's all right. I just dropped him off at the job an hour and a half ago. Before I went to my step class at the—"

"Yes, ma'am. It's somebody else from Langdon we're looking for who might be in contact with Irv. Dale Shuster."

Sydney oriented quickly. "Sure. They had some business recently. Irv bought some machinery."

"We really need to get in touch with Irv." Yeager nodded to the house.

"You'll need his cell." She gave Yeager the number and proceeded to talk, relieved this was a routine visit: "We took a run over to the Dells for two days. It's the rain. The site was too muddy to work. We came back after lunch and I dropped him off to look it over. He figures by tomorrow they can start digging."

"And where's the site?" Yeager asked.

"Prairie Island."

Yeager saw Holly immediately react and flip open his cell phone. At the same time, Broker's eyes went wide and hard. "What is it?" Yeager asked Broker.

Broker moved forward, rasing his hand up to silence Yeager. "Did you say Prairie Island?" he asked Sydney Fuller, his voice struggling to stay calm.

Still smiling, she was made a little uncertain now by Broker's intensity. "Yes," she said, "Irv landed the contract to . . ."

Suddenly she winced and put her hands to her ears. "What's that noise?" she gasped, staring at the way Holly abruptly circled his hand and ran out on her lawn, phone jammed to his ear. Totally unprepared for the Black Hawk appearing in a fury of spinning machinery over her line of evergreens, she screamed and waved her arms. "My flower beds!"

Broker came through the flowers and mulch churning in the prop wash, grabbed her arm, shook her to get her attention, and yelled, "You mean the power plant?"

Aghast at the whirlwind whipping her yard, she shouted, indignant, "Yes, goddammit, the power plant." She yanked her arm away. "Who are you, anyway?"

"Fuck! Let's go!" Broker shouted to Yeager and started to sprint for the chopper. Yeager turned to Sydney Fuller, his face a question mark.

Sydney yelled, "Prairie Island, the nuclear power plant, okay?"

Yeager turned and ran.

Chapter Forty-two

At some point the lull of the tires on the road had tired out the monsters in her mind and put her to sleep. Upon waking, she had a perfectly normal thought. When Kit was an infant and they couldn't get her down, Broker would tuck her in her car seat and set the seat on the clothes dryer. The steady motor chug would ease her to sleep.

Kit.

She pressed down on her elbows, brought up her head, and glared straight ahead. First they'd keep it from her. But someday she'd learn how her mom had died; drugged, smothered, violated.

Can't go out this way. Got to make it a fight.

She heard: "Partly cloudy to sunny. Temperature eighty-three. The prevailing wind direction is steady, seven to eight miles per hour out of the northwest."

He was listening to the weather report, every chance he could, on an all-news station. She looked around. Couldn't see much through the one clear window: treetops, a patch of blue sky. The steady thrum of the wheels on pavement changed, slowed; he was turning in somewhere. More trees rushed by the window. The Roadtrek stopped. He turned off the motor.

Then Dale pulled the curtain to the side and Nina could see out the windshield: treetops, a lot of power lines all ganged together. Closer in, she saw him take pills from two prescription bottles propped up on the dashboard. Pop them in his mouth. Swallow. Wash them down with Coke.

He was humming as he stripped off his work shirt and jeans. But then he took new clothes from a shopping bag and tore off the labels. Watching her from the corner of his eye, he pulled on comfortable baggy jeans and a blue golf shirt that set off his heavy white arms, throat, and face.

The driver's seat swiveled, and now he spun it around and sat down, facing her. "Now, about the bomb," he said.

The word *bomb* cut through the routine terror. She blinked herself alert as he rummaged around on the passenger seat, plucked up a four-by-eight-inch color photo, and leaned far forward, extending his arm so she could see it. She strained up, squinted. It was some big boxy yellow tractor with a shovel bucket on the front. Like you see on construction sites.

"I sold this used 644C to Irv Fuller. He thinks he took me on the deal. But, trust me, he's the one who's in for a surprise." Dale smiled slowly. "That's what I do. I surprise people."

Nina shook her head. Sensed movement. Someone else coming.

"Dale and I have some business to attend to," said George Khari, as he climbed over the passenger seat, stood in the compartment, and nodded curtly.

"Last night . . ." Nina said.

George shrugged, waffled a hand in the air. "Fake left, go right, heh?" He was unshaven, haggard, still wearing the same soiled shirt and shorts. He smiled uneasily at Nina, spreadeagled on the bed. Perhaps she saw a hint of disapproval in his brown eyes. Even disgust. If true, it was the last item on his agenda.

Nina tried to focus on him and got an impression of tremendous tension, but also excitement. The guy was practically throwing sparks as he held up a manila envelope and said to Dale, "Trade you."

Dale handed over the single photo and took the envelope. His thick fingers shook as he opened the flap and pulled out a stack of prints. An almost sweet smile spread over his face.

"Just a peek," George said softly as he held up a set of car keys. Dale nodded, lovingly set the envelope aside, and took the keys. "Now, make the call," George said, again in the soft but firm tone.

"Right." Dale found the cell phone on the dashboard, consulted a slip of paper, punched in the numbers. A moment later he connected. "Hey, Irv. It's Dale. Yeah. I'm here . . . About ten minutes out. You gonna come down to the gate and meet me? . . . Sure. Great. See ya."

George exhaled, his eyelids fluttered, and he raised his hand to the medal attached to a chain around his neck, fondling it, almost sensually. "Just like that," he said under his breath.

Dale gripped the keys in his hand, took a deep breath, and said, "I'll be back."

George clapped him on the shoulder. "Just relax, act natural. It'll go fine."

Dale nodded, spun the seat around, pushed open the door, and exited the camper. George, leaning over the steering wheel, watched through the windshield. Nina heard a car start and then drive away. When the sound of the engine faded, George collapsed into the driver's seat and placed his hand on his chest.

"My God, it's going to work."

Nina waited a few moments, until George calmed down. Then she asked, "What's going to work?"

George studied her, then said, "I don't know that I want to talk to you."

"Why? Afraid you'll get to know me and that'll make it harder to kill me?"

Slowly George removed one of the Cuban Lanceros from his chest pocket and began peeling off the cellophane. "You're some kind of Special Forces, huh?"

"*What's* going to work, George?" her voice cracked, not from fear. She was parched.

George pursed his lips, thought about it, then put aside his cigar. He reached down, grabbed a bottle of springwater, unscrewed the top, leaned over, and held it to her lips. She drank, paused, and drank some more. The water shot through her like a current, waking up some parts, shoring up others. For a brief moment she was stuck on an odd point of captive etiquette: Should she thank him? The moment passed.

He returned the water bottle to the front seat, took out a plastic lighter, and lit the Cuban. After he puffed a few times he sat back and studied her again.

"Dale's really something, huh? I think it's a form of selective retardation, like autism; he's got these big social holes in him." George came forward. "Like, did he say anything about Joe?"

"The guy who killed my . . . partner?"

"Yeah. Dead himself now, too. It was on the radio. The cops shot him at the border." George sighed and shook his head. "Joseph, always too ready with that gun. Didn't work this time. But Dale doesn't care. All he sees is what's right in front of his nose. You know what? This whole country's one big version of Dale. Business can't see past the next quarter. The Army wears berets made in China. One big case of political autism. Blind to the rest of the world."

"Are you Al Qaeda, George? Is this some kind of 'raid on a path,' like it says in the Koran?" Nina asked.

"You mean like Rashid, who couldn't keep his mouth shut? Me? Shit, no. I don't go in for any church. I sell booze as a front and basically I smuggle drugs. I send some money back to Lebanon. From time to time I run people across the border. But it's like this deal, strictly for money."

"This deal?"

"You wanna know? Why not. It'll pass the time. First thing, we got control of Dale."

"How?"

"I found out he's one sick fuck. He had this list of three people he wanted to knock off. Because they teased him in high school. So we agreed to help him—you know, like snatching the woman in Grand Forks. We threw you in extra—you're a freebie. And in return, he agreed to help us." George reached into the passenger seat, took the color prints from the envelope. "And we promised him a new life."

George got up and held a Florida driver's license just inches from her eyes. The name said William Charon. William Charon's photo ID showed a much leaner man than Dale, with dark hair. With a shudder, Nina observed that William Charon looked a lot like Ace Shuster. Then George showed her the prints; front and side shots; some were head shots, others the whole body. But all were magically slimmed down.

"It's all digital imaging. Adobe Photoshop, on the computer. Our people in Winnipeg whipped out the license. Drugs, guns, counterfeiting; it's what we're good at. This other stuff is legit, from a plastic surgeon in Coral Gables who's gonna work on Dale."

"A new identity," Nina whispered

"Yeah, give him a pretty new face and a backpack full of Epipens. Turn him loose on the female population. Hell," George laughed, "he'll be the new Ted Bundy."

Nina looked into George's calm, calculating eyes. *Legit . . . like hell.* She figured Dale was a one-use asset. He had about an hour left to live.

George put the prints and license back in the envelope and returned to his seat. "Things really got rolling," he said, "when Dale explained the possibilities of *this*." He reached down and picked up the picture of the yellow machine. "See those big-ass tires? That's where we put most of it."

"Put most of what?" Nina asked.

"The Semtex."

"How much Semtex?"

"About four hundred pounds in each tire. Tucked a few hundred more pounds here and there. So we put in about a ton."

"You need a power source and a method of detonating it." Nina thought out loud.

"Pagers. Small enough to fit into the valve. We wired each blasting cap to a pager, with a cap booster. Then we deliberately overinflated the tires with foam and capped them up. That way, Irv Fuller would complain that the machine handles stiff, which gives Dale a reason to visit the job site and get in the loader. See?"

George grinned. He reached in his trouser pocket and took out a Globalstar Qualcomm GSP-1600. "I called the phone company and got a group pager number. Just one call and all the charges go at the same time.

"Last thing we did was have the machine power-washed. Then we loaded it on a lowboy trailer. See, that's the only thing they care about at customs on the Canadian border. They're worried about bringing foreign agricultural soil into the States. Gave customs the paperwork and Dale just drove it right on through the port at Maida. Dale and Joe tweaked it some more in Langdon, and then had it delivered to Irv Fuller. We let Irv drive it to the target."

"The target?" Nina said in a numb voice.

"Yeah, it's a construction site. And the funny thing is, if it hadn't been raining it would have blown already, three days ago. But work's been held up because of the mud. So we had to wait till the rain stopped."

"What site?"

George smiled and pointed his cigar out the window. "How

about the Prairie Island Nuclear Plant? It's about two miles that way. Irv Fuller's company won the bid to build a security wall around the reactors. Dale and Irv went to high school together. So . . . Dale sells machines. Irv buys them. That's the connection that made Dale invaluable."

Nina found herself in a new place: dread plus one. "But how do you get it inside?" she whispered.

George laughed. "It's *already* inside. Just sitting there. The construction company brought it in on a trailer, with all their stuff. Their workers have to pass background checks. The guards look inside lunch boxes and underneath vehicles. But they ain't taking tires apart on the machines that came to make the plant safer.

"Yeah, right now Dale is probably having Irv Fuller walk him through plant security—just another vendor visiting the site. The tricky part is, Dale has to move the machine next to the spent fuel pool."

Nina listened, numb. Leaving dread plus one . . .

"Dale comes back, confirms the machine is in position, we drive off thirty, forty miles, and then I make a phone call. You got any idea what's going to happen when a ton of Semtex hits that spent-fuel-pool wall from a range of about six feet?"

Nina strained against the cords in a spasm of inarticulate fury. *So that's why they're so wired into the weather reports. The wind direction. They have to get upwind of the explosion.*

George waited for her tantrum to pass, then he smiled. "The people who built these plants are a little shortsighted. They never figured out what to do with all those fuel rods. So they just cram them into these pools. Dumb shits. Prairie Island's got four, five feet of cinder-block wall. We got a ton of military-grade explosives. No contest."

Spent, sweaty, filthy, with Ace Shuster's dry, caked blood on her chest, Nina could only stare at him.

George narrowed his eyes and tossed his hands in the air. "Boom.

The pool ceases to exist. No more water. The zirconium cladding on the fuel assemblies—about fourteen hundred of them—reacts exothermically. That means they catch fire at about a thousand degrees Celius."

George scratched his chin thoughtfully and pointed at her. "Even the Nuclear Regulatory Commission admits that that kinda fire can't be put out. It would burn for days. We're talking massive radiation exposures."

George stood up, clenched his cigar between his teeth, and said, "So the short answer to what happens is—some people will die fast. On the Arabian Peninsula, we'll watch a whole lot more of you die slowly on Al-Jazeera. Parts of Minnesota, Wisconsin, and Iowa will be *uninhabitable* for the next three hundred years. Impressive, no?"

Then he reached down into the passenger seat again. His hand came up holding one of those damn Epipens. And a roll of duct tape. "Time for your medicine, Nina," he said.

She twisted away but he jabbed at her thigh. She caught a break because George wasn't adept with the pen. Part of the dose dribbled on her skin. Then he tore off a gob of the tape, striped it across her mouth, and said softly, "Sweet dreams."

Nina listened to George leave the camper, then she reared against her restraints, calculating how long she had before the drug took effect. She counted seconds, made it past fifty before the leading edge of the fluffy narcotic cloud bumbled into her blood.

Still, she kept straining. The bedstead jumped on the carpet. Once, twice. A clatter of wood on her right side caught her attention. Weaker now. Drifting. But she had to focus.

Sonofabitch! The dummies, they had too much faith in the drug. She fought for concentration. *Okay. When you strain up off the bed, the motion you feel is the sideboard riding up. No shit.* She visualized the bed's construction, the way the pieces fit together. *If you can get your weight up off the bed and rip upward with your bound right hand while you're in the air, maybe you*

*can yank the sideboard tongue out of the slot in the headboard.
Then . . .*

She blinked sweat, bubbles now. Streaming. Part of her started to float away. The rest of her was turning to cool, dreamy lead. *Fight. Think . . .* Woozy, she stared at the inane appliances in the room: the VCR, the camera, the tripod . . . *This is not how I intend to die—the drugged plaything for these creeps.*

Chapter Forty-three

Who was it said everybody should get fifteen minutes of fame? Dale couldn't remember. But then he wasn't *saying* it, now, was he?

He was no-shit living it.

THE PRAIRIE ISLAND MDEWAKANTON DAKOTA COMMUNITY WELCOMES YOU, said the sign. Some dirty-faced Indian kid pointed a plastic water cannon at him as he drove down a street lined with distressed rez housing. Dale gave the kid the finger. *Ain't you a lucky little shit! Got the Treasure Island Casino across the street like a gaudy pink pile of melanoma; got high-tension wires for a sky; and the Great White Father gave you a mountain of nuclear waste for a backyard.*

His heart started to bang in his chest like a trip hammer when the twin gray domes of the nuclear plant appeared over the treetops. It was located on the river, about half a mile off the road, behind a chain-link fence. Barbed wire on the top. Dale eased the Lexus fifty yards from the nearest car in the visitors parking lot. Parked, got out. Just like George said, act natural.

Two lanes of traffic, one entering, one leaving, motored slowly by a small white guard station. Two guards in brown Wackenhut uniforms monitored the traffic. They wore black Sam Brown belts, sidearms, and one of them had an assault rifle on his shoulder. The other had a mirror on a long pole and was inspecting the underside of an incoming car.

Dale walked up and was challenged by one of the guards. He called back, "Dale Shuster. I have an appointment to meet Irv Fuller at the gate. I'm suppose to be on some list."

"Fuller, the head construction guy?"

"Yeah, that's him."

"We got another construction guy," the guard with the mirror yelled to the one with the rifle.

"I sold him some machines for the job. There's a problem with one of them, so I'm here to take a look. Might have to replace it. Which won't be cheap," Dale said.

The other guard nodded. "My sympathies. Just make sure the badge don't leave his person. If you don't watch them, these guys pass them back and forth going out on breaks."

The guard with the shouldered rifle waved to his partner, then motioned for Dale to remove the items from his pockets. Dale took out his keys, some change, and put them in a plastic basket and had a metal detector passed over him. Then the guard spoke into his mobile radio.

This was the touchy part. He assumed that plant security did their background checks early this morning when he gave his Social Security number to Irv. But what if the Cavalier County Sheriff's office posted a missing-persons bulletin on him? Would this security system monitor such reports after the initial check? Dale and George were betting they would not.

They bet right. After talking for a minute, the guard checked his clipboard, then asked Dale for ID. Dale handed over his driver's license and his Social Security card. The guard consulted his clipboard again, removed a numbered clip-on badge, and gave it, along with the ID, back to Dale. Dale breathed a little easier. He'd been preapproved. Then the guard waved Dale beside the guard shack, into the shade, and said, "Put on the badge and wait here, sir. Mr. Fuller will be out in a minute."

Dale waited, gazing up into the late-afternoon sun, which was starting to flame out across the Mississippi, setting up a gorgeous golden haze over Wisconsin.

Five minutes later a blue Jeep Cherokee pulled up. It had a logo on the side: Holtz-Sydney Construction. A tall man in jeans, boots, and a blue denim designer work shirt got out. Irv Fuller in his styled salt-and-pepper hair looked sports-fan tanned and fleshy. Though not exactly porky, he did have a creeping double chin and the good-time rosettes of incipient gout pooling in his ample cheeks.

"If it's about the rest of the money . . ." Irv said, feigning an apology as he shook Dale's hand.

Dale laughed and waved the question aside with an aw-pshaw grimace. "Hey, no rush. I'm passing through the area anyway. Might as well take a look at that Deere."

Irv cocked his head to the side, grinned. "Just feels stiff, but, you know, it still moves dirt from here to there."

Dale jerked his thumb at the reactors. "Probably nothing. And I wanted to see all this in person, to tell Dad when I get down to Florida, about you and the machines you bought. He always said he'd never sell any big iron to a Fuller. But here we are."

Irv shrugged. "Hey, I needed to have those loaders listed on my inventory to get bonded for this job. Getting them so quick helped save my ass. What the hell. Let's look at that machine. Then I can take a few minutes to show you around. How's that?"

"Great," Dale said, following Irv toward the Jeep.

"And I really appreciate the price you gave me," Irv said as they got in and he started the truck. "I won't forget it. You'll be getting the balance I owe soon's the next quarter starts."

"Hey, I trust you, Irv. Always have," Dale said.

"Well, okay. Here we go. So you never been in one of these things before?"

Dale shook his head.

"Twenty-five percent of the juice in the state comes from nuclear. These two here, and the other one up in Monticello," Irv said as they drove down a narrow road toward a parking lot. Dale had to squint against the bright afternoon sunlight to make out the reactors. A wall of vapor drifted up to the right.

"Pretty much like we learned in high school," Irv said. "Uranium heats primary water in the core. The hot primary water is pumped through steam generators and the heat is transferred to secondary water that flashes into steam. Then the primary water goes back to the core for reheating. Big building on the left is the steam turbines. The smaller building between the reactors is the pool for the spent fuel rods."

"Uh-huh," Dale said. George had made sure he knew the diagram of this puppy by heart.

"Steam turns the turbines to make the electricity. Less than a third of the energy in the core gets used as electricity. The rest vents out in the air or goes in the river. Over on the right, where all the steam is kicking out—those are the cooling towers, four of them. Our job is to build a berm around the reactors, the turbines, and the cooling pool."

"What are they worried about? Some A-rab gonna crash a plane into it?" Dale said it as a joke.

"Not funny," Irv said, rolling his eyes, "Hell, the cooling-pool building is just a glorified pole barn on top. Got a corrugated tin roof. I been in there. Fuckin' sparrows fly in and out. Nah, we're putting up a barrier more to stop a truck-bomb threat. Like the barrier they got over behind those trees, around the storage casks."

"Uh-huh," Dale said, nodding.

They passed through the parking lot. Closer in now, in the shadow of the reactors. To Dale they rose against the sky like giant fat stunted silos. The domesticated cousins of the ICBM silo that had been in his dad's field.

Driving past the lot, they came to the actual construction site. Dale smiled. It was even better than he'd expected. The area to the right of the reactors was in the process of being cleared; several large Morton-style buildings were being dismantled, the top soil stripped off, and the whole site surrounded by a silt fence and another security fence. The big machines sat mostly idle, grazing in the dirt like a herd of huge yellow oxen. But Dale was focused on the tall, square, blue-and-gray structure between the reactors. That was the cooling-pool building. The target.

Irv drove into the fenced site and they passed a broad ditch that had been started—maybe thirty feet wide, ten, twelve feet deep, thirty or so yards long. The dirt had been piled in a rough breastwork about eight feet high, parallel to the ditch, and about a hundred yards from the reactors. Dale could see water still standing in the bottom of the trench.

"What's this?" Dale asked.

"That's the job. The beginning of the barrier."

"Looks kinda muddy," Dale said.

"Yeah. We had to pull out the heavy stuff." He parked next to a construction trailer and they got out.

"We started that excavation before the rain hit. Probably won't get back in full swing till next week. Plan calls for a moat. Use the dirt to throw up the berm. That way we don't have to haul it in by truck. Security is such a drag—drivers coming in and out. The more we can do strictly on site, the better."

"What goes on top of the berm?" Dale asked, to keep the conversation going.

"Big rocks, spaced so a truck can't fit through."

They were walking in among the machines now: excavators, compactors, dozers, fuel and water trucks, belly loaders, graders, shovels, off-road dump trucks. Half the big iron was still on trailers.

He felt a rush of relief when he saw his loaders sitting on dry ground, parked next to a big D-8 Cat dozer. He spotted the one he wanted, with the black X painted on the corner of the cab door.

Not very original. But functional.

"There's the machines I sold you," Dale said.

"Yep. The stiff one's got the X on the door."

"Yeah, okay. The fuckin' Canadians, they probably overinflated the tires. Let me drive her around a little. See how she runs . . . house call, no charge." Nothing but cool.

"Okay, check it out." Irv smiled when he said it, but he also checked his wristwatch. "Just don't go near that plowed-up strip by the trench and get stuck."

"Don't worry. I'll stay right over there"—he pointed to the shadowed area between the pool structure and a utility building— "where it's shady." Dale walked toward the loader, detouring to go right up to one of the reactor containment walls. He extended his hand, placed his palm on the smooth gray concrete, shut his eyes, and felt the brooding fire waiting within.

Waiting for him, like it had been all his life.

The moment passed. He went over to the front-loader, pulled himself up to the cab, opened the door, sat down, and turned the key. The engine belched black smoke, caught, and ran just fine. He raised the bucket, lowered it, and then drove in a semicircle. Then he backed up to the cooling-pool building wall and stopped so there was about four feet between the wall and the rear counter-weights.

Okay.

The wheels felt a little hard but the machine operated normally, just as he'd predicted.

He killed the engine, leaned down, and reached under the seat. The Klein standard NE-type side cutting pliers were still there, exactly where he'd left them. He'd taped another pair under the radiator, just in case. He tucked the cutters in his waistband, under his shirt, swung down from the cab. Then he did a casual walk-around, rubbed the counterweights for good luck—genie in a bottle. When he had the machine between himself and Irv, and was deep in the shadow of the tall pool building, he took out the cutters, leaned into the motor assembly, and quickly cut the battery wires and the fuel line. Then he jammed the cutters up behind the engine, out of sight.

He came around, completing his circuit, and kicked one of the fat tires. He ran his eyes over the site. Not many men in today. The shift was closing down. Guys parking the machines, picking up their lunch coolers, and heading for the parking lot.

Dale moved out around the motor, trailing his hand one last time over the sun-warmed chassis. He walked out and said to Irv, "Looks like she's running just fine. Maybe she rides a little jerky. If it gets worse, let me know."

"It's a deal." They shook hands. "So now what?" Irv asked.

Dale shrugged. "Going to take it easy, see some sights, drive down to Florida and see Mom and Dad. Then I don't know. Maybe I'll try something totally different."

"It'll be a change," Irv said. "I still feel hemmed in, not seeing the sky."

"Yeah, well, down in Florida I figure I can always get on a boat and go out into the ocean."

"That'd do it."

"Well, hey, I gotta hit the road. Thanks for letting me drop by. See what's going on."

"No problem," Irv said and walked him back to the Jeep. As they drove back to the security gate Irv accelerated to beat the trickle of cars that was starting to pull out of the parking lot. Irv pulled over and parked by the security shack. They got out and walked to the side of the shack.

"You going to be here for a while?" Dale asked.

"Yeah, I gotta talk to a couple of the managers. Gotta mark some underground cables and tunnels they're concerned about. And they can't find the right blueprints. You know how it goes."

Dale nodded. "Okay, ah, say hello to your new wife—ah . . ."

"Sydney."

"That's some name," Dale said. He watched Irv carefully. He wanted to remember this moment. All during their visit, Irv had never once mentioned Ginny. The fact that she was reported missing.

"Yeah, well . . ." Irv's voice trailed off as he raked the toe of his Timberland boot through the dust. His attention was already moving off Dale. Irv was cordial but smug. Dale was going out the gate without the balance owed on two front-loaders. The Fullers were sticking it to the Shusters again. "Say hello to your folks for me."

"I will." Dale waved over his shoulder, then he handed his visitor's badge over to a very tired-looking Wackenhut guard. The guard took the badge, checked something on his clipboard, and waved him through the gate. True, he reflected, Irv was sticking him for about twenty grand. Let him enjoy it, for about the next fifty, sixty minutes—which was all he had left.

I, on the other hand, am about to earn a million bucks. More, actually, now that Joe's gone.

When Dale was out of earshot, Irv Fuller grinned and shook his head. "Good old Needle-Dick," he said.

Groggy but awake, Nina heard them celebrate when Dale returned. *Jesus. It's gonna happen.*

Dale hummed as he climbed back behind the wheel after a round of back-slapping and congratulations from George. They proceeded to argue amiably through the open driver's-side door—how far to drive, where to stop. Then George ran back to his car. Dale started up the camper, wheeled onto the highway.

The curtain was still open. Nina arched her neck, saw the dull, gray, rounded shapes loom above the trees, then disappear.

"Dumb," Dale said happily, "They did it to themselves. They could build a belt of windmills from the Canadian border down to west Texas. They could generate enough power to serve half the Midwest. But nooo . . ."

He laughed and pounded the wheel. "You shoulda seen the look on Irv's face. He thinks he beat me out of a few thousand bucks. Boy is he happy. Well, old Irv is in for a big surprise." As he spoke he plucked a page from the high school yearbook off the dashboard, took a Sharpie from among the pill bottles piled on the dash, and blacked out the eyes on Irv's high school picture. Then he came to a red light. He spun in the seat, jumped toward her, and yanked the tape from her mouth. Immediately, he jumped back in the seat, whipped around, and accelerated on the green.

Showing off.

Words were insignificant in the cascading horror, but words were all she had. She couldn't stop from shouting: "You put that thing *in there!*"

"Yep. And in about an hour . . . *poof!*" He tossed his hands in the air. "Now we'll take a little drive, back roads west to Le Sueur, then drop down on 169 past Mankato and pick up I-90 west. Somewhere in there, depending on how the wind holds, we'll make the call. Turn on the radio and listen to the news on the way to Sioux Falls. It's all really very simple. Stay upwind and put a couple hundred miles between us and the plume. Looks like they'll be eating cesium 137 for supper in Milwaukee and Chicago."

Dale wagged his finger. "They're gonna learn the hard way: a spent fuel pool is forever." He laughed at his own joke, watching for Nina's reaction. "You're no fun," he said. He flung an arm back and pulled the curtain shut.

Nina pictured the satellite phone in George Khari's pocket. They weren't kidding. *They were going to set it off with a simple phone call. Jesus . . .*

Nina felt the van move, the rhythm of the road—then cocked her head, picking up a distinctive motor slap, mixed in with the road sound. Then the sound passed over them, faded behind, and was gone.

Weird. Sounded like a Sikorsky Black Hawk.

She refocused on the tension in the cords that held her wrists and ankles. With all her strength, she arched up her whole body.

Chapter Forty-four

Everybody was yelling at once, piling in, falling all over each other as the Black Hawk lifted off Sydney Fuller's lovely lawn and blew her pink wisteria all to hell. The Hawk gained altitude and nosed over, heading south.

Broker lost his footing in the scramble as Yeager punched numbers on his cell. Holly was already talking to whoever he worked for on the fancy radio console. "Northern Route is active. I say again: *Northern Route is active.* We have an event, suspicion is high that there is a device *inside* the Prairie Island Nuclear Plant on the Mississippi River. That's about forty miles southeast of the Twin Cities.

"I need the physical layout of the reactors and the pool. Get somebody on the horn at Prairie Island and patch them through to me . . ."

"I *got* him," Yeager yelled, "Irv, hey, it's Jim Yeager from Langdon. Have you . . . *Holy shit!*" Yeager thrust out the phone like it was hot and pounded Broker on the arm with it. "Dale was *just there* in the plant. Left five minutes ago."

Broker and Holly stopped in place as Yeager's words upped the adrenaline ante. They locked eyes. Holly erupted with a demented laugh, threw his hands in the air, and crowed, "Hey—here's to Kit and her blue poop."

They all joined in a spasm of crazed exuberance. Then the chopper tilted and they all collided as Holly resumed yelling into the radio headset. "I need to talk to somebody on the ground, goddamn it, 'cause we're coming in hot in a Black Hawk and we intend to land inside the plant. I need a ground contact—security, the plant manager, I don't care." He untangled from Broker and Yeager, lurched toward the cockpit. The door was open now. "What's our ETA?" he yelled.

"About ten minutes," the pilot said.

"ETA ten minutes. Get 'em ready for me. Of course we need a reaction team, NBC, EOD, the full schmear . . . No. I don't know what it is, except we think it's already *inside* . . ."

Holly put his hand to the earphones, banged on Broker's arm, and pointed to the pilot. Broker went forward. The pilot had a map out and said, "Tell him I'm flying line-of-sight on the river. We'll come right over it, no messing with the ground clutter trying to read the road net."

Yeager was shouting into his phone. "Irv, Irv . . . Okay, you calm down, too. Look, Dale sold you some machines, right? . . . Yeah, two front-loaders. We think—"

Holly shook his head violently.

"No," Broker put his hand over Yeager's cell, "not till we're on the ground and evaluate those machines. They'll start messing around without knowing what they're dealing with."

Holly said, "Tell him Dale's wanted for questioning in the death of his brother."

Yeager got back on the phone. "Irv. Ace Shuster was shot to death back home this morning. We think Dale was there. So I need to talk to you fast. And could you locate the two machines he sold you? We want to take a look at them." Yeager ended the call, grimaced. "He agreed, but he sounded confused."

"You ain't seen confused. Just wait till we get on the ground," Holly said.

They grabbed handholds on the seats as the chopper pitched forward, picking up speed. Broker felt like the rotors were spinning in his chest. The whole wild day. Dale was out there in front of them somewhere, on the ground. And Broker was sure now he had Nina with him. *Gotta believe that. She's down there on one of those roads in a vehicle.*

Alive.

Without realizing it, he had pulled the crumpled pack of smokes from his pocket. Holly and Yeager reached over and dug out mangled cigarettes, straightened them, and lit up. Broker joined them. Inhaled, exhaled, looked in the pack.

Two left.

Fields and tree lines and housing developments rushed beneath them as they flew southeast with the St. Croix River on their left. They passed over the confluence, where the St. Croix flowed into the Mississippi.

"Any minute now," Broker yelled.

The crazed rush subsided and Holly's face twisted into a disgusted snarl. "Those goddamn motherfuckers. We *told* them. And we *told* them. I helped run the black-hat teams out of Special Ops at Bragg. We'd play aggressor to test nuclear plant security for NRC. Fuckin' private security guards. Bunch of guys who couldn't make it as cops. *Timothy McVeigh* became a private security guard when he flunked the psychological test for Special Forces . . ."

He stared at Broker. "You know what the fuckers did? They canceled the exercise because it was too easy for us to breach security at the plants—when we told them that eighty percent of their guards would shit their pants if faced by a real attack by a serious opponent. Flat run and hide." He shook his head. "But I got a feeling this thing we're heading into ain't something you stop with gates, guns, and guards."

He alerted to the satellite phone next to his ear. "Finally. Plant security." He leaned into the phone. "This is Northern Route Six. I am inbound your position in an Army Black Hawk helicopter. We intend to land as near the reactors as possible. Preferably on the construction site. Have a vehicle waiting and get Irv Fuller, the construction contractor. *This is not a test. Goddammit! It's a U.S. Army helicopter and I am an Army colonel.*"

Holly rolled his eyes, shouted at Broker, "He wants some confirmation. Says we could be anybody."

Holly yelled into the phone. "Listen carefully, Jody; this bird is coming in hot. You start plinking at us, we'll burn you up. We believe your security has been breached. I need to talk to your boss, I need to talk to the most senior person on the site. You must be getting confirmation from NRC, somebody in Washington. This is real serious . . . Well, goddamn it, *find him on his fucking coffee break!*"

Holly lowered his phone and went back to shaking his head, furious. He dug into a go-bag lying on the deck and pulled out a picture ID on a lanyard. He hung it around his neck. "The goddamn French put antiaircraft missiles on their nuclear waste dumps to protect them. The Germans decentralize their waste and bury it in huge bunkers. Our defense amounts to public relations, full-page ads, and hardcore denial. We been telling these assholes at the nuclear plants for ten years, since the first World Trade Center bombing . . . Greedy fuckers, just too damn cheap to—"

Holly interrupted his tirade, cocked his ear to his phone. "Finally, got somebody from NRC. Uh-huh. What's the layout of the reactor and pool? Oh, that's great. Typical. Thanks. Bye," Holly made a face, looked away.

"What?" Broker asked. "The reactors are in hardened containments, aren't they?"

Holly shook his head vehemently. "It ain't the reactors I'm worried about. It's the cooling pool. NRC just told me the one at Prairie

Island is just this big tin shed between the reactors. They say the pool is below grade and bunkered. We'll see."

The cooling pool.

Broker tried to picture it. He summoned a documentary image of this vast watery honeycomb grid. Robotic arms moving the lethal fuel assemblies into the tight-packed cubbyholes. He knew as much about nuclear plants as the next guy—heavy avoidance laced with a whiff of Armageddon.

The pilot reached a hand back and waved.

"There it is," Holly yelled. They crowded forward to get a look.

Two rounded gray towers nestled next to the hazy river fringed with trees and parking lots. A large rectangular building with a blue roof crowded the reactors in the foreground. A lower structure was stitched between them. Across a canal, banks of squat towers released a cloud of white vapor. Past the plant an open rectangular area was surrounded by a landscaped, raised barrier. In the center of the open space a number of tall white cylinders were invitingly grouped like bowling pins.

The Black Hawk banked and descended toward an access road that ran past a parking lot from which cars were starting to leave.

"There." Holly pointed toward a gash of black gray earth in back of the towers. The sun glinted on a chain-link fence erected around the construction site. Coming in lower, they could see the equipment: excavators, bulldozers, and wheel-loaders strewn around the work site.

Several Chevy Blazers jockeyed around on the grass, trying to anticipate the landing point of the incoming helicopter. Holly clamped his cell to his ear. "Finally," he said. "Prairie Island Security? Okay, listen up. This is Northern Route Six . . ."

Holly said to Broker, covering his cell phone with his hand, "Guy's voice is shaking like hell." He removed his hand. "This is Six. C'mon, c'mon, talk to me." Holly shook his head. "Negative. We'll kick up too much dust on the site. We'll put down on the grass next to the fence."

Holly leaned into the cockpit and debated with the pilot. Quickly they picked an open plot of grass near the construction fence. The Hawk descended, flared, and landed with a jolt. Holly, Broker, and Yeager jumped off. One of the Blazers pulled up and three men got out. One wore a natty brown private-guard outfit, duty belt, sidearm. The second guy caught Broker's attention. He wore a dress shirt, tie, and a yellow hard hat. And he had this credit-card-sized plastic gauge in a plastic baggie clipped to his shirt. The card had a gray window in the corner. The numeral zero was displayed in the window. The last man wore jeans, a blue work shirt, and boots. That would be Fuller. All three approached with faces the color of flour, eyes like jelly.

They headed for Yeager, who was in uniform. Yeager pointed at Holly, then shook hands with the guy in the work shirt. He walked Fuller aside and started talking.

While the plant guard and the manager-type struggled with the idea that the guy who looked like a Willie Nelson roadie was a Delta colonel, Broker jogged through the gate in the construction fence. He ignored two heavily armed guards in brown uniforms who nervously flanked him, AR-15s at the ready. Fuck them. He was looking for the front-loader.

He ran past a deep trough and a pile of heaped dirt and saw two 644Cs. One was parked parallel in a rough line with other equipment, some of it still on trailers. But the other loader sat next to the wall of a building between the two reactor towers.

Jesus, just sitting there, perfectly perpendicular to the wall. Like it had been positioned. His stomach tightened as he ran to the machine. When he got within fifty yards he stopped and looked up. The honeycomb image returned with a vengeance, and now the gray domes towered above him like enormous hives. He imagined them buzzing with radioactive killer bees. Aggressive, swarming the containment, insane to get out.

Holly, Yeager, and Fuller came jogging behind him. The guards and the manager followed, somewhat reluctantly.

"I need a big wrench or a hammer," Broker yelled. He sniffed and looked under the loader. "There's a big puddle of gas under here."

Fuller signaled to a workman who was hesitantly approaching, part curious, part nervous. "We need some tools here, fast."

The worker put down his cooler, jogged to a shed next to the construction trailer. Broker pointed to the card around the manager's neck. "What that?"

"Dosimeter. Measures radiation."

Broker smiled tightly, "Might be a good idea to walk around this machine, see if you get a reading."

"You serious?"

Just then the worker returned, panting, with a heavy toolbox. Broker opened it, selected a heavy claw hammer, and immediately began tapping the counterweights on the back of the machine. Broker's first and second hammer blows gave off a dull solid clang. The third strike rebounded hollow, twanging.

The manager, the security guard, and Fuller looked at each other.

"Why is this machine sitting here?" Broker asked.

Fuller said, "Dale put it here. He wanted to see how it ran."

Holly grabbed a wrench from the toolbox, and he and Broker carefully attacked the end of the rearmost counterweight.

"Oh my God," gasped the manager as a crack appeared in the cast-iron weight. Using the open wrench and the hammer claw, Holly and Broker carefully peeled back the thin, milled-out iron. It dropped off in flakes.

Nobody said a word.

They were too busy trying to interpret the shapes Holly and Broker had revealed. Lumps of red clay connected by wires. A flat, dark plastic wafer in a taped plastic bag.

Holly gently scraped at the clay with a fingernail, brought it to his nose, sniffed, then put it to his tongue. He said, "Semtex. Military-grade blasting cap wired to a telephone pager." He turned to the manager.

"Wait a minute . . ." the plant official said. His face was going dreamy and dissociative. His eyes seemed to recede into his head.

"There's another hole like this on the other side. They're angled," Yeager said. "We talked to the guy who milled out the channels for Dale."

"What's on the other side of that wall?" Holly demanded in a steely voice.

"That wall's five feet of steel-reinforced concrete," the manager said, drawing himself up.

"Are there tunnels, subterranean rooms? Goddamn it, how much of the pool is below ground?" Holly shouted.

"Most of it," the manager said, starting to tremble.

"Yeah, right! There's *water* on the other side of that wall. Fucking water. Get it out of here," Holly yelled. "Get the ass end pointed in the river, anywhere, just get it away from this wall."

Fuller scrambled up the step into the cab, sat down, leaned into the controls. Nothing happened. He stuck his head out and yelled, "She's dead."

One of the workmen started checking the engine. He yelled, "Irv, battery wires cut. And the gas line."

Fuller jumped down from the cab, visibly shaken. "This is a fucking boat anchor. Without power the hydraulics are dead, no steering."

"It's a bomb," the security guard said under his breath. He started backing up. The sudden way he moved reminded Broker of something. Then he placed it. The movie *Jaws*, when people in the water thought they saw the shark and started backpedaling, in panic, trampling people. As he backed up, he started talking with barely controlled panic into his mobile radio:

"We have a level-one event. Activate the Emergency Notification

System. Yes, goddammit. Now! Call the city of Red Wing, Good-hue County, the State Office of Emergency Preparedness, Home-land Security, and the governor. And call the St. Paul bomb squad. We may have a bomb next to the spent-fuel pool. Evacuate all nonessential personnel. We have to shut down."

"Shut down?" the manager yelled. "You idiot! WE CAN'T SHUT DOWN THE COOLING POOL!" His knees buckled.

It was starting.

"IT'S A BOMB!" yelled the nearest construction worker, as he started to walk rapidly toward the gate. Broker and Holly stared at each other.

"We gotta move this thing," they both said at the same time.

Fuller gritted his teeth. "Dale was here to check this machine be-cause the wheels felt a little stiff . . ."

"Shit," Holly said. He and Broker stared at each other. "The wheels . . ."

They went to one of the wheel wells and struck at the twist valve cover with a hammer and a wrench. After several strikes it loos-ened. Straining, manic, they forced the cover to turn on its threads and removed it. The wheel was filled with congealed vinyl-like ma-terial. Broker fumbled in the toolbox, found a heavy screwdriver, and probed into the opening.

"Something in here," he said, grimacing, fumbling. Blood ran as he skinned his hand. But he managed to snag a loop of . . . hose. Embedded in the hardened foam. Pulled it out. He peeled away the gunk.

Very lightweight garden hose wrapped in tape. Yeager snapped open a Buck knife and handed it to Broker. He slit the tape and peeled open the bulge of hose. Broker reflexively stood up and backed away—a phobic, reflex firing of muscles. The hose was packed with red Semtex.

"Christ, could be all four wheels." Holly's voice sounded like a dead bolt sliding into place. "That could be . . ."

"A ton," Broker said in a controlled, hollow voice.

"Right," Holly said. He spun on the manager. "You ain't gonna have a *hole* in your pool, buddy. You ain't gonna *have a pool.*"

The plant manager started to tremble. Broker watched his face turn clammy, then he ceased to sweat. His eyeballs enlarged and his pupils contracted. "Wait a minute. What are you saying?" he whispered. "How could that get in here?"

Holly shook his head. "I'm sure you vetted the construction crew, And you checked the bottoms of the trucks these machines came in on. But you didn't disassemble the machines themselves. And even trained sniffer dogs miss Semtex—that's how good those smart Czech bastards made it.

"So basically what we got here is a directional charge of the world's best explosives, maybe four hundred pounds of it aimed directly at the foundation of your cooling pool." Holly clicked his teeth, looked around. "Plus the wheels. This fucker will crater big enough to hold a couple three *Olympic* pools. And it's rigged for remote detonation with pagers . . ."

"One phone call," Broker said, barely recognizing his own voice.

"Yeah," Holly said. "Question is, how big is his comfort zone? How far upwind is he going to travel before he punches in the numbers?"

"We'll . . . just . . . take it apart," the manager said carefully. "We'll disconnect the wires."

"That call is beyond my training," Holly said. "And we can't wait for the bomb squad."

"This can't happen." Slowly the manager lowered himself to the ground as his knees failed. He put his hands in his lap, swallowed, and recited, "An attack on the cooling pool is not a credible event."

Broker and Holly turned their backs on the confused manager. "So let's move this thing," Broker said.

"What if it's booby-trapped to blow if it's tampered with?" Holly gritted his teeth.

"We got no choice," Broker said.

"Agreed. Clear everybody out," Holly said.

Then the siren started. The high-pitched wail galvanized the numb gawkers still standing around the machine. Instinctively, they started to move away.

"Everybody get back," Fuller yelled. His knees had begun to shake and he started to fade away. The plant manger was crawling on all fours. One of the guards helped him to his feet and he joined the exodus, breaking into a jerky run. All over the plant grounds people were starting to walk rapidly toward the gate. The beginnings of an orderly evacuation.

A drill.

Then one of them started to run.

And they all began to run.

"IT'S A BOMB! IT'S A BOMB!" the running workers carried the cry into the parking lot.

Broker took a breath. The air had turned to mush; the old hot and cold fight-or-flight willies ran up and down his spine. It was a strange moment. Broker, Holly, and Yeager were caught up in the momentum and they, too, stepped back, as if swept up in a powerful undertow that sucked them toward the warmth and comfort of the other fleeing bodies.

Hundreds of people in motion now. They watched a guard drop his rifle and run. Not a good omen.

Broker located Fuller a hundred yards away at the edge of the fenced area. Fuller had his hand to his forehead, stooped over like he had a lot of weight on his back. He was talking to three, four of his crew, men in hard hats. They were straining in the bad body language of men caught in a riptide.

Further out, it looked like a big neon sign had crashed down on the parking lot. Horns blared and brake lights sputtered in a snarl of traffic, a building wail of approaching sirens and flashers added to the melee, coming off the highway.

"Yeager, get Fuller over here. We need some of his crew to help us. Gotta rig some chains, fire up those machines, *something*." Broker flung his arm at the line of tractors and bulldozers.

Holly was dancing back and forth, looking over the area. "Where do we put it?"

"We need Fuller," Broker yelled.

So they watched as Yeager sprinted across the wide lot and started an animated discussion with Fuller and his men. After precious seconds of arm waving, Fuller and the other men retreated. One man joined Yeager in a dash back toward the machine. They made a lonely sight, just the two of them doubling back while hundreds ran the other way.

"Jesus," Holly said when he saw their grim faces as they approached. "Hope we don't look that bad."

"Not us," Broker said. He skipped trying to grin. His lips were shaking too bad.

"What exactly is it you want to do?" the big guy with Yeager shouted over the bedlam of honking horns and the siren. A long blond ponytail stuck out the back of his hard hat. He had fatalistic Nordic blue eyes, a square jaw, and the stubble of yellow beard.

"The counterweight and wheels are full of explosives. It's designed to blow out the back," Broker yelled. "We gotta redirect the blast away from the pool and the reactors. Drag the fucker away."

Panting, eyes wide, gushing sweat, the chunky hard hat wore dirty Levis, and a torn T-shirt pushed out in a beer belly; his forearms were the size of Broker's thighs. A faded Marine Corps insignia was tattooed on the left one. *Hadda be Norwegian,* Broker thought. The guy fixed his eyes on the parked machines, pointed to one. "That D-8 dozer should do 'er," he said in a trembling voice.

"Can we drag it to the river?" Holly asked.

"Too much in the way. How about the ditch by the fence, behind that pile of dirt? Dump it in." The hard hat pointed again, this time at the earth bulwark that had been started about a hundred yards away.

"That's it. Let's go," Broker yelled.

Without pause, the hard hat ran toward the huge bulldozer. Broker, Yeager, and Holly chased after him. The guy jerked his thumb back over his shoulder. "The Deere 644 goes around fifteen ton. This big Cat dozer here goes around forty. Piece of cake."

He vaulted up into the seat and in a moment the dozer belched black smoke and its wide treads executed a mechanical pirouette, facing it in the direction of the Deere. He motioned Holly and Broker out of the way. Yeager ran in front of the dozer, stabbing his finger at something, then making a looping gesture. The driver vigorously nodded his head.

Broker and Holly joined Yeager, who yelled, "I spent some time around this shit. Best thing is to use the choker cable on the front." He pointed to a reel of steel cable with a pin clasp on the end. They danced aside while the driver lined up his dozer in front of the Deere, blade to bucket.

Broker heard a second siren. A Red Wing police cruiser skidded through the gate, then fishtailed, knocking down a section of fence. The cruiser slid to a stop, and a young copper jumped out, eyes like shiny ball bearings staring out of his haunted face.

He knew.

Without a word, he jumped forward to help Broker and Yeager thread the thick cable around the bucket arm of the 644. Yeager showed them how to set the pin. Staining shoulder to shoulder they wrestled the cable. Close in. Faces in hell—a local cop, Yeager, the guy with the beer gut and the big arms and the faded Corps tat. He hadn't bothered to give a name. He just started driving the dozer.

Where the hell was Holly? Then Broker spotted him running back from the dirt pile.

The driver pulled back on his controls, stood up in his seat, and inspected the cable rigged to the Deere bucket. He nodded his approval, sat back down, reeled in his cable, and then raised the blade on the dozer. Everyone on the ground stepped back as the driver hoisted the bucket until the cable was taut. Hydraulics screamed, black smoke spewed, and he raised the blade some more until the front wheels of the Deere 644 came off the ground.

They all braced. Nothing happened.

Holly reappeared, climbed up, and had a shouted back-and-forth with the driver. Then he leaped down, briefly took Yeager aside, and then came up to Broker and the cop.

"Me and the driver got it. Everybody else get outta here," Holly ordered as he reached in his jeans pocket.

Broker stared at him. "What do you mean, out of here? Where we gonna go? What the fuck *is* danger-close on a nuclear melt-down?"

Holly pulled a bundle of tiny chain from his pocket, clapped it in Broker's hand. Closed his hand over it.

"What this?" Broker said.

"Nina's dog tags. Hang on to them."

Broker stared at the silver wafer of metal on the beaded chain, shook his head.

Holly narrowed his pale eyes to slits in a mask. Doing one of those fucking warrior-statue numbers. "Listen, asshole," he yelled. "Kit may be down to one parent. I ain't gonna leave her with none. Now move out." A plume of dark smoke framed Holly as the bull-dozer trundled on, dragging the dangling loader on its back wheels toward the ditch.

Broker stuck the tag and chain in his pocket. "You need a ground guide," he shouted.

"I'm guide," Holly shouted back. He motioned, signaling to someone. Stabbing his finger.

Broker moved to protest, then the back of his head exploded—star-bursts fading to black. Going down, he tried to call their names: *Nina, Kit.* But no sound came.

Chapter Forty-five

First Dale took the 500 mg of Prussian blue. Then he took the potassium iodide. Just in case the wind changed on him. But he didn't think it would, because it had been holding steady all day.

He was driving due west on a back-roads two-lane blacktop, holding a steady hundred yards behind George's Lexus. The surrounding farmland was more populated than he was used to back home. Holstein cattle. Dairy farms. Big barns with Dutch gambrel roofs. It was hard to see very far in this rolling landscape, the way everything was close in. He'd lost the sky.

He crossed I-35, the main north-south corridor in lower Minnesota, and continued driving west on the solitary road. Almost half an hour since they left. How much longer? He picked up his cell, tapped in George's number, connected, and said, "Hey, George, let's flip the switch."

"A little more. When we turn south on 169," George said.

Dale put the phone down, sucked his teeth, looked around briefly, then concentrated on the road ahead. The way the land was, they'd never see it go off. Might not even hear it. But it should rattle the windows a little. He turned and looked back at the drawn curtain.

And then . . .

Nina, drenched in sweat, was thankful for sick favors. Dale's excitement had distracted him from sticking her with the ketamine again. She had a lucid window. She listened to the weather report on the radio updating the day's forecast: *Current conditions, sunny; 85 degrees Fahrenheit; dew point 64 degrees Fahrenheit; humidity 49 percent, visibility unlimited; pressure 30.00 inches and steady . . .*

Wind from the north northwest at 9 mph.

So he must be driving west, into the wind, just like he'd told her. How much room did they want between themselves and the . . . Her mind balked at the image of a nuclear plant erupting in a radioactive fire.

Assume the worst. He'll blow the plant. Unless I can get off this bed . . .

And do my job.

She needed to get at least one hand free. She needed him within striking distance of that hand.

The last self-defense course Nina had taken was conducted by an affable Green Beret at Fort Bragg. He began his class with an observation from the current fad of no-holds-barred Ultimate Fighting. He pointed out how there were only two rules in Ultimate Fighting matches: no eye-gouging and no blows to the throat.

In his first class, therefore, he taught Nina how to gouge out an opponent's eyeball. She lay on her back, blindfolded. An instructor straddled her. He wore heavy safety glasses and he held two oranges tight against the goggles, to simulate eyes.

Nina's job was to struggle up, find his head, locate the eyes, and drive her thumb through the orange peel, into the pulp and dig it out. The minute her thumb touched the orange the instructor started screaming and thrashing wildly. The idea was to overcome the normal human resistance to making contact with the visceral fluids and matter of the eyeball. Once you got past the aversion . . . the eye socket being a fertile nest of nerve endings, not only blindness but unconsciousness was a certain result.

She pictured Dale's flat blues eyes as targets.

No problem.

Time to get to work. She visualized the muscles of her arm and shoulder. Angles, leverage, the structure of the bed. *Okay. This time for real.* Painfully, she rotated her right hand counterclockwise in the tightly wrapped cords, encountered the sharp edges of the crimped hooks, and wrenched past them, ripping her flesh to the bone.

Now her palm had turned 180 degrees, so it lay flat along the sideboard. She raised her shoulder, thrust down, and hooked her fingers on the bottom of the board.

Okay.

She had to perform two separate operations. The first was gymnastic, a matter of timing. Slowly, she diagramed the physics involved. She'd brace her left hand and both feet on the sideboards, push down and vault her body up, taking pressure off the mattress and springs. During the split second her weight was in the air she would have to jerk upward with her right hand, dislodging the slotted sideboard as she heaved her head back against the headboard. She had been practicing this move and had felt the sideboard almost come free.

The test would be the second operation, which involved sheer muscle strength. When one end of the board was free, the bottom end would still be anchored in the footboard. She had to drag her right hand, which would still be tightly lashed, along and then off the free end of the detached board. Which meant exerting tremendous pressure to the side and to the rear. Again, she visualized the muscles of her right arm: triceps, the teres major, teres minor, rear delt. They were small muscles and were not structurally suited to perform this unusual movement.

Lubrication would not be a problem. In the process of rotating her wrist against the cord hooks, she had ripped her wrist to shreds. Her right hand was now bleeding freely.

On top of everything else, she had to do it quietly. She couldn't alert Dale before her right hand was free.

Nina blinked sweat from her eyes. Took a deep breath.

Now she focused back several years, on the Russian trainer she'd met in Kosovo. He'd been on loan from the Spetsnaz, the Russian Special Forces. He promoted a concept called "hyper-irradiation," which argued that rigidly flexing all the muscle groups of the body simultaneously was a force multiplier.

She knew her muscles were designed with protective mechanisms—spindle cells and Golgi tendon organs. Their purpose was to prevent damage due to overload by stopping function. Getting free would involve tearing her right rotor cuff to pieces. It would also involve overriding the protective mechanisms, the lactic acid buildup, going past the breaking point.

There was fear, which she was riding like a wave.

And then there was pain.

Which was the shark inside the wave ready to bite.

Go.

Nina poised on the bed, felt her fingers, slippery with blood, hook firmly on the sideboard. She pressed down with her feet and her left hand, took a deep breath, and stopped thinking. Her body knew.

She thrust up her torso and yanked up with her right hand.

Yes.

As the slots came free she extended her right arm to keep the board from tangling in the headboard. The bed slewed to the side as the sideboard thumped on the carpet.

Did he hear? No, the radio covered it.

Now let's see if that Russian knew what the hell he was talking about.

She flexed both feet and her left hand, painfully orienting her soles and her palm against the tight cords. When she had a solid platform, she pressed down on the sideboards. Working up from this tripod, she contracted everything she had: legs and upper body fusing into core abs and glutes. She had to transform the tension into a mighty fulcrum to send more power into the rigid lever of her right arm.

Her breath rasped, panting now. She felt sweat and then veins pop up on her screaming right arm as she strained it back, back. Inch by inch the bloody bungee cord started to slide rearward, toward the open slotted end of the sideboard.

Her strength flashed, so much fire into smoke. All mind now. She visualized every man who ever told her all the things she couldn't do. And some women, too. Every face. Every sneer. Every dirty joke.

She got two more bloody inches from the vivid memory of Johnny Majeski, who wrestled her out of her virginity when she was sixteen in the backseat of a perfectly restored '49 Mercury. And then blamed her because it went too fast.

Good memories, too. Dad. For all the hours in the pool and on the track; for teaching her to throw and jump and climb. For giving her a dollhouse *and* a chin-up bar.

She had two more inches to go.

Willpower gone. Muscles frozen, past spasm into total failure.

C'mon. Must be a few more muscles to call up in this act of self-destruction. She had gone past aching pain to piercing pain to red-hot burning pain to nothing.

All gone.

Must be something, somewhere. Trembling. Arched up. Making the tripod. Squirting sweat. Then in one last surge . . .

Had Kit by C-section. Broker's mom said I'd missed life's main rite of pain. Tap into it now. Bear down. Push.

Her whole right arm began to tremble violently, spasm, overload, maybe torn ligaments.

But the hand was free.

Tears smeared her face, mucus, spittle. Blinking through the blur, gasping, hyperventilating . . . then . . . *holy shit!* She'd been so distracted by her ordeal that she didn't realize the camper had stopped moving. *Christ, not yet.* But she heard their voices. Heard the door opening.

No, please . . .

Immediately, she hauled her right arm in tight, tested her fingers. Christ, her shoulder was burning, feeling loose and disconnected.

The curtain swept aside; Dale swiveled his seat and stared at her. "Aw, jeez, George, lookit this. She broke the bed."

"First things first. Let me show you something," George said as he glanced at her, unconcerned. Nina watched him raise the satellite phone in his left hand. He held a clear plastic cup in his right hand that was half-full of water. He placed the cup carefully on the dashboard and motioned for Dale to turn around. "Now watch the water in that cup," George said. "When I set it off we should see the water level jump, huh?"

"Cool," Dale said, spinning to the front. George eased behind the driver's seat, extending his left arm over Dale's shoulder so the phone was to the left of Dale's head. Nina, way past horror, watched George's right hand slip into the pocket of his shorts and remove a small automatic pistol. It looked like a .32-caliber. A hideout gun. He kept the pistol low against his right thigh. "Here we go," George said as he started thumbing in the numbers.

No, goddammit. No. Nina lurched up and tried to reach for them with her right hand but she was tethered by her left hand. She flung her hand to the left and clawed at the bungee, broke her fingernails.

She heard Dale's awed voice: "No shit. Look . . ."

Then she saw George sweep the pistol up smoothly, stick it pointed up under Dale's chin, and pull the trigger. The gunshot rolled inside the confined camper, knifed her eardrums, as Dale's shoulders and head jerked once and he slumped forward. A spray of red dotted the inside of the windshield.

Efficiently, George withdrew a handkerchief from his pocket and wiped the gun down. Then he placed it in Dale's limp fingers. For a moment he cocked his head, looking out the driver's side window. As he listened he mopped sweat from his brow with the hanky, then put it back in his pocket.

Then he turned to Nina. She glared back at him, pulled herself up by yanking on her fastened left arm; sitting now on the slanting bed, she cocked her right hand.

George grimaced at her. "It's done. I could hear it, you know. Just a faint bump. And the water in the glass did jump a little bit." He bent over the passenger seat, and when he straightened up, he was holding one of Dale's Epipens in his right hand like a dagger. He stared at her for a moment. "Look at you, you're all covered with blood. I'll make this easy on you," he said.

Nina's breathing was still ragged from exertion. No time to think about anything else. She concentrated on his left eye. *C'mon, just bring it closer.*

He twisted the injector, exposing the needle. Then he gestured. "So where do you want it?" His left hand snaked out and pinched at her right inner thigh. "How about somewhere nice?"

"No!" Nina screamed, rearing up, bringing up her free hand.

George laughed, ducked back, and feinted to the right, then changed direction and jabbed the needle into her right calf muscle. As the dose of ketamine entered her bloodstream, Nina started counting, hoarding her strength. *C'mon, you fucker, don't just stand there.*

But he did, he just stood watching. And Nina could feel the first wave of coldness like icy gloves and slippers on her hands and feet. But then he leaned forward and extended his hands, palms out toward her face. "This won't hurt," he said, "I promise."

When he was within her reach she launched her right hand at his face. But the damaged muscles failed, the bloody, rigidly extended forefinger merely slapped his temple weakly and fell away.

George laughed. "See? It was a mistake to send a woman."

As he leaned forward to smother her she put everything into one last explosive surge. She missed again but on the way down, her fingers snagged in the chain around his neck.

The muscles that extended her arm were shot, but she discovered that the contracting muscles still worked. Her bloody fingers found purchase on a medal attached to the end of chain, clamped tight, and yanked. George pitched forward. Immediately, she whipped her bloody arm around his neck, locked her elbow, and jerked him down.

Her biceps and parts of her forearm still worked. George wasn't laughing anymore. Methodically, then desperately, his strong hands clawed to break the hold.

Nina tasted salt and copper and bile as she reached down deep to where the lizard lived. Pure primal instinct now, she embraced him, smelling his minty Binaca breath, the Vitalis in his sleek hair. Their faces almost touched. His dark brown eyes were no longer amused, or even angry.

Fucker's scared.

Good.

Sobbing with exertion, she tightened her arm and drew him close enough for her parted lips to press against his throat. Almost erotic, she hunted for the pulse. Found it. Gauged the depth and bared her teeth.

She relished his scream, the frantic spasm as he tried to pull away. After the powerful bite, with the last of her strength, she tried to rip and gnaw. But her jaw went slack. The ketamine . . .

George's scream ended in a wet slobber as he clamped one hand on his ragged neck. Triumphantly, Nina saw the blood pumping through his fingers. Spurts of it. Streams. But he still had the strength to grab at her encircling arm with the other hand. She was on empty and he stripped her arm away. His stiff hand came down on her throat and she tried to lower her chin, raise her shoulders.

But he was too strong. He shoved the powerful arc formed by his thumb and first finger down into her throat.

Cold bubbles filled her body with floaty pressure. She lost air. She lost light. Her extremities went numb as her chest filled with ice water. She was choking outside, drowning inside. Distinctly, she looked down on a last image of her own body locked in a death hug with George Khari.

Far away.

Chapter Forty-six

Broker woke up in the process of being bodily thrown into the back-seat of the Red Wing cop car. His head throbbed, a knee slammed down on his chest as the car's rear tires threw dirt, accelerating. He looked up. Yeager. Scrambling in on top of him.

"Sorry," Yeager gasped. He was goggle-eyed, panting, shutting the door, looking out the rear window. Broker winced and felt the lump on the back of his head. Yeager held up an old-fashioned braided leather sap. "Me and Holly did a number on you to get you outta there."

There.

Broker lurched up. The cop was hunched over the wheel, floor-ing it. Broker twisted. His vision spun, frantic activity to the front, the Black Hawk was airborne, gaining altitude. Everybody had their mouths open, one long yell. Him, too. He looked out the rear window as they fishtailed through the cyclone fence perimeter. Screened by the silver mesh, Broker saw the deserted site: the black billowing smoke of the dozer, Holly standing at the edge of the ex-cavation pit, vigorously waving his arm next to the Deere and the bigger dozer. The gray domes loomed over the struggling yellow machines, dwarfing them.

The dozer driver was no longer hauling the Deere tractor. He had maneuvered it to the edge of the pit and was now trying to shove it in with the blade. But the two machines had tangled together, sixty tons of grinding steel. The driver stood at the controls, craning his neck to see Holly's hand instructions. Working out some problem. They were mired in the mud, losing traction.

"Jesus," Broker shouted. They were, what?—a hundred yards from the reactors?"

"Yeah, I know," Yeager shouted back.

"How they doing?" yelled the Red Wing cop behind the wheel. His wide eyes filled the rearview mirror, a study in controlled panic.

"Trying to push it in and they got hung up in the mud," Yeager shouted back.

"Not good," yelled the cop, forcing himself to slow down, picking his way through a moving field of running people and vehicles. Headed for the parking lot.

"Hey," Broker said as the Deere teetered over the edge. He saw Holly rapidly waving his arm—urging the dozer driver to drive his machine into the pit. Broker saw the driver jump as the dozer tipped in on top of the Deere. He landed on the ground next to Holly. They started to run . . .

Broker felt the concussion tug the fillings in his teeth—the day shivered, and in that split second Broker grabbed Yeager's neck and pulled him down in the seat. "Duck . . . ," he yelled. Then they were slammed sideways. His mouth and eyes clogged with grit as he glimpsed, but did not hear, the rear window disintegrate. The seat of the cop's pants appeared as he smashed forward over the dash, into the windshield. No one had been thinking seat belts.

Somehow the cop held on to the wheel, flopped back; bleeding from the head, face, neck, and scalp, he fought the wheel. No sound anymore, everything going fuzzy, then opaque with the rolling cloud of dust. They landed back on four wheels, skidded blind, and collided at about twenty miles an hour with something in the churning, silent gloom.

They came to a stop. Broker shook like a dog stepping out of a puddle. Cuts. Blood leaking through his mud-pie hands. Too quiet for all the stuff still flying through the air.

Must have burst his eardrums.

He groped toward Yeager, who was similarly attired in grime and bleeding cuts, tasted the particles of clay and silt and sand that coated his tongue, felt it embedded in his teeth. Just plain old dirt . . .

Then the sheer terror smacked him alongside the head. *Could you taste radiation?*

Was that how it was going to be?

Yeager's lips moved. *"What happened?"*

Broker shook his head. Pointed to his ears. *"Can't hear."* Tried to read Yeager's lips. *"Don't know. It went off."*

Lights probed the murky silence. Shadowy figures sleepwalking, fighting for their balance; cops in blue, firefighters in yellow. They were helping people to their feet. EMT was there. The white of dressings. The red of blood. Some people they left where they lay.

Broker had to know. He struggled out of the car, pushed aside the rescue workers. "Help him, help him," he yelled, pointing to the barely conscious copper in the front seat. He lost track of Yeager.

Go find out. He started back toward the explosion. Clods of dirt were still raining down through the sandy half-light. He tripped on something. The flattened fence.

The next thing he tripped on was a twisted section of tread from the dozer. Like a smashed mechanical snake belly, the grouser pads had been ripped from the cleats, the treads themselves bent by the force of the blast.

Broker grimaced. Holly and the driver . . . They'd essentially been standing under a B-52 strike.

Did it hit the reactor?

Then—*Oh shit*—his feet went out and he tumbled down a slope of loose sand and—*Jesus!*—he hit something metal, red hot, that seared his forearm. Scrambling back, waving his hands in the dust, he tried to see.

Coughing bad now, eyes stinging. Impossible to see.

But he had to find out. Was it safe for his baby? Was it in the air, invisible? He balled his bleeding fists. Swung them in helpless fury. *Somebody better tell me something, goddammit.*

But he was half-blind and deaf, lost in the silent limbo.

Broker sat in a field about a mile from the plant and watched a giant traffic jam still in progress where they were evacuating the Treasure Island Casino. Someone was saying that back in the seventies, the BIA told the Sioux band it was just a steam plant they were being forced to host on their land. Broker, still having trouble hearing, didn't catch it all.

In fact, he wasn't catching much. He was vaguely aware of Yeager, keeping an eye on him. Less vaguely, he was becoming aware that all the stuff that only happened to other people—all that stuff he'd kept isolated in his compartments—had busted out and was creeping over him.

He'd always operated on the theory that someone had to accept the duty of being strong; and, usually, that was him. He ground his teeth. Christ, if he couldn't even bring himself to say Holly's name, how the hell was he going to tell Kit about her mother?

Missing.

Like the walls that used to shield him.

Broker sat and stared. Yeager watched him.

• • •

The men in protective suits had picked their way through the debris field and had checked the walls of the reactors and cooling pool. They returned and took off the suits and assured the exhausted cops, medics, and firemen that some engineers had stayed at their posts, that the damage was minimal. Emergency procedures. Backup systems. Yadda-yadda. They walked through the first responders, showing them the readings on their dosimeters. Very low numbers. Well within acceptable limits. It was under control. No general evacuation order. See?

No one there believed them.

Broker and Yeager had bathed in a makeshift shower, had exchanged their potentially contaminated clothes for baggy National Guard fatigues. They sat numb, dotted with minor dressings, drinking Red Cross coffee. A TV was propped up on the hood of a Goodhue County patrol car, plugged into an emergency generator. The governor of Minnesota was saying everyone should stay indoors, and that it was going to be all right. The hundred-plus cops, firemen, and medics who had been ordered off the blast site did not look convinced.

The governor said most of the blast had been absorbed by the excavation and the heavy dozer. Yes, the shock had caused minor damage to the cooling pool and one of the reactor containment walls. Some of the water pipes in the reactor were affected and there had been a small release of radioactive steam into the atmosphere.

But, the governor assured, it was minimal.

"Sure it was," quipped a cop from Hastings. "That's why he's talking from his desk in St. Paul."

Nine bodies had been retrieved. Eighty or ninety people had been injured, three critically. Most of the deaths and injuries were the results of flying debris and several car accidents in the dusted out aftermath of the blast.

Broker sat and stared, just barely making it out when Yeager started yelling his name.

"What?"

Yeager held up his cell phone.

"What?"

"It's Norm, in Langdon. He'd put out a regional BOLO on Dale Shuster, remember?"

"Yeah?"

"They found him, dead, at a rest stop south of Le Sueur. And that Khari guy." Yeager pounded Broker's shoulder. "That ain't all they found. *She fucking made it, man.*"

All Broker's remaining armor fell off at once and he began to tremble. It took an immense effort to unclench his fist from around the mashed blue cigarette pack. With shaking fingers, he withdrew the two remaining, battered smokes. He gave one to Yeager and put the other in his mouth.

"You got a light?"

The three men in the corridor outside Intensive Care in the Mankato hospital weren't wearing uniforms. Broker thought he might have seen the black one before, that night on the highway outside Langdon. They could have been three Extreme Iron Man competitors who just happened to be in the vicinity. To Broker, they reeked of well-thought-through death.

"Where'd you come from?" Broker wanted to know.

The oldest one came forward, extended his hand. "Dr. Warren Burton. I'm a friend of Nina's."

"I didn't know they had healers in Delta," Broker said.

Burton was affable and rolled with it. "Well, there's always torture." He watched Broker for several seconds with his highly trained eyes. Then he said, "It'll go easier, for you and for her, if you work with us."

Broker nodded. "No problem. Answer the question. How'd you get here so fast?"

"A Minnesota Highway patrolman found her. Shuster and Khari had her in an RV, parked off in the trees at a rest stop. Some people heard her screaming and called nine-one-one. She was tied down and pinned under Khari's body. She'd worked a hand free and fought him. It got pretty intense. He bled out and his body lay on top of her for several hours. She tore out his throat."

"With her hand?"

"No."

After a moment, Broker said, "You still haven't answered my question."

"The cop got her out of there, but she didn't have any ID. She was in deep shock. Still is. All she'd say was her name, rank, and serial number. That's how they got to us," Burton said.

"I want to see her," Broker said.

Burton nodded. "The docs here are good. They're letting me sit in. To prepare you, her face is pretty beat up but it's superficial, just bruising. Her right arm has suffered some major soft tissue and tendon injury and is immobile. We've got her pretty heavily sedated, as you can understand. She's just in here."

Broker started toward the door to the ward. Burton accompanied him. At the door he stopped and said, "I served with Colonel Holland Wood. You were with him at the plant . . ."

Broker didn't trust his voice. So he just stared at Burton, waited until he stepped aside and then went into the ward.

They had her in a corner by a window, screened off. One cheek was bruised and swollen. Purple blood bruises splotched her neck. Her wrists and ankles were bandaged. Her right arm was immobilized in a plastic cuff, an IV drip in her left.

Her instincts were switched on. After this, they probably would be for some time. She jumped alert at the movement when he came around the screen. She tensed and her green eyes acquired him, evaluated him for threat. Then the shrill vigilance sunk back into a quieter narcotic flux.

Did she recognize him? Was that important to her now?

He went to the bed and took her left hand in his.

"Nina."

Her smile faltered. "Don't say anything, about Kit or anything, okay?"

"Okay."

"There's something important I have to tell you about Ace Shuster. But I can't remember it just yet." Abruptly, she pulled her hand away and started plucking at the hospital gown over her chest. A scrubbing motion.

"They cleaned me up," she said, "but it was all over me and I think they missed some here." Her hand went to her throat. "And here."

He decided to wait on telling her that his folks were bringing Kit . . .

Mom's job is making it so people can believe what they want.

Broker shifted from foot to foot, fresh out of tricks. Well, so much for keeping things in compartments. After Vietnam he'd vowed he'd never allow his heart to be broken again.

So much for vows.

"I love you," he said. He held her hand and said it over and over.

He sat with her all night. She had never seen him cry before and he wondered if, later, she would remember it.